TIER ONE

OTHER TITLES BY BRIAN ANDREWS AND JEFFREY WILSON

WRITING TOGETHER AS ALEX RYAN

Nick Foley Thriller Series

Beijing Red

OTHER TITLES BY BRIAN ANDREWS

The Calypso Directive

OTHER TITLES BY JEFFREY WILSON

The Traiteur's Ring
The Donors
Fade to Black

TIER ONE

BRIAN   JEFFREY
ANDREWS & WILSON

TIER ONE

Elite, covert special missions units tasked with conducting counterterrorism operations, strike operations, reconnaissance in denied areas, and special intelligence missions. Their existence is often denied.

PART I

The world breaks everyone and afterward
many are strong at the broken places.
But those that will not break, it kills.
It kills the very good and the very gentle
and the very brave impartially.
—*Ernest Hemingway*

CHAPTER 1

The Arabian Sea
March 13, 0030 Local Time

Jack Kemper ran his fingertip along the place where the jihadist's dagger had carved him to the bone. The scar wrapped his forearm like a serpent, but it had long since lost its bite. It was an old wound, pearly white and smooth, all the pink and tenderness bleached away by sea and sun and time. Sometimes he displayed it brazenly, like a badge of honor; other times he rolled down his sleeves to hide the reminder of the mistake that nearly cost him the use of his left hand. But now, in the dark of night, pride and prejudice were irrelevant.

In the dark, a man could hide his scars.

He watched the water through the open cargo door of the modified Black Hawk helicopter. Below, green rollers and whitecaps whisked past at 150 miles per hour, painted in high-contrast monochrome by his night vision goggles. Somewhere down there was the *Darya-ye Noor*, a cargo ship sailing from the Iranian port city of Bandar Abbas to Aden, Yemen. The *Darya-ye Noor*—Farsi for *Sea of Light*—was registered to and operated by the Khazir Shipping Company. According to the analysts, Khazir functioned as a front company for the IRISL, the Islamic

Republic of Iran Shipping Lines, transporting both legitimate and illicit cargo between Iran and various Middle Eastern, African, and Asian ports. Intelligence indicated that the *Darya-ye Noor* was carrying a cache of chemical weapons to Al Qaeda affiliates in Yemen. The proliferation of WMDs didn't mesh with US counterterrorism strategy, so the brass did what it always did—tasked a team of Tier One operators to take care of business.

Although he had a knack for remembering bullshit trivia, Kemper did not consider himself a "details guy." He really didn't care what JSOC wanted him to blow up, clean up, or pick up; just tell him when and where, and he would get the job done. He had participated in so many missions as a member of the Joint Special Operations Command's covert Tier One SEAL team during the past twenty years that he'd lost count. But the human toll he remembered with perfect clarity—twenty-eight American casualties, fourteen team members wounded or killed in action. He stopped tracing the scar and leaned his head back against the rear bulkhead of the passenger compartment. Tipping his NVGs up away from his eyes, he let the darkness chase their faces away—every last one—until his mind was blank. Regret was an unproductive preoccupation for old men. Besides, he still had work to do.

And debts to pay.

He stared out into the night—so black he was unable to see his leg dangling out the side of the helicopter. The wind buffeted the inside of his calf and thigh, snapping the fabric of his gray utility pants against his skin. The thrum of the rotors and rhythmic vibration of the Black Hawk's superstructure was a wonted lullaby. He yawned as he fished his rope gloves out of his vest pocket.

He felt a tap on his shoulder.

He pulled his NVGs back down and stared at the green-gray face grinning at him beneath a matching set of goggles. Special Operations Chief Aaron Thiel held up a hand—the one with half its pinkie finger missing.

"Five minutes," Thiel said, shouting over the wind.

Kemper leaned in. "You mean four and a half?" he said, gesturing at Thiel's old wound.

Thiel's grin transformed into a smirk, and he flipped his hand over, gesturing now with only one finger.

Kemper laughed and flipped Thiel a bird of his own. Two other SEALs crowded in beside him, completing his party of four for the port-side drop. Four more SEALs clustered on the starboard side. Thiel wrestled the massive bags of rope into place on both sides of the helicopter while Kemper shifted into position, then arched and twisted his spine—cracking the vertebrae to relieve the pent-up tension he'd accumulated during the uncomfortable flight out. Then he rolled his neck, each wrist, and cracked his knuckles. With age, he'd become a cracking addict. He knew it probably wasn't good for his joints, but damn, it felt good.

"Senior Chief," said a voice, barely audible over the comms circuit.

Kemper found the volume knob on the radio clipped to his left shoulder and turned it up. His Peltor earpieces canceled out most of the background noise, but twenty years riding these damn helicopters meant he needed the extra volume. He turned his head to see who was talking to him and found Spaz in his face. "What, Spaz?"

"Help me settle an argument." Spaz's hands flew over his gear, checking his loadout and weapons while he talked. "Pablo thinks that Spider-Man would make the best Tier One operator. I told him only Batman is badass enough to make the teams, much less our unit." He slid the bolt on his M4 partway back to check the round in the chamber, then clicked the power on the holographic sight and infrared laser target designator. "Whadaya think, Senior?"

Kemper rolled his eyes behind his NVGs. "I say you're both idiots. We're on a combat mission, and you assholes are arguing about comic-book characters. Get your heads in the game, for Christ's sake." He looked past Spaz to Thiel and gave the two-finger signal that meant they were two minutes out.

Thiel nodded.

Kemper snapped the sights and lights on his SOPMOD M4 assault rifle and then ran his fingers over his ammo pouches, counting them off in his head. He felt the Black Hawk's nose pull up slightly as it bled off speed on the approach to the target. He sidled up next to Thiel and tightened the straps on his rope gloves.

A moment later, the helicopter pulled up sharply and settled into a static hover. Kemper and Thiel kicked the rope bag together, and it disappeared out the hole into the blackness below. Kemper tightened his grip and pinned the rope between his boots. Then, looking at Spaz, he said, "Everyone knows Spider-Man is a pussy. Without tall buildings for his webby shit, the dude's got nothing. Every SEAL I know could kick his ass . . . every SEAL except maybe you, college boy." With a grin, he slipped out of the helicopter into the cold, black air.

Kemper hit the deck on the fantail of the cargo ship hard. He moved left, dragging the heavy rope bag with him to straighten out any bunches near the bottom. He worked fast, clearing the bottom of the rope just as Spaz landed beside him. Spaz dodged right, and Pablo hit the deck, followed by Thiel a split second later. They moved swiftly to the left, away from the falling rope as it pounded the deck beneath the departing helicopter. The starboard-side team completed its drop with mirror-image perfection. All eight SEALs were now on board, fanning out along the stern of the ship.

Kemper scanned the vessel's superstructure, comparing the reality before him to the reconnaissance photos he'd studied hours earlier. By container-ship standards, the *Darya-ye Noor* was relatively small; her two-hundred-meter length and 2200 TEU carrying capacity were leagues below the size of a typical Panamax vessel. But from his vantage point, looking out across a cargo deck the length of a football field, the ship looked enormous. The *package* was somewhere in the middle of a maze of metal boxes and tarp-covered shipping crates, sandwiched between the soaring bridge tower near the bow and the elevated stern deck on which he stood.

He held no illusions they had arrived undetected. Despite the whisper-quiet stealth technology of the helicopters belonging to the Army's elite 160th Special Operations Aviation Regiment, the *Darya-ye Noor*'s Iranian captain had undoubtedly posted lookouts. A five-second drop time, while tactically impressive, was not fast enough for eight heavily armed operators to descend onto the deck of a moving ship unnoticed. Any second now, he expected floodlights and gunfire.

The key was to keep moving.

The SEALs maintained their port- and starboard-team orientations as they pushed forward—Kemper, Pablo, Spaz, and Thiel working the port side of the ship; Rousch, Gabe, Helo, and Gator split out to starboard. In rapid succession, they descended a short flight of stairs leading down to the cargo deck. At the bottom, Kemper dropped to one knee and covered his three teammates as they passed him. After clearing the next five meters, Spaz took a knee and Kemper took his turn scouting forward.

Hugging the port rail, he checked the first dark corridor between the rows of crates.

Clear.

He advanced to the next row.

Clear.

Fuck, he hated missions like this. It was so much better to land in the suck and get the fight over with, rather than sneaking around waiting for some fanatic to pop up and unload an RPG on your ass.

He checked the next row.

Nothing. Where the hell was everybody?

Based on the overflight drone imagery they'd viewed during the pre-op brief, he'd expected to find shooters patrolling the cargo deck. He'd counted heat signatures for at least a dozen people moving topside.

Sure, that data was ninety minutes old—maybe a little more at this point—but it seemed strange that every asshole with a gun would go inside at the same time. Maybe it was mealtime for the midwatch? Or maybe the ship's captain only ran security patrols during certain hours? The Iranians knew better than that. Hits like this always happened under the cover of darkness.

He quietly keyed his radio. "Demo team, move to the package." Two clicks in his ear told him the other seven SEALs heard him.

Together with Spaz, he scanned the cargo deck fore and aft for movement while Pablo and Thiel disappeared into the maze of boxes with their handheld chemical-weapons sniffers. On the starboard side of the ship, Helo and Gator would be moving to join them, while Rousch and Gabe provided cover.

Kemper waited in silence. It was less than a minute before he heard Thiel whispering over the comms circuit, but it felt like an eternity.

"Sniffer can't find a chem signature."

Kemper grimaced. *Shit.*

Their mission had two objectives: to detonate the package and to collect intelligence. Now he had a decision to make: continue to provide coverage for the demolition team and abort the intelligence-collection task, or proceed to the bridge tower and leave Thiel and Pablo to take care of themselves.

Kemper paused, weighing the risks.

As if his friend could read his thoughts, Thiel's voice said over the wireless, "Lead, Two. We've got this. Go."

Kemper looked at Spaz, who flashed him a crooked grin.

Kemper keyed his mike. "Bridge team, forward."

Two clicks in his ear.

Spaz took the lead. Kemper followed silently up the steel stairway leading to the raised deck. Upon reaching the top step, Spaz spread out prone and Kemper took a knee, sighting over his partner. He fully expected to see sentries in the doorways leading to the bridge tower and crew quarters, but he saw nothing except empty space. He frowned and clicked on his PEQ-4 infrared designator. He confirmed he could spot the red targeting dot—visible only through night vision goggles—on the wall beside the open doorway. Then he tapped Spaz twice on the shoulder.

Spaz moved fast in a low, awkward crouch, covering thirty yards in seconds. Kemper scanned right through his NVGs and saw another SEAL moving parallel to Spaz toward the mirror-image doorway on the starboard side of the raised deck. Once both men were beside the doorways, Kemper sprang from his crouch. His left knee popped, and he silently cursed his thirty-eight-year-old body. He darted across the raised deck while Spaz covered his movement, scanning skyward as he ran, surveying the ladders and catwalks that crisscrossed the superstructure of the bridge tower. All deserted.

They were on a ghost ship.

How could these guys be so stupid as to transport WMDs without a security detail?

He hesitated. It all felt too easy. Why hadn't he heard from Thiel yet? Why was it taking so long to find the package? Something was wrong. They'd missed something.

Instinct and twenty years' experience as an operator took over. He whirled 180 degrees and looked back toward the stern, across the main cargo deck from his elevated vantage point. With perfect night vision clarity, he surveyed the stacks of wooden crates, metal cargo boxes, and tarps flapping in the wind.

The tarps . . .

They were hiding under the fucking tarps.

CHAPTER 2

Kemper keyed his mike. "Demo team—you've got shooters on the cargo deck. Under the tarps. Repeat, shooters under the tarps."

Two clicks in his ear.

A barrage of automatic weapon fire shattered the silence.

And so it began.

Kemper sprinted toward Spaz at the base of the bridge tower and threw his back against the bulkhead. He dropped to a knee and peered up into the open ladder well that led up to the catwalks and the O-5 level. Through his NVGs, he followed the dancing red dot of his IR laser sight as it whipped across the empty runs of metal stairs above.

"It's coming from the cargo deck," Spaz whispered harshly in his ear.

"I know, but I don't want to get shot in the back when we rally aft to cover."

Another burst of gunfire.

"Heavy contact," Thiel's voice barked in Kemper's earpiece. "Heavy contact at the package. Fuck."

Kemper heard a click and then a series of controlled pops from an M4 rifle. Probably Thiel's. More gunfire, this time from an AK-47. The sound danced around the ship, reverberating off the superstructure from every direction. His heart pounded like a timpani keeping time.

Fuck intelligence collection.

His only priority now was to provide fire support to the SEALs trapped in that death maze of cargo boxes on the main deck.

"Bridge team, rally back. Cover from the deck rails," Kemper called into his mike.

Spaz took point and Kemper followed, angling away from the hatch leading to the passageway and moving back onto the raised deck. From the raised deck, they transitioned onto the outboard deck rails, which gave them a slightly elevated firing position compared to the cargo deck six feet below. At a dogleg amidships, Spaz stopped and pressed himself into a corner. He steadied his rifle on the rail slat beside a stairwell leading down. Kemper slid left, looking for cover. He spied a three-foot-tall green box—a small generator, if he had to guess—and crouched beside it. He steadied his rifle and sighted through the railing.

"Fuckin' A," he heard Spaz mutter to his right, as gunfire popped all around them.

Kemper keyed his mike. "Two, Lead—do you want to abort?"

"Negative, Lead. Five is wiring the package now," Thiel's voice came back.

Tracers crisscrossed the cargo deck from three distinct points, all aimed at the center, where four of his teammates were pinned behind a stack of crates—the same crates they were wiring with explosives. A lump formed in Kemper's throat. He wasn't worried about the plastic explosives the demo team was setting; the moldable, green clay bricks could take a direct hit without detonating. But the contents inside the shipping crates were another matter. The assholes were firing at their own chemical weapons cache. Breach a single canister filled with sarin precursors, and it was game over for everyone.

Kemper surveyed the mayhem. The tarps that had been covering the crates were now strewn haphazardly about. Terrorist shooters were popping up and firing from hiding places strategically located around the cargo deck. The multiple firing angles created a wicked crossfire and made escape impossible for the four SEALs pinned down at the package.

Time to do something about that.

Kemper found a target, dropped a bright red dot on the fuck-stick's temple, and squeezed off a single round. The man's head disappeared in a puff of blood and brains painted in night vision green. His body slumped and then disappeared behind a wooden crate.

Sparks flew around Kemper, blinding him for an instant, as bullets slammed into the generator beside him. Enemy shooters had sighted his muzzle flash, and now they were lighting him up. He dodged right two paces and dropped prone onto the deck—the barrel of his rifle now below the bottom railing slat.

Shoot and move—Spec Ops Survival 101.

He clenched his jaw, trying to keep his anger in check as he sighted a new target. *These assholes knew we were coming.*

Trigger squeeze.

Pop.

Another dipshit crumpled onto the deck.

A never-ending stream of tracers streaked across his field of view. He scanned right, checking their escape route to the stern deck. *Shit.* There was no way they could move aft through that much fire. Maybe he and Spaz could cover the demo team up onto the deck rails for an "over the side" drop into the water. Possible, but the *Darya-ye Noor's* freeboard was pretty fucking high. Even worse than the three-story drop, they would be vulnerable to a 180-degree assault while they tried to set up ropes.

Movement to the left grabbed his attention. Sight . . . trigger squeeze . . . miss.

He frowned as the terrorist scurried behind a crate and disappeared from view.

Something slammed into his back—a sledgehammer that sent a tsunami of pain through his entire body. The pain in his spine was so acute, so electric, that it stole the breath from his lungs. He tried to move. Sparks of pain shot through his ass, down his leg, to his left foot. His big toe felt like it had exploded inside his boot. He tried to call out to Spaz, but he couldn't find his breath.

He didn't need to; he heard Spaz's voice in his headset.

"Shooter on the bridge tower! Sniper up on the tower. Lead, Four—are you okay? Are you hit?"

Kemper moved a hand to his radio and pressed the button to transmit on the wider frequency band to include Command and Control on his transmission. He opened his mouth, but all that came out was "Uhhhh." He tried to cough, tried to clear his throat, but he couldn't inhale enough air to push any out. It felt like a car had run over him, and now that same car was parked on his chest.

He heard Spaz again in his ear.

"One is hit. One is down. I'm gonna get him."

"Four—hold," Kemper wheezed. "I'm okay."

The electric shocks in his ass and leg were subsiding, but the pain dead center in his back was debilitating. He finally managed to suck in a deep breath, which radiated a new, heavier pain out along his ribs to both sides of his chest. He tried to move his legs and was punished with another lash of pain down the left leg, but his legs moved.

His legs moved just fine.

If I'd been shot through the spine, I'd be paralyzed.

Despite the pain, Kemper couldn't help but grin. He'd almost left the ceramic plate out of his Kevlar vest when he was gearing up—hating how heavy and uncomfortable the damn thing was. But tonight, prudence had persevered, and that damn SAPI plate had stopped an AK-47 round from punching a hole through his spine.

He counted to three, took a deep breath, and rolled to his right. Pain mushroomed across his back and down his leg as he dragged himself awkwardly toward the metal stairs leading down to the cargo deck. More sniper rounds rained down around him, exploding chunks of stair tread in his face as he belly-crawled. He collapsed at the bottom of the stairs in a heap. Steeling himself, he crawled on his elbows around the staircase, moving outboard until he was behind the staircase and underneath the port deck rail. He pressed his back against the hull of the ship and exhaled with relief. In this position, he was shielded from above and out of the bridge sniper's line of fire.

"Four," he called to Spaz, loud enough to be heard even without the voice-activated mike. "Dude, come to me." Knowing he needed to provide covering fire, Kemper reached up and grabbed a stair rung. Ignoring the pain that shot down his leg, he pulled himself to one knee and aimed blindly up at the catwalks that lined the bridge tower. He thumbed his M4 to a three-round burst and squeezed the trigger. He kept shooting, shifting his aim among different areas of the tower, until Spaz had ducked in beside him. With Spaz safe, he pulled back against the hull with a grunt.

"You hit, Senior?" Spaz asked, looking him over through his goggles.

"Took a round in the back," he groaned.

"You mobile?"

"Yeah, yeah," he said and waved a hand in annoyance. "But I'm not sure where the fuck we're gonna go."

A grenade exploded somewhere in the middle of the deck, showering everything in a fifteen-yard radius with wood fragments and pieces of burning tarp.

"That was one of our grenades," Kemper said.

A second explosion followed, equally satisfying.

"That one, too," added Spaz. "Paradise is gonna get crowded with martyrs tonight."

"Amen, brother," Kemper said with a smirk. He thumbed the wider frequency button on his radio. "Blackbeard Main, this is Blackbeard Actual. Blackbeard Main, Blackbeard Actual." While he waited for a reply, he watched Spaz take up a cover position.

"Blackbeard, this is Main—go."

"Main, Actual—heavy contact. Pinned down and need air support ASAP. Over."

There was a pause that seemed to last an eternity. Kemper could picture Commander Dietrich, the squadron skipper in the Tactical Operations Center, asking the SEAL air-support coordinator for a time check, and then swearing up a thunderstorm when he got the answer.

"Blackbeard, Main—little birds in five mikes. Do you need hot EXFIL from the target, or are you still a go for Alpha?"

Kemper thought a moment. With the little birds hosing the bad guys, they could probably make the water for their plan A for EXFIL. But if they took casualties, then no way. And, if he was dicked up worse than he thought, could he make the swim? He thought of the fractured SAPI plate, the trauma to his back, and said, "Main, Actual—likely Alpha but have Bravo in orbit and available."

"Copy," Dietrich said. "Four mikes. Switch to air."

Kemper would switch to the air channel in a minute, but first he needed a SITREP from his team.

"Two, One—SITREP?"

"Still at the package. Still heavy fire, but no casualties."

Kemper nodded. "Two—hold position. Stay put. Six, One—you off the deck rails?"

"Six—check."

So everyone was clear of the raised deck, and the demolition team was still hunkered down near the package. The Night Stalkers in their OH-58s were coming. With their mini-guns, the helicopter pilots would hose down terrorist snipers on the bridge tower and then lay down suppressing fire, clearing a path from amidships to the stern. Kemper could direct them to use a rocket or two if needed, but that would be a last resort. Better to get off the ship and blow the package from a distance. Safer for *all* the good guys that way.

"Everyone hold. Little birds in three mikes. Let me know if you have to move."

He switched his radio from the tactical channel to the air channel by feel.

"Stalker Two-Five, Blackbeard Actual."

"Blackbeard, Stalker—go."

"Stalker, Blackbeard. Team in two elements. Half at the package on the cargo deck amidships. Half-split between port and starboard below the deck rails. Taking sniper fire from the bridge tower, and heavy contact from the aft cargo deck. Everyone aft of our lights is a shithead."

"Copy," was all the little bird responded. It was enough. Kemper's team worked almost exclusively with the 160th. This was just another day at the office.

Kemper gritted his teeth as he took a knee next to Spaz, pain flaring in his back and leg. He tapped Spaz on the shoulder.

"Relay to the team. I'll monitor air."

Spaz nodded and then repeated the plan to the rest of the SEALs using his radio.

A moment later, despite the din of automatic weapon fire on the cargo deck, Kemper's ears pricked to the familiar whine of the little helicopters. The sound was raspy and higher pitched than the stealth Black Hawks on which they had arrived. The need for stealth was past, and the call of firepower never sounded so sweet.

"Blackbeard, Stalker. Lights on," said the pilot's voice in Kemper's earpiece.

"Lights on," Kemper said to Spaz, as he turned on his strobe.

Spaz nodded, flipped on his own strobe, and relayed the order into his boom mike.

A skinny guy holding an AK-47 popped his head around a crate less than twenty feet away. Without hesitation, Kemper fired two rounds: the first hit the crate, making the insurgent turn in Kemper's direction in surprise; the second round blew off the guy's lower jaw and half his face. The man dropped his rifle and fell twitching backward onto the deck. Kemper continued his sweep of the cargo deck and breathed a sigh of relief as other white strobes began to flash. The SEALs were switching on their helmet-mounted infrared strobes—an ID light visible only with night vision, and a safeguard against friendly fire.

A heartbeat later, two OH-58s screamed across the deck of the ship at low altitude and then pulled up into a static hover.

"Clearing the bridge," Stalker reported in his headset.

"Copy."

Tongues of flame spat from the helicopters as they showered the bridge-wings and catwalks with .50-caliber fury. Tracers in the bullet streams created the illusion of long, fiery orange lassos licking the bridge tower. Entire sections of superstructure exploded, and chunks of metal crashed onto the raised deck. A moment later, a massive span of catwalk groaned and then broke free—tumbling in a roaring cascade of sparks, flame, and twisted metal. Kemper had seen it all before, but the destructive power of the tiny helicopters never ceased to amaze him.

"Clearing the deck for you, Blackbeard," Stalker reported in his headset.

Kemper clicked his mike twice and then switched back to his team's tactical channel. "Get ready to move," he called over the radio. "Rally point Alpha. Prepare for EXFIL."

He shifted into a crouch and sighted over his rifle. He followed the bouncing red dot through his NVGs, looking for terrorist shooters trying to flee the maze of crates. No visible targets. He wasn't surprised, considering the strafing in progress. The OH-58 pilots were using night vision, which meant they could see the SEAL strobes, but they also had their thermals up to spot the heat signatures of any shitheads still hiding under the tarps. Kemper squinted as the two little birds swung around and began to light up the cargo deck. Hopefully Thiel had correctly identified the package, and the remaining crates being obliterated weren't loaded with sarin.

Tracer flares, muzzle blasts, and spot fires turned night into day, and Kemper had to look away to preserve his night eyes. Staring down at his feet, he waited, listening to the sound of wooden crates exploding like geysers, raining fiery chunks of debris across the cargo deck.

And then, as abruptly as it had begun, the firestorm was over.

Kemper got to his feet and assumed a tactical crouch. He raised his rifle and signaled to Spaz to move aft. The first heavy step of his boot unleashed an explosion of pain in the middle of his back and a fresh bolt of lightning down his left leg. Two more strides and his foot felt blown up inside his boot. He paused for a moment and the pain waned, leaving only a throbbing ache in his pelvis and thigh.

Dread washed over him as the severity of his injury finally began to register.

Bullet broke my fucking back.

One bad step, one wrong movement, and the fractured vertebrae could slip, shift, or collapse and cut his spinal cord in half. What the hell was he supposed to do then?

"We gotta keep movin', Senior," Spaz whispered.

"I know," he grumbled and took another step.

Spaz fanned out to the left while he stayed right. He swiveled back and forth in a thirty-degree arc, scanning the path ahead for enemy shooters moving up from the stern. Each turn of his torso brought another red-hot saber stabbing him in the back. He tried to swallow the pain and push forward, but he was beginning to falter.

He was falling behind.

"Movement—port side—aft of last row of pallets," Stalker warned in his earpiece. "You're too close for me to engage."

Kemper swung left and scanned the inboard deck. He spied the row of pallets, but no movement. He surged forward as Spaz widened his sweep. Kemper's IR dot danced with shadows green and gray, but he found no enemies to engage. He held his crouch and moved another three steps. Then, in his peripheral vision, something flashed white; the guttural pop of an AK-47 followed a split second later. He swept the deck and spotted a prone figure holding a rifle. Kemper trained his targeting dot onto the man's forehead and fired twice. The impact flipped the terrorist onto his back, where he stared up at the night sky, one eye remaining in half a head.

"Shit—I think I'm hit," Spaz called out.

Kemper spun to his right and found Spaz sitting on the deck, his rifle in his lap. He took two giant strides to close the gap, adrenaline masking his pain. He knelt beside Spaz. "You okay, bro?" he asked, quickly scanning an arc around their position for other shooters.

"You tell me," Spaz said, looking down at his leg, bewildered.

In the monochrome green of night vision, Kemper saw a black stain spreading on Spaz's gray utility pants. *Not good.* The wound was located on the thigh, just below the drop holster straps for the kid's Sig Sauer P226 9 mm pistol. Kemper reached down with a gloved hand and pressed. His pressure was met with a nauseating crunch and an equally nauseating moan from Spaz.

"Your fuckin' femur's broken," Kemper said.

"Awesome." Spaz coughed through gritted teeth.

"Got a man down," Kemper said into his mike. "I can get him to the fantail, but I need some cover."

Two clicks told him his message was received. Whether he could actually deliver on his promise was a coin flip. His back was completely fucked, but he was a goddamn SEAL, and SEALs do whatever it takes for their brothers.

Whatever it takes.

He helped Spaz recline until he was lying on the deck. Then Kemper positioned the nape of his own neck and plateau of his shoulders across Spaz's midsection. He wrapped Spaz's left arm and bleeding left leg around him, like putting on a sweater. Then he twisted and rolled Spaz on top of him. He struggled to his feet under the crushing weight of his fully loaded teammate. Staying in a crouch, he crossed Spaz's arm and leg together in front of his chest and held them in place with his left hand, freeing up his right to bring his rifle to bear. He scanned the deck, saw no one, and moved forward.

The first step stole his breath, leaving just enough air for an anguished howl. On the second step, his left leg turned to a bag of dead meat. He crumpled to his knees, the explosion of pain in his back dangerously close to making him pass out.

"Fuck," he grunted as he tried to push himself back onto his feet, using his rifle as a cane.

"Put me down," Spaz whispered, his voice ripe with agony.

"No."

Kemper staggered forward, leaning heavily on his right leg and supporting his left with his rifle-cane. Less than fifteen yards to go. He could already see two of his fellow SEALs adjusting ropes on the stern deck ahead of him.

"Put me down, Senior. I can walk."

"Not with a shattered femur, you can't," he huffed. "We're almost there."

Automatic weapon fire echoed behind him, but Kemper couldn't turn, much less return fire. He pressed forward, depending on the other operators to kill the threat. If they didn't—at least his world of pain would end.

Fifteen feet.

Ten.

Seven.

Five.

He collapsed at the feet of two SEALs providing cover fire for them at the railing. Tears clouded his vision. He felt someone lift Spaz off his broken back. Unencumbered, he tried to press up onto his hands and knees, but his left leg was dead.

"You first, Senior. No arguing," said the closer SEAL. It was Rousch, their eighteen-Delta combat medic, who was now in command since this had just become a CASEVAC instead of an EXFIL. "I'll send Pablo down next. Then Spaz. Okay?" Rousch added.

"'K," Kemper said through gritted teeth. "Spaz took one to the right femur. He's bleeding out."

"You carried his ass, Senior, but it's my job to fix him. Now go."

Thiel and Pablo got Kemper to his feet, while Rousch attended to Spaz. Thiel helped him hook a figure-eight descender device onto the rappelling rope, and Pablo clipped it to a carabiner in the center of his kit. Thiel lifted Kemper's left leg over the railing for him and handed it to him like a piece of luggage.

"Might wanna take that with you," Thiel said, the corners of his mouth curling up.

Kemper grunted, leaned back, and pushed off the hull of the *Darya-ye* fucking *Noor*. Rappelling down the side of the ship, he could manage. Finning away with his broken back and useless left leg—that was going to be a bitch.

His gaze on Thiel's furrowed brow and his thoughts on Spaz, Kemper descended into the black.

CHAPTER 3

The instant he hit the water, he knew something was wrong.

Kemper exhaled through pursed lips as ocean water flooded his BDUs, whisking the heat of battle away from his overtaxed muscles. But that old familiar chill—a sensation he'd come to associate with victory and going home—was off-kilter. It took him a second to identify what was missing.

His damn left leg was missing.

Beginning with his left hip, he couldn't feel the cold, or anything else for that matter, all the way down to his toes.

His gray tactical vest hissed and began to fill with compressed CO_2. Gritting his teeth and swallowing his pride, he let the inflatable vest bite into the skin around his neck and underarms. He felt a tug at his chest, which prompted him to unhook his descender from the drop rope to which he was still tethered. Then, using his right leg, he kicked backward out of the landing area.

Bobbing like a cork in the waves, he glanced up at the stern of the *Darya-ye Noor*. A green silhouette dropped toward him from the port side of the ship, and then Pablo was at his side, tugging at his collar.

"You okay, Senior? You need a tow?"

"I'm good," he lied.

"You sure?"

"Yeah. Go help Rousch with Spaz."

Pablo let go of his collar, and Kemper immediately listed to the left from the weight of his dead leg. No matter how he tried to lean, he couldn't compensate. He watched Pablo swim over to Spaz, while kicking lamely with his right leg.

"Am I still bleeding?" Spaz whispered, looking at Kemper. "I don't wanna get eaten by some big fuckin' shark."

Viewed through night vision goggles, all human skin glows with a disturbing green-gray pallor, but at that moment Spaz looked as ghastly as Kemper had ever seen someone who wasn't already a corpse. He shook his head. "If only Spider-Man were here, he could shoot a web under your ass and net that great white I saw circling before he bites off your leg."

Spaz lifted a gloved hand out of the water and flipped him the bird.

That was the reassurance Kemper was looking for.

As soon as Spaz looked away, Kemper shifted his gaze to Rousch for a second opinion.

"Don't worry. I got a tourniquet on him," Rousch said, his voice calm and serious. "He'll be fine."

Kemper nodded, but he could tell from Rousch's tone that the situation was grim. Every SEAL knows that lacerations don't clot in cold water. He wondered if the tourniquet would be enough.

"Starboard team, clear," said Thiel's voice in his ear.

He keyed his mike. "Push out," he said.

Two clicks in his ear.

He kept his eyes on the *Darya-ye Noor* as they finned away. The ship looked so much larger from this perspective than it had during the helo approach. His mood soured as he realized that the ship wasn't getting any smaller. Despite the exhausting effort he was putting into finning with one leg, he was barely compensating for the current. Gritting his teeth, he cinched down on his rifle sling, bringing his weapon tight against his side to free up his arms for paddling.

After a minute of flailing, he felt a tug on his arm.

"Spaz can't make it a mile," Rousch said, cruising along next to him.

Yeah. Me either, he thought. He grunted in agreement but didn't look at Rousch. He was falling behind. Even Pablo, who was towing Spaz, was about to pass him by.

"How much farther?" Rousch asked, forcing the issue.

Kemper looked again at the ship and contemplated how much more separation they needed before Thiel could blow the package. Detonate too early and he risked a lethal chemical drift on top of their position. He considered ordering the team to mask up, but the thought of trying to retrieve his MOPP gear from his pack suddenly seemed too overwhelming.

He keyed his mike. "Two, One. How much farther till we can blow the package? The last thing I want is to take a shower in toxic rain, but this is taking too long."

"Roger that. I say we open another five hundred yards and blow it," said Thiel's voice in his ear.

"Copy."

He looked at Rousch, who was still cruising along beside him.

"Five hundred, but no more," Rousch said, his expression grim.

Kemper nodded.

After a pause, Thiel came back over the radio. "And Jack, just an FYI, we didn't find any chemical weapons on the boat."

"Then what the hell did you wire up?"

"Six crates of Sayyad-2 anti-air missiles."

"Copy that." Kemper turned to Rousch. "Surface-to-air missiles? What the fuck?"

Rousch shook his head. "It wouldn't be the first time the spooks fed us bad intel about a package. Remember the clusterfuck in Fallujah in '07?"

"Yeah, and wish I didn't."

He switched to the air channel and keyed his mike. "Stalker, Blackbeard Actual. Mike Charlie—EXFIL in ten mikes. We have two casualties and we're all lit up."

"Blackbeard, Stalker. Copy."

He reached up with his gloved right hand and confirmed his IR strobe was in the ON position. He was still wearing his NVGs, so he swept the horizon until he counted seven blinking lights in the waves.

He was about to resume paddling when someone grabbed his collar and began tugging him along. He arched his neck and saw it was Rousch. Instead of biting his head off, Kemper sighed and accepted the tow to the pickup point.

Once Thiel's team of four had melded with theirs, he checked his GPS and glanced back at the ship.

"Whatcha think, Jack?" a voice said to his left.

He turned his head, and now it was Thiel finning alongside of him. "Blow it."

Thiel gave him a thumbs-up, rolled onto his back, and retrieved a tablet computer in a waterproof case. Kemper watched him tap out the detonation instructions on the keyboard, while somehow managing to keep pace with the group. After the last tap, Thiel averted his eyes.

Kemper and the rest of the team followed suit.

Thiel's charges detonated, and the *Darya-ye Noor's* main cargo deck erupted like a volcano. A split second later, a deafening boom hit him like a slap in the face, followed by the unmistakable squeal of steel tearing from steel as the hull of the container ship absorbed the shockwave. Unable to resist, Kemper tipped up his NVGs and looked. Black smoke, lit from below by towering walls of flames, spiraled skyward.

Another burnt offering to the God of War, compliments of the Tier One SEALs.

He flipped his NVGs back down into place and keyed his mike on channel three. "Stalker, Blackbeard Actual—set for extraction. Two urgent surgicals will need special attention."

He'd phrased the message so the Stalker boys would know that they'd need help getting Spaz and him into the bird. By switching to the CASEVAC plan, they were assured of having advanced medical care aboard, including some Air Force PJs who were on assignment to their joint task force. It also meant command would send two birds, both old school MH-60M Black Hawks instead of the cramped stealth birds they used for INFIL.

"Blackbeard, Stalker. Flight of two—gotcha in sight. Eight strobes."

The Blackbirds were reliable workhorses, but far from stealthy. He heard the helicopters at about the same time he saw their IR strobes winking just above the horizon. He double-clicked twice and then tilted his head back to look at Rousch. "Thanks for the ride, dude."

"No problem, Senior," he said and let go of Kemper's vest.

Seconds later, the first bird settled into a hover above them, kicking up sea spray in a forty-foot disc. At the same time, he heard Rousch on channel three, barely audible over the whine of the engines and the rotor wash. "Need litters for both," Rousch shouted.

"I don't need a litter," Kemper barked, tilting his NVGs off his face to glare at the medic.

"Yes, you do," Rousch hollered back. "Don't be a dumbass. You have a fucking spine injury."

Kemper wanted to yell something back in protest, but he held his tongue instead. Rousch was right. His back was a mess. If he wasn't careful, he might end up needing a cane. Or worse. What would he do if the injury was bad? Unfixable bad. So bad that he couldn't be a SEAL anymore. Every operator has a shelf life. Was tonight proof that he'd passed his expiration date, like a package of rotten deli meat? This was a question he'd been mulling over recently, but the pain from this injury was like a judge's gavel pounding in his mind before the pronouncement of his sentence:

Senior Chief Jack Kemper, Tier One Navy SEAL operator and twenty-year Naval Special Warfare veteran, is hereby sentenced to retirement, where he will spend the rest of his days as a civilian, telling anyone who will listen that he is still important, while living vicariously through his active-duty teammates as he hobbles his way toward senility and irrelevance as an independent government contractor for hire.

"You still with me, Senior?" he heard Rousch ask. "Don't black out on me, bro."

Kemper gave Rousch a thumbs-up and looked skyward at the two litters dropping from the hovering helicopter above. He stared at the coffin-shaped metal cages as they swayed and twisted in the turbulence while making their parallel descents. A heartbeat later, two Air Force PJs splashed down into the water. Twenty yards away, the second bird arrived and flared into a matching hover. Lines dropped and the other five SEALs hooked up; within seconds that helicopter had drifted clear. While a PJ helped Rousch maneuver him into the litter, Kemper watched his fellow operators disappear into the night, dangling from ropes like . . .

He laughed.

Like fucking Spider-Man.

CHAPTER 4

Masoud Modiri folded his hands in his lap and waited patiently while Israel's ambassador to the United Nations, David Arnon, addressed the committee members. Modiri had listened to Arnon's arguments so many times over the past six months that he could recite them in his sleep—in English, no less.

". . . And I cannot overstress that Iran's nuclear program—which Mr. Modiri and his government claim exists solely for peaceful purposes—has been a matter of international concern since 2003, when we discovered that Iran had been concealing uranium enrichment and heavy water-related development activities for nearly two decades. This activity is in direct breach of the Nuclear Nonproliferation Treaty, to which Iran is a signatory. Since the ill-advised Joint Comprehensive Plan of Action was pushed forward by the United States, Mr. Modiri continues to demand that all sanctions be lifted—some of which predate the JCPOA and have been in place since 1979 to address decades of treaty noncompliance. The lifting of sanctions under the terms of the JCPOA has resulted in nothing more than funneling cash into the coffers of a rogue nation. Moreover, by lifting sanctions mere weeks after Iran performed overt missile testing, the council has set a terrible precedent of non-enforcement and emboldened Tehran to continue its weapons-development program. How can this council deem a nation that publicly calls for the destruction of Israel and flagrantly disregards international law to be a benevolent and peaceful state? Let us not forget that Iran lied about the very existence of its weapons program and continues to deny its existence in the face of indisputable proof. Let us not forget its recent missile testing is a breach of the JCPOA, a breach that was dismissed without consequence. So I ask you, what cause does the council have to lift additional sanctions when we have proof that Iran deceived the world about its nuclear weapons program, and continues to deceive the world about fulfilling its obligation to dismantle it?"

Modiri listened, politely and without interrupting, while Arnon spewed his rhetoric. When the Zionist finally finished speaking, all eyes shifted to him. He smiled, leaned forward in his chair, and said, "What my counterpart from Israel seems to have forgotten is that we have moved beyond talks. Whether Mr. Arnon likes it or not, the Joint Comprehensive Plan of Action has been signed. The government of Iran has agreed to all of the conditions, including providing all requested information on the Gchine mine in Bandar Abbas, on the heavy water-production plant outside Arak, and on the Natanz fuel-enrichment plant. In addition, we have permitted managed access to these facilities by IAEA inspectors. Furthermore, over seven thousand centrifuges have been destroyed or dismantled to date. If this is not cooperation, if this is not trust, then I ask the committee—what is? The longer these unfair sanctions are in place, the more the people of my country suffer. The majority of the frozen assets released by the JCPOA have been used to settle Iranian international debts. Yet despite taking immediate steps to meet our fiscal and trade obligations, Iran is met with renewed distrust. Iran is not the nation of radicals that Ambassador Arnon suspects.

Instead, Iranians like myself and the new leadership in Tehran wish only for our nation—and our people—to flourish in peace. Economic stability and independence are the keys to that peace. Freeing us to conduct commerce with other nations not only rebuilds our economy, but also rebuilds relationships with those nations who have publicly committed to investing in Persia, the future of our people, and our mission of peace."

Instead of rebutting, the Israeli glanced at the US ambassador, Felicity Long. She nodded at Arnon, but to Modiri's astonishment, she did not respond in the manner he expected.

"While I agree with Ambassador Arnon that talk of lifting all sanctions against Iran is premature, I think it is important to recognize that progress has been made since the signing of the JCPOA. For the first time in a decade, UN inspection teams have been permitted open access to Iran's nuclear facilities. Dismantling activities, while behind schedule, are progressing steadily. If Iranian compliance continues at this level, I'm confident that within three to six months, the IAEA Board of Governors will be able to assure the international community that Iran is in full compliance. Should this happen, the United States will support lifting all UN Security Council sanctions against Iran, and the six signatory members of the JCPOA, the United States included, will suspend all economic sanctions not already lifted under the terms of the JCPOA."

Modiri stared dumbfounded at the woman, not trusting his ears. He glanced at Arnon. The pulsing veins in the man's forehead were all the proof he needed. The Jew wasted no time launching into a heated rebuttal, but it didn't matter. Ambassador Long had just played a perfect concert-pitch A. She had tuned the orchestra, and the musicians were ready to play.

Music was inevitable.

He smiled.

Discussion among the delegates continued for two more hours, but the quality of the dialogue had changed. The timbre, the tempo, the dissonance were different now. The world was ready to embrace a repentant Iran. Reformed, remorseful, and well behaved—this was the Iran the new administration would present to them. And when they were all convinced—all except for the Zionists, of course—then Persia would finally become the true seat of Islamic power in the Middle East.

In the world.

This was all part of the plan.

The recent election of President Hassan Esfahani was a strategic opportunity—one that Modiri and his fellow true believers intended to exploit. All war is strategy, and Iran's political posturing over the past decade had been the country's greatest strategic failure. Thanks to the outgoing Ahmadinejad government, Iran's political capital in the Middle East and Europe was exhausted. Had it not been for Ahmadinejad's inflammatory rhetoric and acerbic belligerence, the United States and the Zionists would not have succeeded in rallying the public support needed to enact the crippling economic sanctions that had brought Iran to its knees. A Muslim who cannot control his tongue has no business being the leader of a nation. If only he could convince the Supreme Leader and the mullahs to curb their inflammatory rhetoric as well!

Ahmadinejad's shortcomings as a leader had gone beyond his failed diplomacy. He had handed Esfahani the reins to a country in financial ruin, with inflation at 42 percent, millions of young people unemployed, and a GDP held captive south of $500 billion. The wanton corruption and incompetence that had plagued Ahmadinejad's government was an affront to Islam and an affront to the people of Persia. Allegiance required full bellies and warm homes, and the last administration had made that all but impossible. Esfahani meant to change all that. His number one priority as president was to reinvigorate the economy and return Iran to solvency. But to do this, his administration had to first convince the UN Security Council and the West to lift all sanctions. And to do that, Esfahani needed a new voice inside the UN.

Eight months ago, behind closed doors, Esfahani had approached Masoud. He could still feel the great man's hand on his shoulder. He could still hear the echo of Esfahani's sanguine voice in his ears:

"There is much work to be done, and even more work to be undone. I'm counting on you, Masoud, for the latter. That's why I've chosen you to serve as Iran's ambassador to the United Nations under my administration. The countries of the world are an ecosystem. Iran cannot prosper in isolation. Islam cannot spread its roots and blossom in the shade. My predecessor did not understand this. Your predecessor did not, either. Cooperation is a prerequisite for effective subterfuge. We cannot achieve our goals without tapping the economic arteries of the West. This is not shameful. It is not blasphemous. It is reality. Without material sustenance a body withers, becomes weak, and eventually dies. Without economic sustenance, a nation suffers the same fate. A prosperous Iran is a strong Iran.

"Make no mistake, my friend, what I am asking of you will be difficult. In the course of your assignment, there will be times when you will feel like you are betraying your family, your country, and your God. But Allah sees inside the hearts and minds of his servants, and he knows the truth. Will you do this great thing that I ask of you? If not for me, for Persia and for Allah, praise be his name?"

His answer had, of course, been yes. An overwhelming, tearful yes. His wife, Fatemeh, had also cried when he told her the good news. Even the dogmatic, militant Kamal, his elder son, had seemed genuinely impressed, his soldier's eyes glimmering as Masoud recounted Esfahani's speech over a shared pot of Turkish coffee. No longer was he a spectator of government, watching other men play the world's most dangerous game from outside a fence. He was the Iranian ambassador to the United Nations—plugged into the highest levels of world government. He understood Kamal's anger and his thirst to do battle for Allah. It was his dream that one day such violence would not be needed—that the world could live in peace under Allah, as promised by the prophets. Those same prophets had predicted that blood would have to be shed to achieve such a world, but perhaps they were now on a path beyond such violence. Perhaps even Kamal would be able to live in peace.

During his brief tenure as ambassador, he had already accomplished great things. Brokering the JCPOA with the West and politicking for the partial lifting of sanctions had won him respect from Esfahani. More important, it proved that he, Masoud Modiri, was a pivotal disciple in fulfilling Allah's will for his people. Yet despite all his accomplishments, there was still much to be done. The $60 billion in unfrozen assets were but a pittance of the funds necessary to rebuild the Iranian economy. He needed direct investment in the Persian oil infrastructure by the West, and direct investment was still forbidden by the remaining sanctions. He needed to secure unrestricted trade, both import and export, or else the Persian economy would stall and his detractors in Tehran would call for his replacement. He would not let that happen. His rhetoric, his relationship building, his negotiating skills were the only reason Iran had risen so far so fast in the eyes of the world.

He was startled from his thoughts by movement around him, and glanced up from where he had been tapping his mechanical pencil absently on the edge of his laptop. Around him, his fellow diplomats were gathering their things to leave. The Zionist's ranting rhetoric was predictable and redundant, but he wondered if others in the assembly had marveled as he did at the US ambassador's response. He prayed silently to Allah that Ambassador Long's words bespoke an official US policy shift, and were not just the bravado of a new ambassador—not unlike himself—trying to win the attention of the council. He would read the transcripts, of course, but he had a gift for finding the true but oftentimes obscured meaning behind a person's words. Long's gaze was earnest, her mannerisms telling.

"We have much in common," a woman's voice said.

Surprised, he turned to see Ambassador Long approaching him from the semicircular row behind him. Unlike the two scowling brutes flanking her, she was smiling at him.

Modiri swallowed his revulsion at the sight of this woman behaving as Allah intended a man to carry himself. She was even dressed like a man. He wondered if she lusted after women, as men do—an abomination rightfully punishable by death in sharia. He smiled back with great effort, then took her hand and shook it firmly, swallowing his disgust and the other, more disturbing feeling that surprised him at the touch of her soft, warm hand.

"Ambassador," he said, and released her hand quickly under the guise of trying to gather his things. "Your support of Iran and rebuttal of Ambassador Arnon's misguided fears is appreciated."

Her smile tightened. "I'm not sure *support* is the right word," she cautioned. "But I do believe that your government is on the right path. And I believe in your sincerity, Ambassador. I'm hopeful that together, we can take the necessary steps to lift all remaining sanctions."

Modiri nodded—almost a bow. His pulse quickened with shame and anger. The feeling of humbling himself before this woman—an ambassador of the Great Satan—was unbearable. "I look forward to that as well," he said, forcing himself to look her in the eyes. "As you said, we have much in common."

She shifted her red-leather handbag on her shoulder. "Not only do we both bring a fresh perspective to the council but I believe we also represent a growing and sincere belief that a lasting peace can only come from diplomacy. Past administrations have confused peace with compliance. Compliance through force and violence is, of course, not peace at all. Wouldn't you agree?"

"Yes, of course," he said, nodding. With the pleasantries out of the way, now it was his time to push. He could not afford to waste this critical opportunity. The UN Security Council sanctions were *not* the problem keeping President Esfahani and the Supreme Leader up at night. The remaining economic sanctions were. Time was of the essence. They had momentum, but another administration change was around the corner in the United States, and the rise of ISIL and its so-called caliphate had made the American people nervous. A new administration could undo much of what he had accomplished. He could ill afford to let that happen. The prize was in sight; he needed to push hard to win the game before someone decided to change the rules. "But I caution you that there can be no peace without cooperation, and as you Americans are fond of saying, cooperation is a two-way street. For the citizens of Iran, time is of the essence. By your own admittance, Iran has eagerly cooperated with the IAEA requests for transparency, and we have just as eagerly complied with the additional concessions demanded under the new treaty. While we appreciate the partial lifting of sanctions under the JCPOA, there are still economic sanctions levied against Iran. Over the past year, we have suffered a ten percent devaluation of our currency—this on top of an already devastating sixty percent fall over the past four years. Your government states the remaining sanctions are designed to cripple Iran's nuclear development, but the truth is they are designed to cripple the Persian economy. Iran is cooperating fully in the pursuit of peace; do you not think it is time for America to do the same?"

Long nodded. "I understand," she said, still wearing the noncommittal smile to match her noncommittal words. "You have my word that I will communicate your concerns to the White House and Congress, but please communicate to President Esfahani that the National Security Council is particularly impressed with his administration's recent efforts to help crack down on terrorist activity in the Middle East. Continued cooperation in this arena will go a long way toward helping the members of the National Security Council build a case to convince the president that economic sanctions of any kind are no longer needed."

Modiri suppressed a scowl and held her gaze with strength and confidence, despite the fact that he had no idea what she was talking about. There was important subtext to her statement, but the true message was veiled to him.

"The West has a perception that all Iranians are radicals and terrorists," he said at last. "But this is not true. We are a proud people, maybe sometimes too proud, but it is peace and progress that we seek, not war and terror."

"Of course, I know that," the ambassador replied quickly.

Despite the damage done by the fanatics in ISIL, Islamophobia was taboo in the Western media. The Americans' penchant for guilt was a weakness he could exploit. By subtly playing the victim, he had ended the dialogue with her by gaining the upper hand.

"You may call upon me anytime," he said.

"Likewise."

With a victorious smile, he nodded to her and her stone-faced companions. Feeling decidedly less subjugated than he had at the beginning of the conversation, he strolled confidently out of the General Assembly Hall. Ambassador Long might indeed represent the country with the greater power, but he felt that in this exchange, Iran had gained ground—proof that women should not occupy roles that Allah deemed the right of men. As he walked to the secure parking area, he thought about what he would say in his report to President Esfahani. Today, real progress had been made, but not progress that was measurable. Not progress that was concrete. The shift in sentiment was a real victory, but it was victory felt in the soul, not in the text on a computer screen. Would Esfahani be convinced?

Modiri felt a headache coming on as he approached the black Mercedes sedan idling in his assigned parking spot. As a delegate from a Permanent Mission at UNOG, he was afforded the privilege of a parking permit at the Palais des Nations. That did not mean he drove himself, however. He detested driving automobiles—a menial activity best performed by a menial mind. His driver, an IRCG brute trained in the methods of tactical driving and killing people, opened the rear passenger door for him. He nodded at the man, ducked his head, and slipped into the leather-appointed backseat. The driver returned to his seat, put the transmission into gear, and piloted the Benz out onto Avenue de la Paix. After a few minutes, Modiri noticed that instead of taking him south, into the heart of Geneva toward his hotel, the driver had merged onto Route de Lausanne and was driving north along the western perimeter of Lake Geneva.

"What are you doing?" he asked in Farsi. "You were supposed to take me to my hotel."

"I have other instructions, Ambassador Modiri," said the driver.

"You work for me," he said, seething. "Do you understand? Now turn this vehicle around and take me to my hotel."

The young Persian ignored the order.

"You work for me," Modiri said again, harshly.

"I drive for you, but I work for General Ghorbani," said the driver, meeting his gaze in the rearview mirror. "And the General instructed me to drive you to a meeting. An old friend is in town and has asked to see you. It won't be much longer, sir. I apologize for not informing you in advance, but my instructions were explicit."

Modiri turned and stared out the window at the steel-blue water of Lake Geneva and the snow-draped French Alps in the background. The driver had spoken one of seven acceptable code phrases used to communicate covert instructions when traveling outside Iran. There was no point in trying to guess who was waiting to speak to him or what the subject matter concerned. Whatever the reason for this impromptu meeting, he had no doubt it was important.

Fifteen minutes later, the driver slowed, signaled a turn, and pulled off Route de Lausanne into the gated driveway of a lake house. Modiri stepped out of the backseat, not waiting for the driver to open his door.

The front door of the modest two-story house swung open before he could knock.

"Amir?" Masoud said with surprise, seeing the man in the doorway.

"Masoud," said his younger brother, embracing him. "It is good to see you. Come inside. We have much to discuss."

The driver tried to follow him inside, but Amir stopped him with a hand on the chest. "No. You wait outside."

"But it's freezing," the young man said.

"You have a Mercedes. Turn on the seat heater."

Masoud heard the door slam behind him as he surveyed the modern, utilitarian decor. The owners of this property were definitely not Persian. "What is this place?" he asked his brother.

"A rental house. It was the best I could do on such short notice. Booked over the Internet," Amir said, gesturing for him to have a seat on the sofa. "Don't worry, it's clean."

Masoud sat and exhaled slowly through pursed lips. Amir worked in the upper echelon of Vezarat-e Ettela'at va Amniat-e Keshvar, also known as the Ministry of Intelligence and Security. VEVAK functioned as Iran's equivalent of the American CIA, the Russian FSB, or the Mossad in Israel. For Amir to travel personally to Geneva for a face-to-face meeting meant that something was wrong.

"Tell me, brother. What is going on?"

Amir sat down in an armchair opposite him. He said nothing for several seconds, then reached across and took Masoud's hand. "Kamal is dead—martyred in service of Allah. I wanted to be the one to tell you."

Masoud had known this day would come. He had tried to prepare himself, but now that it had come to pass, he was overwhelmed with emotion. His knees began to shake. "How . . . how did it happen?"

Amir let go of his hand, stood, and began to pace. "Do you know what I do at VEVAK?"

"Yes, of course. You're the Director of Foreign Operations."

"And do you understand the duties that position entails?"

He shook his head. "I have an idea, but we should not be talking about it here. This conversation is dangerous."

Amir straightened his posture, closed his eyes, and inhaled deeply. "I am the reason Kamal is dead."

"What are you talking about?" Masoud said, staring at his brother.

"Two days ago, twenty-four Sayyad-2 anti-aircraft missiles were loaded onto the *Darya-ye Noor*, bound for Aden. American drone activity in Yemen has increased threefold over the past eighteen months, resulting in some regrettable losses in midlevel Al Qaeda leadership. The Sayyad-2 was specifically designed to take down the American drones. This operation was to be a critical demonstration of the missile's capability."

"I understand," Masoud answered. "The American drones are a problem. But how is this connected to Kamal?"

"Kamal, as a member of Quds Force, was assigned to train the Yemenis how to mobilize and operate the missiles. But last night, while the ship was crossing the Arabian Sea, the Americans ordered a strike. We don't know all the details, but we do know it was a SEAL team that hit us. The missiles were destroyed and we lost twelve operatives."

A hard lump formed in Masoud's throat as he asked the question he already knew the answer to. "And Kamal was one of them?"

Amir nodded. "Your son fought bravely and in service of Allah. Do not worry, my brother. The reward of Paradise is his."

Masoud slid from the sofa to his knees and began to pray. Tears blurred his vision and sobs choked his lungs, but he prayed until he'd made his peace with Allah. Then he looked up and met his brother's eyes. Rivulets of tears glistened on Amir's cheeks, disappearing into his thick black beard. "Is this the first time the Americans have deployed the SEALs against our operations?"

"The first time?" Amir laughed, his tone obscene and incredulous. "In Damascus, their Tier One operators raided our covert operations safe house. In Lebanon, they intercepted a crucial weapons shipment and killed an elite Hezbollah unit in the process. And beyond my comprehension, they somehow managed to sabotage one of our Kilo class submarines—while it was docked in Bandar Abbas no less—preventing it from completing a highly classified surveillance mission against the US Navy's Fifth Fleet."

Masoud clenched his fists. "If the American military is a viper, then their Special Forces are the fangs. Pull out the fangs and a viper becomes just a worm."

"An interesting metaphor, but impossible to follow through," said Amir.

"Why is it impossible?"

"They are ghosts. We never know where they are, when they are coming, or what they are going to do. I even told Kamal to expect a raid. He prepared a trap on the cargo deck in case the SEALs came, but it made no difference. Like I said, they are ghosts."

Masoud shook his head vehemently. "No. They are men—men with superior training, information, and tactical support. The rest is mythos, perpetuated by their success." He stood and began to pace. Not thirty minutes ago, he had been smiling and discussing the path to peace with Felicity Long. What a fool he'd been. She was the Great Satan's ambassador, practiced in the art of deception. All her talk of cooperation was nothing but lies. Her words of support in front of the assembly, nothing but a diversion to buy America time to continue its attacks on Iran. Did she know about his son's murder? Is that why she had sought him out—to mock him to his face? Competing emotions—vengeful rage and debilitating sorrow—made it difficult for him to think clearly. He looked at Amir. "Will you help me, brother? Help me to avenge my firstborn son's death?"

Amir looked down at his feet. After a painfully long pause, he said, "I will not lie to you, brother. A terrible mistake was made. By presidential order, we have been providing their American military commanders with leaked information—real information—in order to establish trust. Until now, we have only leaked intelligence pertaining to affiliate activities in Lebanon, Syria, the Arabian Peninsula, and North Africa. The Americans were supposed to be tipped off about a Libyan ship smuggling the last cache of chemical weapons out of Syria. There is great demand for sarin on the black market, especially now that Assad's stockpile has been extradited by the Russians. But one of my analysts mixed up the shipping manifests and mistakenly leaked information about *our* ship smuggling the Sayyad-2 missiles. We did not learn about the error until after the SEALs hit the ship. My heart is broken to have to tell you this, Masoud, but you deserve to know the truth."

Instead of hot rage, an icy calm washed over Masoud. Now Ambassador Long's National Security Council comment suddenly made sense. *This* was the cooperation she was alluding to, not Iran bowing to IAEA pressure for transparency and nuclear-site inspections. Amir's secret program was what had grabbed the American president's attention. A terrible epiphany occurred to him as he put the second piece of the puzzle together. He felt light-headed and braced himself against a chair. "So this program is responsible for my son's death?"

His brother shook his head softly. "I know the pain of losing a son must be terrible. But we cannot put our personal need for revenge above the needs of our country and Islam. We cannot destroy the bridge of trust we have built with the Americans until the time is strategically right to do so."

"A mistake was made, but the mistake did not kill my son. The Americans did. Kamal's blood is on the hands of the Navy SEALs who assaulted the ship. We must avenge my son's death, Amir. Defang the serpent that you yourself said is the bane of your existence," Masoud said, shaking his fist, "and avenge Kamal's death."

Amir rubbed his beard in silence for a very long time. Finally, he spoke. "I will only agree if we can devise a trap that has plausible deniability and keeps my source in play with the Americans."

Masoud nodded. "The losses on their side must be commensurate with the losses on our side."

"That will be difficult."

"And dangerous."

"It will require many martyrs. Men of consequence and importance."

"Allah rewards the faithful and the brave."

Amir stood, walked to Masoud, and embraced him. "I will try to do this thing you ask of me, my brother," Amir whispered. "For Kamal."

"And for Persia," added Masoud.

"And for Allah, praise be his name."

CHAPTER 5

"It's my job to take your vitals, Mr. Kemper. Would you please just let me do my job?"

The nurse glared at him, cheeks flushed, one hand on her hip and the other on the machine that would take his pulse and blood pressure, if only he would let her.

"And I told you I'm fine. I just want to rest, but you keep waking my ass up with that damn machine to check if I'm still alive. Well, I'm alive . . . see?" Kemper said, waving childishly at her. "My ticker is beating; my blood pressure is just dandy. Now, please go, so I can get some sleep."

"Your doctor wants vitals every four hours," she said, but her voice had lost all its fight.

"He's not my doctor," Kemper said for what seemed the hundredth time. "My doctor is—"

"Right, right, I know," the nurse said, giving up and tossing her stethoscope onto the machine. "Your doctor is the lumberjack with the fake name who drops by and pisses the real doctors off. Thank God you're leaving today."

With that she rolled the machine out, mumbling obscenities under her breath.

Thirty seconds later, his hospital-room door swung open again, and this time in strolled "the lumberjack." Today, Commander Dan Munn looked nothing like an esteemed Navy doctor who rated silver oak leaves on his collar. Munn's unmarked BDU pants, untucked gray Columbia shirt, and Oakley desert boots screamed, *Don't fuck with me. I've earned the right to look like this.* The two-week beard growth he sported was the exclamation point. Munn was a former enlisted SEAL who, instead of retiring, had taken a detour into medical school, followed by a tough surgery residency, and finally an even tougher trauma fellowship. And now here he was, back with the teams, still serving the brotherhood, but in a distinctly different role.

"'Sup, bro?" Munn said, hands in his pockets.

"Shouldn't you be in North Carolina with Cathy, visiting her family before you deploy?" Kemper asked. "You're going down range in a few weeks, right?"

"Yeah, but she's probably glad to have a couple days away from me," Munn said, which they both knew wasn't true. "It's good for her to have some private time with her folks. Plus, I wanted to stick around until you discharge. Someone's gotta make sure you head home and not straight to the bars."

"Nothing to worry about. I rarely hit the party scene like I did back in the day."

It was true. Being a member of a Tier One unit nowadays meant keeping it low key. When he partied, he partied with his unit. And when he really wanted to cut loose, he'd do it at a friend's house rather than in public. It was better for everyone that way, except for maybe the lucky wife enlisted as the evening's designated driver.

"So when am I out of here?" he asked Munn.

"Admin is working on your discharge paperwork as we speak. An hour, two at the most."

"An hour, huh? Guess that means you're my ride?"

"Nah, Thiel insisted that he and the boys had that honor." Munn glanced at his oversize Suunto wristwatch. "I'm supposed to meet the gang in the lobby in fifteen."

"Cool," Kemper said and looked out the window at Hillsborough Bay and the silver-spired downtown Tampa skyline.

So what happens next? Rehab and a desk job?

Munn placed a hand on his shoulder, reading his mind. "Doctor Platz, the spine guy, thinks you'll have full recovery."

"My vertebra was cracked in half, Dan."

"Yes, but with the bone fragment back in place, your spine will heal. Now that we have the inflammation under control, you should be feeling a helluva lot better. Left leg feeling normal?"

"Almost," he said. "Still feels kind of heavy."

"That should go away completely in a few days."

Kemper eyed him with suspicion.

"Okay, two weeks tops," Munn said. "The bone fragment was pressing on the nerve, and now the nerve needs time to calm down. Plus, you had a ton of pressure in the spinal cavity from the swelling and blood and shit. Platz assured me he saw no damage to the nerve. A little physical therapy after the bone mends and you'll be good to go. Hell, I've got twenty bucks wagered that you'll be operational before Spaz."

That perked Kemper up. "Wager with who?"

"Gabe."

Kemper shook his head. "Dumb kid. When's he going to learn that experience trumps youth every time?"

"And that you never make a wager with a doctor who has confidential medical knowledge of *both* patients," Munn quipped.

After he'd stopped laughing, Kemper asked, "So, what's the verdict on Spaz?"

"Metal plates to rebuild the femur, and a vein graft to bypass his superficial femoral artery. He has a tough road ahead of him—anywhere from a three- to six-month recovery."

"You do realize when you collect the twenty bucks on that wager, the drinks are on you."

"I wouldn't have it any other way," Munn said.

Kemper looked down at his legs. The muscles in his thighs already looked flabby. Was that even possible? He hadn't been in the hospital that long.

"You okay, Jack?" Munn asked, his tone turning serious.

Kemper forced a smile. "Yeah, I'm good. Just don't bounce like I used to."

"True for us all," Munn said with a chuckle and a slap on the shoulder.

The hospital-room door flew open. "The sign says don't fucking disturb," Kemper barked without waiting to see who it was.

"Didn't think that applied to me," a baritone voice answered.

Kemper opened his mouth to assure this jackass that it applied to Air Force docs most of all, but then the tall figure stepped past Munn into his field of view.

With his neatly trimmed gray hair, pressed suit coat, and open-collar dress shirt, Captain Kelso Jarvis bore little resemblance to the rugged, bearded, mountain-man look of current operators. As if sensing the disparity, or remembering it, he shrugged off his suit coat, draped it over the back of a nearby chair, and began rolling up his sleeves.

"Snuck up on a Tier One operator. Not many men can say that. Men who are still breathing, that is," Jarvis said.

"Doesn't count when the man doing the sneaking happens to be a former Tier One SEAL commander, sir," said Munn, extending his hand to the man who was arguably the most legendary SEAL in the US military's secret Tier One umbrella. Kemper noticed the cords of muscle rippling across the former CSO's right forearm as he shook Munn's hand. Clearly, Jarvis still had it. His level of fitness cut at least a decade off his fifty years of age.

"Once a SEAL, always a SEAL," said Jarvis. "Been a while, Dan. Good to see you."

"Likewise, sir," said Munn. "I assume you came by to rib Kemper?"

"Absolutely." Jarvis turned toward Kemper. "So, how is our guy, Doc?"

Munn glanced between them. "Well, he's doing everything in his power to win the title of most belligerent SOB on the ward, but other than that, he's on the mend."

"That's a relief. I'd hate to think that same belligerent SOB who made my command tour miserable had gone soft in his old age." With a smile, Jarvis added, "It's good to see you, Jack."

"You too, sir," Kemper said, extending his right hand to his former boss.

Jarvis gripped his palm and then clasped his left hand against Kemper's forearm. "You can cut the 'sir' shit. You never called me that in Bosnia or Iraq, so why the hell start now?"

Despite the divergent paths they'd taken since Jarvis's retirement, the man would always be "Skipper" to Kemper. If Jarvis wouldn't let him say "sir," then he'd have to deal with the other. "In that case, what brings you to Tampa, Skipper?"

"I was in the neighborhood visiting SOCOM and thought I'd drop by and see my old LCPO. A little bird told me you'd had an accident."

"Minor setback," Kemper corrected, borrowing Jarvis's favorite line—the one he'd made legendary when making SITREPs to the brass.

While Jarvis laughed, Kemper wondered what a retired SEAL commander working in the civilian sector had going on at SOCOM. Anyone who knew Jarvis never believed he would stay out of the game for long.

"What's new with you?" Kemper asked. "How's civilian life treating you?"

"Relax, Senior. This is just a social call, nothing else," Jarvis said. Then, screwing up his face, he added, "And yes, that's right, I'm aware that you're *still* a fucking Senior Chief."

"Not gonna command a desk just to make Master Chief," Kemper said with a shrug. Jarvis understood. Rather than putting on a star and going soft pushing papers at the Pentagon, Jarvis had retired and moved on.

"Mind if I sit for a few minutes and shoot the shit? Swap a few lies?" Jarvis pulled up an empty chair next to Kemper's hospital bed.

"Be my guest," Kemper said, straightening. The movement sent a stinger down his back. Nothing like the pain he'd experienced on the *Darya-ye Noor*, but sharp enough that he fought the urge to grimace. No matter the situation, he refused to show weakness in front of Kelso Jarvis.

Munn shuffled backward toward the door. Checking his watch, he said, "I think I'll go intercept the ass clowns—er, I mean highly trained, elite, tactical operators—gathering in the lobby. Give you guys a few minutes to catch up before they crash your party."

Jarvis waved a hand. "No need to rush off, Dan," he said. "I swear this is just a social call."

Munn laughed. "You've always had a lousy poker face, Skipper," he said, heading out the door.

After the door shut behind him, Jarvis casually propped an ankle up on his knee and smiled at Kemper with his slate-gray eyes. "Doc's gone, Jack. How are you, really?"

"I'm fine. Really. Sore as hell, but the spine guy says after the bone heals I'll be a hundred percent. Fully operational."

"Requals?"

"Nah, should be back on line before that much time elapses."

"Good. Going through requals is a pain in the ass," Jarvis said, nodding. "How much time you got left?"

"Time?" Kemper asked, confused.

"Yeah, time," said Jarvis, knocking the edge off his words with his trademark Jack Nicholson chuckle. "What? You planning to stay in forever? Even *you* have a shelf life, Jack."

There it was again—*shelf life*.

"Hadn't really thought about it," he lied. "I got my twenty in, so I suppose I could put in papers anytime. But I still got a few good years left."

"I'm sure," Jarvis said. "But when the time comes, I might have a place for you." He uncrossed his legs, leaned forward, and propped his elbows on his knees. "Does Kate know you're here?"

Kemper hated when Jarvis did that—opened Pandora's box with one hand and, while you were gawking at it, tossed you a live grenade with the other. His current teammates knew better than to float his ex-wife's name—or mention his son, now sixteen—but by rank or history, Jarvis obviously felt he'd earned the privilege.

"We haven't talked in a long time," he said, hoping to leave it at that.

"I'm sorry to hear that. She was good for you. Tough girl, Kate. Funny, too. I always liked her." Jarvis continued, unbidden. "I knew you were divorced, but I'd heard you were dating her again—whatever the hell that means for two people who shared a life and had a son together."

"We were," Kemper said, silently wishing to end the conversation. "That changed after the thing in Afghanistan a couple of years back. She wanted me to get out after that. Something about straws and camels' backs."

Jarvis nodded, a frown tightening his face. "Gotcha," he said. "How's Jacob?"

Better off without me.

He sighed. "Honestly, Skipper, I have no idea. Like I said, we don't really talk."

Jarvis simply nodded. Every operator knew the toll the job took on families. Jarvis lived alone—or used to, back in the day—so he was intimate with the sacrifice. And the regret.

The door burst open, and Munn returned with six rowdy mountain men in tow. Kemper's brothers in arms. His family.

"Kinda nursing this shit, ain't ya?" Thiel said and high-fived him. The slap ignited a stab of pain in his back. This time it stayed concentrated at the surgery site, rather than radiating down his spine.

"Anything for a med chit to get out of PT, huh, Senior?" teased Pablo, with a scratch of the ridiculously thin beard that painted his chin. "Ain't you heard, man? The only easy workout was yesterday."

"I could whip your ass in a swim right now," Kemper fired back, goading the much younger three-time Iron Man competitor. "But why bother, when I could just whip your ass?"

Jarvis laughed at the dig, and the guys turned to stare at him en masse, as if they'd just noticed him for the first time.

"This your lawyer, Senior?" Rousch asked.

"No. This is Captain Kelso Jarvis," he said, and reveled in the gaping jaws all around—except for Thiel, who knew the Skipper and just shook his head with pity at the others.

"Honor to meet you, sir," Rousch said, regaining his composure and reaching out a hand. Only a SEAL would breach the protocol of waiting for a senior officer to extend his hand first. And only a blooded SEAL like Jarvis would expect it.

"Honor's mine," Jarvis said, rising. "Pleasure to meet the poor ass-holes charged with following the Senior Chief into battle. God bless you guys."

After shaking hands all around, Jarvis abruptly said, "Well, fellas, I should probably get going."

"Are you sure, Skipper?" Kemper said. "After I check out of this dump, we're gonna grab some beers. You're welcome to join us."

"I appreciate the offer, but it's time I go pretend I have a job," he said, donning his suit jacket and making for the door. "Left a number for you, Jack. Call me if you need anything, and for Christ's sake, keep me apprised of how you're doing, okay?"

"Will do, Skipper," he said, glancing at the business card Jarvis had left on the tray by his hospital bed.

Jarvis paused at the threshold just long enough to make eye contact with Kemper before disappearing. He didn't say anything, because his eyes said it all: *Don't forget about my offer.*

Kemper nodded deferentially and then shifted his attention back to the guys.

"Holy shit, fellas. Was that really *the* Captain Jarvis?" Rousch blurted out once the doorway was clear.

"Yeah, nice work, dipshit," Gabe said, leering at Rousch. "'Is that your lawyer? Smooth, dude. Fucking smooth."

Gator elbowed Gabe. "What a dumbass," Helo chimed in.

The others piled on, slamming Rousch until his cheeks were crimson.

"All right, all right. Cut a brother some slack," Kemper said.

"What time you outta here, boss?" Thiel asked. "I got a tee time, ya know."

"In that case, let's go," he said, and swung his legs out of bed. He winced, unable to mask the spear of pain from the twisting movement.

"Hold on there," Munn said with a laugh. "At least let the nurse get your friggin' IV out, bro. I'll go get her," he said, and disappeared out the door.

"You sure you're okay?" asked Thiel.

"Good as new. Thanks to Munn and that quack there," Kemper said, gesturing to Rousch. "If it wasn't for you, Spaz and I might not have made it. You're the real deal, Rousch. Bravo fuckin' Zulu, dude."

Rousch shrugged, and quickly shook Kemper's outstretched hand, clearly uncomfortable with such a healthy dose of praise from his team leader in front of the group.

"Now, let's go grab a beer," Kemper said, and rolled his arm so the IV was in Rousch's face. "Pull this fuckin' needle out, Doc."

While Rousch removed the IV, Pablo fetched a wheelchair from the adjacent room. Two minutes later, Kemper was strapped into some poor bastard's missing wheelchair, with the rest of the gang running at his side hooting and hollering. He tilted his head back to look at Rousch, who was propelling him down the corridor at ludicrous speed.

"Driver, we need to make a detour by Room 178 on our way out of this dump."

"Sure thing, Senior," Rousch said. "What's the mission?"

"Operation Spaz Attack." He turned to Pablo, who was jogging next to him. "Did you bring the two items I requested?"

"You mean these?" Pablo said, holding up a Spider-Man doll in one hand and a rubber shark in the other.

Kemper flashed Pablo his broadest Cheshire cat grin and then said to the group, "I heard from one of the nurses that Spaz was lonely. The least we can do is drop off his two best friends to keep him company while we go party."

CHAPTER 6

Jamkaran Mosque
Qom Province, Iran
March 24, 1321 Local Time

Masoud watched the young man's fingers tremble as he tried to tie the knot. Like hundreds of thousands of Shia Muslim pilgrims before him, Reza Pashaei was leaving a private message for the Twelfth Imam at the Well of Requests. Masoud had waited fifteen minutes for young Reza to compose his wish on a piece of the ambassador's private UN stationery. Then, as was the custom, the young man had folded the paper, fixed it with a string, and proceeded to tie his note for the Mahdi to the metal grate atop the well. In trying to complete the deed, Reza's nerves appeared to be getting the better of him.

"It is okay to drop the note in the well, Reza," Masoud said, placing a hand on his shoulder.

"I know many people do that, but I want to tie it as is the custom."

"Then let me help you."

"Thank you, but that is not necessary," Reza protested, cheeks flushed as he continued to fumble with the string.

Masoud noticed that the paint on the metal grate was worn and scraped—rubbed to a polish by millions of Persian fingers. The mosque kept no official accounting, but he imagined the number of notes left for the Mahdi surely reached the hundreds of thousands. Finally, not being able to stand it anymore, he snagged the ends of the string from Reza's fingers and deftly completed the knot. When he'd finished, he looked at Reza and smiled.

"The first time I left a message for the Mahdi, I was as nervous as you," he said. "Yours is an important message. But don't worry. I have faith your request will be granted."

Reza nodded but said nothing.

"Walk with me," Masoud said.

"Yes, sir."

He led young Reza to his favorite spot, a location fifty meters in front of the main facade, where one could marvel at the architectural beauty of the newly renovated Jamkaran Mosque. Masoud had visited this holiest of places at least half a dozen times since the renovation, but despite his familiarity with the complex, the experience had not lost its magic. The iconic onion-shaped dome, painted robin's-egg blue with gold adornments, was the most recognizable architectural element of the mosque. But his personal favorite had to be the twin minarets. Painted in Khatam style—ornate, geometric, and multihued—these towers were distinctly Persian. Many Iranians had criticized the Jamkaran renovation project for being excessively expensive, but Masoud believed the people of Persia needed a monument that represented their unique cultural and Islamic spirit. What better choice than the mosque dedicated to the Twelfth Imam—the promised one who would someday spread Islam to all corners and countries of the world?

"Can I ask you a question, Ambassador Modiri?" Reza said, breaking the serene silence.

"Yes, of course."

"Do you believe the Mahdi is coming soon?"

Masoud thought carefully about this question before answering. He decided that the boy was not in fact asking a question, but rather trying to convince himself he had made the right decision volunteering for the mission on which he was about to embark.

"Why do you ask this question? Are you afraid that by carrying out your task, you will miss the Mahdi's imminent return?"

Reza nodded.

"That is a perfectly valid concern for a man of your years, but take it from one who has spent thrice your lifetime waiting for al-Mahdi to return: no one can predict the date the Twelfth Imam will choose to reveal himself. Even the Supreme Leader does not know when the chosen one will usher in the new era of peace. A wise man does not concern himself with the when. A wise man does not focus on the waiting. Instead, a wise man devotes himself to living a life of piety and service to Allah, knowing that the only *certain* opportunity to bow before al-Mahdi is in the afterlife."

Reza, considering this, nodded.

"Let me ask you a question now," Masoud said.

"All right."

"If you fulfill the obligation you have to Allah and bring jihad to the apostates and nonbelievers, do you think the Mahdi will be blind to your actions?"

"I suppose not."

"And when you complete your mission, do you think he will somehow forget about your sacrifice?"

"I hope not."

"Allah sees all the deeds of men. Action does not pass unnoticed. Bravery does not go without reward. Your sacrifice will bring honor and glory to your family, to Persia, and to Islam."

Reza looked at him and smiled. "Thank you, Ambassador, for bringing me here today. I know you are a very busy and important man, and I am just a boy soldier. Your generosity and your wisdom give me strength."

Masoud draped his arm around the young man's shoulder. "Come, it's time to go. The drive back to Tehran will take two hours, and my wife is expecting us for dinner."

As they walked back to the car, Masoud thought about his own life and the choices he had made. He thought about his time in university, and his decision to pursue a career in politics rather than soldiering. He thought about his wife, Fatemeh, and how much he loved her. He thought about his sons and how much pride and happiness they brought him. And then he thought about Kamal—his most beloved lost treasure. The hole in his heart from his firstborn son's death was still gaping and raw. Like Kamal, Reza was a member of Quds Force. Like Kamal, Reza was brave and pious. According to Amir, Reza had volunteered for the suicide mission in Djibouti. When Amir told him that Reza's only request had been a one-day leave to visit the Holy Well at Jamkaran before deploying, Masoud had insisted that he be the one to take the young man.

He felt tears welling in the corners of his eyes as they walked.

Martyrdom is essential to jihad, he told himself. *The plan cannot succeed without sacrifice.*

The truth is sometimes ugly. The truth is sometimes painful.

Would he trade places with Reza, if given the opportunity? Would he sacrifice his wife and only remaining son?

Masoud wiped his eyes with his sleeve.

He was not that brave. He was not that young.

CHAPTER 7

Kemper skipped the buffet and went straight for the beer. Gabe, aka Special Operator First Class Gabriel Stein, had filled an aluminum tub to the brim with ice and at least five cases of beer. Kemper plunged both hands into the icy slush and retrieved two Budweiser Black Crown longnecks. As he made his way back to the table, he stopped to marvel at Zachary Stein's bar mitzvah cake.

Expertly crafted to resemble a Torah scroll being unfurled, the multilayered cake sat untouched in all its glory on a pedestal table beside the buffet. MAZEL TOV, ZACHARY! proclaimed the blue frosting letters set against a background of white fondant. A six-pointed Star of David and an impressive Navy SEAL trident insignia decorated with gold icing gave the cake a personalized touch. In the hierarchy of elaborate party desserts, this cake was a title contender.

Kemper felt a tug on his pant leg and looked down. He was greeted by a gap-toothed smile and an unholy mop of curly black hair.

"It's not time for cake. My mom said no one can have cake until after we dance, and that she's the only one allowed to cut the cake," said Samantha Stein, Zach's little sister.

"Don't worry," he said. "I'm just looking."

"Do you like chocolate? The icing is vanilla, but the inside is chocolate. Chocolate is Zach's favorite flavor."

Kemper made a show of licking his lips and said, "Mmmm, mine, too. What about you?"

"Chocolate is okay, but pink is my favorite flavor."

"Is pink a flavor?"

"Yep," she said, and then put her hands on her hips. "My mom said that the kids get cake before the grown-ups because bar mitzvahs are for kids, and last time when we had the Super Bowl party, the grown-ups ate all the cheese pizza, which was supposed to be for kids. I only got one piece of cheese pizza, and I cried."

Kemper nodded sympathetically. "I remember Pizza-gate well. You were not a happy camper. I'll tell you what, Samantha. If you're still hungry after you eat your piece of cake, and if there are no pieces left, I'll give you some of mine."

"Really, Mr. Jack?"

"Really. That way, we can call it even for what happened with the cheese pizza."

"Cool, thanks. Maybe I'll even let you dance with me. Bye," she said, and disappeared in a blur.

Kemper watched her go, his mind filling with pictures of Jacob. He had missed so much time when his son was an infant and toddling around in diapers, but he had spent almost a whole year at home recovering from an injury when Jacob was Samantha's age. Subconsciously, he rubbed the scar on his forearm. That year had been about rehab, requals, and family. He remembered savoring the little moments, falling deeply in love again with his wife, and bonding with his son. When it had been time to go back to work, Kate had supported, encouraged, and pushed him forward. And when it was time for him to leave and head down range with the team again, she had cried, perhaps realizing she had been instrumental in rebuilding him only to send him away again.

When he returned six months later, she had cried again—but this time because the man returned to her had reverted to the badass, door-kicking SEAL who had been sliced open in Iraq, not the attentive, caring husband and father she had loved during that year. The operational tempo picked up after that, and the time and the miles took their toll. Kate began to think of herself as a single parent, and he let her.

He let her . . .

He shook his head to scare away the ghosts of regret. The past was a sinkhole, and he wanted to be here, in the moment, with his brothers. He walked over to where Gabe was sitting, a beer in his hand and little Samantha squirming on his lap. Gabe's wife sat on one side, Rousch and his wife, April, on the other.

"I couldn't help but overhear Sam giving you the gouge on the cake," said Gabe. "We Steins can be a little high-strung when it comes to food, if you haven't noticed."

"Oh really? You mean like the time you nearly ripped Rousch's head off for eating one of your PowerBars?" Kemper asked, dropping into the empty chair next to Diane Stein.

"Or the time you sent your porterhouse back at Bern's three fucking times because it was too pink inside?" teased Rousch.

April socked Rousch in the arm. "Watch the language," she scolded. "This is a kid zone, not a war zone."

"Jeez," Rousch said, pretending to massage his arm, "there's more rules hanging with the wives than briefing in the SCIF."

"And while we're on the topic of language," Diane piped in, eyeing Gabe, "in addition to being a profanity-free bar mitzvah, this is also an acronym-free bar mitzvah. No one but you guys knows what a 'SCIF' is. If I hear one more sentence with more acronyms than actual words, I'm going to scream."

"You should hear our dinner conversations," said April. "I'll ask Mike about his day, and he'll say something like: 'Well, the CSO told my LCPO that an NCDU deployed with the JTF got a BZ from JSOC, blah, blah, blah . . .'"

"All you do is fight fire with fire," Diane said. "As soon as Gabe goes into Team Speak Mode, I immediately switch into Text Message Mode. He says, JSOC SCIF, I respond with OMG RUS—it works every time."

Kemper looked at Gabe. "What did your wife just say?"

Everyone at the table burst into laughter.

Pablo wandered over, a half-empty beer bottle dangling from two fingers. "So your little dude is a man now or something, Gabe? He ready to head for BUD/S and then down range, or what?"

"And when does his dad become a real man?" Rousch chimed in, earning a high five from Pablo.

Gabe made sure Samantha wasn't looking, then flipped his team-mates the bird. "A bar mitzvah is a rite of passage."

"So, it's sorta like a SEAL pinning on his trident after completing quals?" said Pablo.

"Except it's a rite of passage without the sleep deprivation, HALO jumps, extreme dive training, and explosive ordnance instruction," added Rousch, garnering another round of laughs.

Over the next twenty minutes, the conversation wandered, and so did Kemper's mind. His thoughts turned back to Jacob. His boy was also becoming a man, but without a father to guide him. He admired Gabe and Rousch. Somehow they had managed to be Tier One opera-tors and still be great family men. Like him, they were absent all the time, but unlike him, they found a way to not be *absent* when they were home—something he had never mastered. For him, to excel as a Tier One SEAL meant never turning off the switch. Why? Because he was afraid he wouldn't be able to turn it back on?

Suddenly, the hip-hop music the DJ was spinning stopped, and a familiar folk rhythm began to play over the loudspeakers. Kemper felt the energy of the crowd ignite. Within seconds, half the guests were on their feet—clapping, cheering, and dancing.

"'Hava Nagila,'" said Zach, jumping out of his chair. "Come on, fellas, it's Hora time!"

Kemper looked at Diane and raised an eyebrow.

"It's tradition to raise the boy up on a chair and dance. C'mon, Jack, it's fun."

Kemper smiled and politely waved her off. "You guys go. I'll watch from here."

"Suit yourself," Diane said with a fleeting glance as Gabe pulled her away by the arm. She and Kate had been friends—best friends, actually. He wondered what Gabe's wife thought of him. He wondered if Kate and Diane were still close.

Thirty seconds later, he found himself alone at the table—the only Tier One wallflower at the party. If Kate and Jacob were here, he'd be out there on the dance floor whooping it up like an idiot, too. A knot formed in his stomach as it occurred to him that not a single one of the wives had asked him about Kate or Jacob. After too many rebuffs, they'd given up any hope for a reunion. Bravo Squadron was stuck with him, the gloomy, non-Hora-dancing, broken-back sonuvabitch.

As he watched the families dancing and laughing, a strange thought occurred to him. Instead of cursing his broken back and numb leg, maybe he should think of the injury as an opportunity—a golden ticket out of life in the unit and back to the life he had given up. If he couldn't do both—and he had more than proven that he couldn't—then maybe it was time to hang up the trident and head home. He would have his pension and . . . he slipped his hand into his pocket and retrieved the business card that Jarvis had given him:

JOINT INTELLIGENCE RESEARCH GROUP
CAPT. KELSO JARVIS, USN (RET)
DIRECTOR

No street address. No website. Just a name and a title, with his mobile phone number hastily hand-scrawled in pen on the back. And what the hell was the Joint Intelligence Research Group? He slipped the card back into his pocket. Jarvis had made the transition to civilian life, and the man certainly didn't look broken. Quite the opposite, in fact. Maybe recent events were signs pointing his life in a new direction . . .

He felt a tug at his pant leg.

He looked down expectantly and found a very familiar gap-toothed smile and an even more unruly mop of curly black hair.

"Yeeees," he said.

"My mom says that everyone has to dance, including you, Mr. Jack, and if you don't dance, then you won't get any cake, and if *you* don't get any cake, then that means when the cake runs out, I don't get any *extra* cake, so you have to come dance with me, right now."

"Oh really?" he said, narrowing his eyes at Samantha Stein.

"Yes, really."

"Well, in that case, let's go," he said, taking her delicate fingers in his bear paw of a hand. "No man can refuse a dance from a girl as beautiful as you."

With a giggle and a twirl, she led him to the circle of people dancing. As the beat of the music picked up tempo, so did the clapping and the hooting and the hollering. Before he knew it, Kemper felt himself swept away in the counterclockwise rotation of the crowd. For thirty seconds, he forgot about the pain in his back and the pain in his heart, and he just danced—danced in celebration of life and friendship and a young boy becoming a man. And for thirty seconds, his life was perfect.

He felt something buzzing—an angry hornet clipped to his belt.

He looked right and saw Gabe palming a pager in his hand, shaking his head. He looked left and saw Zach being lowered to the ground, his chair gone still. The folk music was playing, but the main attraction had ground to a screeching halt.

They had been summoned.

All of them.

Something had gone to hell somewhere in the world, and Tier One had been tasked to fix it.

Kemper felt his heart sink. Not for himself, but for Gabe and Diane. For Samantha and all nine of her cousins. And most of all, for Zach. He watched Diane burst into the center of the circle and clutch Gabe's arm. He couldn't hear her voice, but he could read her lips: "Please, don't go. Not now. Just this once, Gabe, stay. Please, please . . . please."

"What's happening?" Samantha said into his ear. "Why is my mom crying?"

He set her gently onto the ground. Taking a knee in front of her, he said, "Nothing's wrong, sweetheart, except that your daddy has to go to work. We all have to go to work."

CHAPTER 8

Tampa, Florida
March 30, 1830 EDT

Kemper tapped the pager clipped to his belt with the side of his thumb—keeping time with the sound of the tires as they rolled over the concrete seams in the road.

Tap. Gurthump, gurthump. Tap. Gurthump, gurthump. Tap. Gurthump, gurthump.

Gabe and Pablo were in the front, and Thiel was beside him in the backseat of Pablo's jeep. They were crossing the Gandy Bridge, which stretched across the clear, blue-green Florida waters of the Hillsborough Bay, connecting St. Pete with more urban Tampa.

No one was talking.

To the rest of the modern world—a world flooded with Apple iPhones, Samsung Galaxies, and Motorola Droids—the pager was as appreciated as a paperweight. But to Tier One operators, the pager transcended its low-tech capability. It was a part of being. Never lost, and never to be lost. Never forgotten. Never forsaken. It was their battle cry. Their stoic good-bye. An invisible tether. A calling together. It was an amalgam of intangibles—powerful and contradictory and personal.

Three little beeps, and then the rituals started. Last call. Time to go. Don't worry. I'll be fine. One last hug. One last kiss. One last glance . . .

Leaving was easier for Kemper than for the others. Coming home—well, that was another matter altogether. He stared out the window at Hillsborough Bay. Pablo had the windows down, not because the air was cool and dry this time of year and it felt nice, but because Pablo always drove with the windows down. The wind buffeted Kemper's cheeks, and he squinted at Skyway Bridge stretching from Tierra Verde to Bradenton. It felt good—really damn good—to be making this ride. To think that just fifteen minutes ago he'd been contemplating leaving the teams. No way. Not an option. He couldn't do it.

He wouldn't do it.

He gripped his pager. "This is my fucking life, and I'm keeping it," he mumbled.

"What's that, Kemp?" said Thiel, glancing over.

"Nothing," he said. "Just ready to get it on."

Thiel held out his fist. Grinning wide, Kemper slammed his knuckles into it.

They approached MacDill Air Force Base via the main gate at the end of Dale Mabry Highway. The sprawling base occupied the entire southern tip of the South Tampa peninsula. Fueled by the events of 9/11, Central Command had expanded to near-biblical proportions to support the war on terror. As a theater-level unified combatant command, CENTCOM was responsible for the planning and execution of all joint military operations in the Middle East, North Africa, and Central Asia. In addition to CENTCOM, thirty-six other major and subordinate tenants called MacDill home. One of these tenants was the US Special Operations Command.

Like CENTCOM, SOCOM was a unified command, with the mission of overseeing Special Operations warfare for all branches of service. Unknown to the residents of Tampa, and even to the military personnel on base, Kemper and his teammates fell rather loosely under the SOCOM umbrella. They had been known by many code names over the years, but whatever the brass changed their name to, they were the Navy's elite and secret special warfare team. Along with their Army sister unit, Delta Force, they were designated as "Tier One" Special Forces. The best of the best. The most versatile and lethal counterterrorism weapons the United States had.

Unlike the rest of the Special Operations community, the Tier One units had the shortest possible chain of command and often received orders directly from the White House. Once tasked, they operated with unprecedented autonomy within their mission parameters. The secrecy around the unit—and often the rumors and false information that circulated—made it easier to do their job, but also much more dangerous. *Only one link in the chain separates us from the top dog,* Kemper often joked with Thiel. *Whadaya think would happen if that link broke?*

At the gate, Pablo gathered up their military IDs and passed them to the Air Force Military Police. The guard stared at each of them, comparing their faces to photographs, and then scanned each ID with a handheld scanner. A second MP walked a complete circle around Pablo's Jeep, surveying the vehicle. As usual, their long hair and beards prompted closer scrutiny of their credentials and the vehicle. Finally satisfied, the MP waved them through.

Pablo weaved past the commissary and then followed an access road along the expanse of airfield ramps and runways. They drove past rows of KC-135 aerial refuelers belonging to the 927th Air refueling wing—the only resident flying unit since the F-16 fighters departed years ago. Halfway down the two-mile-long runway, Pablo turned the truck onto a smaller, unlined road, past the sign that read "Authorized Personnel Only. Use of Deadly Force in Effect." After fifty yards, the road doglegged sharply to the right and then disappeared into a thick grove of brush and mangrove trees. After another hundred yards they were forced to snake among a series of concrete barriers that deliberately slowed approaching vehicles to a crawl. A runaway vehicle at sixty miles an hour was a hell of a weapon. After exiting the serpentine gauntlet, the road opened onto a large blacktop parking lot serving a small brick building. The lot was deserted, except for the desert camo Humvee and its .50-caliber machine gun pointed at the approaching road. Pablo drove them past the Humvee, gave a nod to the unseen occupants, and proceeded to another guard gate. Like MacDill's main entrance, this portal was equipped with twin hydraulic metal barriers, but it was the unseen surveillance equipment and invisible barriers that made it different. Presently, the massive steel plates were flipped up at forty-five-degree angles, blocking access to the road just beyond.

Pablo stopped short of the barrier and put the Jeep's transmission into park.

"Gents," said a guard clad in black Nomex, his finger on the trigger guard of his short barrel SOPMOD M4.

"'Sup, bro?" Pablo said and handed over all four special IDs within their hard plastic cases.

The guard nodded and scanned the IDs with his handheld scanner, linked to a computer log controlling access to the secret compound.

"Having a good week?" the guard asked, staring into Pablo's eyes with a gaze that suggested he couldn't care less.

Pablo nodded and gave the programmed response. "About average."

This was one of four acceptable responses. Had they answered differently, a dozen armed men would have converged on the vehicle from the woods a few yards away, and life would have gotten infinitely more interesting for everyone.

The guard's shoulders relaxed and he flashed Pablo a legitimate smile. "Have a good one, guys," he said, and waved them through. The steel panels lowered into the ground, and a superfluous wooden arm flipped up, clearing the path for them to enter.

Kemper smirked at that. *It's the little touches . . .*

The "compound" on the other side was underwhelming—three small one-story brick buildings clustered around a common parking lot. A simple wooden deck, replete with bench seats and an oversize gas grill, spanned the gap between two of the buildings. As far as passing aircraft and satellites were concerned, this little back corner of MacDill held nothing of interest.

Nothing to see here, folks, nothing at all.

Above ground, that is.

Kemper pursed his lips. Today, the parking lot was full, with twice again as many vehicles parked in the weeds along the tree line. This was not just a gathering of the squadron on 0300 alert. This was something big.

"What the hell?" Thiel said as Pablo found a spot along the tree line. "Last time I saw this many vehicles—"

Kemper shook his head, cutting him off.

Not now.

Their summons had officially taken an ominous turn. Kemper was unsure whether to be nervous or excited. Either something horrible had happened or JSOC was planning something big. He leaped out of the rear seat of the Jeep and hit the ground with a thud. The resulting stinger in his spine recalibrated his mood. He looked again at the full parking lot. Pain be damned—he would tell the docs whatever they had to hear to be sure he was at the front of the pack for whatever the hell this was. No way was he going to watch from the sidelines.

A black SUV skidded to an angry stop in the grass next to Pablo's Jeep—Rousch's ride—and the remaining four members of the team popped out. Eight brooding SEALs converged on the center building and entered through a set of tinted glass doors. Kemper brought up the rear, following Spaz who, in only two weeks, had mastered the operation of his wheelchair as if it were a drift racer. If someone were to offer Kemper a wheelchair ride, he might actually take it, because the dull ache in his back had turned sharp and fiery. The combination of the Jeep's off-road suspension and Tampa's shitty roads hadn't done his spine any favors. If only he'd listened to Munn and stayed on his pain meds instead of tossing the bottle like a macho dumbass.

Inside, a young Third Class Petty Officer, whom Kemper recognized but whose name he could not remember, sat beside the quarterdeck desk. Beyond him stretched an office floor—government-issue banal—partitioned with lifeless gray cubicles. The four offices along the perimeter were similarly deserted. The doors were shut, the windows dark.

Odd, Kemper thought. *Thirty vehicles outside and up top is a ghost town.*

"Hey, Senior," the young Petty Officer said. "Captain Thomas said to head directly down to the SCIF. Everyone else is already down there."

Kemper nodded, resisting the urge to ask what in the hell was going on. The young support sailor could not answer the question anyway. The kid's ID, dangling in a plastic case from a lanyard around his neck, sported a green border around his name: EM3 RUSSELL, MICHAEL. Green indicated that Petty Officer Russell held a Top Secret–level clearance. TS access meant something to the rest of the world, but it didn't buy a ticket to ride in the Tier One carnival.

Kemper walked to his office and dumped his keys and cell phone into the top desk drawer. He held the drawer open, and the rest of the team followed suit. He shut the drawer and led the gang to an elevator in the far corner of the building. He swiped his red-bordered ID badge across the wall-mounted card reader beside the elevator. When the light turned green, he pushed the down button, and the elevator doors whisked open.

He often wondered how far underground the Tier One compound was located. The elevator plunge took six or seven seconds, and this lift was not some slouch commercial rig. One story per second, he figured, which put them at least fifty feet under.

Probably more.

The doors slid open, revealing a steel door five paces away, painted green and labeled SENSITIVE COMPARTMENTED INFORMATION FACILITY. Flanking the stout green door stood two armed guards dressed in full battle rattle and clutching rifles slung combat-style across their chests.

These boys weren't much for small talk.

All business, Kemper handed the right-hand guard his ID. The guard scanned it with his iPod-size scanner, and the system assigned a digital-entry time stamp. Later, when Kemper left the SCIF, an exit stamp would be logged, thereby giving the system the ability to inventory the status of all persons granted access to what was the most secure space on all of MacDill Air Force Base. The guard rotated the scanner in his hand and offered it to Kemper to image his left thumb and right index finger. The scanner flashed green. His fingerprints were a match. The stone-faced guard entered a rotating code into the keypad beside the green door.

The door hissed open, and the left-hand guard waved him through.

Cavernous and serious, the dimly lit SCIF buzzed with all the clandestine self-importance and urgency one would expect from a place where decisions that change the world are routinely made. A star-shaped conference table dominated the center of the room—the six spokes of the star formed by three long tables joined in the middle. And around this polished mahogany Polaris, several clusters of SEALs worked huddled over laptops. Kemper spied the unit's Chief Staff Officer, Captain Thomas, seated at the opposite side of the table, talking with three men in civilian clothes. And while their clothes screamed Wall Street executive, their chiseled chins and athletic builds suggested they were anything but. Kemper recognized the suit seated to the CSO's right; he'd run into the guy a few times down range. The name escaped him, but the guy had made a solid first impression in the field. Competent, with balls as big as any team guy. From their prior interactions, Kemper had pegged him for a spook working for the Activity—the secret intelligence unit based in Fort Belvoir, Virginia. Like wolves, spooks preferred to travel in packs, so maybe the other two guys were also Activity. Feeling Kemper's gaze, the suit looked up. Recognition flashed in the man's eyes, and he gave a nod before returning his attention to the discussion at hand.

Kemper stood with his team and waited until Captain Thomas beckoned him with a wave.

"What the hell is going on?" Pablo asked.

"Looks like it's time to find out," Kemper said. "Be right back with the gouge."

While he headed over, Pablo and the rest of the team smartly stayed put, clearly assuming that a private conversation requiring their Senior Chief was above their pay grades. Kemper scanned a wall of flat-screen monitors, looking for some clue as to why so many Special Warfare assets had been mobilized. Five ninety-six-inch flat-screen displays were tuned to various feeds, including CNN, Fox News, BBC, Al Jazeera, and an eight-way split screen showed camera feeds from the approaches to the compound, the upstairs admin spaces, the elevator, and the green access door. The televisions offered no hints of what had brought both of the Tier One squadrons, a couple of dozen operators from partner agencies, and a pack of spooks to the SCIF on such short notice.

"How are you doing, Jack?" Captain Thomas said, extending his hand.

Expecting to find the CSO grim and serious, Kemper had braced himself for bad news. Instead, the Captain's tone was crisp; his mood eager and infectious.

"Skipper," Kemper said with a firm handshake. "What the shit is happening?"

"Opportunity of a lifetime, we hope," Thomas said. "I think you know Shane Smith from our friends up north?"

"That little victory in the Hindu Kush, right?" Kemper said, certain that the spook's actual name was neither Shane nor Smith.

"Good memory," Smith said. "We ran into each other in Ramadi, also."

Put a shaggy beard on this guy—and bingo. Memories of the longest eighteen-hour clusterfuck of his life came rushing back. He flashed a broad smile and gripped Smith's forearm as they shook hands. "That's right, that's right. It's been a while. You were Daniel then, I think."

Smith shook his head with a sly grin at the inappropriate comment.

"I owe you big from that night," Kemper added.

"From what I remember, I'd say we're even."

"Now that we've established you fellas have a crush on each other," Thomas said with a shake of the head, "maybe we can get back to work?"

"Absolutely," said Kemper. "Whatcha cooking up, Skipper?"

"Jack, we have a real chance to do something big here, but I'll need all hands to execute the plan. I know you're not fully operational, but we could use your help in the N3 shop with mission planning. Shane here will bring you up to speed first, then we'll reconvene in about fifteen mikes. Solid?"

"Good to go, Skipper." He felt his heart sink. "Not fully operational" meant the CSO knew he wasn't fit to fight. He pushed the self-centered thought aside. Executing the mission took priority. He followed Smith to a breakout room. Smith shut the door behind them and grabbed a chair next to Kemper at the small table. He pushed the room's silver-colored secure phone to the side to make room for his notebook computer.

"I'm gonna go fast, Senior. Just the down-and-dirty overview," the spook began, flipping open his laptop and angling the screen to share the view. "Most of what I'm showing you comes from source data above my pay grade, but I've seen the raw intel, and trust me, this is all solid shit."

Kemper took Smith's comment to mean he would not be sharing any of his source data, but that was hardly unusual. Source data was compartmentalized and fiercely protected. In the case of human intelligence (HUMINT), source data might come from an asset whose identity was known by two people in the entire US intelligence apparatus. Some of the team guys hated the fact that *they* couldn't validate source data for missions they would be risking their lives on. Thiel, for example, only trusted intel from the Group Ten Special Activity Units, which were staffed by fellow SEALS. In Thiel's mind, Group Ten source data was pure, and the only intel he was willing to bet his life on, no questions asked. Kemper, on the other hand, had no such hang-ups. He had no desire to pore over raw data. The intelligence community had scores of folks much better suited for that kind of analysis than he was. If the intel was vetted by his Head Shed, then Kemper considered it actionable. His job was to capture, kill, rescue, or destroy whatever target was packaged for his team. Sure, sometimes the intel was wrong, and sometimes that sucked hard for guys like him at the pointy end of the spear, but that was the business he'd chosen. He was a Tier One operator, not a spook.

"I understand," Kemper said. "Whatcha got?"

Smith clicked on a thumbnail, and a satellite image of a compound filled the screen: brown buildings surrounded by brown walls, in a sea of brown land. The bottom edge of the screen showed a sliver of blue surf breaking against a shallow cliff.

"Definitely Middle East," Kemper said. "If I had to guess, I'd say this is somewhere in Yemen."

"Correct. This particular compound is located southwest of Al Mukalla in southern Yemen. For several years now, it's functioned essentially as a rest stop for Al Qaeda and other groups moving along the coast and in and out of the country. Shitheads from the Horn of Africa traveling to or from Oman, for example, often stop over here. Lately, we've observed points of interest from the other side of the Gulf using this compound to both shed gear and gear up before disappearing into whatever hole they choose to hide in.

"We keep this place off the list of targets for drone strikes and counterterrorism action because it gives us a nice spot to monitor movement, look for activity, and the like. Activity has increased in tandem with the drone tasking because the shitheads think this place is off the grid."

Kemper nodded, rubbing his beard. "It looks familiar. I'd swear I've seen this place before."

"Could be," Smith said. "These shithole compounds all look the same to me, but this one could have popped up on any number of your prior action briefs. If you were operating in the remote areas farther south and west, this compound could have been the source for a bad-guy QRF. A handful of low levels are in residence at any given time, with the head count surging periodically. But because the compound serves a waypoint, it houses a robust weapons cache at all times."

Kemper marveled at how much the spooks knew about every little nook and cranny of the enemy's operation.

"The important thing is that, as far as we know, it has never housed anything but low or occasional midlevel operatives."

"AQAP?" Kemper asked, referring to Al Qaeda members occupying the Arabian Peninsula.

"Almost exclusively," Smith said. "In total, we figure there's six hundred-plus AQAP fighters in Yemen at any given time, plus maybe half that number on the other side of Yemen's northern border with Saudi Arabia."

"That's a lot of shitheads." Kemper wasn't sure where Smith was going with this. The Special Warfare community had been asking for permission to strike the low-level bad guys in Yemen for years but always met a stonewall. "Why are you showing me this? Please tell me this means we finally get to go after these guys in their breeding grounds."

"Activity in Yemen has always been limited to high-value targets only," Smith said. "And unfortunately that has not changed."

Kemper shook his head. A bullshit policy. Why limit yourself to attacking the head of the snake, when savaging the body could yield equally effective results? A dead snake is a dead snake. To his surprise, the right corner of the spook's mouth curled into a crooked grin.

"As far as hitting HVTs, well, permission is not an issue," Smith said. "That's where this little shithole comes in."

He zoomed out on the imagery until Kemper could see the town of Al Mukalla—the fifth largest city in Yemen, with a population of three hundred thousand. Kemper studied the roads and topography around the city in relation to the compound. The compound was located twenty or thirty miles southwest of the city, within a few clicks of the N4 coastal road. It was built at the base of a modest-size mountain, with the terrain spreading out flat in every direction into empty desert. While twenty-five miles was meaningless in the Western world, traveling that distance in Yemen was a haul.

Kemper pointed to the mountain. Even without knowing what the mission was, his mind had shifted to operational planning. "Nice high ground for an approach," he said.

"I was thinking the same thing, but it's rough terrain, so you'd need to INFIL ahead of time to position."

"HALO INFIL at night. North of here and then a tough hump over," Kemper said, tapping a ridgeline. "But you'd be the night," he added, meaning the approach would have stealth.

"Surface of the moon behind you," Smith said, nodding. "Rest of the force from the water."

"Yeah," Kemper agreed. "Night HALO with RIBs to hit the beach in the dark and coordinate with the northern team. Two teams of twelve." He watched Smith's face for a sign that would give away the target.

Smith stayed quiet, still not ready to drop his drawers.

Kemper shrugged it off. "Command comms?"

Please don't say satellite relay. He'd been fucked by shitty satellite comms more than once.

"Airborne command and control relaying to the TOC in Djibouti. Real time, for all intents and purposes. This shithole is definitely not a place you want to lose comms."

Kemper was impressed. The higher authority was apparently in wish-granting mode, which meant this op had been blessed by the White House. He could barely stand it anymore, so he pressed. "How many guys per team?"

Smith leaned back in his chair and stared at him. After a few seconds, he finally broke. "You'll want everyone for this one, Senior."

After two decades in the teams, very little surprised Kemper—and that surprised him. "Both squadrons?"

"You'll need 'em. Pull this off and Tier One will go down in history as the guys who ended the war against Al Qaeda."

Smith leaned forward and began clicking the touch pad on the computer. Kemper watched as Top Secret files popped open on the screen—page after page, image after image, HVT after HVT. Most of the head shots were familiar—ghosts and murderers from the hundreds of operations and briefs he'd participated in during the past fifteen years. His pulse quickened, and he felt that old familiar surge of adrenaline.

"You're telling me that all the bad guys in these pictures are going to be at this compound at the same time?"

Smith grinned.

"And we know when?"

"We're positive. We have inside guys—sources and operators—embedded in all of the parent organizations confirming this. We're talking about an AQ fucking convention—leadership from all the worst cells. We think this is an attempt to unify the myriad of splintered factions together."

"But why?" Kemper asked. "These guys have always hunted in small packs, and that was actually what made them hard to fight. They must know that."

"Two words: Islamic State," Smith said. "The nut jobs in Syria and western Iraq are spreading through the region like a cancer, as you know. Bad for the good guys, but it turns out bad for Al Qaeda as well. With ISIS getting all the press, both recruitment and funding are drying up for the AQ affiliates. Business as usual is becoming unsustainable for them. We think this is a summit to pull the factions together and plan something dramatic that gets them back on the front pages." Smith rose and paced for a moment, his excitement almost palpable. "Guys like you and me—guys who have spent years of our lives, lost our friends, sacrificed our marriages, and spilled our blood hunting these assholes—are finally going to get our day in the sun."

"I don't know, it sounds . . ." Kemper stopped himself. The opportunity seemed almost too perfect, but that feeling was natural when you didn't have all the information. Smith had shared only a small fraction of the intelligence that had been aggregated. This was how the game worked.

Smith sat back down and leaned forward, propping his elbows on his knees. "Look, dude, I wouldn't be here with you if I didn't believe this, and my boss sure as hell wouldn't have sent me. We're not chasing unicorns. This opportunity is the real deal—the op that could change it all."

Kemper shifted in his chair and felt a twinge in his back. The biggest operation in Naval Special Warfare history and he would be on the bench. All the years he'd logged since 9/11, grinding it out in the field to get to this moment, all wasted. Jack Kemper would be watching his brothers end Al Qaeda from a TV in the TOC.

"You okay, Senior?" Smith asked. "I thought you'd be doing back-flips over this shit."

Kemper nodded slowly. Smith was right. This wasn't about him. This wasn't about glory or personal retribution. Terrorism was the plague of the twenty-first century. Jihad was the disease. Whatever the sacrifice, he had sworn to make it. Whatever the contribution, he had sworn to give it. On September 11, 2001, he had made a promise to protect the lives of innocents, not just in America but everywhere Al Qaeda tried to sow death and misery. He had never reneged on that promise. He wasn't about to now.

He met the gaze of the man whose name he'd never truly know.

"Tell me everything you can," he said. "We have work to do."

CHAPTER 9

Gulfstream G550
Southeast Bound over Central Europe
April 2, 0130 GMT

Kelso Jarvis finished reading the Yemen operation debrief for the third time—an events summary drafted by him, addressed to his boss, for a mission that hadn't happened yet. In the world of Special Operations, he suspected he was the only person masochistic enough to spend time writing post-op debriefs for future events, but he found the exercise extremely insightful. Just as world-class athletes visualize performing the movements and mechanics of their sport before each competition, Jarvis visualized every mission parameter, start to finish, before the actors were set in motion:

Terrain maps, satellite coverage, drone flight and strike plans, INFIL procedures, team movements, firing solutions, kill-order criteria, target response, target evasion, counterinsurgency probabilities, first-level backup plans, second-level backup plans, abort criteria, and EXFIL procedures . . .

So many moving parts.

So many contingencies.

Normal people did not possess the mental horsepower to do his job, but Jarvis had never considered himself "normal." From a very young age, he'd recognized that he perceived the world differently than other people. Not just the way numbers and letters had colors associated with them, making them easier to remember and combine into strings, but also in the way he comprehended life's complexities. Times and dates occupied spatial positions. Geopolitical events stacked themselves into pyramidal hierarchies. Options and variables for complex problems automatically organized themselves into ladder diagrams with logic gates in his mind. He no longer included the color-coded graphical representations of his thought processes in his reports; it was far too frustrating and time consuming to explain such things to other people. He often lamented the fact that synesthesia was so rare, because life was too fascinating a journey to travel alone. But he was alone, and had been for a very long time. In fact, in fifty years he had only crossed paths with one other synesthete. And while she shared some of his traits—they both perceived the letter *A* and numeral *9* as red, for example—he had quickly assessed her gifts as inferior to his own and lost interest.

He simply could not imagine perception without sensory cross-connection.

Without intuition.

Without affect.

Early in his military career, Jarvis had learned the danger of sharing his intuitions with his subordinates, his peers, and even his superiors. His perceptions and intuitions had a tendency to rattle people. Military operations determined life and death, not just for American soldiers and foreign combatants, but also for noncombatants and civilians. *Mortality is not math, Jarvis,* his first CO had lectured. *You need to learn to trust your gut.* Outwardly, he had laughed and thanked the man for such sound advice, but inside, he'd found the suggestion repugnant. When someone says, "Go with your gut," what they're really saying is that they prefer to obey the rudimentary reflexes of their vestigial limbic brain rather than utilize their highly evolved mammalian cerebral cortex. In other words, "Me think like lizard. It much more easy."

After that experience, Jarvis learned the importance of wearing masks. In the beginning, it was exhausting trying to emulate the type of people who occupied all the different worlds he traversed back and forth between his personal and professional life. But over time, his skills improved, and eventually changing his persona became as automatic as a chameleon changing the color of his skin. Kelso Jarvis was not simply Kelso Jarvis. He was many different men to many different people. Jack Kemper and his fellow SEALs idolized Kelso Jarvis, the Tier One operator, who talked their talk and walked their walk, but they would not feel the same connection with Kelso Jarvis, the politician's ass-kisser. He loved Kemper and the team, appreciated them for who they were and the strengths they brought to the party, but they didn't carry the same burdens he carried. They didn't interpret data, identify problems, and create solutions the same way he could. And most important, they didn't have an understanding of the big picture.

His computer screen saver turned on—a passive-aggressive taunt to stop zoning out and get back to work. He pushed the secure laptop away in disgust, sighed, closed his eyes, and leaned his head back against the plush, leather-appointed headrest. The Gulfstream's cabin was so well insulated that despite traveling at nearly six hundred miles an hour, he did not need earplugs. This particular jet, on loan from supporters over at CENTCOM, was way too luxurious for his taste. Actually, he didn't mind luxury per se. What he minded was the appropriation of luxury for the intercontinental transportation of government employees. It was akin to giving a garbageman the keys to a Range Rover and telling him to make his rounds. He would have been perfectly happy stretched out on a sleeping bag beside Kemper and the Tier One SEALs in the back of a C-130.

Footsteps.

He opened his eyes. A female attendant, with curves that even her green flight suit couldn't hide, approached him from the galley.

"More coffee, sir?" she said with a smile, stopping next to his seat.

"Yes, thank you. Use this, please," he said and handed over his stainless-steel tumbler.

"Cream and sugar?"

"Black."

"Yes, sir."

He watched her go, wondering what modeling agency CENTCOM had plucked her from. Maybe the coffee service on this VIP transport was a luxury he could grant exception to. He glanced at his watch. Two hours and they would be on the ground at the joint base in the Republic of Djibouti on the horn of Africa.

He hated Djibouti.

Both the country and the base.

He had nearly lost his Tier One command because of a mission out of that place. Why? Because he chose to disregard the asinine orders of a paper-pushing civilian in the TOC while he was fighting for survival on the ground in Ethiopia. That fiasco had happened more than a decade ago, but he remembered the details as if it were yesterday. Information and perception were so tightly linked in his mind that time did not erode his memories the way it seemed to for everyone else.

Phil McDonald had been the spook's name.

What a jackass that guy was.

When Jarvis was an operator, he'd often fantasized about what could be accomplished if he—rather than some pencil-neck politician—was granted both the means and authority to protect America without having to fret over political fallout. Someone important apparently had similar thoughts, because opportunities that had previously been sequestered had suddenly become available to him. According to his boss, an unofficial, unwritten mandate had been issued to speed the transition of experienced operators into civilian leadership positions bestowed with secret authority. Whether this had come down from POTUS, the JCS, or SECDEF, Jarvis did not know, but someone with serious swag believed that empowering men like him was critical to the future success of US clandestine operations. And now that he was on "the inside," Jarvis considered it his personal obligation to purge the chain of command of people like Phil McDonald and replace them with people like Shane Smith.

The polished mahogany door separating the passenger cabin from the aft sleeping quarters cracked open. Jarvis looked up.

Speak of the devil.

Smith stepped into the cabin, rubbing his eyes. Jarvis had hand-picked the former Delta operator for the joint interagency counterterrorism task force he now commanded, and was in the process of mentoring him for bigger and better things. Like Jarvis, Smith was retired from active duty and worked as a civilian for the Joint Intelligence Research Group. Over the past three years, his young prodigy had become more than just a trusted subordinate—he had become a friend. At least as much of a friend as a chameleon can have. Despite the difference in age and positional authority, Jarvis trusted Smith implicitly.

As his operations officer slipped into the seat beside him, Jarvis slipped into his operator persona. "Get some sleep?"

"A little, but I've got so much spinning around in my head it woke me up," said Smith, shifting uncomfortably.

"What's on your mind, Shane?" Jarvis asked, holding the man's eyes in a way he knew would be intimidating, but familiar from his time in Delta Force. "I didn't drag your ass out of that shithole in Mogadishu and all the way to this task force so you could hold back. Talk to me."

Smith nodded and took a deep breath. "It's the data stream. Not the data itself, but the stream that's bothering me."

Jarvis pursed his lips, mostly for effect, but secretly he was intrigued to see where his Ops O was going with this thread. Maybe, just maybe, with enough tutelage, Smith might develop the skills and knowledge necessary to succeed him as Director. "What do you mean?"

"The data seems solid, don't get me wrong. If it weren't, I would say so," said Smith, tapping his armrest. "The intersecting streams support everything we'd expect to see for a high-level meeting. We have embedded assets in most of the camps, and they not only confirm that a meeting has been called, but they are now confirming movement of the principals. The movement in force and size is consistent with what I'd expect for an incursion into Yemen. Also, the movements are not coordinated. The different groups are moving in accordance with their unique SOP fingerprints. For example, Mohamed Al-Badari is traveling through Iraq, and his border team is in place as expected in Jordan, near Al Qaim, while Raheem Mufar is following his typical protocol of switching identity in Kosovo, playing that tired Eastern Bloc businessman we all know by now. The point is, all those different cells have very different signatures of communication and movement, and we are seeing those fingerprints. It makes it impossible to conclude this is a ruse promulgated by a single source."

"I thought you said something was bothering you, but instead of playing devil's advocate, you just outlined all the reasons this mission should be a go. What's your—" He stopped as the blonde flight attendant returned with his tumbler in one hand and a carafe and extra cup in the other. "Thank you," Jarvis said as she handed him his thermos.

"You're welcome, sir." To Smith she asked, "Would you like coffee, sir?"

Smith flashed her his best cool-guy smile and said, "You came prepared."

"Always," she said, unfazed by his charm.

"Coffee would be great, thanks. I take it black."

She nodded and deftly poured a stream of steaming Columbian roast into a Styrofoam cup, which she then handed to Smith.

The chemical formula of polystyrene (C8H8)n, popped into Jarvis's head, accompanied by a mental image of an expanded hydrocarbon chain of hexagonal phenyl groups. He watched Smith take a sip from the Styrofoam cup and resisted the urge to wrinkle his nose at the endocrine-disrupting styrene oligomers being released by the hot thermoplastic and subsequently ingested by his prodigy. *These* were not the type of things that Tier One operators worried about, so the topic was not something the "retired operator" Kelso Jarvis would interrupt the conversation to mention.

"Anyway," said Jarvis, slipping deeper into his SEAL-self to make it easier for Smith to speak freely, "you're doing a pretty shitty job of raising red flags for me, Shane."

Smith chuckled and shook his head. "I know, I know."

"It's the data stream, you said, that bothers you?" Jarvis prompted.

"Yeah, but not even the individual streams," Smith said, rubbing his temples. "It's more the way they intersect. They come together so damn well."

"And that's bad?"

"Not necessarily bad," he said, shrugging. "Just worth discussing."

Jarvis had considered a similar hypothesis himself and dismissed it. He was impressed that Smith had thought of it. He was also impressed at how quickly the former door-kicking Delta operator had taken to intelligence analysis. Unfortunately, Smith was still uncertain of his capabilities, and he was hesitant to challenge any of Jarvis's ideas. Now was a good time to do something about that.

"Okay, then let's stop pussyfooting around and discuss it. You're thinking it, so why don't you just fucking say it. You think the meet is a ruse. You think we're being set up because all the data streams show principals moving like they're supposed to. Am I right?"

Smith nodded.

"I considered that possibility. But the communication styles and methodology have remained unique to each principal from the beginning, which tells me that it's unlikely one puppet master could be pulling all the strings."

"What was the data source for the hit on the Iranian ship in the Gulf last month?" Smith asked.

Jarvis met the other man's gaze. His first reaction to Smith's probe was to fire back a "need to know" dodge, but it was becoming clear that criterion had already been met. "Original data or confirming?" he asked, buying time as he decided how much he should share.

"I know the confirming data. Hell, I developed half of those assets, and I run the cell in Hindu Kush. No, I mean the original data."

Jarvis split the difference between full disclosure and a lie. When in doubt, only go halfway. "I have a very reliable asset with close connections to the Deputy Director of Clandestine Operations in VEVAK."

"Why don't I know about this asset?"

"Why did you need to know before now?"

Smith didn't say anything for a moment. "I suppose I didn't," he finally agreed. "That was the source for the hit on the *Darya-ye Noor*?"

Jarvis nodded. It was more complicated than that, of course, but that was basically the truth.

"Who works that asset?" Smith asked.

"I do," Jarvis said, watching Smith's response, partially interested, partially amused.

"Personally?"

"Yes. Me and me alone," he answered, sipping his endocrine-disrupting, styrene oligomer–free coffee.

Smith looked impressed, but less surprised than he would have expected. Then, he asked the next obvious question. "And the source data for this meeting in Yemen?"

Jarvis cocked an eyebrow. "You want to know if it is the same source point? It is not." The answer, again, not a complete lie, but the shades of truth here were pretty spectral.

Smith sat back and took a sip of his poisoned coffee, then rolled his head in a slow circle, cracking vertebrae in a sign of visible relief. He looked past Jarvis and out the oval window into the black. "Do you think the *Darya-ye Noor* was a trap?"

"If it was, then it was a pretty shitty trap. No RPGs, no anti-air fire support of any kind. Amateur effort at best. Sometimes in our line of work, shit just happens," he said, in full badass SEAL mode now. "Look, Shane, the shitheads are learning how we operate. Most likely, the shitstorm on the mission was just a shipboard security–driven effort trying to prepare for a number of *What-if* scenarios. There's nothing to suggest they knew specifically that we were coming."

"I don't like it," Smith murmured, still staring out the window.

"Neither do I," Jarvis said. "Our enemies are always learning and adapting, never forget that."

He wondered if there was anything to Smith's data-stream concern. If there was, why didn't he perceive the problem? Based on his assessment of the data, his trusted source in VEVAK, and his track record of sound judgment, Jarvis had gotten presidential authority to mobilize heaven and earth to spring a trap in Yemen and break Al Qaeda's back. God forbid he was actually wrong.

That seemed pretty unlikely.

He was a details guy. He didn't make those kinds of mistakes.

CHAPTER 10

Joint Special Operations Task Force
Camp Lemonnier
Djibouti, Africa
April 4, 1745 Local Time

Reza Pashaei said a silent prayer—perhaps the two hundredth of the day—for Allah to give him strength. He asked Allah to make his face a stone mask, concealing the anxiety in his heart, the fear in his mind, and the pain in his abdomen. The burden was so heavy, each step was a trial, and he felt so very, very ill. They'd told him he would be nauseated, and the doctor had given him medication that was supposed to help, but his unit commander had cautioned him. *"If you take the pills, do so sparingly, as they will make you drowsy and dull your wits."* Reza had dumped the pills down the toilet. He'd made a promise to the Mahdi on a slip of paper at the Jamkaran Mosque. To fulfill that promise, he needed to be clear of mind and strong of heart.

He tried to walk normally as he approached the gate to the Joint Special Operations Task Force compound. When the gate guard smiled at him, he returned the gesture with great effort.

"Hey, June," said the young American soldier, as he unlocked the gate. "How's your mom, dude?"

"She is well, thank you," Reza said.

A sick mother in Pakistan was the excuse he'd given for the short absence from his duties on the sprawling base in Djibouti. Best known for housing the Combined Joint Task Force—Horn of Africa, the base was home to a number of much less advertised commands, including the small and unassuming compound where he'd worked for several years. The hard plastic ID around his neck—worn and scratched from years of service on the filthy base—said his name was Junaid Ahmad. But nobody called him that. The Americans wasted no effort trying to pronounce his Pakistani pseudonym, and by the end of his first day on the job he had been forever dubbed "June."

"You back for good?" asked the American, an Army intelligence specialist named David. It was no coincidence that so many Americans were named for Jews.

"Yes," he said, as the specialist closed and locked the gate behind him. "Maybe we play backgammon tonight?"

David flashed him a sly grin. "If you think I'm gonna let you whup my ass again, you're sorely mistaken."

"Okay. Then this time, I will let you win," Reza said, returning the gibe.

He liked David. After four years working at the base, he found it impossible not to like many of the young men he'd met. Over time, his perception of the Americans had changed. How they led their infidel lives was just as offensive to him today as it was the day he started his assignment, but now he viewed men like David as victims, rather than the true enemy. Yes, they were part of the West's attempt to subjugate Muslims—the true heirs of the earth—but as individuals they were oblivious to this fact. They were blind servants of the Zionists—puppets unable to perceive the strings controlling their every move. A part of him was sad that these men served a cause obscured from them, and worse, that they would die in a war they were preordained to lose.

He watched as David searched his worn leather shoulder bag, riffling through the contents with both hands. Not that it mattered. He carried nothing of consequence in the bag, just his books and mobile phone, no incriminating items. His mobile phone was just a mobile phone, with no special technology or spy components. While his mission would surely fail without it, he was not worried. His phone had been cleared for use on the base. The real danger was hidden inside him, packed in sealed, sterile bags deep inside his abdomen.

The inspection was quick and cursory. David trusted "June."

"See ya, buddy," David said, handing the bag back to him. "Come by the hooch if you want to make some of that badass coffee and get a game on. I'll be off duty in another hour or so."

Reza smiled broadly and nodded but didn't answer for fear that if he did, he might vomit or, worse, soil his pants.

The American gave a small wave and they parted company.

He had shared many meals with David over the last few months, and the American had told him all about the girl he hoped to marry "back in the States" and the job waiting for him at his father's company if he ever left the Rangers. The girlfriend apparently wanted him to stay at home. Always the Americans shared the details of their private lives with such uncomfortable abandon. As instructed by his Quds commander, Reza had shared invented stories in return—humorous tales of his fictitious family back in Islamabad and aspirations both vulnerable and hopeful of going to England to study computers. Much of June's backstory was based on Reza's real-life dreams as a teenager—a technique taught to him to help avoid inconsistencies. He had dreamed of going to England, having heard amazing stories about life in the UK from his cousin, Ahmed, who had actually attended King's College London. But those foolish dreams were before he had learned the truth about the West. Before he understood how the Jews and Christians used money, sex, and drugs to woo good Muslims from their faith. His cousin was dead now, at the hands of Reza's uncle; with justice served, at least Ahmed's soul had a chance for salvation.

"You okay, June?" said a voice, baritone and close.

Reza started and looked up. The man wore no markings on his uniform. The dirty brown cargo pants and a black T-shirt were not really a uniform, but Reza knew, from scraps of conversations, that this man was a Navy SEAL assigned to the intelligence unit on the base.

"Yes, I'm fine," Reza said. He tried to swallow but couldn't. The achy heaviness inside him was getting worse, and so was the constant feeling that he had to defecate. "I am quite tired from my trip."

"Right," the man said and scratched the short beard on his face. "Sorry, I forgot. How's your mom?"

"She is well, thank you." Reza felt sweat beading on his forehead. He glanced nervously at the now-setting sun and said a silent prayer that the coming darkness would better conceal his condition.

"Good to hear. I hope she stays healthy, because I'd hate to lose our best 'terp," said the SEAL. "Take it easy, June."

Reza exhaled with relief and wiped his brow with the back of his hand as the SEAL departed. He looked beyond the row of trailers housing the showers and toilets and spied his target: the brown stucco building, unremarkable by all accounts, with no windows and a flat, green door. It looked like the other four buildings in the small compound, the only differentiating features being the thick bundle of cables snaking into the east wall and a cluster of antennae and satellite dishes fixed to the roof. Reza had never been in this building, which he knew to be the Operations Center for the Special Forces soldiers. It was a restricted compound, a base within a base, where the SEALs launched their strikes at his brothers in the region. No foreigners were permitted near this building. The building was surrounded by a row of waist-high concrete barriers, and always had a small group of Army Rangers shuffling about, trying to appear casual despite their loaded weapons and body armor. Thanks to the hard work of his brothers in Iran and their tireless research on enhancing explosive yields, he would not need to be inside the building for the mission to succeed. He would not even need to be close to it. His commander had told him that anything inside thirty meters was likely to achieve success. Within twenty meters, success was guaranteed. Twenty meters would not be a problem. The row of trailers where the enemy relieved himself was not much farther than that.

He forced his eyes away from the target.

In his mind, a warning played like a song: *If you want to keep your job, Reza, never approach the Special Forces operations center. Never let the Americans catch you looking at it. Pretend it does not exist.* This had been the advice from the "cousin" who had arranged his transfer from working as a menial laborer at the main barracks to his current coveted position as a "cultural interpreter" for the intelligence specialists. He regularly volunteered as an interpreter for the Special Forces teams, and over the past three years he had worked hard for the Americans, building relationships and earning trust.

His VEVAK handler had pressured Reza to seek embedded assignments with the SEAL teams so that one day he would have the opportunity to inflict damage to the infidels' most prized soldiers. But his small size, and the affection many of the older soldiers had developed for him, had kept him from such assignments. This lost opportunity had made him feel like a failure, and more than once caused him to question his faith. Now that Allah had unveiled his true purpose, it all made sense. He, Reza Pashaei, the eldest son of Aftab Ali Pashaei, devoted disciple of his holiness the Twelfth Imam, servant of Allah, had been chosen for the greatest and most esteemed honor a soldier of jihad could ask for.

His prayers had been answered.

A spasm of pain shot through his pelvis and back, so sharp it made his man parts burn and his eyes fill with tears. He clenched his buttocks, fighting the powerful urge to defecate. He considered for a moment going to the toilet in search of relief, but his last four efforts to relieve himself had resulted in pain but nothing else. Sweat streamed down his forehead, mixing with the tears. His face felt flushed. They had told him he would most certainly develop a fever. What if the Americans sent him home ill? Or worse, what if they thought he appeared anxious and might be a threat? He bent at the waist to wipe his face with his shirt, and a nauseous spasm caused him to stumble to the left and crash into something hard.

Or someone.

The impact sent pain through his lower belly and knocked him off balance. He was falling—a vision of his belly tearing open and his insides spilling out onto the dirt flashed in his mind. He would not survive a fall; the mission would fail.

A powerful hand gripped his left arm, keeping him on his feet. He looked down at the muscular forearm. A thin white scar twisted around the golden flesh, like a snake coiled around the trunk of a tree. Reza shrank in the cold shadow of fear. The mark of the devil—this man was a demon lieutenant of Great Satan, sent to kill him in the moment before triumph. Reza tilted his head up, expecting to find the muzzle of a pistol pointed at his forehead.

Instead, he found a square-jawed, bearded scowl.

"Shit, dude. What are you doing?" said the demon soldier.

"I'm so sorry," Reza said, steadying himself. "I was not paying attention."

The soldier released his vise grip on Reza's wrist. "No problem," said the American, but he didn't smile.

Reza recognized this man: he was a Navy SEAL like the last one, but this operator was older, and the most revered by the other soldiers. This man was a decorated servant of the devil and, Reza realized, his final test. The SEAL's gaze seemed to go through him, probing and diagnosing, like an X-ray scanning his insides. Fear surged through him, and a putrid foulness roiled up from his stomach into his throat. He swallowed down the vomit, took a breath, and steeled himself for the delicate battle of words and wits he had no choice but fight.

"You're the 'terp from the intel shop, right?" the SEAL asked in a voice that was more interrogating than social.

"Yes," Reza said, extending his hand in the easy, American style. "I'm called June."

At that, the man's face softened a bit. "I remember you from last year."

"Yes, the problem in Somalia."

The American demon nodded thoughtfully. Then he spoke. "You okay? You look green, son."

"Green?" Reza asked, panicking inside. "Funny, I've always considered myself brown."

The SEAL stared at him for an awkward moment, then burst into laughter and clapped him on the back. The blow, which normally he would have found offensive but only mildly physically irritating, sent a fresh wave of nausea rippling through his body.

"Next time, June, try to watch where you're going."

"Yes, of course. My apologies."

Trembling, Reza watched the SEAL marked with the sign of the serpent walk away. Once he was certain the man would not turn around, he closed his eyes and exhaled. He had won; he had passed his final test. The devil has sent his most lethal and discerning lieutenant to stop him, and Reza had disguised himself in the mannerisms and humor of the enemy to make himself invisible. Deception, not soldiering, had always been Reza's greatest talent. Allah had seen this in him, which was why he had been chosen for this task.

He pressed firmly into his abdomen, which made the pain ebb, giving him a few seconds of much-needed relief. A small reward for his victory over the devil's disciple. He glanced at his wristwatch—a Casio G-Shock given to him by a SEAL called Pablo after working forty-eight hours without sleep to support a difficult operation last year. He smiled at the irony as he wiped the sweat from his burning forehead. All the symbols, all the clues, all the enemy's deceptions, were so obvious to him now. He had never experienced such clarity of mind. This was Allah's work. This was Allah's will. This was Allah's gift to him before his death and resurrection in Paradise.

He turned to look upon the plain brown building that, Insha'Allah, would soon be a flaming temple of victory.

He took a step toward it.

Then another.

The pain was back.

It didn't matter . . . the time for suffering was almost over.

CHAPTER 11

The cheap, wobbly roller chair was the most uncomfortable thing Kemper had ever had the misfortune to sit on. He couldn't decide which was more painful: the emotional toil of being confined to this particular chair while the rest of his team deployed on the greatest counterterrorism mission of all time, or the physical toil of occupying a chair whose only design criteria was to inflict agony on persons recovering from spine trauma. He pressed the adjustment lever, hoping to find some relief for his hunched and aching back by raising the seat height. With a long, slow hiss, the chair sank to the lowest setting. He tugged upward on the seat, but the pneumatic cylinder refused to budge, stubbornly keeping the seat cushion fourteen inches off the ground.

He stood and kicked the chair aside. "Stupid piece of shit."

A couple of team support guys sitting at computer terminals nearby turned to look at him. Beside him, Spaz chuckled from his wheelchair.

"Sorry," he mumbled. "Having a disagreement with an inanimate object over here."

He started pacing.

He glanced at the mission clock mounted among six giant flat-screen monitors on the east wall. Only two minutes had passed since he last checked the time. The waiting was killing him. He needed a task to keep his mind occupied, but every one in need of doing was already being handled by someone in the TOC infinitely more qualified in operational oversight than he was. He had already checked in with both squadrons twelve minutes ago. He fought the urge to check in again, not wanting to be *that* guy. Why was he so wound up? Everything was progressing according to plan. Nothing to worry about.

Whiskey squadron had deployed by HALO drop and was now on foot, moving down from the mountains into position north of the AQ compound. Scotch squadron had deployed by sea, but they had closed the distance to shore a little too quickly in their quiet boats. Scotch was now burning time in a holding pattern before making their final approach to the rocky shore. Together they were Crusader—an appropriate, though politically incorrect, name for the op. After the kick, both teams would fall under Thiel's direction as Crusader One and strike the compound from opposite directions.

Kemper looked around the TOC, taking the emotional temperature of the room. The environment was quiet and confident. Military calm. Only he was frenetic. Only he was an engine revving at redline rpm with the transmission stuck in neutral. Across the room, Commander Dietrich and Commander Perez—the squadron commanders for the Tier One SEAL teams—sat forehead to forehead in quiet discussion. Kemper watched the two men for a moment. Words couldn't express the admiration he held for these two officers—men whose mettle and fidelity had been tested hundreds of times and never faltered. Dietrich laughed at something Perez said and patted his compeer on the shoulder. Then, he stood and began his signature pre-op stroll around the TOC. Like a pilot conducting a preflight checklist, Dietrich verified every detail and mission parameter before putting his squadron in harm's way. First stop, the air-support and med guys, who were constantly on secure phones. Next stop, the "eyes guys," who were responsible for coordinating the satellites and drones. His third stop was Kemper's station.

Kemper stopped pacing and anchored himself to his desk—leaning forward and placing his palms down on either side of his computer keyboard. Intel flash populated his monitor, but the feed had gone stale, the latest being fourteen minutes old. He felt a hand on his shoulder just as his wireless headset crackled. Dietrich started to ask him a question, but Kemper held up a finger, hushing the senior officer.

"Crusader Main—Scotch Actual. Feet wet."

Thiel's hushed voice brimmed with excitement. "Scotch," Kemper said into his mike, "call feet dry." He heard two clicks in reply and then looked over his shoulder and grinned at Dietrich. "Scotch is in the drink," he said. "Feet dry on the rocks in twenty-five minutes—plenty of time for the guys to make the kilometer-and-a-half swim." He was still amazed at the thought of the whole squadron moving in together.

"Whiskey?" Dietrich asked.

"In position and holding," Kemper answered.

Even the emotionally flat Peter Dietrich could not keep his grin bottled up. "The head count from the thermal on the drones suggests all the guests have arrived. You can see it on the middle monitor. Every goddamn one of them is inside that compound."

"I wouldn't believe it if I wasn't staring at the imagery with my own two eyes," said Kemper. The situation was so insanely perfect, it was starting to make him paranoid. "Nothing new from our OGA friends?"

Dietrich shook his head. "Everyone who was supposed to be here showed up, and they all moved in predictable ways. It's the first bona fide AQAP convention in Yemen."

"Yes, sir," he said.

"Anything to add, Spaz?" the officer asked.

"Watching and learning, sir," the younger SEAL said.

Dietrich nodded and moved on to his next stop, leaving Kemper alone with his computer and his anxiety.

Predictable ways?

Maybe that was what bothered him. That and something he hadn't yet put his finger on.

He shrugged. Worst-case scenario, different terrorists show up than the ones they were hoping to nail. Did it really matter when hell's fury was about to rain down on every-damn-body in that compound? A dead shithead was still a dead shithead. He wished he could be there to see it go down. The operator side of him hoped the bastards fought to "the last soldier of Allah," as the jihadists always promised. He would love for Thiel and the boys to send every one of them straight to hell. The calmer, practical side of him hoped that, instead, the SEALs would nab a bunch of key guys with intimate knowledge of AQ operations and future terror plots. If Shane Smith was right, then the intelligence yield alone from this op could drive a stake into the heart of Al Qaeda.

Kemper looked around. Where the hell was Smith anyway? It wasn't like a spook to miss the big surprise party. Then again, spooks were weird dudes. He wouldn't be surprised if Smith had already been tasked to sniff out the next big stinking plot to kill Americans. It could be months, even years, before they crossed paths again.

The dull ache in his spine reminded him that he was still hunched over the desk. He straightened, feeling the impulse to twist his shoulders and crack his back like he always did. But that was before the injury; he didn't dare try that now. He'd made that mistake once and paid dearly for it with debilitating spasms for the rest of the day. He cracked his knuckles instead and looked around for someone to bug.

"Air?" he called out to the flight suit–clad soldier at the console across the desk from him.

"Good to go," the pilot from the 160th SOAR answered with a thumbs-up. "Times two," he added, referring to the backup team on the USS *San Antonio*, circling offshore in the Gulf. They had an additional Marine air attachment, AV-8B Harriers for air support if the shit hit the fan, and two additional CH-47s in case they struck gold and had an assload of crows—aka insurgent prisoners—that needed to be hauled out of the compound for interrogation.

"Med?" Kemper asked the SEAL medic beside him.

"All set." The Senior Chief Eighteen Delta medic was just as pissed off as Kemper to be running med ops from the TOC and not out there kicking in the door with the team. "JMAU is fully staged aboard the *San Antonio*. I got the CASEVAC birds farped there as well, but they'll be airborne at the kick."

Kemper nodded.

Yes, he was irritating as hell asking people questions he already knew the answers to, but damn it, what else was he supposed to do? He started pacing again and felt eyes on his back. He glanced over his shoulder and saw Dietrich gesturing for him to relax and take a seat. Kemper shook his head, too amped up to sit. He checked the clock. Ten minutes had ticked by. He looked at the real-time thermal imagery from the Predator drone displayed on the center flat-screen. After a few minutes of that, he shifted his gaze to the separate feed from the dedicated drone following Whiskey's movement. Whiskey team was dug in like ticks on a deer, scattered across the rocky face of the closest hill outside the compound. He saw very little movement—just the occasional shifting of numb feet, a routine he knew intimately from cramming himself in cracks and dugouts for hours on end. Scotch didn't have dedicated drone coverage at the moment—no real reason to watch them swim. The primary Predator would pick them up once they were "feet dry" on the beach.

He looked back at his computer screen and wasted a few more minutes scanning through the intel bullets.

Time passed.

Slowly.

Thiel's voice crackled in Kemper's ear, taunting him from the field: "Main, Scotch Actual—feet dry. We're Crusader Actual."

Thiel was now Crusader One, the voice of two squadrons merged under his leadership. Kemper pictured Thiel switching his radio over to check in with Whiskey and bring the other squadron on a single frequency—one big, happy, lethal team. He turned to the drone feed and watched multicolored silhouettes moving among the rocks at the water's edge. Scotch thermals held much more blue and green than the operators to the north, their bodies cool from the water approach. Only the center of each man glowed with a tiny yellow-and-red bull's-eye. But that would change. By the time they reached the compound, their thermal signatures would match their brothers'.

Angels of death, glowing hot like flames in the cold, black desert.

"Main—copy. On time," Kemper said, acknowledging Thiel's report. After the teams performed buddy checks on gear and weapons, they would begin the swift but silent move toward the target. It wouldn't be long now.

"Little birds are up," Air Ops called out. "CASEVAC up in ten mikes."

"Scout Two is back in orbit. Standing by," the drone coordinator called out, informing everyone in the TOC that they were on single drone coverage because he had moved one drone to a higher altitude orbit. This was done both for contingency and to conserve fuel.

Kemper glanced at the monitor with the satellite feed. The imagery was so crisp, they might not need the drones, but for tonight's op, he was glad to have three independent sources of coverage. He tapped his foot on the floor, aware the sound was annoying, but he couldn't help himself. The nervous energy was like a bomb in his gut, ready to explode. He never felt this way in the field—only now, trapped in the

TOC, forced to worry and watch "through the window," like an old lady in her rocking chair.

A hush fell over the TOC. Kemper turned and saw Commanders Dietrich and Perez standing shoulder-to-shoulder in front of the wall of monitors.

"Go?" Perez asked.

This was the last chance for anyone on support to call out a problem. Whenever Kemper was in the field, there was always something that delayed the op. A drone glitch, loss of satellite imagery, comms problem with a helo. Something. Tonight, the room was miraculously silent. Kemper scanned the room, looking for new faces, but Shane Smith was still AWOL. And where the hell was the unit CSO, Captain Thomas? Kemper couldn't believe—

"Go," Dietrich said, breaking the silence.

Perez nodded.

Dietrich looked at Kemper.

Kemper met his gaze and said, "All green. No changes. We're go."

Dietrich nodded. "All right, gents, let's go make some history we can't tell anyone about."

The room responded with nervous laughter. Kemper was finally getting pumped. He balled his hands into fists and had to restrain himself from barking out a *Fuck yeah!* Beside him, Spaz mumbled just that under his breath.

Still looking at Dietrich, he keyed his mike and said the words, "Crusader Actual, Main—all green."

"Main, Crusader Actual—roger that."

The second hand of the clock began its painfully slow sweep, torturing everyone in the TOC for the next two and a half minutes while the teams closed on the compound. Kemper heard a shuffle in the back of the room. He turned and saw Captain Thomas crossing the threshold.

About fucking time you showed up, Skipper, he thought.

Thomas entered the TOC with none of the fanfare his O-6 rank and command would demand elsewhere in the Navy. They were all SEALs here. That was enough. Thomas nodded at Kemper first, then at Dietrich and Perez. Kemper nodded back and returned his attention to the center screen. He watched two clusters of colorful heat signatures rise in unison, then like a choreographed ballet, the silhouettes spread apart, only to converge a moment later as the SEALs advanced on the target compound. From the bird's-eye view of the drone camera, their movements looked slow and graceful, but Kemper knew this was a deception. The SEALs were moving fast and working hard.

The drone operator cleared his throat.

Air Ops made a hushed call to his helo teams.

Kemper shifted his gaze to the left monitor and watched the scene unfolding all over again in the distinctive green-gray imagery of the satellite feed, which lagged a few seconds behind the drone feed. He tapped his foot with increasing tempo as the teams converged on the perimeter wall of the compound. The overhead perspective was misleading; Kemper guessed the wall was much taller than the imagery suggested. Three meters high. Maybe four. Inside the compound perimeter, there were only a couple of notable thermals: a security patrol moving along the wall, and the yellow glow of a pickup truck engine—the last vehicle to arrive and still cooling down. As far as thermal imagery was concerned, there were no guards patrolling outside the wall. And from the detailed satellite imagery, the wall lacked sniper towers. The compound proper had three windows on the second story with line of sight on the team approaching from the northern mountains. It was difficult to tell in vertical 2-D whether any of the dozens of thermals milling around inside the main building were on the second floor or the ground level. Almost certainly, the shitheads had spotters at the window, but without night vision, he doubted they would spot the assault team. Even if they did have night vision and they did spot the northern squad, it wouldn't change the outcome. This wasn't a normal mission with only a handful of SEALs. They weren't worried about footprint here—speed and size and firepower would rule the night.

"That's it, looking good," someone murmured, but Kemper didn't look up to see who'd said it. The two teams were along the north and south walls now. The most dangerous part of the approach was over and seemingly without compromise. The half-dozen figures in the yard of the compound were still milling casually about. The heat signatures inside the main building were typical social aggregate. No one was panicking. No one was running for weapons or taking defensive positions.

The two teams spread along the north and south perimeter walls, bunching to the sides and leaving a gap in the middle. In the gap, a single silhouette remained. These were the breachers, setting charges to blast access holes for the SEALs to penetrate the compound perimeter. Time slowed to a crawl, and Kemper became aware of his breathing, his pulse thumping in his eardrums. He watched. He waited. Charges set, the two breachers cleared their respective blast zones, and in unison, rejoined their teammates on opposite sides of the compound. On the north wall, two unlucky fuckers had stopped their patrol to chat and smoke a cigarette—the spot they chose was directly opposite where the charges were set.

Three heartbeats later, two bright flashes appeared on the drone feed, the two guards on the north wall disappearing in the light. For Kemper the experience was eerily unnatural, watching the explosions on the monitors in complete silence. Lightning without the thunder. In the field, you felt the power. It hit your chest. You expected it. You wanted it. The satellite feed flashed then—the same blast in time lag, erupting in bright light-green hues. The monitors refreshed and Kemper watched his teammates pour through the gaping holes in the walls on both sides of the compound. As the SEALs streamed through the northern breach, they stepped over blobs of orange—what remained of the jihadists who had been smoking. Kemper figured they were the lucky ones, considering what was about to happen to their brothers inside.

The image on the center screen became momentarily obstructed as two helicopters from the 160th streaked over the compound several thousand feet beneath the drone. The helos circled, then settled into complementary orbits to provide air support. On the ground, the picture had changed. The SEAL force was now divided. As the assault teams closed on the main building, two smaller groups remained behind outside the perimeter wall, ready to fend off any Al Qaeda QRF in the event the enemy called for help.

Gunfire flashed as the four remaining guards in the yard tried to return fire, but within seconds the figures lay still, sprawled out on the dirt, their thermal imagery cooling.

"Get some," growled Spaz from beside him.

"Fuck yeah," Kemper mumbled to himself. Across the room, both squadron commanders had begun pacing, but their eyes were glued to the screens on the wall above them. Beside them, Captain Thomas stood perfectly still, arms folded across his chest. Kemper realized that the CSO was the only man in the room wearing an actual uniform—desert digital khakis with an embroidered black trident above his name. Thomas looked iconic. Archetypal. The image hung with Kemper, and he had to shake his head to snap out of it.

Back on the center screen, he watched the thermal images of at least two dozen high-level bad guys moving to the center of the building. They appeared now to all be standing on the same floor. Strangely, they were lining up, putting themselves in symmetrical rows, and then their images seemed to become compact—in unison. Kemper felt his heart skip a beat.

They're kneeling.

His throat went tight.

Oh shit.

"They're kneeling!" he yelled, pointing at the center screen. "They're praying. Pull the team. Pull them back!"

Perez and Dietrich both turned and stared at him. Dietrich's eyes went wide with comprehension. He reached for the headset on the console beside him. The center screen turned white. For a moment, Kemper thought they'd lost the drone feed, but then the left screen—the satellite feed—flashed bright yellow.

Perez dropped his headset.

"What the fuck?" someone shouted.

"What was that? What just happened?" Captain Thomas belted.

"Crusader Actual, Crusader Actual—SITREP."

The voice was Dietrich's, calm and flat, in Kemper's headset.

Kemper did not key his mike. There was nobody left on the other end to answer the call.

The image in the center screen refreshed. A bright ball of red streaked across the frame and then abruptly stopped. That was one of the two Night Stalker helicopters crashing and bursting into flames north of the compound. When the screen refreshed again, Kemper was looking at nothing. No structure. No stone wall. No scattered body parts. Just clumps of yellow and red that had been his teammates. His best friends. His family. Instead, the entire area glowed a homogeneous orange, the heat from the massive explosion turning what had once been a terrorist compound in the Yemen desert into a burning Hell on Earth.

"Crusader Actual—Crusader Actual."

"Night Stalker Zero One—Zero Two—this is Homeplate."

Someone in the room began to sob.

Kemper stumbled, dropping to one knee. He rose and walked away from his station; he felt a tug as his headset jerked off his head and fell to the floor. Spaz grabbed his sleeve, but he shook the hand off without looking at his teammate and barreled into the double doors. He was going to be sick. His boots found the dirt, and his stomach lurched. He heaved, vomiting as he stumbled into the darkness outside the TOC.

He became acutely aware of the stench enveloping him. The stank of puke on his beard. The stank of the Horn of Africa.

He started running. Running from the pulsing evil orange screens in the TOC. Running to escape the smell of this place. His stomach muscles cramped violently as he dry-heaved, and he began to stumble. The lurching caused his back to spasm and sent pain shooting down his left leg. He didn't care. The pain was real, everything else a dream. He tripped and caught himself before crashing into a pair of skinny legs. Looking up, he saw an eerily familiar face staring down at him with wet eyes. Eyes full of pain. Beads of sweat ran down the boy's forehead, and for a moment Kemper thought the young man was going to puke as well. This boy was one of *them*. Rage erupted inside him. He wanted to rip the kid's Arab head off his stinking Arab body. His palm found the butt of the pistol in his drop holster, but he willed himself to push on before he did something he would regret later.

"Open the fucking gate," he said to the Army Ranger standing beside the padlocked gate.

"You okay?" the soldier said as he spun the lock on the chain. "Dude, what's wrong?" he asked, looking back at the TOC.

Kemper shook his head and shoved his way past, slamming the heavy gate full open against the fence. He ran, just ran, down the dirt road toward the flight line, his path lit by anemic moonlight, and the ambient light of the compound fading into the distance behind him.

Then, abruptly, he stopped.

All the voices in his mind—screaming, sobbing, and begging—fell silent. The noise and pain were gone, replaced by a memory:

You're the 'terp from the intel shop, right?

Yes. I'm called June.

I remember you from last year.

Yes, the problem in Somalia.

You okay? You look green, son.

Kemper turned around.

In the haze, he saw the boy—still staring at him from the other side of the fence. Their eyes met. The boy called June fished something out of his bag. A grenade? No. A mobile phone. He pressed buttons on the phone, then raised a hand toward Kemper.

Kemper took one step toward the JSOTF compound and screamed.

June pressed another button with his thumb.

The Army Ranger drew his weapon.

Lightning struck.

Then came the thunder.

The shock wave sent Kemper flying. There was heat, a horrible smell, and pain.

The docs will put me back together, he thought as the world went black.

The docs always did.

PART II

In the dark, a man can hide his scars.

CHAPTER 12

He is jogging along the beach, shirtless and barefoot, trying to ignore the searing burn on his neck and shoulders. He's stayed in the sun too long, and now he can almost hear the chiding he'll get about not wearing sunscreen when he gets back to the beach house. The wagging finger, the pouty lips, the one fist pressed against a curvaceous hip . . .

The thought of Kate scolding him makes him grin like a schoolboy.

He picks up the pace in anticipation.

His calves ache, especially his left calf. Actually, his entire left leg is killing him. The pain snakes all the way up to his ass and across his lower back. This should mean something, a voice in his head says, something more than the lactic burn from pushing his thirty-eight-year-old body too hard during a morning run on the beach. He shuns the idea as soon as he sees Kate waiting on the wooden steps of the beach house. God, he loves Nags Head in April—too early for the crowds, but just warm enough for a frogman to go swimming in the ocean. Kate waves at him, and he heads straight toward her. The burn along his neck and shoulders is starting to creep up the back of his head toward his scalp.

He keeps his speed on all the way to the steps, where his wife is waiting with a coy smile and a cold beer. She opens her arms to him, and he sweeps her off her feet, spinning her in a circle like he used to do on homecomings after long deployments. She laughs, loud and unabashed—a little girl's laugh—as she clutches him about the neck. The cold aluminum can is pressed against his skin, and for a moment it quenches the burn on his charred neck. When he sets her down, she looks up at him, wanting. He smiles at her, feeling a familiar stirring as she steps into him.

"You're sweaty," she breathes, pressing her pelvis against him. "I love it when you're sweaty."

He bows his head and brings his lips to her forehead. He buries his nose in her mane of chestnut hair, closes his eyes, and inhales. "I miss the smell of you," he whispers, sliding his right hand over her skimpy bikini bottoms.

"Senior Chief Kemper," a voice booms from above. A drunk voice. "Your presence is required at the barbeque."

He looks up the wooden steps and finds Thiel's arms open expectantly—a bottle of beer in one hand and a spatula in the other.

"I put my life in that man's hands every day. But it appears I can't trust him with a gas grill," he says to Kate with a smirk. Then, he yells up the stairs, "Gimme the SITREP."

"There seems to be a problem with the fuel-to-air ratio, resulting in inadequate combustion," Thiel calls back. "Translation: your fucking grill won't light, and there are seven hungry SEALs up here about to gnaw their fingers off if we don't get some dawgs cooking."

Kemper rolls his eyes and stops groping his wife.

"Go save the day," she says, and gives him a swat on the ass. "It's what you do best."

"Yes ma'am." With a wink, he swipes the beer from her outstretched hand.

Up on the deck, Pablo is dancing while Gabe plays Jimmy Buffett on an old, beat-up Gibson. The entire squad is there—even Spaz with his busted leg healed up good as new. Kemper scans their faces, taking it all in. His friends, laughing and drinking. Lounging and bullshitting. He spies Kate, sitting next to Gabe. She looks so relaxed. So young. God, when did life get so good? Both his families together, at last.

This is the way it's supposed to be.

This is the way it's supposed to be.

This is the way it's supposed to be . . .

"You just gonna stand there gawking, or are you gonna light this sonuvabitch?" Thiel's voice says behind him, but when he turns, the man standing behind him is not his best friend of ten years. He is not even a man, but a boy wearing a dusty tunic, clutching his stomach.

"Whatcha gonna do, Kemper?" the boy says, tears streaming down his cheeks.

Then the boy explodes.

The explosion knocks him to the ground. His ears are ringing, and the light is too brilliant to open his eyes. When at last he forces his eyelids open, he finds himself on his hands and knees crawling through a puddle of blood. His fingers brush up against something wet. He looks—Thiel's left hand, the team-issued Suunto watch still clasped to the severed wrist.

He gags.

Next he finds a boot.

He begins to hyperventilate.

Ten toes, perfectly pedicured, step into his field of vision.

Kate?

He's afraid to look up, afraid to see what's missing.

"They're all gone, Jack," she says.

He forces his gaze upward.

Is she . . . ?

Oh thank God.

He begins to weep and extends a hand to her. "Help me."

"I can't help you, Jack," she says, her voice flat and cold. "No one can help you now."

She turns and begins walking away.

He tries to crawl after her, but his arms and legs aren't working properly. Suddenly, his right arm can no longer support his weight, and his forearm snaps above the wrist. He collapses into the puddle of blood and realizes he's burning. The flesh on his neck and scalp is on fire.

"Please, don't go. Don't leave me . . . not like this!" he screams as all the color bleaches from the world.

CHAPTER 13

Gulfstream G550
Northeast Bound over Europe
April 9, 1440 GMT

"Is he all right?"

"Dreaming, I think. I can give him some more Ketamine to keep him comfortable."

"Please."

"Are you sure he's the right guy for this?"

"It depends on what's left of the man when he finally wakes up. What other option does he have? Where else can he go? Everyone is gone, but him . . ."

Kemper didn't wake up.

He simply emerged, regaining awareness very slowly from a nightmare so raw it oozed. It felt like someone was dragging him out from beneath two tons of dirt—dragging him out of the grave.

His head throbbed. His joints ached; his body was too heavy to move. He felt a searing pain across the back of his head and neck, and he tasted the copper tang of blood in the back of his throat. And his mouth—God, his mouth—was so dry his swollen tongue was stuck to the roof of it.

He opened his eyes. The gray mist from his dreams was still there, but now was transformed into a thin veil of gauze over his face. Was he bandaged? He couldn't tell. He wanted to rip the gauze away, but his arms were impossibly heavy. Where was he? Was he in a hospital? He stilled his breathing and listened.

A whining drone . . . vibration . . . feels like an airplane. A mobile hospital in the belly of a C-17 Globemaster or C-5 Galaxy.

He knew the rumbling hum of those planes from countless trips back and forth between Europe and Iraq. They had been "Lifts of Opportunity" for the men who moved in the shadows and blind spots of the conventional military. Men like him—undocumented passengers, hitching a ride with the Military Airlift Command to their next assignment or a safe place to recuperate. Thankfully, he had never been a MEDEVAC patient on any of those flights. Was he now?

The world around him jostled—abruptly and violently—then went still.

Turbulence. I'm definitely on an airplane.

He listened intently, and heard a muffled conversation—like the ones that had intruded on his nightmares, but farther away. If he called out, maybe someone would help him. He tried to speak, but only succeeded in croaking out a dry burp.

Water. Need water. He mouthed the words, which at the moment was all he could manage.

He waited.

No one came.

Where am I? What happened to me?

He closed his eyes. To find his way to the here and now, he would have to retrace his steps, back through the nightmares. He winced at the prospect, but he had no choice. He forced himself back into the dark places.

I remember the beach, and Kate and everyone together in Djibouti. No, no, it was North Carolina . . . there was an explosion and Thiel's boot. And a boy name June, who conned me with a joke. Oh God . . . But did he? Everything was all jumbled. He felt his pulse picking up—a war drum pounding in his ears. The imagery was too raw. Too painful. He was panting now, and with the oxygen rush came clarity. Then it all came back, like a dam break flooding his mind with too much information.

Both Tier One squadrons had been on a mission in Yemen. He had been watching from the TOC in Djibouti. A flash of light on the flat-screens, and then everyone was gone. He had vomited on the steps outside the TOC, and then he had run with rage and grief he had never felt before. There was that Muslim boy with the strangest look on his face. Pain and redemption and satisfaction. The boy's plan had come to him, like a slap in the face, but a few seconds too goddamn late.

Tears pooled in Kemper's eyes, unable to run off because of some slime on his face. He tried again to call out, this time loud enough to be heard over the jet engines, but his voice failed him a second time. He focused all his energy on raising his arms. Maybe if he waved, he could get someone's attention. But his left arm wouldn't budge. It felt bound: his left wrist was secured to whatever it was he was lying on. His right arm simply didn't work at all.

Was he a prisoner?

A surge of fear electrified him. Had he been left behind? Had he been taken? His mind flashed to a memory as gruesome as his dreams— the video of American journalist Daniel Pearl being decapitated. Dying in combat was easy, but to go like that . . . He shuddered as his imagination presented him a vision of his own head being sawed off with a butcher's knife by a hooded jihadist. This was every SEAL's nightmare.

"I think he's waking up," said a woman's voice. In English, not Arabic, thank God. It was a soft voice, tinged with compassion. Or was it pity?

He felt a comforting squeeze on his shoulder, and immediately his raspy breathing slowed. He felt the muscles in his neck and arms relax. He was with the good guys. He was safe.

"Hey, Jack," said a man's voice. The timbre was familiar, but he could not conjure the face. "You're okay, bro. You got pretty banged up, but you're gonna be fine."

"*Wrrwrr,*" he wheezed, his bone-dry vocal cords unable to articulate the word.

"Yeah, yeah, of course. Can he get some water?" said the man.

There was rustling, and then he felt a tube press against his lower lip, which hurt more than it should have.

"It's a straw," the woman's voice said. "Drink slowly."

Kemper tried to comply, but that was impossible. He sucked eagerly, flooding his mouth and throat. The first few swallows burned like grain alcohol, but the coolness and the moisture soothed the pain and quickly put the fire out. The next long pulls on the straw were sweet ecstasy. He swirled the water around his mouth with his tongue and felt a nasty layer of paste dislodge and slide down his throat with the water. It reminded him of the crap leftover in the bottom of the pot after cooking oatmeal. The thought made him shudder.

"Dan?" he mumbled, hopeful that his old friend Commander Munn had flown to his rescue once again. "Is that you?"

"'Fraid not," said the man.

"I can't see," Kemper whispered, deflating.

"You have bandages over your eyes," said a new voice, not Munn's, but one equally galvanizing. Captain Jarvis. "You suffered some corneal abrasions. Nothing serious, but the doc put antibiotic ointment on your eyes. They're probably healed by now. You also have burns and lacerations on your face, neck, and head."

"How bad?" he croaked.

"You weren't so pretty to begin with, Jack, so I wouldn't worry about it."

Kemper grinned despite himself, and felt his dry lips crack open. He licked them, tasting fresh blood. God, he was a mess. He cleared his throat and swallowed. "How long have I been out?"

"Five days," said the other male voice, which he now recognized as belonging to the spook who called himself Shane Smith.

"Take this shit off my face," Kemper demanded, jerking his left hand against its binding. "And untie my fucking hands."

Soft hands—hands that could not possibly belong to Jarvis or Smith—loosened the strap on his left wrist. Then, someone removed the shroud of gauze from his face.

"Fuck," he grumbled, raising his left hand to block the light now blazing above him like a thousand suns. Reluctantly, his pupils remembered what they were supposed to do, and the light began to pale. He squinted, but the world stayed blurry.

"That's the antibiotic," said an angelic face hovering above him. She was lit from behind, and for a moment he swore she wore an angel's halo. "Blink hard to clear it."

He did as instructed, squeezing the goo out the corners of his eyes. When he opened his eyes, the halo was gone. Not an angel . . . just a smoking-hot brunette in a green-bag flight suit. "Thank you, Nurse," he said and tried to smile.

"Doctor," she corrected. "I'm the surgeon who packed off the bleeding in your liver while the bone guys plated your arm and set your ankle."

"Thanks," Kemper said, embarrassed.

"You're welcome, Soldier," she replied without smiling. "I've got to be honest with you. You're a train wreck. Besides the broken bones and internal bleeding you suffered, you've got a bunch of partial thickness burns, you're bruised head to toe, and we had to sew up at least two dozen deep lacerations. What I'm saying is, you're going to have a lot of pain."

"Where?" he asked and tried to sit up.

Pain erupted everywhere.

"Everywhere," she confirmed.

He gave up and collapsed back onto the thin mattress. After a moment, Smith pressed a lever and raised the back of the trauma bed. Being up thirty degrees felt so much better—that is, until a familiar ache crept along his spine.

"Can we have a few minutes with him alone, please?" Jarvis asked.

"Of course," the doctor answered, and rose from her seat beside Kemper. She handed him a cord that ended in a white plastic bullet with a red button on the end. "This is a PCA," she said. "If you have a lot of pain, push the button and it'll give you some morphine. It has a lockout so you can't accidentally OD yourself. Press it enough and you'll drift off to sleep."

"Thanks, Doc."

He watched her walk away. When she was gone, he turned to his old CSO. "Where am I?"

Jarvis took the seat beside him where the doctor had been. "Dead," he said. "But we'll come back to that. Is your head clear enough to talk?"

Kemper nodded. The fog in his mind was burning off, but the pain was creeping in to take its place. He looked at the PCA button for a moment and considered. He dropped it on the mattress next to his leg. "Talk to me."

"What do you remember?" Jarvis asked.

Kemper swallowed hard and felt tears fill his eyes again. "Everything," he mumbled. "They're all dead, aren't they? The whole unit?"

"Yes," Jarvis said flatly. "Everyone on the ground and both aircrews from the 160th were lost."

"It was a trap?"

"Yes."

Kemper closed his eyes, and his mind filled with memories from the TOC: thermal imagery of jihadists kneeling en masse, a flash of white, then the heat signature of glowing carnage after. Then, he thought of body bags, and folded American flags, and closed coffins with gleaming tridents hammered by hand into the wood. He watched the parade of faces on the backs of his eyelids of his friends who would be laid to rest.

He opened his eyes and looked at Jarvis.

"How many died in the TOC?" he asked.

Jarvis let out a slow breath. "All of them."

His reply was a sword through Kemper's heart. But this time, instead of grief, his chest burned with homicidal rage.

"Who?"

Jarvis leaned back and crossed his legs. "We don't know yet, Jack," he said. "We're working on it."

With anger sometimes comes epiphany.

"Who's 'we'?" Kemper growled. "And what the hell are you doing here anyway, Captain Jarvis?"

Smith stepped in and put a hand on his shoulder. For some reason, that really pissed him off, but he didn't shake the hand off. Moving hurt too much, and he wanted to resist the *little red button* as long as humanly possible.

"I couldn't tell you before, Jack," the spook said. "Now I can. Captain Jarvis is my CO. We've been working together for a little over three years now."

Kemper shifted his gaze from Smith to Jarvis. Of course—it all made sense now. The sly reference Jarvis had made to being in Tampa for meetings with SOCOM; his knowledge of Kemper's CASEVAC; the thinly veiled job offer in the hospital. Kelso Jarvis as head spook? He couldn't believe it.

"You're with the Activity now?" Kemper said, his tone more accusation than question.

"No, not hardly," Jarvis said, and almost looked amused, despite the somber atmosphere, before morphing back into the battle-hardened visage Kemper knew. "Don't get me wrong, the Activity does great work.

But with all the meddling civilians and admin pogues in the Pentagon, it has become increasingly difficult for even the best covert-intelligence groups to do their jobs. Shit, even our Tier One military assets are bantered around on the news, with politicians claiming credit for their successes and cursing their failures like *they* own the teams."

Kemper clenched his jaw. Although neither one of them said it, they were both thinking about Yemen. When Kemper joined Tier One fourteen years ago, only a handful of people even knew of the unit's existence. *That* was the original charter for Tier One operations. Covert special warfare at the most elite level, coupled with unprecedented anonymity and autonomy. Their successes would be credited to others, and their failures would never see the light of day. Ironically, it had been the war on terror that had changed everything. The insulating buffer between the Tier One operators and the political paparazzi had eroded, jeopardizing their anonymity and autonomy. After the raid on Bin Laden's compound, Kemper and his fellow operators went to work every day with the feeling they had targets painted on their backs. The carnage in Yemen and Djibouti was proof that they did.

"I don't give a shit about the bureaucrats and the media. Let the talking heads talk. They don't own me," Kemper mumbled.

"But they think they do, and therein lies the problem." Jarvis leaned forward, elbows on his knees. "Which is why we are having this conversation."

Kemper nodded. *Go on.*

"Three years ago, I was tasked with standing up a new unit—a unit that does not report to JSOC or SOCOM. We are completely outside of the Pentagon's chain. The same goes for the CIA and DHS. You will not find us on any DoD org chart. There are no dotted lines connecting us to anyone or anything. We are black—black in a way that hasn't been possible in decades. I can count on one hand the people outside this conversation that know of our existence."

"What the hell are you saying, Jarvis? That *you*, and you alone, somehow broke the shackles, and now you have unprecedented clandestine authority?"

"Yes. That is exactly what I'm saying."

"What do you call yourselves?"

"JIRG—the Joint Intelligence Research Group."

"Did you come up with that?"

Jarvis smirked. "Innocuous, banal, and forgettable—perfect for what we're trying to do."

"And what is that exactly?"

"Collect the type of actionable intelligence that the CIA did in its prime. So far, we're succeeding. You would not believe how much JIRG work has translated into tasking for our old unit."

The reference to "our old unit" was not lost on Kemper, and it sparked fresh anger inside him. "Does that include the Yemen op?"

Jarvis paled. "Yes."

"Then you're fucking compromised, or you swallowed some asshole's bait—hook, line, and sinker. Either way, your group is seriously fucked." The bark in his voice burned his throat. He reached with a trembling hand for his cup of water.

"We don't think we're compromised," Jarvis said coolly. Then, glancing at Smith, he added, "The intel on Yemen was streaming in through too many channels from too many end users to be attributed to single-point failure."

Kemper screwed up his face and shook his head. "What the hell does that mean?"

Smith stepped in. "We think that whoever did this was targeting your team, but that they didn't have a specific route for the intelligence in mind. It was like they propagated the lie through every back channel—from senior AQ leadership, to field operatives, all the way down to the goddamn errand boys. Whoever was behind this hit gathered HVTs from across the entire region. This was not just some bullshit tribal meeting in Yemen; they recruited key guys from Syria, Gaza, Palestine, Saudi Arabia, Egypt, and Iraq and brought them to that compound. That's the genius of the plan. It didn't matter who sifted the data on our side; they knew it would work its way up the chain to SOCOM, and the op would ultimately be assigned to Tier One."

"What are you saying? That somebody put up a neon sign and simply bet that my unit would come?"

"In a manner of speaking, yes," Smith said. "But here's the thing, Jack. We're getting chatter that suggests even the highest-ranking leaders of these various shithead groups are as surprised by this hit as we are."

Teeth clenched, Kemper stared at Jarvis. Over the past few years, all the teams had encountered scenarios in the field that felt like ambushes, but no *verifiable* counteroffensive plot targeting the Tier One units had ever been uncovered. This reinforced the business-as-usual mentality— operational freedom with impunity. Maybe the teams were victims of their leadership's arrogance and meta-think. The invincibility of invulnerability, and all that crap. If so, that strategic insensibility would apply to the man beside him, wouldn't it?

Jarvis held his gaze.

Kemper wondered if his former CSO could read his thoughts. Of course he could. Jarvis was way too smart to be outmaneuvered by the likes of him. Kemper broke eye contact first. This strategic, political bullshit was exactly the sort of thing he had devoted his career to avoiding. He was an operator. He didn't have the heart or the wits for the lying game. He picked up the PCA bullet and pressed the red button. Swallowing, he waited for the morphine to kick in before looking back at Jarvis. "You were saying?"

Jarvis sat back in the chair. He folded his hands together in his lap, his index fingers forming a steeple. A singsong voice from Kemper's childhood told him that he could *"open the doors, and see all the people."* Kemper shook his head. Stupid, damn morphine.

"Our group does more than just analysis or HUMINT aggregation. We have field assets; we conduct surveillance. We manage a variety of assets throughout the world that require me to recruit men like Shane for fieldwork. Sometimes, we plan events and take action to change the tide in favor of the good guys."

Kemper rolled his eyes at the politically correct description. He expected a former operator like Jarvis to tell it like it was: *And sometimes we kill people.* If Jarvis noticed his reaction, the man gave no sign of it.

"What we don't have," Jarvis continued, "is a force of operators. We can take out the occasional target of opportunity, but that's where our capabilities plateau. For the big stuff, we aggregate the intel, put together a plan, and then coordinate with JSOC for Tier One assets to execute operations spawned by our activities. That arrangement worked great, until now."

Shane paced behind him, and Kemper began to suspect that "Smith" was more than just a foot soldier. He had real authority in the group. Maybe he was Jarvis's XO.

"Thing is, Jack," Smith said, taking the lateral from his boss, "with the catastrophic loss of your unit, we're left only with Delta. Problem is that Delta—and even the white-side SEALs—are in an indefinite time-out while the Pentagon tries to figure out how their go-to black-ops team got wiped off the face of the earth."

Jarvis snorted. "It doesn't matter how much data they crunch at the Puzzle Palace, they're never gonna figure out who did this." He clasped a hand on Smith's shoulder. "*We* are the only people with the skills and autonomy to uncover the truth."

Kemper shook his head. "In that case, use your assets to find the bastards responsible, and when things calm down, use Delta to take them out."

"You're still not getting it," Jarvis said, exasperated. "The game has changed. Forever. From this point forward, the tasking of Tier One operators will not be the streamlined process it once was. Now, there will be bureaucratic oversight, administrative red tape, second-guessing, double-checking, multiparty signatory approvals, and every other roadblock the pencil-necks can think to pile on. Do you see where I'm heading with this? Tier One used to be a point-and-shoot asset, but now, by the time you unlock the trigger guard, the opportunity will be lost—the target will have disappeared into the ether."

Kemper nodded. He got the point. He just didn't want to imagine that world. "If what you're saying is true, how do you propose to solve the problem?"

"By integrating Tier One operations capability into our task force. We will be the Alpha and the Omega, the shadow and the flame, and no one will see us coming."

"You want the JIRG to own Tier One? And I thought I was the one who got blown up," Kemper laughed. "That'll never happen."

"We're not talking about a large assault force, nothing on the scale of a SEAL team," Smith interjected. "We want a small, highly skilled group that can operate outside normal channels and stay impervious to whatever leaks exist in Washington and the Pentagon. We need assets who can change hats at the drop of one—be that operator, intelligence analyst, or asset manager—depending on the need. We need a field team that can function as assaulters as well as covert operators, execute tasking on a moment's notice, and make decisions in real time without bureaucratic oversight."

Kemper felt the heat ratchet up several notches on his neck and head, and he knew it was not because of his burns. "What do you want from me?"

"I want you to lead that team," Jarvis said with an intensity and certainty that Kemper found unnerving.

"Why would I do that? I'm no spy. I'm a frogman—a straight-up warfighter. Give me the target and I'll blast it, but the rest of the shit your people do is not me. Sorry, Skipper, you have the wrong guy."

Jarvis narrowed his eyes. "I served with you on the teams for seven years, Jack. I watched you operate in situations that would shred lesser men into mental hamburger meat. Some people call it instinct. Others call it a sixth sense. I call it situational awareness. I call it tactical fucking superiority. How many of your judgment calls saved lives in the field? How many of your orders turned failed missions into successes?"

Kemper looked down at the PCA button. "I don't know."

"I do. Too many to count. You're smart, Kemper. No matter how much you try to act like some SEAL jock made to hang out in biker bars, it doesn't change the truth. You're a tactician. You're a field marshal. You're a one-man, ass-kicking retribution machine."

Kemper had heard enough. He was done. He needed the morphine as much for his spinning head and mauled heart as he did for his broken body. For God's sake, how could Jarvis not recognize he'd sacrificed enough for his country? There was nothing left to give. He picked up the PCA cord and rested his thumb on the red button. "Even if that were true, why should I join your band of merry men? You said it yourself. Everyone I care about is either dead, or thinks I'm dead. What can your unit possibly offer me?"

"Justice. That's what I can give you. From this day forward, my number one priority is to find every person with a hand in murdering our brothers in Yemen and Djibouti and then erasing those sons-of-bitches from the face of the earth. I can think of no one on this planet better qualified to execute that mission than you."

Kemper dropped the PCA button back onto the sheets beside him as the endorphins from Jarvis's words numbed his pain better than morphine ever could. "And when it's over, when every last one of them is dead, then what?"

"We can cross that bridge when we come to it."

"What about Kate and my son? What am I supposed to tell them?"

Jarvis looked down at his feet. "Whoever planned this wanted the Tier One SEALs gone. If you walk away from this as Jack Kemper, sole survivor, you'll spend the rest of your life with a target on your back, always wondering when some asshole with a suicide vest is going to find you and finish the job. If you and Kate were still together, we could give you and your family a relocation package and new identities. But you're divorced, Jack. And besides, is that really the life you want to force on Kate and Jacob? Always moving, always looking over your shoulder, always worrying? I'm sorry, Jack, but your old life is over, whether you want it to be or not."

A bitter pill . . .

Kemper took it, swallowed it, and said, "Okay, I'm in. What do I have to do?"

When Jarvis smiled, his eyes were lit with a fire Kemper had not seen since their time down range together. "First things first," his new boss said. "Let's get you buried in Arlington, like you deserve."

CHAPTER 14

Virginia Beach Convention Center
Virginia Beach, Virginia
April 14, 1400 EDT

Jarvis ran his thumb across the brass insignia pinned to his dress blues—an eagle, wings spread and head bowed, clutching a pistol in one foot and Neptune's trident in the other, superimposed around an anchor. The SEAL trident. "The Budweiser." A badge of honor. A badge of readiness, of freedom, and of the sea. A badge sought by many, but earned by few.

How long had it been since he'd worn this uniform?

Too long and not long enough.

He took a deep breath, refocused, and put on his SEAL persona. The transition was easier than he expected, given the morbid circumstances. Captain Kelso Jarvis. Retired. Former Tier One operator, badass down range, and tactician in the TOC. A legend in his own right throughout all of Naval Special Warfare. Why? Because he'd killed more evil motherfuckers with the fewest friendly casualties of any unit commander in Tier One SEAL history. Now, he was back. Reunited with his men in this most horrific of venues. A mass memorial for those he had lived, fought, and drunk with over the years. Maybe they had never really known him, but he sure as hell had known them. For a man like him, they had been as much a family as he could ever hope to have. He'd admired them, and a part of him had even envied them. The simplicity of their lives, the single-minded clarity of purpose. Sometimes, in the middle of the night, when insomnia and obligation held sleep at bay, he imagined being unencumbered by the burdens of his mind. If he did not see the patterns he saw, if he did not *understand* the world the way he did, then maybe, just maybe, his casket would be awaiting entombment, and someone else would be giving the eulogy today.

"Retired Navy SEAL Captain Kelso Jarvis is a legend in the Special Warfare community and has been a friend, a colleague, and a mentor to many of those we honor here today . . ."

Jarvis straightened his tie and tried to filter out the words of the JSOC Commander introducing him. He found the words distracting. Not just distracting—irritating. He hated when people introduced him anywhere, preferring to meet people cold and manage the transfer of professional and personal information himself. All information should be dispensed on a need-to-know basis. All information. He swallowed his annoyance and told himself that the JSOC Commander was not sharing anything that couldn't be found in his military bio. Yet it was everything missing from his bio that made this engagement so painfully ironic. Of all the men the Navy brass could have asked to memorialize these SEALs, they had asked the very man whose secret task force was culpable for their deaths.

But if not him, who else was alive to speak for them?

"It is with great pride and a heavy heart that I turn the podium over to Captain Jarvis."

Jarvis took the steps onto the stage slowly, somberly. He paused for a moment at the podium and made a show of straightening the index cards in his hands. Speechwriting was a superfluous activity for him;

the index cards were blank. The words would come to him, no matter the circumstance, no matter the venue. His first draft was his final draft.

He cleared his throat and looked for a long moment out at the crowd. Hundreds and hundreds of people filled the convention-center ballroom, but less than a quarter of the crowd was in uniform. He knew that, in addition to the families, colleagues, military personnel, and politicians who were present, many local celebrities and political types had solicited invitations. Virginia Beach did so love their SEALs, even if they didn't truly know or understand them. Of course, no one could acknowledge that the supposedly secret unit to which these men belonged had been based out of a classified compound in Tampa, and not in Virginia at all. In the official Navy press release, the departed would be forever memorialized as simply "East Coast–based SEALs."

Ironic, he thought. *In life, they would have appreciated that. Maybe even liked it.*

"What can you say about these men?" he began. "What do you say about men who choose duty over safety, country over normalcy, honor over family, and commitment to a cause over the sanctity of their own lives? What do you say when America's heroes fall?"

Jarvis paused for the audience to consider that.

"I knew these men. I fought with these men. I laughed with them and cried with them. They were my brothers. They were my family. But what can I say about them?"

He spent the next twenty-five minutes saying exactly what the audience, especially the families, needed him to say. He gave them the most precious gift he could give—his memories. He told stories of courage under fire, and triumph over terror. He told stories of fraternity and teamwork. He told stories that made them laugh and made them cry. Anecdotal stories that filled their hearts with pride and made them remember the good times, while forgetting the bad. When he finished and looked out over the crowd, he was satisfied. Never once did he speak a name, a rank, or a call sign. To every wife, he celebrated her martyred husband. To every parent, he venerated a lost son. And to every fatherless child, he took off Clark Kent's eyeglasses to reveal that their dad was, and always would be, Superman.

A strange paralysis settled over the assembly. All eyes were fixed on him. They wanted more. They were not ready to let go. And when the JSOC Commander stood and clasped a hand on Jarvis's shoulder and replaced him at the podium, they began to weep and hold each other. They ignored the words that followed, introducing the Secretary of Defense. Instead, they watched Jarvis with wet, grateful eyes as he walked past the front three rows where the widows, orphaned children, and parents and siblings of the lost were seated. They watched him until he took his seat in the fourth row, behind them. Those within reach shook his hand. Others nodded or mouthed a silent "Thank you" as he walked by. In the end, the Secretary of Defense was made to wait—wait for a man he had never heard of.

Eventually, the memorial regained its banal rhythm. Jarvis let the ramblings of the SECDEF become background noise as he reconsidered the data and the decisions that had sent his fellow SEALs to their deaths. The mental exercise was not about assuaging his guilt—that was neither possible nor necessary. It was about formulating a plan to use the event to unmask those responsible, so that the sword of justice—*his* sword—could exact vengeance. It was up to him to solve the unknown variables and balance the equation. Everything in life was an equation, and unbalanced equations set off chain reactions and became chaos. In a perverse sense, he considered himself a bookkeeper, maintaining the ledgers of madness that mankind perpetually unleashed on itself and the world at large. When the books were balanced, a fragile sort of peace persisted until the tireless agents of entropy began their work anew.

What is peace but war held in check?

What is life but entropy held at bay?

He could not remember when the thought first occurred to him that good and evil could be—must be—understood in mathematical terms. Entropy is the true devil in the universe, not some cackling, fiery satyr with horns and a pitchfork. Entropy is the great destructor, the root of all disorder and chaos. What are the seven deadly sins, if not a failure to resist the decay of one's moral fiber? What is war, if not an alliance with entropy to bring chaos and destruction to an ordered world? It took 182 years to build Notre Dame de Paris—182 years of effort, energy, and discipline to construct a magnificent cathedral from sand, wood, and stone unhewn. But with only one Mark 83 general-purpose bomb, this beautiful triumph over entropy could be reduced to rubble. Would the bombing of Notre Dame be a sin, even with no human casualties? Yes, because the very existence of such a structure in the universe is good. Life, in all its forms, is good. Because life, by definition, is the endeavor to persist against the forces of entropy, always nibbling and clawing to redistribute life's energy and matter into the cold, homogeneous ether.

The Secretary of Defense finished his remarks and introduced President Warner. Everyone in the audience perked up as the president took the stage—everyone except Jarvis. As usual, he expected the president to speak many words but say very little. Judging from the pacing of the poorly focused drivel he was hearing already, Jarvis guessed he had at least eight or nine minutes to devote to something more important than listening to the most powerless powerful man in the world. He let his eyes glaze over as he looked inside and resumed dissecting the question that had been plaguing him day and night for the past week: Who was the puppet master behind the SEAL massacre?

Supposition number one: someone with access to, and control over, critical channels of information inside the Al Qaeda network.

Supposition number two: someone with authority to direct multiple data streams through multiple sources in a way that would fool not only the Americans, but also those allies whose actions he wished to control.

Supposition number three: someone not interested in publicly taking credit for the attack, and therefore someone occupying a powerful position in either an Al Qaeda parent organization or a Middle Eastern government that supported terror activities behind the scene.

Al Qaeda was fractured, partially by intent, partially by economics, and partially by culturally rooted Islamic differences. Al Qaeda in Iraq was not the same as Al Qaeda on the Arabian Peninsula, which was not the same as Al Qaeda in the Islamic Maghreb. As the saying went, "All politics is local." That same aphorism applied to terrorism. Which was why Jarvis still struggled with the idea that someone had unified the sectarian terror cells and conducted an operation of unprecedented scale and sophistication against the US military. Were he still alive, even Bin Laden would have had difficulty managing a coordinated feat such as the SEAL massacres in Yemen and Djibouti.

Tired of fixating on the complexity of the operation and the data streams, Jarvis decided to simply go back to the beginning. The rise of the Islamic State was a powerful inducement for the factions of Al Qaeda to cooperate. ISIS had grabbed the world's attention, and to stay relevant, Al Qaeda needed a big win. The initial tip that AQ factions were gathering in Yemen had come from his VEVAK source in Tehran. By itself, that meant little or nothing. Just because the source reported the meet, and the meet turned out to be a trap, did not guarantee the source was supplying counterintelligence. Most sources lived in the middle of the food chain, where they made opportunistic intelligence grabs. This particular source had consistently provided valuable leads—despite the fact that his intel often had holes or inaccuracies. The tip about the *Darya-ye Noor* was the perfect example—right ship, wrong cargo, but a big win nonetheless. Because of this tip, the SEALs had been able to destroy a cache of surface-to-air missiles bound for Yemen and guarded by Iranian security forces. For an Iranian source to provide intel that resulted in Iranian deaths was a powerful validation of the source's loyalty. At first blush, Jarvis was inclined to believe his source had been an unwitting pawn in the massacre. And yet . . . a spymaster must always remain cynical.

On paper, Iran had much to gain from wiping out the Tier One SEALs. Not just because of its covert support for jihad against the West, but also the necessity of removing barriers to Persia's ascension to the head of the caliphate and a new era of global Islamic domination. Since the creation of the JIRG, the uptick in actionable intelligence gathered had resulted in the Tier One SEALs being tasked regularly and often. Over the past several years, Tier One had repeatedly kicked Iranian black-ops collective ass all over the map. Together, his task force and brother SEALs had foiled countless MOIS and IRGC operations outside of Iran's borders. Had Tehran finally decided to punch back? Had he and Shane terribly underestimated the strategic prowess of President Esfahani? He found it impossible to believe that the bureaucrat who'd championed nuclear cooperation with the West could also be the architect of such a brilliant and subversive plan. But maybe he'd misclassified the man. Perhaps, Esfahani was not the puppet Jarvis had assumed him to be. After all, Esfahani's charm offensive had worked on the White House. Just last week, the Warner Administration had praised Iran on its progress since the implementation of the JCPOA and had even hinted that the remaining long-standing economic sanctions levied against the former regime might be lifted soon as well. He'd even heard US ambassador Felicity Long refer to Esfahani as "a moderate voice of reason in an ever more turbulent Middle East." Jarvis shook his head. How could the politicians not understand that there was no such thing as "moderate" when it came to the ruling powers in Iran?

Yet, pegging Esfahani as the mastermind behind the SEAL massacre raised more questions than it answered. With the ongoing inspections of Iran's nuclear facilities, why would Esfahani engage in such overt warmongering? The timing couldn't be worse. Moreover, why risk the ire of the Pentagon when the United States was on the verge of ending an era of Iranian sanctions? There were other issues to consider as well. Had Esfahani used VEVAK to manipulate the various Al Qaeda factions? If so, how had he managed logistics of such an operation without a single leak?

Jarvis had an informal agreement with an old friend—recently "retired" from the Israeli Mossad—to exchange critical intelligence on matters of joint concern. The Mossad had reliable assets embedded in both the MOIS and IRGC. If Harel had heard anything, anything at all about a move against the US military, he would have warned Jarvis. But Harel had been quiet for a while now, and had not contacted him in the days since the massacre. Given the magnitude of the loss, Jarvis would have expected at least a phone call. Strange.

Something in this equation definitely doesn't balance.

President Warner finished his remarks, and the crowd stood. They gave him subdued, respectful applause as he looked out at them with a stoic face. Jarvis rose to his own feet noticeably late. He had not processed a single word of the president's speech, but now he was paying attention. President Rand Warner made an obvious point of wiping away a tear, probably imaginary, and then gave an awkward salute to the entire crowd, equally inappropriate, before leaving the podium. He took his place back between SECDEF and his chief of staff, Robert Kittinger. Jarvis had not yet met this president, but he'd done his homework on the country's newest Commander in Chief. Admiral Kenneth, who sat on the Joint Chiefs of Staff, had recently shared his observations with Jarvis over a bottle of bourbon:

"He's always in campaign mode. In public, he's a master bullshitter and knows how to leverage his good looks and charm to win both critics and detractors over to his side. Behind closed doors, he's a megalomaniac with a short fuse and a deep distrust of flag officers. But he's neither lazy nor stupid. Unlike his predecessor, he has a tenacious appetite for information and a memory for detail. Shit, in that respect the guy reminds me of you, Kelso . . . the sonuvabitch doesn't forget anything. But the similarity ends there. Warner does not see the world like you and me. Hell, the Iran treaty

is proof of that. If he's willing to bow to Tehran, then there's no telling what he's capable of."

Jarvis shifted his gaze from the president back to the podium, where the chaplain from NAVSPECWAR Group Two stood ready to close the proceedings. The crowd bowed their heads and listened to the chaplain recite a brief prayer—vague and generic enough to offend no one, which, of course, resulted in offending almost everyone. Then everyone stood for a moment and looked around at one another as if uncertain what to do or where to go next. For many of the families, this was the first in a long series of painful events meant to honor their lost loved ones. There would be a private ceremony back at the command. There would be individual funerals. There would be ceremonies at commissioned memorials for many months to come. It would be a long time before they'd be allowed to let go.

For the leadership, however, the next stop was Congress and their goddamn hearings to decide whom to blame for the tragedy. It would be a circus, with both sides of the aisle pointing at each other until some poor SOB—probably one of Jarvis's friends—was offered up as the sacrificial lamb. He doubted that he would be summoned to the witch hunt. As long as he ran JIRG, he was vapor. But that didn't make him immune from self-flagellation. He knew who to blame for this.

Himself.

And the enemy he planned to hunt to the ends of the earth.

He moved to the end of his row and waited for the occupants to sift past in single file. He had one final obligation to fulfill, and it was bitter. Head bowed, he waited for the former Mrs. Kemper to exit her seat in the front row.

He only had to wait a moment.

Their eyes met, and he took her by the elbow—leading her and her son into an empty row. "I am so, so sorry, Kate."

She nodded, tried to speak, and then shook her head. Her chestnut hair, which he remembered as always pulled back into a sporty ponytail, hung limp and heavy to her shoulders, framing her ashen, tear-streaked cheeks. Her hazel eyes, usually so bright and vibrant, looked tired and bloodshot. And yet despite the angst, she had not lost her inner strength. She stood tall, her petite chin raised.

Beside her, Kemper's sixteen-year-old son stared at the floor, his mouth half-open and his eyes far away. The boy had Kemper's same tawny-brown hair, but wore it long and unkempt—a Kurt Cobain homage. He had Kate's eyes and narrow nose, but Jack's square jaw. He stood five foot nine or ten, but he still had the skinny, gangly body of a teenager with a nuclear-powered metabolism. He carried none of his father's hard-packed muscle, but give it a couple of more years, and that would change.

"Do you remember me, Jacob?" Jarvis asked, placing a hand on Jacob's slumping shoulder. The boy looked up, stared at the trident on Jarvis's chest for a long moment. Finally, the boy's bloodshot gaze met his own.

"You used to be my dad's boss," he said, in a voice younger than his age.

"Yes," Jarvis said. "And I never stopped being his friend. With the exception of you and your mom, I knew your dad better than anyone on the planet. I knew him enough to know how very much he loved you and how very proud of you he was. He showed pictures and video clips of you all the time—playing soccer, at your wrestling competitions, even a YouTube clip of you playing the guitar. He never stopped talking about you. I know he was counting the days until the war was over and he could be with you again."

"Really?" the boy said, in a voice full of pain and hope.

"Really," Jarvis said. "Can we spend a few minutes together so I can tell you some things you need to know about him?" He glanced at Kate for a mother's approval.

She answered him with her eyes: *Thank you for this, thank you . . . thank you.*

Jarvis put an arm around Kemper's son, and they sat side by side on the cushioned folding chairs. He talked for forty minutes, recounting the odyssey of Jack Kemper—SEAL, father, hero—blending truth and fiction so that by the end, the son, and his eavesdropping mother, had heard what they needed to hear. When he had finished answering all their questions, he retrieved Kemper's trident insignia from his coat pocket and pressed it into the palm of Jacob's hand.

"Every SEAL owns a handful of these, but this one is special. This trident was your dad's first, pinned onto his chest the day he officially became a SEAL. He had been saving it for the right time to give to you . . . I know it's not the same, but that honor now falls to me."

With tears streaming down his cheeks, Jacob clutched the brass insignia in his hand and threw his arms around Jarvis. Jarvis hugged the boy back, hugged him like the son he would never have.

After a long moment, Kate stood and gently laid her hand on Jacob's shoulder. "It's time to go, Jake."

Jacob released his bear hug. Jarvis did the same.

"If you ever need me," Jarvis said, not sure what else to say.

Kate leaned in and kissed him cordially on the cheek. "You were a good friend to him, Kelso." She was about to say more, but the tears came rushing, and it was time.

He watched them disappear into the crowd, and for an instant, he lost himself in the charade and felt his eyes moisten. He blinked, and the hair stood up on the back of his neck.

Someone tapped his shoulder.

The tap was not a tentative tap. Not an "Excuse me, but you're blocking the aisle" tap. This was the tap of a man with something to say. The tap of a man who was not afraid of anything a former Tier One SEAL having a very bad day might do to him. It was the tap of an equal, and someone just as lethal.

Jarvis turned and found himself face-to-face with the last man on earth he expected to see.

CHAPTER 15

Tehran, Iran
April 14, 1722 Local Time

Triumph is a jubilant elixir. It is bright and fleeting, like fireworks on New Year's Eve. Grief, on the other hand, is something altogether different.

Grief lingers. It stains. It weighs.

Ten days ago, Masoud Modiri had been so very, very happy. Thanks to his vision and his brother's impeccable planning, America's most elite Special Forces unit had been decimated and the will of Allah satisfied. The infamous Tier One SEAL unit was no more, and his son's death had been avenged forty times over.

Persia had triumphed over the Great Satan.

The Modiri brothers had bloodied the most powerful nation on Earth and done so in perfect anonymity.

Fireworks.

But now, the feeling was no longer within his grasp. Lost, like wind through his fingers. Lost, like Kamal. Five hundred, or five thousand, or five million dead Americans would not bring his son back. Almost a month had passed since that dreadful day when he had learned of

Kamal's death, and still his wife wept. She wept upon waking; she cried herself to sleep. When he tried to comfort her, he had trouble keeping his own tears at bay. He had stopped bargaining with death, and it had left him weary.

Death was no man's companion.

He leaned his head back against the leather seat of the Mercedes sedan and closed his eyes. Traffic was heavy today; the driver had told him the commute would take ten to fifteen minutes longer than usual. He was exhausted—physically, mentally, and emotionally. He let himself sleep, until the sound of the passenger door opening roused him.

"Will you be needing the car tonight?" the chauffeur asked him.

"No," he said, climbing out of the sumptuous backseat. "See you in the morning at the regular time."

"Yes, sir."

He walked to the front door, turned the handle, and stepped into the entryway of the ambassador's residence, the residence he now called home. Echoing from the kitchen was a howling sound so terrible it made his stomach drop. Fatemeh was wailing. Without bothering to shut the front door behind him, he dropped his attaché case and ran to the kitchen. He stopped abruptly at the threshold to the kitchen, gazing open-mouthed at the scene before him. Not wailing, but laughing—she was laughing—a sound so alien to him that his mind had mistaken it for suffering. Sitting next to her was his brother, Amir, a wry grin snaked across his face. They both looked up at Masoud in unison.

"Oh good, you're home. Come have tea with us," Fatemah said, smiling, and standing to greet him. "Amir was just telling me the funniest story about an argument he and Maheen had over a pomegranate. I haven't laughed that hard in months."

Emotion in triplicate washed over Masoud—relief, gratitude, and a pang of jealousy, all at once. In twenty-six years of marriage, he could not recall ever making Fatemeh laugh like that. And for Amir to pull Fatemeh from her well of sorrow made the feat all the more impressive.

As boys, Amir had always played the comedian, charming their parents and winning favor with the teenage girls. But comedy, especially at the expense of other testosterone-charged boys, often led to balled fists and puffed chests, and that was where Masoud, the young diplomat, had first exercised his special gift. How many broken noses had he rescued Amir from? How many faculty warnings had he staved off to preserve his younger brother's golden status in the Modiri household? Was this Amir's repayment of those debts, or was it some secret revenge? *Don't be absurd,* he told himself. *This is only Amir being Amir. You should be grateful for this kindness. You should be happy to see your wife's smile after so long an absence.* A diplomat's words, no matter how pragmatic and empathetic, are a poor substitute for humor in moments when the soul needs a jump start.

Diplomacy was cerebral.

Amir poured a fresh cup of tea in a lonely third cup waiting on the table. "You look tired, brother. Come, sit, have some tea."

Masoud nodded and forced a smile. Looking at Fatemeh, he said, "The pomegranate story is a good one. It always makes me laugh, too."

"I had not heard it before," said Fatemeh, wiping her checks with a paper napkin. "I will never look at pomegranates the same way again."

Masoud accepted a white ceramic teacup from his brother's outstretched hand. "How is Maheen, brother? We have not seen her since . . . well, you know."

"Maheen is Maheen, very busy. Even when all the work is done, she finds six more chores to do. Always buzzing, my little Maheen."

"Yes, that is Maheen. The queen bee of the Modiri hive," agreed Fatemeh. After a brief pause, she added, "Are you sure you don't want to stay for dinner? I promise it is no intrusion. Besides, when I cook, I can't help but make extra portions. Conditioning from raising a household of hungry boys, I suppose."

"Thank you for the kind offer, but no. A few words with Masoud, then I must fly straight home to the hive. I don't want the queen bee buzzing at me."

Masoud took a sip of his tea and said, "We can talk in the garden."

Leaving Fatemeh behind in the kitchen, he led his brother to a tiny, walled courtyard behind the town house. Groutless sandstone tiles covered the dirt, and no fewer than ten potted exotic plants flourished in the corners—a surrogate flock for a mother with no children to tend. Two aluminum benches—painted to look like aged cast iron— sat two meters apart, facing each other. Masoud gestured to one of the benches and took a seat in the other. Before sitting, Amir removed his mobile phone from his pocket and powered it off. Masoud followed his brother's lead and did the same.

"How were the cabinet meetings today?" Amir asked.

"Stressful," Masoud answered, rubbing his beard.

"Tell me."

"Esfahani wants to know why discussions have stalled with the Americans on lifting the remaining economic sanctions."

"Have the discussions stalled?"

"What do you think? Of course they have."

"When was the last time you spoke with Ambassador Long?"

"Three days ago, before I came back to Tehran."

"How were things?"

"Cold as ice."

Amir blew air through his teeth. "We expected this."

Masoud nodded. "It is only a matter of time until Esfahani finds out what happened. And when he does, he will come after us."

Amir smiled. "That's why you're going to tell him before that happens."

Masoud stood up. "Are you mad?"

"Not mad, brother. Just pragmatic. What we did may never make the news, but glorious whispers will circulate through the back channels, eventually reaching Esfahani's ears. It is best that you take credit for bringing the intelligence to him first."

Masoud began to pace. "You want me to admit to the president that we subverted his plans to win the Americans' trust at the most pivotal time by conducting a strike against their SEALs without his permission or knowledge?"

"No, Masoud, I want you to tell the president that you have learned through a reliable source that our Sunni cousins on the Arabian Peninsula have done this remarkably brazen thing and dealt a serious blow to the Americans. I want you to tell him that since the strike, the Americans have suspended all special warfare operations. Did you hear me? All operations have been suspended until they can figure out what happened. The Minister of Intelligence and Security has already informed the Supreme Leader of this development. This is a golden opportunity for VEVAK, and we are going to be very, very busy for the next few weeks taking advantage of the situation."

Masoud shook his head. "How did you manage to hide our involvement?"

Amir laughed—a loud, condescending laugh. "This is what I do, and I am very good at it. All planning for this operation was conducted in face-to-face meetings. Zero electronic communication. Since I became chief of the Foreign Operations Directorate, this is the way I do things. The NSA is always listening. GCHQ is always listening. Unit 8200 is always listening. Only four people in the entire world know what we've done, and two of those people are in this garden."

Masoud sat back down on the bench, folded his arms across his chest, and said nothing. In retrospect, their plan had been so ambitious it bordered on insanity. Had he not been blinded by grief and rage over the loss of his son, he would have never partaken. The fact that the plan had worked still boggled his mind. "There is something I don't understand, Amir. How did you know the Americans would send in their SEALs, rather than simply blow up the compound with a missile from one of their drones?"

A shadow washed over Amir's face, and he seemed reluctant to answer the question. Finally, he said. "That was always a risk, but risks can be managed. What I'm about to tell you, we will never speak of again. Understood?"

Masoud nodded.

"I have an American ally, someone plugged into the highest levels of US military command and control. The confirming information I needed to make the operation a success was communicated to me."

Masoud smiled and shook his head. "Even now, as grown men, you never stop amazing me, little brother."

"Now, do you trust me?"

"Trust has never been the problem," said Masoud. "My trust in you is absolute. It is everyone else I worry about. Common sense tells me it is only a matter of time until someone discovers what we have done."

Sensing his doubt, Amir tacked. "Don't lose sight, Masoud, that we serve the Supreme Leader, not President Esfahani. Esfahani is a wise man, but he is a strategic figurehead meant to lure the West into complacent cooperation. The American people are tired of war. They don't want another one with Iran. The Pentagon needs a scapegoat, and you're going to give them one. I will provide you with intelligence proving that Al Qaeda was responsible for the ambush. Then, I want you to present the documentation to Esfahani and encourage him to share the information with the Americans. The sharing of intelligence will be perceived as an olive branch. It will help improve relations between Tehran and the White House, and also create opportunities for dialogue between you and Ambassador Long."

Masoud sniffed. "This proof you give me better be indisputable."

Amir smiled. "Leave the details to me. All you need to do is what you do best—use your diplomat's tongue to keep everyone distracted and oblivious."

CHAPTER 16

Jarvis blinked, but the legendary Mossad spymaster did not disappear.

"Levi?" Jarvis said, trying to hide the incredulity in his voice and failing. "What are you doing here?"

"I came to see you," Levi Harel said with his hallmark rapid-fire cadence and heavy Israeli accent. "Why else would I come?" Then Harel embraced him like a brother. The hug was very strong and very brief. "There are no words for a tragedy like this. I know you loved them like brothers. I'm sorry, Kelso. Truly."

Jarvis inhaled through his nose and exhaled through his mouth, centering himself. "Yeah, me, too."

"Walk with me."

They walked side by side in silence to the main entrance of the convention center. Once they'd stepped outside, Harel immediately lit a cigarette.

"I'd offer you one, but you always say no."

"Last time I was in Tel Aviv, you told me you'd quit."

"I'm a spy. We lie and we smoke—what can I say?"

"When did you arrive stateside?"

"This morning."

"When do you leave?"

"This afternoon."

Jarvis nodded.

"I came only for this, Kelso. We need to talk."

"I know," Jarvis acknowledged, but when Harel didn't respond, guilt compelled him to say, "Look, I'm sorry I didn't tell you about the op, but . . ."

"*Pssffssst.* I don't give a shit about that. It was your party, and I would have done the same in your shoes. Besides, even if you had tipped us off, it wouldn't have changed anything. We saw the comms traffic and put the puzzle pieces together. Like you, we came to the same erroneous conclusion."

Harel's admission that he and the Mossad had also been duped made Jarvis feel a little better. It shouldn't have, but he was human, and misery loves a party. Instead of forcing his friend to ask the next question, Jarvis answered it preemptively. "No, I haven't found the bastards who are responsible yet."

Harel took a long, last drag from his cigarette, flicked the butt onto the sidewalk, and stomped it out with a twist of his black-leather loafer. He turned and looked at Jarvis with angry, weary eyes. "You're not the only one with problems, my friend. Things are changing. The cowboy days are over. The enemy is getting smarter. Worse, he has become more patient and more careful. In the past six months, we've lost two informants, one field operative, and three deep-cover assets. All murdered. And two weeks before your tragedy in Yemen, S-13 lost three guys during a raid because Hamas knew we were coming. I'm telling you, Kelso, I don't like what I'm seeing."

"Maybe you have a mole problem."

"No, that's not it. It's fucking VEVAK. I'm certain of it. There's been a policy shift; they've gone on the offensive. Do you remember April 2012?"

"When MOIS announced they'd busted up your spy network in central Iran?"

"That was no bullshit, Kelso. We lost a lot of good people, and we still haven't fully recovered. Iran was a difficult environment to place assets in before, but now it's almost impossible."

"Do you think VEVAK was behind the hit on our Tier One SEALs?"

"I'm telling you that I think Tehran is a good place to focus your attention."

Jarvis sniffed.

"What's that sniff supposed to mean? You disagree?" Harel scowled. "Don't tell me you're one of the converted. Maybe your president has invited you and his new best friend Hassan Esfahani to Camp David for beers and pretzels? What—you think Prime Minister Shimon hasn't noticed the shift in White House sentiment? Warren is making a lot of people in Givat Ram very nervous. Me included. What is the expression you Americans like to say? 'You can put lipstick on a pig, but it's still a pig.' Iran will *never* be a friend to the United States. Never. And I'm not just saying it because I'm an old, cranky Jew from Tel Aviv."

"Look, Levi, I don't trust Esfahani, either, but Oval Office policy is way outside my area of influence. Besides, we both know that political rhetoric and black-ops policy are two very different animals."

"Well, in Israel we have a saying, too: 'Better a slap from a wise man than a kiss from a fool.' I think your president needs a good slap, or one year from now, you and I are going to have a lot of blood on our hands."

A raindrop hit Harel in the middle of his forehead. Both men instinctively looked skyward. A second later, an FA-18D Superhornet screamed past at low altitude, racing ahead of the spring thunderstorm growling in from the Atlantic Ocean. Jarvis watched the jet break steeply overhead—condensation trails spiraling off the wingtips in a tight, high-G turn—as it circled on approach to Oceana Naval Air Station only a few miles away. Jarvis pulled his officer's cover lower over his eyes as more raindrops began to fall, breaking against the brim.

"A storm is brewing," Harel said, lighting another cigarette.

"A storm always is," Jarvis replied, regarding the Israeli as they walked. Harel was a man who had weathered a thousand storms and had the mettle to weather a thousand more. He'd be a fool not to use this opportunity to tap the former Mossad Operations Director's vast network of managed assets—especially now that his source in Tehran had gone completely dark. "What if I told you I had a friend in Tehran and, hypothetically speaking, I'd lost touch with this friend? Given recent events, I'm worried my friend has gone missing, which is unfortunate, because I very much need to talk with him."

"In that case, I would tell you that there is a girl in Frankfurt who knows a Persian man who might know what has happened to your friend. Hypothetically speaking, of course."

Jarvis nodded. "Good to know." He paused a moment, looking at the streams in his mind, the ones that never faded. "Is that Persian in the energy business perchance?"

Levi Harel smiled and nodded. "Of course you would know of him."

Jarvis shrugged. "We lost interest in him, but perhaps that was a mistake."

"Perhaps. I can arrange for you to speak with friends of mine who still find him interesting."

"I appreciate any help you can give, old friend."

Harel stopped walking and turned to face Jarvis. "I would not normally say this, because it should not need to be said—but if there is anything at all you need."

Jarvis extended his hand to the man from Tel Aviv.

Harel shook it.

"Thank you, Levi. It means a lot that you came today."

"They were good men. The world is a darker place without them." With that, Levi Harel turned on a heel and headed to a long black car waiting at the curb.

Jarvis checked his watch. He had one hour until his flight to DC left the private side of Oceana Naval Air Station. In his peripheral vision, he saw a black Lincoln pull away from the curb farther down the block just as Harel's limo pulled away. He had instructed the driver that delivered him to the memorial to wait. As the Town Car crept toward him, Jarvis raised his hand and stepped toward the curb. The rain was coming down harder now, and his dress blues were beginning to soak through. But when the car pulled up next to him and he squinted through the tinted, rain-spattered glass, he didn't recognize the driver. A pulse of adrenaline set his senses on fire.

Someone had been watching him talking with Harel. With an annoyed expression, Jarvis waved the driver off and pretended to signal another car farther down the block. He moved away from the car at an angle, keeping his peripheral vision fixed on the rear passenger window as he reached through the faux pocket in his coat. His fingers found the butt of the compact Sig Sauer P239 in the holster snug in the small of his back.

The rear passenger window of the Town Car rolled down.

Jarvis slipped the weapon from the holster, keeping it concealed inside his coat. He twisted his torso toward the vehicle and repositioned his feet for what was about to come next.

"Captain Jarvis," a voice called from the backseat.

It took a second for the face to register: Robert Kittinger, President Warren's chief of staff. Jarvis felt his blood pressure plummet as the threat evaporated. What the hell was Kittinger doing following him?

"Yes, sir."

"A moment of your time, Captain," Kittinger said, his tone indicating this was not a request.

"Now?"

"Yes, now. For Christ's sake, get in. I'm getting wet."

Jarvis reached for the door handle with his left hand, while subtly slipping the Sig back into the holster with his right. He climbed into the plush leather backseat beside Kittinger and slammed the door.

The bureaucrat slid as far away from Jarvis as the cabin and his considerable girth would permit, while wiping beads of water off the fabric of his expensive suit. Jarvis looked down at his own drenched uniform coat. *Afraid of a little rain?* The thought of this guy in the mountains of Afghanistan or the back alleys of Mogadishu made him smirk.

Kittinger tapped the driver on the shoulder. "Around the block a couple of times," he said. He pressed a rocker switch to raise a soundproof, bulletproof glass panel between the front and rear compartments. Kittinger straightened his tie and jutted his chin—a mannerism Jarvis loathed—and then smoothed his jacket with flittering, pudgy fingers. "Horrible thing, this SEAL tragedy," he said. "Just horrible. The worst disaster in military history." He paused. "Well, obviously Pearl Harbor was a terrible loss, but in terms of irreplaceable assets—you know, human assets—this is horrifying. The whole team. Maybe the most important weapon in the war on terror the country has ever had. Gone." He shook his head again. Then at last he met Jarvis's eyes. "I know these men were your friends . . . I'm truly sorry."

Ironic. Levi Harel had said almost the same words to him not five minutes ago, but when Harel offered his condolences, the words had actually meant something. Not that Kittinger's sympathy wasn't genuine—Jarvis didn't know the man—but empathy without friendship or fraternity felt unctuous to him. Robert Kittinger had never spent a minute in a uniform, much less combat, and patriotism without sacrifice, well . . .

"Thank you," Jarvis said at last. "What can I do for the White House?"

Kittinger sniffed. "I know that your task force was involved in the operational planning for Yemen. I'm sure that hurts like hell." The jab was less than subtle—something between a dig and a threat. The investigation into Yemen was still open—plenty of time for bureaucrats like Kittinger to spin stories and assign blame. Jarvis held Kittinger's gaze but said nothing, wondering if his neck was on the proverbial chopping block.

Kittinger shrugged off the silence. "Do you have any new intelligence indicating who's responsible for this?"

"No, sir, but we are working around the clock to find out."

"Of course."

Jarvis couldn't decide if the tone was meant to be smug, or if Kittinger was just toying with him. Feeling compelled to say something else, he added, "We're pursuing several leads. As soon as I have something concrete, I promise—"

"Do you think it was the Iranians?" Kittinger interrupted.

"As I said, we're working on it, but the last thing I want to do is speculate with so little concrete data. We're looking at every angle and every possibility, I assure you."

Kittinger glanced out the window. "It was those Iranian lunatics," he said, nearly spitting the words. "I'm certain of it. They're the next Third Reich, Jarvis. Make no mistake about it. We can't be fooled by this new asshole, Esfahani, spouting rhetoric and lies about cooperation and treaty compliance. They're all closet Twelvers—radical Islamic zealots—every last one of them. And with the feckless IAEA rolling over on compliance, the Iranian regime is more emboldened than ever before. The minute we lifted sanctions, I swear they started executing dormant plans to slit our throats in the name of destiny. They can't be trusted."

Jarvis blinked. Had he really just heard the president's chief of staff rail against the Iranians? And it wasn't just the words, but the venom in Kittinger's voice that shocked him. A logic bomb went off in his brain, scrambling all the equations he'd worked so hard to balance.

"Well?" Kittinger said, turning to face him. "Say something."

"I didn't realize this was the White House's position on the matter," Jarvis said, treading lightly, waiting for the trap to spring. "Especially given President Warner's recent speech praising Iran's progress in dismantling their centrifuges, and innuendo about Persia rejoining the international trade community."

Kittinger shook his head in disgust. "They told me you were a genius, but Jesus fucking Christ, you're no different than the others."

"Excuse me?"

Kittinger rapped on the glass window, and a half second later, it opened six inches. "Pull over. Captain Jarvis is getting out."

"Wait," Jarvis said, surprised at the urgency in his own voice.

Kittinger turned his head just enough to make eye contact.

"We're on the same page," Jarvis said with a little nod.

The chief of staff smiled and rapped on the window again. "Never mind. Two more times around." When the window was up, he said, "Do you think the president of the United States is a moron? Hmm?"

"The thought has crossed my mind."

Kittinger howled at this and reached over to squeeze Jarvis's shoulder. Jarvis tensed. Now that was where he drew the fucking line. He took a deep, cleansing breath, and swallowed his repugnance at the gesture. "That's the first genuine thing you've said since your eulogy."

Jarvis feigned a fraternal laugh.

"The president is not a moron, Captain Jarvis, but sometimes he plays one on TV. That's how it works. That's how the game is played."

"So you're saying the nuclear cooperation agreement with Iran is all a ruse for the sake of bolstering White House public opinion?"

"Hell no. Nothing could be further from the truth. Iran was at the economic breaking point. Something had to be done or the Middle East was going to spiral out of control. If we didn't act, France, Russia, or China would have, undermining our authority. The United States leads, never follows, and so the president decided to act. The agreement buys us time. It gives IAEA inspectors access to facilities we haven't been able to penetrate for years. Nobody believes Tehran'll come into compliance with all the tenets of the agreement. The Supreme Leader will make certain of that, but politically we are obligated to give him the rope he needs to hang himself."

Jarvis narrowed his eyes at the president's right-hand man. He couldn't believe what he was hearing. Either Kittinger was the best bullshitter he'd ever crossed paths with, or the Warner Administration was not the administration he thought it was.

Kittinger plowed ahead without missing a beat. "Is it possible that the Iranians were behind the hit in Yemen?"

"Anything is possible," he answered, guardedly.

Kittinger narrowed his eyes. "I know you have an asset inside VEVAK you've been running. I want to shake that tree and see what falls out."

Jarvis felt his chest tighten. How the hell did Kittinger know about his VEVAK source, and why was he discussing it outside of a SCIF? The Director of National Intelligence was the only person Jarvis had told. "We're shaking lots of trees, sir. That's all I'm prepared to discuss at the moment."

Kittinger sighed. "I'm beginning to lose my patience now. This is not a fucking poker game, Jarvis. When your boss asks you a question, you answer him. I would have thought that after twenty years of decorated military service, you would have a solid fucking grasp on the concept of chain of command."

Jarvis stared, dumbfounded, at the man. What the hell was he talking about? In principle Kittinger was right—everyone under the DoD umbrella worked for the Commander in Chief—but as far as chain of command, his boss was the Defense Intelligence Agency Director. Since the beginning, his direct line of communication was with the DIA Director and no one else.

Kittinger smirked. "You didn't know, did you?"

"That I work for you?" Jarvis said. "No, I was not aware of that detail, especially given the fact this is the first time you and I have spoken."

"Well, that was by design, of course. But the JIRG was my idea. As soon as the president was elected, and we were read into this dysfunctional disaster known as the Intelligence Community, I realized we had big problems. It didn't take me long to convince the president that we needed an intelligence activity immune to Congressional oversight. He snapped his fingers, and the Joint Intelligence Research Group was born. I handed the JIRG over to the DIA and said, 'Congratulations, Dad. Don't drop the baby.'"

Jarvis raced through the timeline of JIRG's genesis. The data points matched. The DIA Director, a Marine Corps General with MARSOC roots, had approached him almost three years ago to the day, during the first one hundred days of Warner's first term. Jarvis knew that all the intelligence the JIRG collected was funneled to the president and the National Security Council, but he'd never contemplated that President Warner—the man he'd written off as a witless puppet—was the JIRG's maker and greatest ally.

"The problem is," Kittinger continued, "the DIA did drop the baby—well, actually, you did—and now somebody's got to take the blame. So, Captain Jarvis, you're fired. As of this moment, the Joint Intelligence Research Group is shut down."

Kittinger's words were a blow to his gut. Jarvis's mind shifted immediately into damage-control mode. "We suffered a setback, yes, but I don't see how shutting us down solves anything. In fact, scuttling the JIRG now will only hinder the country's ability to collect the kind of actionable intelligence the president needs . . ."

While Jarvis pleaded his case, the president's chief of staff opened his briefcase and retrieved an envelope. Instead of handing it over, he set the envelope on the seat between them and began tapping it impatiently with his index finger. When Jarvis kept talking, Kittinger interrupted.

"Let me stop you right there. This isn't complicated. Everything you were doing before doesn't matter now. What does matter is finding the bastards who hit our Tier One SEALs. That is the president's number one priority. Captain Jarvis, look me in the eye and tell me if you're the right man for that job."

Jarvis locked eyes with Kittinger. "Yes, sir, I am."

"Good. Consider yourself retasked. The Joint Intelligence Research Group was the most successful intelligence-gathering team in the history of the war on terror, but now it's tainted. The JIRG is dead. Long live the JIRG. Congratulations, Captain Jarvis, you now have a new team."

Jarvis took a slow, deep breath. This conversation was getting more interesting and insane by the minute. "A new team?"

Kittinger tossed the bulky envelope into Jarvis's lap. "Say hello to Task Force Ember." There was a fire in Kittinger's eyes that seemed out of place. The bureaucrat began to laugh, his double chins jiggling. "Poetic name when you're in the black, don't you think?"

Jarvis nodded, only half listening, as he fought the urge to tear open the envelope.

"I expect you to run Ember with the same tenacity and spirit with which you ran the JIRG. And I expect the same results—no, I expect better results. This is more than just a rebranding. Now, you work directly for the president of the United States. You will communicate with me and only me, and I will safeguard your group's secrecy and autonomy. You will work only on tasks I assign, and you answer to no one but the president. The knowledge of Ember's existence will be limited to the president's inner circle, and the White House will provide you with blanket protection from prying eyes."

Jarvis gritted his teeth. The *idea* of operating outside the Pentagon and the greater Intelligence Community was a covert-operation paragon—no paralyzing administrative red tape, no decision making by committee, no political pissing matches over conflicting agendas, and no fighting for resources and autonomy. But the *reality* of being "unte-thered" was sobering. When the proverbial shit hit the fan, which it invariably did, he and his team would be on their own. The moment it was politically profitable to do so, Kittinger would smile and deny any connection to, and knowledge of, Task Force Ember.

Still . . .

"I understand. Please, go on."

"You're the Director, and I'm giving you the flexibility to manage the operation as you best see fit. You can continue with a hands-on leadership role like you had in JIRG, or you can assume an oversight position and appoint an Operations Director to manage day-to-day minutiae. You can keep any of your existing analysts, but every team member needs to be screened as if a new hire. Polygraph and the works."

Jarvis raised an eyebrow.

"If you had any leaks in JIRG, this is our opportunity to close those holes without raising anyone's suspicion in the group."

"Understood," Jarvis said. "What about poaching?"

"If there are assets within any other agencies you want, I will secure them for your team. And"—Kittinger paused for effect—"I want you to expand your operational capability. We can't have you relying on other agencies to execute the president's orders. Which means you'll need to grow that side of your house quickly."

Jarvis smiled. He had never intended to tell anyone his plans for using Kemper as an operator, but this change played perfectly into his vision.

"Inside the packet you'll find everything you need to get started. I want you close—arm's-length distance—so set up shop here, in Virginia. I have people already working on the secure server drops, and by the time you assemble your team, the facility will be ready to occupy. I've arranged for space and blocked time at the Farm for any training your people might need—the details are in the files on the encrypted thumb drives in your packet, as are the details of the new facility. You're responsible for the internal and external security, but a nonofficial cover is detailed in your packet. You have air assets for travel, which will be ready within forty-eight hours. Both aircraft have the ability to function as covered medical and covered air, and both are licensed through established, real-world companies to provide optimal cover. The parent companies are patriots, but they're blind as to the use of the assets they provide. Your packet also details a dozen or so nonofficial cover identities to use through those same companies if you like, though you are free to establish whatever NOCs you need."

Jarvis felt his head spinning. His dream task force had just been dropped into his lap, but things were moving too fast. He hadn't even started and already felt out of control. "Wait—the OPSEC is all over the place. Who is the curator for those assets and identities?"

Kittinger shrugged. "Don't worry. I ran them by the National Security Advisor. You're a resourceful guy, Jarvis. Use them, or manufacture your own instead. I don't care." Kittinger handed him a business card. EMBER CORPORATION was printed at the top in clean, block font. Beneath it, Jarvis saw his own name and the title CEO. There were phone numbers in Arlington, London, and Dubai, as well as a company website and an e-mail address.

Jarvis looked at the card, then at Kittinger, and nodded.

"You have your tasking—connect this massacre to Iran. Give the president the ammunition he needs to punish Tehran and expose the regime for what it really is. Once that's done, you will hunt down the parties responsible for Yemen and Djibouti and eliminate them. Make sure there is no connection to the US government or our allies."

"Simple enough," Jarvis said, smiling.

"You have six months and forty million dollars to do it." Kittinger held out a hand.

Jarvis gripped Kittinger's hand. The bureaucrat's hand was so soft and mushy; he was afraid he'd turn it to pulp if he squeezed.

Kittinger tapped the glass behind the driver and they pulled to the curb, right in front of the convention center again. "My secure mobile number is in the packet. But as a general rule, don't call me. I'll call you."

Jarvis nodded and reached for the door latch.

"Oh, one more thing, Captain. There's a plane ticket to DC in your packet for tomorrow. You have an appointment at Anacostia."

"Excuse me?"

Kittinger smiled wryly. "Go throw yourself on your sword, and make a convincing spectacle of it. You will recommend that the Joint Intelligence Research Group be disbanded. You will state that you believe the task force may be compromised. An internal leak may have contributed to the breach in OPSEC that led to the massacre of the entire Tier One SEAL force. Don't put up a fight. Take full responsibility. Let the General save face. I'll mop up afterward."

Jarvis swallowed the revolting bile that had refluxed up into the back of his throat. "Yes, sir."

Envelope in hand, he opened the rear passenger door.

"Good luck in the private sector, Captain Jarvis," Kittinger said as Jarvis stepped out of the car. "Thank you for your service."

"Thank you for this opportunity. Please let the president know I won't let him down."

The chief of staff flashed him an odd, crooked smile. "I'm counting on that."

CHAPTER 17

St. Petersburg, Florida
May 2, 2045 EDT

Kemper stared at the ocean, his hands stuffed into the pockets of his cargo shorts. Cool water lapped against his shins as the gentle tide surged and receded. Surged and receded. He breathed in the salt air and the quiet. This was his favorite place in the world at his favorite time of day. Eventide, his bookish wife had called it once. *Ex-wife*, he reminded himself. Eventide on St. Pete Beach, the time after sunset when the sunbathers were long gone, but before the rowdy bar- hopping crowd spilled onto the shore to party barefoot in the sand and do *other* things in the darkness.

A memory of Kate skinny-dipping in the moonlight invaded his mind; he chased it away, the voice in his head a snarling, rabid dog. He resisted the urge to look over his shoulder and lament the waterfront condo that was no longer his. Jarvis had told him not to come here. Told him that even after the surgery that peeled away his burns and altered his appearance just enough to fuck with facial-recognition soft- ware, there was still a chance someone could recognize him. Kemper doubted that was true. The only people who knew him well enough to look past this new face and see Kemper were his dead brothers.

And Kate and his boy.

They would certainly know him. By his gait, by his shape . . . by the love in his eyes. But they were miles away across the bridge in the small house Kate had bought in South Tampa. He wondered if there was someone filling the void he'd left—an impostor—catching a baseball with his son and keeping Kate warm at night. The thought turned his stomach to acid. A sudden desire to hop in his rental car and drive to Kate's house welled up inside. When she answered the door, he would sweep her up in his arms, kiss her again and again, and tell her the nightmare was finally over. He was alive. He was home. And this time, he would never leave her and Jacob again . . .

I'm not ready to let go.

Not yet.

He had always believed that when he finished his Tier One obligation, he would reclaim his old life. He would retire and dedicate all his time to winning Kate back and being a proper father to Jacob. In his heart, he was certain they'd understand why he'd made the sacrifices he had. It was because of that understanding that they would be able to start again—this time as a real family. It was this dream that kept him going, no matter how difficult, how dark, or how dangerous the mission. Ironic, because now that dream was dashed, and the mission he was about to embark on was the most difficult, darkest, and most dangerous of his career.

And while he was off meting vengeance in the shadows, Kate would move on.

She should move on.

With the death benefit from the Navy, and his sizable USAA life insurance policy, she would be able to pay off the house and still have a tidy nest egg to start her new life. His GI Bill would pay for Jacob's college, and . . .

He sighed—a heavy, raspy sigh.

Despite the warm breeze blowing in from the Gulf, he began to shiver. He was already thinking like a dead man. He was a ghost, walking among the living, self-aware and feeling, but cold and unseen. Jack Kemper, and the life he'd spent four decades building, was dead and buried—along with almost every friend he'd ever had. He would never be Jack Kemper again.

Not even in his own mind.

"You don't live here anymore," a voice said behind him.

Kemper didn't startle, nor did he bother turning around. "Fuck off, Smith."

He felt the spook's eyes on his back. Still, he didn't turn. Eventually, he heard a series of splashes and Smith was standing beside him—boots and all. Kemper looked down at the watermark creeping up the other man's khaki pants. "You're a strange dude, Smith."

"So I've been told." Smith shoved his hands in his pockets and matched Kemper's gaze out at the sea. "And it's Pozniak."

Kemper turned and looked at the spy.

"What?"

"My name," he said. "Once upon a time, I would've said you can call me Barry."

"Barry Pozniak? That's your name?" Kemper snorted. "Jesus, I woulda become Shane Smith, too."

"I figure if a man's giving up his name forever, the least I can do is tell him mine," Smith said.

"I appreciate that," Kemper said. "But I still don't trust you."

"I don't trust you, either," Smith said. "But I trust Kelso Jarvis, and he trusts you, so here we are."

"Yeah, here we are."

"Did you drive by her house yet?"

"What are you talking about?"

"Kate," Smith said, his gaze still fixed on the horizon.

"What kinda question is that?"

"You're here. Don't tell me the thought hasn't crossed your mind."

Kemper exhaled. "Fuck off, Smith."

"You already said that."

"I meant it then, too." Kemper turned to face him. "Why are you here? Did Jarvis send you to talk me off the ledge—is that it? Does he think I cracked? That I'm going to run home to my ex-wife and ruin the brilliant plan the two of you cooked up during my MEDEVAC? Gimme a break. You fucking spooks are all the same."

Smith didn't answer.

"That's what I thought," Kemper said with a victorious scowl.

"I was Army," Smith said, after a long pause. "Fifth Special Forces Group, and then over to Delta after 9/11. We spent a lot of time in Afghanistan and Iraq—just like you guys. After that, I was sent to Ethiopia with some guys I thought must be OGA, except they really had their shit together. They were spook types, but you could tell they'd been operators. We got tasked with 'asset management' and setting shit up for obliteration." Smith drifted for a moment. Then, he shook his head vigorously, as if shaking off stars from a right hook. "Anyway, three years ago I got a visit from this weird dude, a former Tier One SEAL commander that you might know. He gave me this pitch about a special project I could join. He went on and on about how they were doing stuff I couldn't imagine, making a difference in the war on terror, blah, blah, blah." Smith took his hands out of his pockets and folded his arms across his chest. "He was right. Since I signed on, we've done some absolutely amazing shit. Incredible things that no one knows about, even at the highest levels of the Pentagon."

"You were Delta?" Kemper asked, zeroing in on the piece of Smith's story that held the most weight in his book.

"Yeah," Smith said with a proud, nostalgic smile he tried to hide and failed.

"Do you miss it?"

"All the time. Every day. It was a simpler life with simple rules. And I slept a helluva lot better back then," he said with a hesitant chuckle. Then he turned to Kemper, all the humor gone from his face. "Here's the thing, Jack. I've done more to affect the security of this country in the last two years than the culmination of my efforts over the decade before I joined Jarvis. Promises are an occupational hazard in our business, but I'll make you one tonight: our group will never replace what you had with the teams, but I promise you'll never regret the decision to join us. Even if you could go back to Tier One, you wouldn't."

Kemper looked down at the water swirling around his calves. "I got nothing left to go back to, man," he said, and then silently cursed the tears pooling in his eyes.

"Yeah, it sucks," Smith said softly. After a long, awkward moment he spoke again, his voice now conspicuously light. "I know you SEALs are all about the water, but can we get out of the surf now?"

Kemper forced a laugh. "The ocean is your friend, Smith," he said as they waded back to the beach. "It's what connects us to every continent on the planet."

"The ocean scares the shit out of me. Give me a perfectly good airplane to jump out of and I'll take that any day over a scuba INFIL."

"Has anyone ever told you," Kemper said, shaking his head, "that you're a strange dude?"

"I get that a lot," Smith said. "And 'fuck off'—don't forget that."

Kemper followed him up the beach, pausing only to scoop up his Oakley desert boots along the way. As they trudged through the sand toward the parking lot, Kemper decided he still didn't trust Smith. Being former Delta helped, but unconditional trust had to be earned. Hopefully, it would happen organically in the coming months as they worked together. They were, after all, the same breed—a couple of Smiths forged by fire in Tier One units, only to wake up one day, inexplicably, as spies.

CHAPTER 18

Kemper clenched his jaw and narrowed his eyes.

Mindful of the position of his feet, he closed the gap to his adversary. He drove forward with the full power of his legs to unleash a brutal combination—left jab, right cross, elbow. Had the target of his rage actually been a man, this person would now require plastic surgery, but as it was, the heavy bag simply shuddered in mild protest and begged for more. Sweat poured from his scalp and forehead, running over his burn wounds and stinging like a Portuguese man-o'-war. He swallowed the pain and focused all his attention on pummeling the vintage-leather Everlast bag hanging from a ceiling joist in the basement of Shane Smith's house.

The fingerless mixed martial arts gloves he wore protected his knuckles; the wrap tape added stability and rigidity to his wrists. He reveled in the tightness in his forearms and the ache in his heavily muscled arms. He exhaled and moved through a rapid series of katas, each designed to neutralize a specific threat—a man with a handgun, a man with a knife, two men with rifles, finally ending with a jihadist bastard in need of an ass kicking. The lactic-acid burn was becoming a raging fire in his overtaxed pectoral and deltoid muscles, but he kept pounding the bag. For the first time in months, he felt alive. He felt strong and lethal. He felt like a fucking SEAL. His sweat had a tangy odor, undoubtedly due to the unusually large quantity of alcohol he had been consuming over the past week and the daily cocktail of meds he was slowly weaning himself off. Exercise was the catharsis his body craved, not mind-numbing booze and painkillers. He'd often heard the saying "As goes the mind, so goes the body," but the inverse was also true. It was time to start rebuilding.

Kemper slowly circled the bag, planning his next assault. His bare feet—now raw from an hour of shuffling on the cement floor—made a whisking sound as he shifted his stance. Normally, he would be pounding the bag with kicks and knee strikes, but he wasn't sure if his back was ready for that. His spine was feeling almost normal again; he saw no reason to risk putting himself in traction over a heavy bag workout. His left foot felt normal, except for his numb big toe, which he had decided would be that way forever. His right fibula, which had cracked four inches above his ankle, was still nagging him, which the docs said he could expect for several more weeks. The right side of his neck itched incessantly where the skin graft was finally healing, as did the other surgery sites on his face. Soon, the plastic-surgery scars would be impossible to see—faded into the weathered creases of this old new face whose reflection he still didn't recognize. If there was one thing two decades on the teams had taught him, it was this: flesh heals, but imperfectly. Some of his wounds would ache forever, nagging reminders of a dark night on the *Darya-ye Noor*, and the darkest of all nights in Djibouti.

As he drew back his right fist, he heard the floorboards creak overhead. He froze and listened. Footsteps—someone walking in the kitchen. Almost certainly it was Smith, but he was not in the mood to play roulette today. Using his teeth, he tore loose the Velcro wrist wraps on the borrowed gloves and shook them off onto the floor. He continued to pummel the heavy bag barehanded while angling left so that the Sig Sauer P229 pistol resting on the nearby table was within arm's reach. He quickly scanned the basement, noting an emergency-egress window fifteen feet to his right. Keeping the bag between himself and the basement steps, he waited. A moment later, he heard feet on the unfinished wooden stairs. Black boots appeared, then 5.11 Tactical cargo pants. The gait was casual, nothing akin to infiltration or combat movement.

A second later, Smith's head entered Kemper's line of sight. When the spook reached the staircase landing, he turned and nodded a "What's up" in Kemper's direction.

Kemper gave a single nod in return and circled the bag. Setting his feet, he reengaged with a series of punches, elbows, and hammer-fist strikes—a final, brutal sequence to end his workout. In his peripheral vision, he saw Smith take a seat on the landing, a beer clutched in each hand. Completely spent, Kemper finished his final three-strike combination, then leaned his forehead against the bag, panting.

"Good Lord," Smith said, clicking the two beers together in applause. "You hit like Jack Dempsey reborn."

Kemper laughed and wiped the sweat from his face with the back of his hand. "Thanks," he said. "I suppose I'll take that as a compliment."

Smith set the beers down on a step, grabbed a hand towel hanging on the banister, and tossed it to Kemper. "You do know who Jack Dempsey was, right?" he asked as Kemper toweled off.

Kemper nodded. "I've heard the name."

"Heard the name?" Smith said, shaking his head. "Shit, Kemper, the man is a legend. They called him the Manassa Mauler. He won more than fifty of his fights by knockout. Seven years as a world heavyweight champion. Dempsey was one of the greatest boxers of all time."

"Sounds like you're a boxing history buff," Kemper said, walking toward the steps.

Smith handed him a beer. They clinked bottles and Kemper took a long pull.

"Yeah, I've always been fascinated by that period in American history—the gangsters, the Roaring Twenties, and the golden age of boxing. They don't make fighters like Jack Dempsey anymore."

"Sure they do," Kemper said with a grin. "They're called Navy SEALs."

Smith blew air through his teeth. "Er, I think you mean Delta."

"Oh no, I definitely meant SEALs. Delta is for pussies and guys who can't swim," he said, sliding comfortably into the ball-busting rivalry between the brother Tier One units.

Smith laughed and sat back down on the landing.

Kemper took a seat on a folding chair beside the end table and his Sig. He took a long pull on his beer, then eyeing Smith, he said, "How much longer are we going to do this shit?"

Smith looked surprised at the comment. "Do what, Jack?"

"This," Kemper said, waving his hand around. "As in nothing. How much longer are we going to sit on our collective asses wasting time when we should be down range, putting Al Qaeda assholes in the dirt?"

Smith made a show of checking his watch. "One hour."

"What do you mean *one hour*?"

"I picked up some Chinese food for lunch. It's on the kitchen table," Smith said, getting to his feet. "Why don't you get cleaned up? We'll pound some sesame chicken and rice, and then I'll drive you to your appointment."

"What appointment?"

"With the doc."

"Oh, c'mon, Smith," Kemper huffed. "You just saw me working the heavy bag. Do I look like someone who needs more convalescence? I'm good to go, man. It's time to kit up and hit the road."

"Not that kind of doc, Jack."

Kemper rolled his eyes. "A headshrinker? Are you fucking kidding me?"

Smith shook his head. "Boss's orders."

For Tier One operators, psychologists were reviled almost as much as terrorists. He'd never met a shrink he'd liked. They were all the same—find a scab and pick, pick, pick until the wound opened up and started bleeding. How in God's name was it therapeutic for him to be forced to relive all the pain and anguish from his darkest of all days in Djibouti? How did a compulsory stroll down memory lane—reminding him of everything and everyone he'd lost—help him move forward?

Kemper felt the fury boiling up inside. But instead of erupting, he practiced his four-count tactical breathing and bottled his rage—bottled it up tight for later. Psychological evaluations were standard protocol after traumatic events, and what he survived in Djibouti qualified a hundred times over. Jarvis had to play it by the book, which meant so did he.

Just keep your cool and say what the doc wants you to say. Let the vampire nibble, check the box, and move on.

Kemper flashed Smith his cockiest smile. "Just kidding. I love fucking with those guys."

"Hooyah," Smith barked, visibly relieved this hadn't turned into a battle.

"Hooyah," Kemper echoed back. He peeled off his sweat-drenched T-shirt, chugged the rest of his beer, and belched loudly. Then, he exchanged the empty beer bottle for the Sig on the table and headed for the stairs.

"Just one more thing," Smith said.

Kemper stopped, halfway up the basement steps. "What's that?"

"After you finish up with the doc, we have one more stop to make."

Kemper rolled his eyes. "Let me guess—you scheduled me for a colonoscopy?"

"No." Smith laughed. "Nothing that invasive. Actually, I thought you might like to swing by the office and meet the rest of the team."

Kemper grinned from ear to ear. "It's about fucking time."

CHAPTER 19

Ember Corporation Executive Hangar
Patrick Henry Field
Newport News, Virginia
May 4, 1442 EDT

Kemper surveyed the nondescript, windowless, metal building from the passenger seat as Smith parked the SUV. A lone gray door faced the parking lot; the sign above read EMBER CORPORATION in unadorned black letters. From the size of the structure, Kemper estimated the hangar could house two midsize biz jets—maybe three—plus still have room enough left over for tow vehicles and maintenance equipment.

"Are we flying somewhere?" he asked Smith as he climbed out of the Chevy Tahoe. Gravel crunched underfoot as his boots hit the ground. He slammed the passenger-side door and trotted to catch up.

Smith paused at the hangar entrance. "How'd it go with the doc?"

"You tell me."

"You're here, so that says something."

The appointment with the headshrinker had gone better than Kemper expected. Unlike most of the clowns he'd dealt with in the past, Dr. West seemed like a pretty good dude, but he'd never admit that to Smith.

"We just gonna stand here like a couple of idiots," Kemper snorted, "or are you gonna let me in?"

Smith smirked—enjoying himself entirely too much—as he punched a five-digit code into a generic twelve-button keypad mounted beside the door. Kemper arched his eyebrows as the entire panel slid upward to reveal a black glass surface beneath.

"I haven't seen *that* before. Very James Bond," he said, with just enough condescension to gauge Smith's reaction.

Smith ignored the comment and pressed his left hand against the glass. An instant later, Kemper heard a beep, followed by a click as the magnetic door lock released. Kemper recognized this particular brand of security door—hardened, with reinforced internal hinges, and a magnetic lock that made it impossible to bust open by force. He scanned the overhung eaves above and noted the security-camera "eyeballs" in dome mounts. A servomotor whirred, and the keypad retracted back in place, concealing the palm reader. Smith opened the door and gestured for Kemper to enter the hangar.

Inside, the first thing Kemper noticed was the polished concrete floor, and how it reflected the halogen lights evenly spaced and mounted in the truss-work overhead—dozens of little yellow suns, shining from above and below simultaneously. Two corporate jets sat ready, doors open, each behind its own tow vehicle already attached by a yellow tow bar. From the kerosene smell in the air, and the *tic-tic-tic* of cooling turbofan blades, he guessed the smaller jet—a Learjet 35—had recently arrived. The other jet was a model he didn't recognize, but from the size and configuration, he figured that bad boy was outfitted for intercontinental travel with enough room inside for an eight-man team and plenty of gear.

Thirty feet away, a middle-aged man in a pilot's uniform was chatting with another guy in coveralls beside the smaller jet.

"Hey, fellas," Smith said with a wave.

Both men waved back and smiled, unperturbed by Kemper's presence.

Kemper nodded cordially and followed Smith over to a gray metal cabinet set against the far wall.

"Nice digs," Kemper said, gesturing to the hangar and the jets.

"Wait for it," Smith said, grinning like a kid.

Smith opened both cabinet doors and picked up what looked like an oversize calculator tethered to the top shelf. Kemper watched while he punched in a code, returned the device to the shelf, and shut the doors. After a two-second delay, the entire cabinet disappeared into the floor with a *whoosh* that reminded Kemper of an old *Star Trek* sound effect and caused him to jump backward. He peered through a gap in the wall into a space the size of a walk-in closet, behind where the cabinet had been moments ago.

"What the hell is this all about?" Kemper asked.

Smith continued his annoying variant of the silent treatment, and motioned for Kemper to step inside. Kemper rolled his eyes. He hated this cloak-and-dagger spook shit, but he walked over the top of the file cabinet into the darkened closet without protest. Once inside, his perspective changed, and he immediately realized he was standing inside an elevator, not a closet. Instead of a keypad, this elevator had a palm reader similar to the unit at the front entrance. Smith pressed his left hand firmly against the glass until a green LED in the wall flashed twice. An overhead light switched on, and a pair of elevator doors began to close. Through the shrinking gap, Kemper saw the metal cabinet rising up into position to conceal the access point after their departure. A motor purred underfoot, and Kemper felt the elevator descending. The experience was uncannily reminiscent of the SCIF at MacDill.

A moment later, the elevator cruised to a silent stop, and the doors opened, revealing a sleek, modern tactical operations center. Kemper tried not to look impressed as he stepped into the TOC, while at the same time resisting the urge to scratch the itch that never quit beneath the bandage on his neck.

First impressions matter, he told himself. *Try not to look like some nervous rookie with a contagious skin affliction.*

Similar to the MacDill SCIF, a large wooden table was the focal point of the ops center. Replete with built-in speakers, ultrathin computer screens, and individual video cameras and microphones, this table was undoubtedly set up for multiparty, ultra-secure videoconferencing with any number of similar "war rooms" in other undisclosed locations. Kemper counted twelve leather task chairs encircling the round, polished mahogany table. Maybe the team was bigger than he'd thought.

He surveyed the rest of the space: to his left he saw a door labeled LOCKER ROOM, a small kitchen, and what looked like a bunkroom with half a dozen cots; to his right, he spied an arms locker, a server room, and a door labeled MECHANICAL. On the far wall, seven flat-panel LED monitors hung on angle brackets near the ceiling, mounted above a set of double doors set in black glass. All the screens were dark, except for the center unit, which had quad split-screen streaming security-camera feeds of two different angles inside the hangar—one of the parking lot, and one of the flight line on the airport side of the hangar. Presently, a King Air 350 was taxiing toward the runway.

Kemper returned his attention to the center of the room, where Kelso Jarvis leaned over the table, talking with two young men dressed in blue jeans and T-shirts. Jarvis whispered something in the ear of the closer kid, who nodded and snapped his computer screen closed into the table. *Jesus,* Kemper thought, *these guys don't look a day out of college.* Finally, Jarvis waved him over. Instead of waiting for an introduction, the two kids gathered their gear and disappeared through a set of blacked-out double doors. Kemper dismissed the brush-off with a shrug and extended his hand to Jarvis.

"How are you doing, Jack?" Jarvis asked, shaking hands.

"Fine, Skipper. I still don't recognize the guy in the mirror, but for someone who recently got blown up, I can't complain."

"How'd things go with the doc?"

Kemper shrugged. "I'm here, so I guess I passed muster."

"Good," Jarvis said. Then, with authority, he added, "Now try to put all that out of your head, because today is about new beginnings. For all of us. I'm gonna kick things off with introductions and then explain the charter of this new task force. Not just for your benefit, but for all the principals. You're not the only newbie in the group. On top of that, several of the priors from the JIRG don't know all the details about what happened in Yemen and Djibouti."

Great. I get to relive the worst day of my life twice in one day.

But instead of protesting, Kemper just nodded. "Sure, I understand."

"All right, good. Now, the moment of truth," said Jarvis, with an expectant look on his face. "Jack Kemper is dead. You will not hear that name from my lips ever again. So, who are you?"

Kemper shrugged. "I didn't realize I had a say in the matter. I figured I'd show up here and you'd hand me an ID with my picture and a new name."

"Well, in that case," Smith interjected, surprising both of them, "I'd like the honor."

Kemper had no idea what was involved in becoming someone else—in starting a new life with a new identity—but Smith had already crossed that bridge. From operator to spook. From born to reborn. Maybe it made sense for Smith to be his baptizer. Or maybe he'd regret letting a guy named Barry Pozniak pick his new name. Either way, did it really matter? It was just a NOC, after all—what difference does a name make?

"Fine," Kemper said, with another shrug. "You can call me Sister Mary Francis for all I care, so long as you put me to work."

"All right, then, your fate is in Shane's hands," said Jarvis with a little ironic smile. "Follow me to the conference room, gents."

Jarvis led them from the roundtable into a room behind blacked-out glass doors. Inside, Kemper scanned the faces of the most unlikely group of people he'd ever seen assembled in a TOC. The two college boys from earlier were huddled at the end of a narrow rectangular conference table, jabbering over an iPad like chipmunks fighting for a giant acorn. Next to them stood a tall, lanky professor type, dressed in an expensive suit, intently observing their conversation. A young Asian man with crazy hair and trendy eyeglasses occupied the spot to the professor's right. After him stood two operators: a bearded, twenty-something Latino and a clean-shaven, middle-aged African American who Kemper pegged as at least six and a half feet tall. Beside this brute, stood an angel. Or maybe, the devil herself. It was impossible to say which, but whoever she was, the girl was smoking hot. And angry. He'd never seen a face so beautiful saturated with so much venom. She was dressed like an operator, except her cargo pants, shirt, and boots were all black. Her auburn hair was pulled back in an unforgiving ponytail; she wore no makeup. Her pale blue eyes never wavered from their target—Kelso Jarvis.

"Please, everyone, take your seats," Jarvis said, interrupting Kemper's look around.

Kemper took a seat next to Smith, and realized he was grateful to have the former Delta operator on the team. The world of spies and OGAs—"other government agencies" as they were known by operators—was outside his wheelhouse, and he was not familiar with the various protocols and personnel roles in a civilian task force like this one.

"Welcome to Task Force Ember," Jarvis announced once everyone was seated. "In part, this task force is the reincarnation of the Joint Intelligence Research Group, which was officially disbanded a few days ago. Some of you already know one another, but for the sake of our new additions, I'd like to start off with introductions. To my left is our Director of Operations, Shane Smith. Shane is my right hand, and he's responsible for overseeing all facets of task-force operations. All data and reports should flow through him, and in the event I'm unreachable, he's in charge."

Smith nodded to the group.

"Shane, why don't you introduce the head of our new Special Activities Unit?" Jarvis said.

Kemper found himself gritting his teeth at the prospect of his new name. Damn it, why hadn't he given Jarvis a name when he'd had the chance five minutes ago? Something simple and forgettable, like Mark Jones. Instead, he'd flubbed it, and now Smith had control of his fate. He shouldn't have called Delta guys pussies this morning. *Shit.* Smith was going to make him pay for that. He could hear it coming. *Hey, everybody, meet Jack Goff. Or, I'd like to introduce Erick Shin. The possibilities for lifelong shame were endless: Holden Johnson, Wayne Kerr, Dick Short, Rick O'Shea,* and those were just the doozies he could think of on the fly—

"Everyone," said Smith, giving Kemper's shoulder a squeeze, "this is John Dempsey. Dempsey is a former Tier One Navy SEAL, and like the famous boxer he shares a last name with, he's an all-around badass. We're fortunate to have him on the team."

Kemper breathed a sigh of relief and nodded to the group. Then he met Smith's eyes and gave a subtle nod of gratitude. Maybe it was time to start trusting this guy. With stand-up moves like that, Smith seemed like a team guy more and more every day.

Jarvis gave no visible reaction to the impromptu christening—at least none that Kemper could see. He waited for Smith to take his seat before continuing.

"On my right is another new addition, Sal Mendez, who will be working in Special Activities with Dempsey."

Kemper pegged Mendez for a Marine. Probably a former critical-skills operator. Mendez sported a heavy black beard—at least two weeks' growth. Give that beard two months and send Mendez and his Latin complexion to Miami Beach for a week, and the guy could easily pass for an Arab. That could be useful. Mendez flashed the group an easy, confident smile that reminded Kemper of Spaz. He liked the guy already, but he knew he should bury the feeling. That sort of thinking was dangerous. He didn't know shit about Mendez. It didn't matter what Jarvis or Smith thought of any of these people. Anyone who was going to be part of his team would need to be vetted by him personally before earning his trust.

"Also new to Ember," Jarvis continued, "is Elizabeth Grimes. She will be part of the leadership here, although her exact role is still evolving."

Unless his ears were playing tricks on him, Kemper swore he heard the redheaded beauty actually growl at that comment. With her pale-blue irises locked on Jarvis and a voice so cold the room went numb, Elizabeth Grimes said, "I believe what Director Jarvis meant to say was that I will also be working with Dempsey's Special Activities Unit."

Unfazed, Jarvis held her gaze. "As I said, your role is still evolving. Should you happen to find yourself with the title of Director, then you can call the shots. Until then, I will decide in what capacity you serve this task force."

She made no rebuttal, and Jarvis dismissed her with a glance.

Kemper watched the muscles ripple along her hard, perfect jawline as she ground her teeth together in bitter, silent enmity.

What the hell was that all about?

Kemper raised an eyebrow at Smith, who responded only with a sniff.

"Next is Mr. Quinton Thomas. Mr. Thomas is the head of both internal and external security, not the least of which is the physical security of our new facility here. He will be checking our three newbies into the system and running biometrics. Later this afternoon, he'll brief all hands on the protocols for this compound, discuss our two dedicated aircraft, and give you a walk-through of the comms and computer systems. For all you legacy members, there are a number of important changes to the way we're doing business in Ember, so pay close attention."

Thomas gave Jarvis a cordial two-fingered salute, but his face was all business as he looked around the table. Kemper could not help but stare at the big man's ridiculous physique. Thomas looked like he could pick up Smith and break him over a knee like kindling. The man's neck was thicker than his head, for Christ's sake. How was that even possible? After intimidating all the non-operators at the table, the big man looked at Kemper and winked, a hint of a smile lingering still on his lips.

Thomas is enjoying this way more than he should be, Kemper decided. *Definitely a Marine.*

"Next up is Ian Baldwin, our chief data cruncher and analysis demigod. Baldwin keeps our analyst team on task and on target, which includes the two kids beside him." Jarvis gestured to the two geeks seated beside Professor Baldwin. "I call them Chip and Dale. I encourage you to do the same." Both of the junior analysts rolled their eyes at the nicknames like high school freshmen just told to clean their rooms. "All kidding aside, Baldwin's team is second to none. Data analysis is our differentiator. It was the lifeblood of JIRG, and it will continue to be so with Ember."

Dempsey nodded at Chip—or was that Dale?—who raised a hand to wave before being elbowed by his partner.

"Which leaves us with Richard Wang," Jarvis said, gesturing to the Asian kid sitting next to one of the chipmunks. Wang had the lean physique of a triathlete, but he didn't have the hard eyes of an operator. *Cyber tech and comms? Probably,* Kemper decided, *but he can't be a day over twenty-three.*

"I poached Mr. Wang from US Cyber Command before they could make him head of the Southeast Asia division. Since then, he has reluctantly adapted to our low-tech task-force environment, and somehow manages to carry on as our ITO chief." There were some chuckles from the organic members, suggesting this was some sort of inside joke.

"A couple of bamboo sticks and a roll of copper wire is all I need, boss. No, seriously, though, first order of business—I'd like everyone to turn in your existing phones and laptops, and I'll get you set up with some nice Chinese Huawei phones and Hasee computers," Wang said, barely cracking a smile.

Wise guy, huh? Kemper liked him immediately. But in the field, not knowing what you don't know was every rookie's greatest liability. As long as Wang stayed in the back and followed orders, his inexperience could be managed.

"For you new guys—and girls," Jarvis said, with an exaggerated look at Elizabeth Grimes, "this is a small, elite team. We do the impossible with an impossibly small number of people, so there will be a lot of crossover training. I'm not saying I expect you to be interchangeable assets—we are a team of specialists—but I do expect you to have an *operational* understanding of one another's roles. I'm an optimist, but also a realist, and in this business, attrition is a fact of life. When gaps appear on our roster, I need existing members to step up and fill those gaps. Under our new charter, everyone in this room needs to be prepared to work in the field. With that in mind, I've scheduled ops training to begin on Monday up the road in Williamsburg. You can think of today as a fam day, if you like, to get used to our new home, the new gear, and one another."

Kemper noticed Baldwin and the two analysts exchange nervous glances. For men accustomed to working in the ironclad safety of a TOC, the prospect of being thrown into the wild would be terrifying.

Jarvis tapped the table with the Naval Academy ring he wore, jolting everyone awake from their private daydreams.

"Why are we here?" he asked.

Kemper considered the question. The words were rhetorical, but the tone in Jarvis's voice was not.

No one answered.

"Why are we here?" Jarvis repeated.

Kemper was about to open his big mouth, but Jarvis turned to Smith and nodded.

Smith picked up a remote control on the conference-room table and pressed several buttons. The conference-room lights dimmed, and a large flat-screen TV flickered to life. The screen was configured in a four-way split, streaming video that made Kemper's stomach churn. Each quadrant showed a different cable-network news piece depicting the massacre of "two dozen" Navy SEALS during an operation in Yemen. CNN, Fox News, NBC, and goddamn Al Jazeera. Fucking unbelievable. The story had been leaked into the wild. Even with the fictitious losses—fewer than half the true number of casualties—the idea that actual footage from the Yemen mission had found its way onto television infuriated Kemper. Secrecy and anonymity had been the government's promise to the Tier One operators in exchange for the sacrifices they made every day. Once again, that promise had been betrayed to satisfy some nameless, faceless political agenda. Ironic that the bureaucrat responsible for this leak got to maintain his anonymity, while the safety of the Tier One SEAL family members were put in jeopardy. Kemper listened in disgust as the various news anchors "memorialized" the gallant men who'd lost their lives by reading off their goddamn names and ranks! His chest tightened with rage. He started bouncing his right leg under the table, toes on the floor, heel moving up and down like a piston—trying to relieve the angst brewing inside.

"I ask you again," Jarvis said, his voice hard and baritone. "Why are we here?"

"To find the bastards responsible and send them straight to hell," Kemper said, clenching both his fists.

"I couldn't have said it better myself," said Jarvis, standing. "Dempsey just spelled out our charter in one sentence. Live it, breathe it, and don't forget it. The massacre of our nation's Tier One SEAL unit will forever be the legacy of the Joint Intelligence Research Group. But not this group. This group will make things right."

Jarvis paused for a moment to look around the table. "What happened in Yemen and Djibouti can only be explained by a breach in operational security. Was the JIRG compromised? Maybe. Does this event highlight a systematic vulnerability of the DoD intelligence apparatus as a whole? Most definitely. I say this because the intelligence collected that led to the mission in Yemen was vetted through multiple channels, flowed from multiple sources, and was screened with the highest level of care—most notably by half of the people sitting in this room. Our group was secure, and it was black. Its existence in the outside world was known only at the highest echelon of the intelligence community. Even that was not enough."

Kemper looked around the table. This was the confirmation he'd been dreading—Jarvis and his Joint Group were intimately involved in the operational tasking for Yemen. His immediate reaction was a strong compulsion to blame the people in this room. If they were the ones responsible for handling the data, didn't that make them responsible for the massacres? He forced himself to take a deep breath. And then another. Would blaming Jarvis, Smith, and the young analysts across the table bring his dead friends back to life? No. Would hating the people in this room ultimately accomplish anything? No. Blaming was unproductive. Blaming was living in the past. He needed to focus on the now. He needed to focus on the *real* bad guys—the fuckers who compromised the OPSEC and sprung the trap. That was why he was here. That was why Ember was born.

Jarvis must have read his mind. "Disbanding the JIRG was a necessity. Whoever pulled this off not only ambushed our brother SEALs in Yemen and the TOC in Djibouti, but also exploited the workings of our entire intelligence and counterterrorism infrastructure. Despite its minuscule footprint, the Joint Group was still plugged into the system. And that system is compromised."

"How is this group any different?" Grimes asked, leaning forward on her elbows. "What makes you certain that history won't repeat itself?"

"Because this group is unplugged. This group does not report to the Pentagon or DIA or DHS or the CIA, or any official intelligence-collecting entity that falls under the US government command-and-control umbrella. We have no official name except our NOC—Ember Corporation. We have no constraints on how we gather intelligence, and no constraints on how we prosecute the enemy. There are two people outside of this room who know who we are and what we are doing. We're well funded and well equipped, but we have no perpetual charter. Our only task is to find the masterminds behind the hits in Yemen and Djibouti, discover how the hell they did it, and then eliminate them. We have no other mission, no other priorities, and no distractions from this singular quest. Unlike the Joint Group, we have the personnel, the authority, and the autonomy to act on the intelligence we collect. With Dempsey's field unit, we will hunt down and destroy those targeting our nation's elite Special Forces. With the Tier One SEALs gone, who's to say they won't go after Delta next?"

"Unless we find these bastards, Delta might as well be dead," Smith said, taking his turn at the pulpit. "JSOC has put an indefinite hold on all counterterrorism Tier One Spec Ops. Without our Tier One units out there in the wild, our enemies will become more brazen and more active. I expect to see a spike in terrorist activity in the coming months, the likes of which we've not seen in a decade."

Heads nodded in agreement around the table. Smith was right. Before Yemen, nearly all of Kemper's team's missions had been counterterror related. He couldn't imagine a world where ISIS and Al Qaeda were left to run amok.

Jarvis nodded at Smith, and Smith worked the remote control. The lights in the conference room brightened, and the TV screen went dark.

"I don't give pep talks. The hard work starts now. What happens after we succeed is for the bureaucrats. Any questions?"

"I have a question," said Grimes.

Kemper shook his head. *Great, here we go.*

"You said two people outside this room know of Ember's existence. Are you planning on sharing their identities with the team?"

Jarvis pursed his lips. "If I wanted to share that information, I would have."

"You thought things were secure with the JIRG, and look where that got you," the redhead said, steepling her fingers. "If we're out in the wild and things go wrong, don't you think the team has a right to know who decides our fate?"

"Every person in this room is here by invitation and of their own volition," Jarvis said. "And every person in this room needs to understand the inherent risk of being disavowed when you're operating in the black."

Kemper remembered that tone from the teams. *Oh boy, the shit is about to hit the fan.*

Instead of escalating, Jarvis took a deep breath and smiled. "If you have reservations about this group that will prevent you from doing your job, then by all means, you're free to go. If you think you're not a good fit, then please, leave. But do it now, because once Thomas completes your security indoc, you're with us to the end. Either way, the NDA you signed this morning gives me the authority to prosecute you for treason, should a breach occur."

"Either way?" Grimes said, her voice even colder than his. "Is that a threat?"

"That is protocol," Jarvis said with a condescending smile. Then he looked away, dismissing her with his body language. "Mr. Thomas, show Ms. Grimes to my office so she and I can discuss her role on the task force. Then, you can start checking in Mendez. As for the rest of you, pick a locker, get moved in, and wait your turn for indoc with Thomas."

Thomas slid his chair back and stood up, towering over everyone. "Yes, sir."

Jarvis turned his attention back to the redhead. Kemper noticed that now she was wearing the same condescending smile that Jarvis had been moments ago.

"I'll be along in a few minutes, Ms. Grimes," Jarvis said. "First, I need to speak with my new head of Special Activities."

Grimes said nothing and *let* herself be escorted from the conference room. Beside Thomas, she looked like Little Red Riding Hood playing dress-up in 5.11 Tactical clothes. After everyone else had cleared the room, Jarvis collapsed against the backrest of his chair.

"What a bitch," Smith said, laughing beneath his breath. "Boss, who the hell is she, and what is she doing here?"

"*She* is our devil's advocate in residence," Jarvis said, rubbing his temples. "With the castle came a queen. Don't worry; I'll make her my problem."

Kemper got the sense that Jarvis had more than just misgivings about Her Highness, Lady Grimes, but he knew better than to push. Still, he couldn't help wonder who this woman was. Like his new name, he assumed Elizabeth Grimes was a pseudonym. With the exception of Kelso Jarvis, undoubtedly every person he'd met today was using a nonofficial cover.

Welcome to your new family, Kemper. A family of strangers.

"Soooo," Jarvis said, smiling at Kemper, "you're John Dempsey now, huh? You ready for that?"

Kemper leaned forward, his elbows on the table. "I'm ready for anything, Skipper," he said. "So long as you let me pull the trigger on the assholes responsible for Yemen. After that, I don't really care."

"There may not be an after, Dempsey," Jarvis said. "Therefore, we need to keep our focus on getting this mission right. Shane will give you a tour of what we have here in terms of equipment and support. Tomorrow you'll meet some of the other folks you'll be interfacing with on your operations. Keep a mental list of anything else you think you need. We have to pull this shit together fast, before the bad guys responsible all disappear like ghosts. You have a lot to learn, and even more to *unlearn*, in a very short time. This isn't kicking in doors, clearing the room, and evacuating the survivors off the X, John," said Jarvis.

It wasn't lost on Kemper how Jarvis kept using his new name. Familiarization and repetition formed the cornerstone of the Kelso Jarvis training handbook.

My name is John Dempsey, Kemper told himself.

My name is John Dempsey.

Jack Kemper is dead.

I am John Dempsey.

"This is an entirely new world for you, John. This is making someone disappear from bed while his wife is sleeping beside him. This is deciding to let a friendly take a bullet while you save some shithead's life. This is a world that requires compromise, sacrifice, and surgical precision—without SOPs, without little birds, without MEDEVACs, and without the power and security of JSOC behind you. Do you understand what you've signed up for?"

"Yes, Skipper," answered Dempsey. "I understand."

"All right," Jarvis said. "After you finish your security indoc with Thomas and your tour with Shane, you and I are going to have a sit-down. I want to hear your thoughts on how we find the assholes responsible for Yemen."

"You want *my* thoughts on how to find them?"

"Yes," Jarvis said with a crooked grin. "You're more than just a point-and-shoot asset on this team. Time for you to start contributing strategically."

Dempsey nodded, holding his tongue about his true feelings on the matter.

"Shane will bring you up to speed on the operational parameters for your group. The team will grow organically over time. You will be able to recruit new members, but for the immediate future, you're running a team of five."

"Roger that," Dempsey said, standing up.

Smith was already standing by the blacked-out double-glass doors, waiting to start the familiarization tour. The news that Dempsey could recruit other guys he trusted bolstered his mood. Dan Munn's name immediately came to mind.

Before stepping through the doors, Dempsey paused. Turning back to Jarvis, he said, "You said five, but I only count four—me, Smith, Mendez, and Wang."

Jarvis clasped his fingers together and stared at him without reply.

"The redhead?" Dempsey asked, incredulous.

Jarvis smirked. "The redhead."

CHAPTER 20

"Shane, when was the last time you saw Dempsey?" Jarvis leaned back in the leather chair behind his desk and rolled his head in slow clockwise circles, trying to alleviate stiffness in his neck and the pounding headache that came along with it.

"Ten minutes ago, in the equipment room," said his Operations Director. "You should see him. The dude is like a kid in a candy store. I think handling the gear is making him feel less out of his element."

"Good. Give him a few more minutes before sending him in here to chat with me about our hunting strategy."

Jarvis knew that John was adaptable—something he suspected the former SEAL Senior Chief did not know about himself. The only way to truly measure Dempsey's adaptability was to put him to work. Trial by fire, so to speak.

"Will we get him into our playbook in time?" Jarvis asked. He had his own opinion on the matter, but he wanted to observe Shane thinking through these issues with him.

Smith nodded. "He'll be ready. Dempsey is smarter than he thinks."

"And more stubborn than you think," Jarvis cautioned. "And emotional. Dr. West called me after their session."

"Dempsey told me it went fine," said Smith. "Hell, if I didn't know better, I'd say he even liked the doc. Did West say otherwise?"

"West said what I already suspected—Dempsey has a long road ahead. What happened in Yemen and Djibouti hit us all hard, but nothing like it did for Dempsey. He's been traumatized in ways that will take years to sort out. In the short term, his anger could affect his judgment in the field and thereby jeopardize the team. Keep a close eye on him during the scenario-based training at the Farm. Dempsey has a wealth of surveillance experience and a keen mind for observation, but a tactician he is not. My goal is to challenge him during the coming weeks and see what wins out—his emotions or his wits."

"Roger that."

"He's also going to look to you for clues on how to handle the transition from Tier One operator to clandestine operator. It's a paradigm shift, and not one that every SEAL or Delta soldier can pull off."

Smith nodded. "The hardest part of going spook is the subtlety. Recognizing what's different from SPECOPS and what's not. After the first couple of screwups, the temptation is to go overboard and think you need to chuck all your Tier One training out the window. That is a mistake. The same principles apply, even when the environment has changed."

"Our world is more kinetic," Jarvis said.

Smith shrugged. "Different kinetics . . . for me at least."

Silence lingered a moment between them. Jarvis saw Smith shift uncomfortably in his seat. "What is it, Shane?"

"Well, I was wondering." Smith leaned forward. "Your asset in Iran—have you reached out to him? It would be helpful if we could vet any new theories we generate with someone on the inside."

Jarvis knew Smith was looking for more than that. He was wondering if the Iranian asset had a role in the SEAL massacre. Robert

Kittinger and the president were probably wondering that as well. But Jarvis doubted Kittinger cared one way or the other so long as Ember found a way to prove Iran was the architect of state-sponsored terrorism against the Tier One SEALs, thereby giving the White House the justification it needed to sway world opinion. Then and only then would America have the support it needed to reverse course on the treaty with the Iranian regime. But, unfortunately, Jarvis wasn't any closer to finding the truth than he had been a few weeks ago.

"I've been unable to contact my asset since the attack," Jarvis said. "At this point, I think we can safely assume he's in the wind, or he was captured or killed."

"Or that we were played," Smith said. There was no judgment in the statement. It was part of the game and the risk of doing business.

"Or that," Jarvis agreed, his voice catching in his throat. "It's good that we restructured. Make sure that all bridges to the JIRG are burned. If the bad guys come looking for us—which undoubtedly they will—we need to make sure the trail stops at a cliff looking down into the abyss."

"I took the initiative and already shut down all bank accounts, data servers, e-mail accounts, phone numbers, safe houses, and contract obligations we had. All subcontractors have been canceled, and all our managed assets were issued new contact protocols. But I'll task Quinton with a final sweep to confirm I didn't miss something."

"Perfect," Jarvis said. "Now tell me, Operations Director, what's our next move?"

Smith laughed. "I thought deciding next moves was your job."

"Only until I die or get fired. What's our next move?"

"Start shaking trees and see where the nuts fall?"

"Exactly, which brings me to an interesting conversation I had with a friend at Mossad," he said, watching Smith's face closely.

Smith nodded. "Levi Harel."

Jarvis smirked. *Sneaky bastard already knew.*

"You know I keep a detail on you, sir. It's part of my job."

"And you know I slip them when I have to," Jarvis countered.

Smith shrugged. "If the mission demands it?" he said, his tone a tad incendiary. "What did the former head of Mossad have to say? Something helpful, I hope."

"Harel is too busy to waste time not being helpful," Jarvis said. "It appears our friends in Tel Aviv have been managing an asset in Frankfurt who has developed a relationship with an Iranian national. Harel believes the Iranian is a midlevel operative with VEVAK and could provide us information concerning the fate of our asset in Tehran."

Smith nodded, leaning forward. "How long has Harel's girl been working the Iranian?"

"How do you know Harel's asset is a woman?"

"Call it an educated guess," said Smith, scratching his neck. "Harel made a name for himself by successfully deploying more female assets than any other Mossad chief."

Jarvis nodded, impressed. *The kid has been busy taking initiative and doing his homework. Excellent.*

He grabbed the iPad off his desk and opened an encrypted file Harel had sent him early that morning. Then he passed the tablet computer to Shane. "For now, this is for your eyes only. We can bring the rest of the team up to speed on a need-to-know basis."

Jarvis watched Shane's pupils dart back and forth as he scanned the text, scrolling with his right index finger as he read. "Do you want me to make contact with her and arrange a meeting?"

"Absolutely not. Never risk burning an asset—especially someone else's asset—unless you have no other alternative."

Shane looked up from the iPad, confused. Then his eyes brightened with understanding. "Observe the girl until we ID the Persian, then we put HUMINT and SIGINT on the target?"

"Exactly. And we coordinate all this with Mossad in Frankfurt so they understand our intentions. Then, once we've learned the Iranian's routine and travel schedule, we kidnap the sonuvabitch."

Shane let out a whistling sigh. "There is a lot of risk in taking a VEVAK operative. As soon as we take him, all the spiders will scurry back into their holes. Even if we learn everything about his operation, we may find ourselves unable to act on that intelligence."

Jarvis nodded, a little disappointed that Shane was back to thinking inside the standard DoD box.

"That would be true," he conceded, "if they knew we had taken him. Brainstorm me a screenplay."

Smith frowned. "The Dream Makers are a CIA asset. I severed that link when we shut down the JIRG. We don't have access to that group anymore."

"I know. Which means you're going to have do it in-house. Get creative with it," Jarvis continued. "Find me a way to get this guy to Virginia without anyone in VEVAK thinking they've been compromised."

Jarvis slid a thumb drive across the desk to Shane.

"Here's the file on the Mossad asset in Frankfurt. Harel offered to mobilize his permanent team in Germany if things go bat-shit crazy. If that happens, then VEVAK will undoubtedly blame the Mossad for their agent's disappearance, while we walk away with a nice cover story. Hopefully, we don't go down that road, but it's a scenario we need to consider."

"Understood."

"I know you've got a full plate, but work through it quickly. You know how these things go. Short fuse, then boom. I need Dempsey and the rest of the team ready to go, ASAP."

"You got it, boss," Smith said, and turned to leave.

"Shane," Jarvis called after him.

Smith turned back, his eyebrows raised.

"Stick close to Dempsey. He's most vulnerable while we're in work-up mode. Once he's on mission, he'll be a heat-seeking missile. But right now, he's got too much fucking time to think."

"You got it, sir. I'm turning over the keys to his house and car today, but I'll stay close."

"Have Quinton keep a detail on him until I say otherwise."

Smith nodded, but looked disappointed by the order.

"It's not a trust issue, Shane. Just being careful."

"I know."

"And put a detail on Grimes."

"I already did. I can tell you every time she takes a leak and how she likes her coffee in the morning."

"Good," Jarvis said. "I'm particularly interested in any outside contact."

"Understood. So far, she's had none. Oh, have you heard what Dempsey's calling her?"

"No," Jarvis said. "What?"

"The Lady Grimes."

Jarvis laughed. "Think she'll have a sense of humor about it when she finds out? Because they *always* find out."

"Probably not," Smith said with a grin. "Good thing Dempsey knows how to duck a punch."

As soon as Shane was gone, Jarvis picked up his iPad. He closed the file on Mossad's asset in Frankfurt and entered a five-digit security code to access the Ember personnel records. He scrolled through the list until he found the entry for Elizabeth Grimes. With a double-tap of his index finger, her classified CV filled the screen. He stared at her official White House headshot and bio:

Kelsey Clarke is the Assistant Director of Intelligence Programs for the National Security & International Affairs Division of the Office of Science and Technology Policy. Her charter is to pursue innovation and excellence in the technical support of US defense, intelligence, and national-security objectives. Her work focuses primarily on ensuring that science-and-technology issues are given proper consideration during policy and budget-development processes in the domain of national security. Current areas of interest include cyber security, counterterrorism, defense against biological and chemical threats, nuclear deterrence, emergency response and communications, international relations and counterintelligence, and other matters relating to the future of national security.

Ms. Clarke is a graduate of the US Military Academy at West Point. After completing two tours of service in the Middle East, she left the Army as a Captain to pursue graduate studies at Harvard University, where she earned a JD-MPP from Harvard Law School and The John F. Kennedy School of Government. Immediately prior to joining the OSTP, Ms. Clarke worked at the Brookings Institution as an instrumental team member on the Twenty-First Century Defense Initiative, where she conducted research, analysis, and outreach addressing the future of war, the future of US defense needs and priorities, and the future of the US defense system.

Jarvis shook his head and laughed. The page might as well read: Kelsey Clarke, aka Elizabeth Grimes, the most talented, brilliant, pain-in-the-ass woman imaginable. He scrolled farther down the file and scanned her military-service record, marksmanship scores, and fitness report. Oh, and don't forget: type A personality to the third power, movie-star good looks, and deadeye shot. Christ, no wonder Kittinger selected this woman to act as his personal mole in Ember. He wasn't an idiot. No one hands over $40 million, two corporate jets, a bat cave packed with guns, and a mandate to go kill people with no strings attached. Grimes was Kittinger's ace in the hole; she was his insurance policy. She had the smarts to judge Jarvis's decisions, and the mettle to question his authority if she deemed it necessary.

The bigger question was: Why did she want to be here—almost desperately, it appeared? She didn't seem the type to jump at the chance to be a bureaucrat's mole. She wanted something—everyone did. Maybe Kittinger had some dirt on her?

He scrolled back up to her picture and blew air through his teeth.

You're going to make my life miserable, aren't you, Elizabeth Grimes?

CHAPTER 21

Dempsey fidgeted in the leather passenger seat of Smith's Tahoe, trying to ignore the terrible itch that had been tormenting him all day. The burns on his neck and shoulder had been the most severe and the last to transition from the pain phase of healing to the itching phase. He preferred the pain. An itch that couldn't be scratched was like—

"You've gotta stop doing that," Smith said, glancing over at him.

"Doing what?"

"Tracing that scar on your left forearm. I noticed you doing it in the TOC at MacDill months ago, and you were at it again during Jarvis's brief earlier today."

"Old habit, I guess," Dempsey said with a shrug. "I didn't even realize I was doing it."

"You have to do a better job policing your mannerisms. That behavior is something Jack Kemper did. You're John Dempsey now. John Dempsey doesn't do that. The shape of the scar is distinctive enough; you don't need to draw people's attention to it by rubbing it."

"Got it," Dempsey said, a little irritated at being henpecked, but Smith had a point.

"As a Tier One operator, you relied on habits forged by your training and experience to save your ass whenever all hell broke loose. For a clandestine operator, habits are dangerous. Habits lead to patterns. Patterns are recognizable by the enemy. Also, habits dull situational awareness and promote operational laziness. Even the most effective agent can be undone by practices that, while useful in certain situations, evolve into habits. Trust me, I'm speaking from experience on this one. My goal is not to preach, but to hopefully help you from making the same mistakes I did."

Dempsey nodded. "Makes sense. I'll keep that in mind."

They rode in silence for several minutes until Smith spoke again, this time his tone markedly more upbeat. "What did you think of the hangar?"

Dempsey was about to answer, but the sight of a black GMC Yukon parked in Smith's driveway stole his attention. He reached for the pistol holstered in the small of his back. "You expecting company?"

Smith shook his head. "Relax. I've got a couple of surprises for you."

He pulled up beside the Yukon in the three-car driveway. Dempsey grabbed his duffel bag from the backseat and slung it over his shoulder. He looked admiringly at the large SUV in the drive, the windows tinted as dark as Virginia state law would allow.

"Who are we meeting?" he asked, his curiosity growing.

"No one," Smith said, and tossed a set of keys to him. "That's your new ride."

Dempsey caught the keys midair in his right hand. "So, there are some perks to this job, huh?"

"Not enough to compensate for the wear and tear, but yeah, Jarvis knows how to take care of his people. You can check out the Denali in a bit; first, I have some other things to show you."

Dempsey followed Smith to the front door. In the past, they'd always entered through the garage. Up close, he noticed for the first time that steel bars were inset in the frosted glass. Smith unlocked the door, pushed it open, and pointed to small metal circles spaced every twelve inches in the door frame. The perimeter frame was heavily reinforced, and clearly designed to slow down an intruder using anything short of a breacher charge. Smith motioned Dempsey inside, away from any prying neighborhood eyes.

"The door is red oak, with a bulletproof-glass center panel, and a reinforced steel retainer that mates with the doorjamb. The entire house is framed with one-inch steel rebar running laterally through steel studs and set into concrete pillars spaced every six feet. Lock that door and the house is virtually impenetrable."

"Dude, you've taken home security to a new level of paranoia."

Smith ignored the dig, and Dempsey decided he'd have to work harder if he wanted to get Smith spun up. Pushing his teammates' buttons was what he did for fun—besides fast-roping out of stealth helos and shooting automatic weapons. Of course, those days were over, and maybe so were his button-pushing days. Nah, fuck that. If there was one morsel of Jack Kemper that needed to survive, it was his sense of humor.

"Over here." Smith waved Dempsey over to the ADT alarm panel mounted next to the front door. "You can operate the alarm system here at the foyer panel and also in the main control room."

"Control room?" Dempsey asked, cocking an eyebrow.

"I'll show you that in a minute. First, something else I think you'll like."

Smith punched a code into the alarm panel, and the buttons turned yellow. Then, a small biometric panel popped out from the side of the panel with a click.

"Left thumb," Smith said, motioning toward the biometric sensor.

"You're giving me access?"

Smith nodded.

Dempsey placed his thumb on the sensor, and the control panel beeped. To his right, another click and another magic reveal—this time a rectangular panel hissed out from one of the two fluted columns that flanked the front door. Dempsey tilted his head for a better view and noticed the butt of a 9 mm pistol protruding from the column.

He pulled the weapon free from the shuttle panel. "Okay, now *that* is pretty frickin' cool." He pulled the slide back a few millimeters and confirmed there was a round in the chamber, then placed the weapon back into the shuttle-panel holster. He slid his thumb across the bio-metric reader again, and with a hiss the weapon was gone.

"There are five panels like this throughout the house, which I'll show you, and each has the same weapon—a Sig Sauer 226, which I know is a SEAL favorite."

Dempsey shook his head. "Dude, that's awesome, but why are you showing me all this? How long are we going to be roommates?"

"Getting to that," Smith said. "There's a small armory in the control room that doubles as a panic room, and like these panels, it is remark-ably well hidden. Let me show you the rest of the house and we'll end the tour there."

Dempsey followed Smith through the house, making mental notes as he went. Strange that Smith was giving him the tour now, weeks after he'd moved into the guest bedroom. The home was new construc-tion—no more than a year old, he surmised, from the lack of wear and tear—but the fit and finish put to shame the builder-grade crap he was used to seeing in Florida. He guessed the floor plan was more than three thousand square feet. The second floor housed three bedrooms, connected by a shared transverse hallway. One of the bedrooms had been converted into an office, but Dempsey had yet to see Smith use it. Dempsey scanned the office, noting a couple of framed degrees on the walls and a bookshelf stacked with titles on leadership, business, finance, and self-help: *How to Win Friends and Influence People, The Big*

Short, Blink, Understanding Derivatives, Option Trading for Dummies, The 7 Habits of Highly Effective People . . .

"Please tell me this is for your NOC and you don't actually read this crap."

Smith smirked, evading yet another one of Dempsey's attempts at levity. "C'mon, let's go."

Dempsey followed him out of the office and down the hall to a cantilevered balcony that looked out over the curved staircase into the foyer, living room, and dining room below. He immediately saw the tactical implications of this particular design feature. It provided a 180-degree field of fire to defend against a breach through the front door or windows. The waist-high safety railing was constructed of glass panels, spaced at regular three-inch gaps, and topped with polished steel tubing. Dempsey tapped a glass panel with the toe of his boot, making a dull thud that echoed in the open foyer above.

"Ballistic glass with muzzle slots?"

"Something like that," Smith said, and trotted down the curved staircase.

Dempsey took the stairs two at a time. In the hearth-room kitchen, Smith picked up the remote control for the sixty-inch flat-screen above the stone fireplace. He hit the "Mode" button and then punched in some numbers.

"Zero-one-one-two-zero," he said. "It works on all five of the TVs in the house." The TV transformed to an eight-split screen with live feeds from the surveillance cameras. One of the feeds was from a camera looking down on them. Dempsey scanned the room trying to find the lens, but the techs had done their job well, hiding it somewhere in the built-in bookshelves flanking the hearth.

"I'll show you how to program the cameras and everything else from the control room," Smith said, and changed the TV picture to ESPN SportsCenter.

They left the hearth room and headed for the master-bedroom suite.

"I will not be lured in there," Dempsey said, pausing at the threshold. "Your *GQ* man cave shit may work on the chicks, but not on me."

Smith laughed. "Don't worry, John. You're not my type."

Inside the expansive master bedroom, he pointed to an alarm panel with the same setup as the panel in the foyer. Then he showed Dempsey how the top drawer of the right nightstand opened to expose a steel pistol box with the same biometric reader. The box clicked open to Dempsey's thumbprint, revealing another Sig and two extra fifteen-round magazines. "There's an MP5 in a coded lockbox in the master closet."

"Okay, you're James-fucking-Bond. I get it. But I gotta tell you, it makes me a little nervous being roommates with a guy who thinks he needs this much firepower at home. Even the most trigger-happy SEALs I know don't pack this much heat."

"You've got it backward, John. You haven't been my roommate— I've been yours."

Dempsey gawked at the spook. Forget the firepower and security. This house was so far above his pay grade it made him uncomfortable. "What the hell are you talking about? I can't afford this place."

"I know. That's why we're renting it to you for nine hundred dollars a month. C'mon, there's more."

Smith led him through an insanely large bathroom with a Jacuzzi tub and cavernous walk-in shower enclosed by glass on three sides. The walk-in closet through the opposite door held rows of clothes—jeans, cargo pants, and a variety of shirts by 5.11 Tactical, Columbia, Merrell, and Oakley—all the outfitters loved by operators. Shoes, boots, and even flip-flops were lined up neatly on the floor. In the left corner hung several coats and sweaters. To the right, Dempsey spied a rack of suits.

He made a snorting noise and gestured. "When the hell would I wear that shit?"

"When the tactical situation demands," Smith said, his tone low and serious. "You aren't a team guy anymore, remember? You're part of a task force that will demand you be able to shift among a variety of personas. You have a lot to learn about your new life, my friend, and training starts tomorrow. You need to learn to be more than just an ass-kicking shooter, John. Ember is not the teams. Going forward, your new motto needs to be 'Patience, patience, patience.' In our line of work, you have to let the plays evolve in real time, often to the point where you think you've fucked it all up. We're going to teach you how to disappear, watch, and wait. Once you can reliably do those three things without blowing your cover and charging into battle, you'll be one of us."

Dempsey sighed heavily.

Smith read his mind. "Jarvis and I handpicked you for Ember. Not all of our reasons are self-evident to you now, but someday they will be. Trust me."

Dempsey wanted to believe that. He needed to be part of Ember, but he had doubts. Self-doubt was not something he was accustomed to. Not since Phase I of BUD/S had he felt this uncertain about his choices and the unknown future hurtling toward him.

He followed Smith out of the bedroom and down into the basement. At the bottom of the stairs, Smith stopped, and Dempsey looked past him. The basement looked different from when he'd last seen it. More exercise equipment had been added. Some free weights, a rowing machine, and a stair-climber/elliptical hybrid now occupied the far corner. In the near corner, the heavy bag still hung exactly where he'd last seen it. Thank God for that, because he needed something to pound the shit out of tonight.

To his right, beside the stairs, he spied another unassuming ADT alarm panel. He had lived in this house for three days; how the hell had he not noticed any of the integrated security features? He punched in the code—zero-one-one-two-zero—and then slid his thumb across the biometric scanner. Instead of a weapon popping out of the wall as he expected, he heard a click. Then a hiss, like gas escaping from an uncapped soda bottle. A hidden wall panel swung open, revealing a gap of several inches. Dempsey pushed the panel into the wall and peered inside the void.

The hidden room looked like a miniature version of the Ember TOC, but a TOC intended for one or two people. Everything in the dimly lit room glowed an eerie blue, illuminated from backlit LED seams along the top of the walls. A simple black desk occupied the far wall and held three flat-screen computer monitors, each with its own keyboard. Inset in the left wall, he spied a rack of tactical-assault rifles protected by a glass panel. He stepped closer for a better view—an old-fashioned SOPMOD M4 favored by the SEALs, and three other high-tech models he was familiar with. Beneath the assault rifles, he saw two shoulder-held grenade launchers and a box of grenades. Above the rifles sat a long row of pistols, starting with the bulky Sig Sauer P226 on the left and progressing to an effeminate concealable pistol that could probably fit in his pants pocket along with a set of car keys. Finally, he surveyed the variety of folding and sheathed tactical knives mounted on the side panels.

"The gun shelves slide to the left, and behind them you'll find personal-protection equipment. Body armor, low-profile vests, flotation devices, dive gear, jump gear, and even MOPP gear. Most of that stuff came right from your personal cage at your last command, so it's worn to your body. Inventory it all tonight and make sure you have everything you need, and let us know if anything needs to be replaced."

Dempsey blinked. Twice. It was like Shane Smith had somehow entered his brain and built him the perfect weapons room. He felt the strong and overwhelming compulsion to give Smith a gift in repayment. "The SUV, the house, and now this. I don't know what to say."

"How about 'Thank you, American taxpayer. And I swear to anni- hilate the deranged bastards trying to destroy our country, our God, and our way of life, or I'll die trying.'"

Dempsey clenched a fist and held it up at chest level. Smith slammed his fist into it.

Both men stood looking at each other for moment, until Smith broke the silence. "Any questions?"

"Yeah, a million. I'll start with the obvious one. Why build this for me? A double-wide with a couple of oversize gun safes would have suited me fine."

Smith shook his head. "Ember is not like the teams. You'll be work- ing from here at least thirty percent of the time."

"I don't understand. I thought we all worked at the hangar?"

"Nope. We can't have thirty people showing up to work every day at a small, quiet hangar at the airport. It would compromise everything we're trying to do."

"I thought . . ."

"That Ember was just comprised of the people you met today? No. We have a staff of thirty-one, but those thirty-one are highly compart- mentalized. Only ten of us are authorized to enter the hangar at will. However, the number of folks with hangar access will undoubtedly grow as we bring more people onboard."

"Does everyone in Ember have a house like this?"

"Only the principals, but the other members all have black rooms. When we're not in the field, most of our work is done virtually from black rooms."

Dempsey nodded, but he didn't like what he was hearing. Teams should work as teams, together, face-to-face, shoulder-to-shoulder. This felt cold.

Alien.

Smith tapped the space bar on one of the keyboards, and all three monitors woke from hibernation. "This is your homework assignment.

The first file is a detailed history of John Patrick Dempsey. I want you to study it tonight and start getting all this shit in your head. Dempsey can't be someone you're pretending to be. You have to be him all day, every day, until the day comes you can't even remember that other name."

Smith tapped the screen again. "When you meet your neighbors, you're John Dempsey, military veteran and security specialist for Ember Corporation. You work long hours and travel frequently overseas. It's all in here—family background, romantic history, the first car you owned, where you went to school, yada, yada, yada."

"I went to Virginia Tech?" Dempsey said, speed-reading the file.

"Yeah. We were roommates there, by the way, so we still hang out a lot. Everything you need to know about yourself is in that file. You have two days to know it cold. Beginning tomorrow we'll challenge you on your history during training. Stress and distraction will blow holes in your memory, so instead of memorizing facts, John Dempsey's life should be a narrative. Imagine living his life, from high school to the present. Celebrate his victories, and suffer his failures. Emotional bonding is the key to becoming someone else. If you don't care about John Dempsey, you'll never convince anyone that he's real."

Dempsey nodded. The passion in Smith's advice resonated with him, and he felt a strange gravity pulling him—almost against his will—toward the desk.

Smith put a hand on his shoulder. "Later," he said softly with a smile. "The other file you need to pay attention to is the one the CI guys put together about the Ember NOC, detailing all of the company's business activities. Thomas will be pimping you on that file first thing tomorrow morning. Also, sometime, I need you to take a crack at the retrospective data we have on Yemen. Our policy is that all eyes scan the data. You never know whose eyeballs will see something the others have been blind to."

"Oh, is that all?"

Smith laughed. "Not hardly, but that will get you started. Tomorrow afternoon we have a block of time at the Farm for some scenario-based training to get you up to speed on clandestine operating protocols. Kicking in doors and clearing the room with flash-bangs and rifle fire is your old life. Your new life is about finesse."

Dempsey glanced at the computer—at his new life.

"You're gonna do great," Smith said. "Let's go grab some dinner."

"I would, except my boss gave me all this work to do."

"Oh, c'mon, Dempsey. There's a Bonefish Grill five minutes from here, and they have killer shrimp tacos. I'm buying."

Dempsey pulled out the task chair and planted himself in it. Then, while scanning the text of his bio, he said, "Sorry, dude, but John Dempsey hates shrimp tacos."

CHAPTER 22

Geneva, Switzerland
May 6, 0844 Local Time

Masoud Modiri stood at the shore of Lake Geneva watching the eastern sky.

In his experience, the greatest beauty was most often born in the moments of greatest transition. At the junctions where opposites collide, the contrast is rich and profound. It is the battle for dominance over the sky between day and night that paints the sky brilliant—retreating indigo and fading purple make the oranges and reds of the waking sun all the more magnificent. Spring's color parade is all the more striking set against the gloomy backdrop of winter's dearth. This morning, Switzerland was ablaze with the color of transition, and he did not want to look away.

His brother was waiting for him inside—waiting to finish the breakfast conversation that Masoud had walked out on. He crossed his arms, not ready to go back inside the rented lake house on Route de Lausanne—a house he had come to despise. With its brown wooden cabinets, brown wooden floors, brown furniture, and brown carpet, the house was suffocating. Brown, brown, brown, everywhere he looked.

He felt the brown seeping into him, soiling his soul. He remembered learning to mix acrylic paints as a schoolboy to make different colors. Mix yellow and blue to get green. Red and blue for purple. Yellow and red yield orange. But mix every color together and the result is brown. The color of digestion, of decomposition, of homogenization, of—

"Your mind is somewhere else today, brother," said Amir, from somewhere behind him. "Talk to me."

"My mind is here, but my heart is in Tehran," Masoud said at last. "With Fatemeh and Cyrus, and the ghost of my dead son, Kamal."

"I understand. You've been through a great ordeal the past two months, but look at how much we've accomplished. US Special Forces are still grounded, and you are engaging in regular, productive dialogue with the West."

"Yes, but sanctions are still in place. My intelligence-sharing through back channels with Ambassador Long did not ingratiate us with the White House as you had hoped. And the rest of the world still does not trust Iran. Despite all of your covert victories, from a political perspective, nothing has changed for Persia."

"Which is why it is time to take this next step. Just like before, we will secretly use Al Qaeda to inflict a terrible blow on America. And just like before, we will pretend to be America's ally in the aftermath of the carnage."

Masoud did not look at his brother. His pride wouldn't permit it. "What you're asking of me is too dangerous, Amir. I'm sorry, but the answer is no."

Instead of getting angry, which is what Masoud expected would happen, Amir took up a position beside him to watch the sky. After a long moment of silence, he said, "Do you know the story of how I met Maheen?"

Surprised by the question and the change of topic, Masoud glanced at his brother, but Amir kept his eyes straight ahead, looking at the sunrise. "You met her while you were at university. You told me that the first time you saw her, you knew she was going to be your wife."

"You have a good memory, but that is not the whole story. There is a part I've never shared with anyone before."

Masoud wondered what this secret could be, and he was intrigued. "You can trust me with the secret."

"Of this, I hold no doubts," said Amir. "When I first saw Maheen, the voice of Allah spoke inside my head. He told me that this girl was destined to be my wife, and that I would have a son and a daughter. At first I was afraid, because the Lord had never spoken to me before. I was afraid that I was losing my mind, but at that moment, Maheen, who was then still a complete stranger, turned and looked in my direction. We made eye contact, and she smiled at me. Immediately, all the fear subsided, because clearly this was Allah's will. She was so very beautiful, and the young lover in me wanted to possess her in every way a man can possess a woman. But after a moment, she looked away, and the fear returned. Now, instead of fearing Allah's voice, I was afraid of losing this girl. I was afraid of losing my destiny."

"What did you do?"

"I walked over to her and told her the truth. I told her that Allah had spoken to me, and that we were destined to be married and have a family together."

"What did she do?"

"She laughed at me—she literally laughed in my face."

Masoud tried to imagine the scene. His brother had always been the smooth talker when they were young men. All the girls had swooned over Amir because of his good looks and brash confidence. The thought of Maheen laughing in Amir's face was unimaginable to him, and yet immensely satisfying. It gave Masoud a perverse sense of pleasure to know that Amir had not won Maheen's heart without effort and a few bruises to his ego along the way.

"What happened after that?" Masoud asked.

"I asked her to have lunch with me, and she said no. I offered to walk her to class, and she said no." He smiled. "Thankfully, on my third attempt, she finally said yes."

"Allah has never spoken to me directly," Masoud said, aghast as the words flowed from his mouth. He felt his chest tighten with fear. What would his brother think of him after such an admission? Would Amir judge him a faithless Muslim, or worse, an apostate? "I should not have said that," he said quickly.

Amir turned to him, his dark espresso eyes full of compassion. "Are you afraid that I would judge you for telling me the truth? You have no reason to fear me, and more important, you have no reason to fear Allah. I did not tell you this story to advertise my piety or question yours. I told you because that day marked a transformation in my life. From that moment, I was no longer Amir Modiri, the boy. In my soul, a transition had occurred. I became Amir Modiri—husband, father, and devout disciple of Allah. While none of those things had yet come to pass, I knew with absolute certainty that they would. It was not a question of if—only a question of when. This shift in perception may sound subtle, but it is not, I assure you. Do you understand what I'm talking about?"

"Destiny," Masoud said, slowly nodding. "You're speaking of destiny."

Amir flashed him a bright smile. "Yes, exactly. Just because a man has not fulfilled his destiny does not mean he cannot recognize it and pursue it. For Allah does not distinguish between the past, the present, and the future. He sees a man's life in its entirety, from birth to death, and this is why he can know a man's soul."

Masoud took a step back. He had never heard his brother talk this way before. Amir sounded so . . . enlightened. "Has Allah continued speaking to you since that day?"

"No. Over the years, while I strove to fulfill his will, He has been silent—that is, until today."

Masoud turned to face his brother, eyes wide. "Our Holy Lord spoke to you today?"

Amir nodded. "He told me I should share with you my experience to give you the reassurance you need to serve him faithfully and trust in his will."

"Why does he talk to you about my destiny, instead of talking to me directly?"

Amir put a hand on his shoulder. "It is not my place to question Allah's will or his methods. I am his vessel, not his critic. What I can tell you is that I will see his will done, whether you accept this mission or not."

"If the world discovers that Iran is responsible for what you're planning, the consequences will be unimaginable."

"Where is your faith, brother? This is my plan, but it is Allah's will. We succeeded in Yemen and Djibouti, why not this?"

"But it's the UN, Amir," Masoud protested. "Must this be done?"

"The ethos of the United Nations mirrors the ethos of the world it represents, but the inverse is also true. To summon al-Mahdi, we must first destroy the temple of the Great Satan. Destroy the sanctity of the UN, and the world will fall into chaos. Only when chaos and civil war have consumed the world will Allah send Imam al-Mahdi to usher in a new era of peace. When the Guided One arrives, Persia will be ready to light the way and take its rightful place at the head of the new caliphate."

"The plan seems a contradiction of goals."

Amir smiled. "That is because you still do not grasp its beautiful simplicity. Our faith demands that we do everything in our power to hasten the Twelfth Imam's arrival . . . but until that time comes, we must also take action to further Iran's global standing and influence. Behind closed doors, we are the architects of the West's destruction. But in front of the Western media cameras, we are a beacon of cooperation and hope in an Islamic world gone mad. All war is deception, big brother. Surely you have realized this by now."

Masoud took a deep breath. *The greatest beauty is born in the moments of greatest transition,* he reminded himself. A future where the Twelfth Imam rules supreme, dispensing the peace and justice of Islam to all the world's people, would be a beautiful future indeed. "Okay, what do you want me to do?"

"I'm proud of you, Masoud. I knew we could count on you," Amir said, gripping Masoud's shoulder. "You're not a soldier. I realize that, but you must learn. I'm sending a man from Frankfurt to train you. He will teach you everything you need to know to complete your mission."

CHAPTER 23

Roanoke Regional Airport
Western Virginia
May 17, 1930 EDT

Dempsey was furious.

Jarvis had promised that after the team completed a two-week intensive training module at the Farm, he would turn them loose to do the job Ember was chartered to do. But graduation was two days ago, and were they hunting down the bastards responsible for blowing up his friends? No, they were not. Instead of pursuing Al Qaeda in the Middle East, they had been tasked with some domestic bullshit operation right out of the gate. To Dempsey's dismay, Jarvis had toed the party line, making the typical excuses with carefully curated managerial buzzwords. Now, Dempsey was forced to face the hard truth. Ember's charter was fantasy. They were no different from any other OGA task force—a tool for the bureaucrats in Washington to use for crisis management. This operation should have been assigned to the FBI, but because some senator's reputation was on the line, the tasking found its way to Ember.

Keep it quiet. Keep it black.

Dempsey exhaled and unclenched his jaw. The mission was on, and now it was time to get his head in the game. He tried not to look at Grimes and Smith as they strolled past, walking hand in hand and laughing like lovers on a weekend getaway. According to the instructors at the Farm, "The most common mistake a field agent can make is trying to look like someone trying not to look." Keeping this in mind, Dempsey fumbled with his wallet as he headed toward the Alamo Rental Car counter.

Nothing to see here, folks—just a harried businessman running late.

No subterfuge, no false identity, no semiautomatic weapon in the roller bag.

The two-week stint at the Farm had been a real eye-opener for him. The simulations had been so real and convoluted that even after debriefing he still wasn't sure which people were agents and which were ordinary citizens. He'd heard rumors of spooky shit going on in Williamsburg—a town famous for its colonial life reenactments—but now he joined the select few who knew the truth. Williamsburg regularly served as an unwitting extension of the nearby Armed Forces Experimental Training Activity. During his Tier One days, Dempsey had participated in a few joint training exercises with his CIA counterparts, but none of those experiences had prepared him for the intensive, scenario-based training he'd endured over the past two weeks. Now, here he was on a real domestic operation, and his mind was still swirling with subterfuge and scenarios.

"Welcome to Alamo," the desk attendant said with a forced smile. "Your name?"

"Jason Worth," Dempsey said, laying a printed reservation on the rental-car counter. On top, he placed a driver's license and credit card bearing the same name.

"Thank you," the attendant said, collecting the cards. After a fair bit of clacking on his keyboard, the man looked up. "Here we are, sir. A one-day rental of a full-size SUV. Will that work for you?"

"Yes," Dempsey said, resisting the urge to fidget. He was not accustomed to wearing tailored suit jackets, and he found this one borderline claustrophobic.

"Would you like the insurance, sir?" the attendant asked.

"No, thank you."

Dempsey noticed the attendant glance at his watch.

Must be close to the end of his shift or coming up on a break.

He was working hard to employ techniques from the "detail drills" he'd learned—a system for observing and cataloging details around him. He already, unconsciously, took mental notes about exits, allies, and potential threats—an occupational habit from his years on the black side of the teams. Now, he was training himself to notice other, less overt details, critical for surveillance and detection.

He signed the rental agreement and then initialed beside all the Xs—*JW* and not *JD* or, God forbid, *JK*. With his keys and rental contract in hand, he boarded the blue-and-yellow shuttle bus for a ride to the rental-car lot. After waiting the requisite five minutes for other customers who never came, the driver took his seat and piloted the clumsy shuttle bus away from the curb. Dempsey flipped through a copy of the *Wall Street Journal*, forcing himself to actually read the articles. Apparently a trained observer could tell the difference—thank God he was alone on the bus.

He practiced multitasking, rehearsing his memorized schedule with one part of his brain while reading an article about the housing-market correction with the other.

Phase One: Pick up the rental car, drive to the target location and survey, then check in with the TOC. Phase Two: Swing by the Sheraton to pick up Wang, then back to the target for a SIGINT collection. Phase Three: Back to the Sheraton to pick up Mendez, swing by the Lucinda House Bed

& Breakfast to grab Smith and Her Highness Elizabeth Grimes, then drive the crew to a strategic location to prep for the mission and wait for the green light from Jarvis.

Now, recall three facts per paragraph, just like they taught me:

Florida, Nevada, and Arizona have been the slowest markets to recover, 12 percent gain in thirty-six months, the national thirty-year fixed mortgage rate is . . . Shit.

He couldn't remember the rate.

The bus jerked to a stop, and Dempsey popped to his feet. After thanking the driver, he located his green Ford Expedition in spot A35, unlocked the doors with the key fob, and deposited his roller suitcase on the passenger seat beside him. He fired up the ignition, placed the transmission in drive, and departed the rental lot. He turned right on Hershberger Road, leaving the regional airport behind. Steering with his left hand, he unzipped his bag with his right, gaining access to a black metal gun box. He slid his thumb across the biometric reader, and after two beeps the bolt slid back. At the first stop sign, he opened the box and retrieved the compact Sig 239 inside. He installed a clip and released the slide, advancing the first round into the chamber. Then he slipped the weapon into a thin waistband holster and jammed the holster between his seat and the center console, where it would remain until he could put it on without wrecking his rental car. The two extra magazines went into the left pocket of his suit coat.

As he drove northeast on Route 11, he pulled out one of the two burner phones from his inside jacket pocket. He dialed the 577 area-code phone number from memory. After two rings a woman's voice answered.

"Hello?"

"Hey, sweetheart. It's me."

"Hey, me," said a warm and loving voice, a voice he'd never heard before. "You got in okay? How was your flight?"

"Great," he said. For an instant, he imagined Kate on the other end of the line, but he shook the pointless, distracting fantasy out of his head. "How are the kids?"

"Playing like maniacs inside. I'm about to put them in the tub. They have school tomorrow, ya' know."

"I know," he said.

"What time is your dinner meeting?"

"Not until later this evening. Eight thirty. I'm just out for a drive to kill some time. Looking around in case they really do transfer us here."

"Bleah," the woman said with a chuckle.

"I know, I know," Dempsey said, trying to make his rehearsed lines sound spontaneous. "I love you, baby," he said. "I'll call you after dinner."

"Okay. Love you, too." And the stranger was gone.

The entire conversation had been code. Now his Ember support team back in the hangar knew that he was on time, on target. By mentioning the kids were *playing like maniacs inside*, his female collaborator confirmed that satellite and overflight drone imagery had located the "package"—an annoyingly sterile term for the terrified woman possibly being held hostage by a domestic terrorist cell. By saying the kids had school in the morning, she conveyed that Jarvis was giving the green light for Dempsey to drive by the target facility. His responses informed her that after the drive-by, he would proceed with the plan to pick up the IT guru, Wang, at 2030 for a surveillance stakeout after sundown.

When he was a SEAL, after being briefed on the mission objectives, all he had to worry about was INFIL/EXFIL contingencies and hosing down bad guys. Now, he was overwhelmed with information. He had sat through hours of briefings on the package—Sarah Reed, daughter of Henry Reed, US senator from the Commonwealth of Virginia. He knew intimate information about the twenty-three-year-old Georgetown graduate, details he felt uncomfortable knowing. Like the fact that Sarah had been molested as a child by a trusted family friend, and that this psychological trauma had precipitated a period of heavy drug use and rampant promiscuity during her high school years. Like the fact that her younger brother was gay, but—for the sake of Senator Reed's political career—still locked in the closet. And like the rumor that Sarah's mother was having an affair with one of the partners from Henry Reed's old law firm.

Dempsey understood that digging through the Reed family skeleton closet was relevant to characterizing the package, but having so much personal information swirling around in his head was terribly distracting. He felt sorry for Sarah Reed; he couldn't imagine the angst the girl must carry around in her heart every day. So when Jarvis theorized a possible link between Sarah and the Islamic terror cell suspected of kidnapping her, Dempsey had balked. On what grounds did Jarvis draw this conclusion? On the grounds that Sarah had traveled to the Middle East during the summer between her junior and senior years of college? Or was it because she had dated the son of a Saudi diplomat for a short period of time during her sophomore year? Dempsey thought the connection was a stretch at best. He didn't understand how Jarvis could be so bold as to connect this girl to a terror cell without any hard evidence. Because Sarah Reed had been molested, that made her an Islamic radical? Yeah, right. If working for Ember meant he had to become cold, calculating, and paranoid when investigating fellow Americans, then maybe he'd made a mistake signing on.

He turned the SUV onto Read Mountain Road and took a left on Cloverdale Avenue, following the route he'd memorized. The road banked sharply to the right and became Second Avenue after the turn. Dempsey followed Second Avenue to a circular gravel drive leading to a modest house with two cars parked in front. Behind the house loomed a large warehouse—its corrugated steel roof dappled red with rust. He braked to a stop but left the transmission in drive while he made a show of pulling out a sheet of paper and calling up Google Maps on his mobile phone. Scratching his head, he pretended to reference the map program while cataloging the details of his surroundings. After a total stop time of thirty seconds, he drove away in the direction from which he'd come, retracing his route in reverse. Half a mile down Read Mountain Road, he pulled into a church parking lot. He got out of the Expedition and made a show of looking up and down the street, while pressing "Redial" on his burner phone.

"Hello?" said the woman's voice.

"Man, I really hope they don't transfer us here. This place is Hicksville, baby," he said with a good-natured laugh. "I'm in the parking lot of a big church in a neighborhood that doesn't have two decent houses on the whole block."

I surveyed the target, and there were two vehicles present.

"Is the church nice?"

"Yeah, nice enough, but I can't speak for the congregation."

The target could be breached by our team, but not without risk.

"Can I talk to the kids?" he asked.

Are we a go?

"They're in the tub. Can you call again in a little while?"

Undecided. We'll let you know at the next check-in.

"Okay," he said. "I'm gonna check in to my hotel. I'll call you when I'm all settled."

Roger. Will proceed to pick up Wang.

"Love you."

"Love you."

All is well.

Dempsey climbed back into the Expedition and drove out of the church parking lot toward Route 11. After picking up Wang at the Sheraton, they would return so the tech genius could conduct electronic surveillance. The idea that Dempsey would cross-train in Wang's job seemed preposterous. It had taken him half a day to operate the new-generation GPS that had been issued to the teams last year. Hacking into computers and turning people's mobile phones into listening devices was hopelessly beyond his IT capabilities. He would watch, he would try to learn, but most likely he would fall asleep.

Thirty minutes later, he was back at the target with Wang. SIGINT collection proceeded exactly as Dempsey imagined, with Wang losing himself in ones and zeroes while Dempsey did everything in his power not to doze off. Using two laptops and an oversize PDA device, Wang somehow recorded voice information from *inside* the target house and the warehouse at the same time. They listened to the static-filled conversations together—Wang nodding enthusiastically under his noise-canceling headphones while Dempsey grimaced, unable to understand anything but a random word here and there. By combining Wang's pirated voice data with the thermal imagery from the overflight drone, Ian Baldwin and his data nerds back at the TOC were able to confirm that Sarah Reed was inside the warehouse with two Arabic-speaking males. Baldwin also determined that two other people—a man and a woman—occupied the house in front. If not for Wang and his IT kung fu, Dempsey decided, the SIGINT stop would have yielded zero actionable intel.

With the package confirmed at the target, Dempsey made another round trip to the hotel to pick up the rest of the team. Another thirty minutes burned, and once again he found himself driving north on Route 11 toward Cloverdale in the dark—only this time the Expedition was fully loaded with operators and gear. He wasn't worried about the man sitting beside him in the front passenger seat. As a former Delta operator, Smith had Tier One skills and experience. In a shitstorm of bullets, blood, and confusion, Dempsey knew he could count on Smith the same way he had Spaz, Rousch, or Thiel. Wang was also not a concern, because his job was to stay behind in the SUV and monitor comms from the driver's seat. If things went bad, Wang would assume the role of evac driver. Dempsey looked in the rearview mirror at Wang, who was fixated on Grimes's chest while she stared out the window. The

SUV bounced over a divot in the road, and he saw Wang grin like a high school kid peeking into the girls' locker room.

Well, maybe I should revise my assessment. As long as a chick with a great pair of tits doesn't walk by during the op, Wang should be okay.

In the cramped third row sat Mendez, looking like every Marine Dempsey had ever known—all business. Face taut, unblinking eyes staring into space, the Marine was running over his responsibilities and preparing for the rescue op. If they got the green light, Mendez would be ready—psychologically, at least. Tactically speaking, Dempsey would have to wait and see. A Marine with MARSOC training should be able to handle a weapon as well as any white-side SEAL.

He hoped.

And that left Grimes.

He studied her in the rearview mirror. Her face was stone, but the rapid rise and fall of her chest told him she was nervous. Best-case scenario, she would only be a *limited* liability. Worst-case scenario, her presence would put the entire mission in jeopardy, along with the lives of her teammates and the hostage. During their Farm training, Grimes had been a complete pain in the ass. She seemed to lack all sense of tactical posturing and repeatedly put herself into compromising or vulnerable positions. She hesitated when she should have moved, and moved when she should have held. She overthought every scenario, and questioned all his decisions during the exercises. Worst of all, she felt compelled to play Monday-morning quarterback in the debriefs, pointing out how every screwup could have been avoided if Dempsey had simply listened to her. Admittedly, most of her strategic insights had proven to be right, but it was her holier-than-thou attitude that pissed him off. She was the queen, and they were foot soldiers—unenlightened brutes who would do well to listen to her wisdom. Frankly, he was shocked she wasn't running her mouth right now, driving everyone crazy.

He drove past Read Mountain Road—the turn that would have taken them back to the target—and continued on another quarter mile to Updike Lane. He turned left on Updike and followed it until he reached Mickey Lane, where he pulled the SUV into the empty parking lot of a brick building with a sign that read ROANOKE CONSTRUCTION INC. He piloted the SUV to the back of the lot and parked under a large oak tree to block the glare of a nearby street lamp.

"Let's see what we can see," Smith said with a grin.

Dempsey looked over his shoulder at Wang. "Get me an imagery update from Mom."

Wang opened his laptop and clicked through several windows. "As of fifteen minutes ago, the overflight drone still had the package in the warehouse. She's unrestrained and moving around. She's with two men. From body movements, Baldwin believes one of the men is carrying a rifle."

"Comms update?"

"There's a TV on in the room. Everyone is speaking English. The package is doing very little talking. The chatter is primarily between the two men. No tactically relevant conversations to report."

"What about the house in front?"

"A man and a woman are camped out in the kitchen, and have been on every pass, suggesting this is a sentry position against a forward entry. They also appear to have rifles."

Dempsey closed his eyes and tried to picture what Wang was describing. He imagined two Middle Eastern men in the warehouse, one pacing back and forth with a rifle slung across his back, the other armed with a handgun tucked in his waistband. The sentries in the front, he pictured armed with automatic weapons—AK-47s or AR-15s, most likely—staged within arm's reach.

"Traps?" Smith asked.

"Well." Wang scratched at his sparse goatee in a way that reminded Dempsey of Spaz. "They've been in and out of the back door on the east corner of the warehouse several times, so that's an unlikely site for a booby trap. The front door has also had tons of traffic. The woman in the house left to get food a few hours ago, which she shared with both groups—the package ate, by the way, for what that's worth—and they've been out to the cars a couple of times since. I think those doors are your best bet for entry."

"Any other vehicles?" Smith asked.

"Nope," Wang said.

"Anything else you want to add?" Dempsey asked.

"There's a TV on, like I said. The noise helps you guys, right?"

"Right," Dempsey said.

"I've run through everything I can see. Mom has new information still in analysis. Chip and Dale opened the mike on a tablet computer through an Internet connection, but they lost it when the device was turned off. Dale said the sound quality sucked, so Ian is trying to clean it up now."

"Any fires we need to worry about?" Smith asked.

"I had SIGINT running on a one-mile radius, but there's a neighborhood with several hundred homes, and that's a lot of traffic to parse. Mom doesn't have the manpower she had in the JIRG. Still, nothing we've heard suggests that these assholes have another site standing by to help out. Only one phone call in the last hour, on a burner to another burner—that was from the dude in the main house. According to Baldwin, it sounded like a pickup request, but not for at least a couple of days, which seemed to piss everyone off. I'm confident they don't have any help nearby you need to worry about."

Smith nodded and looked at Dempsey. "JD?"

Dempsey scowled. He was getting used to his name but wasn't ready for a nickname yet. "All right, let's brief it, then I'll make the call for the green light."

"Agreed," said Smith.

Dempsey turned in his seat so he had everyone's eye. "We're going to run Plan Two from the tactical brief: Smith and Grimes go in through the front to neutralize the sentries and stop them from making an outbound call for a QRF. Mendez and I go in the east door to the warehouse, put the shitheads in the bag, and bring the girl out with us. Each team tries to take one crow," he said and looked over at Smith, who nodded in approval. They had been drilling into him for a couple of weeks the importance of leaving with information. Taking two prisoners off the X would be a great source. "But if that slows us down, or endangers anyone on the team or the package, then we just smoke 'em all and harvest whatever intel we can from the girl."

He paused and noticed Grimes staring at him. Unblinking. Silently judging.

He quickly shifted his gaze to Wang. "INFIL will be on foot to the north corner where we'll kit up and then split into pairs. Mendez and I will wait until Smith and Grimes get into position. That gives you plenty of time to reposition the Expedition. When you hear the GO, drive the SUV in *front* of the target vehicles. No one leaves unless they're with us. On EXFIL, we'll come to you. Got it?"

Wang nodded.

Dempsey paused long enough for comments but got none. "Our biggest external threat is local police response, but out here response time should exceed fifteen minutes. However, in the unlikely event some Barney Fife is patrolling a nearby neighborhood, the response time drops to under five minutes. So I want our total mission time well south of that number. From kicking in doors to on the road should be under three minutes. Questions?"

He scanned their faces. Grimes raised an eyebrow at him, and Dempsey hated that it made her look pretty. Her lips parted, and he could see the wheels spinning in her head, but for once she held her tongue. His pulse quickened at the thought of a gunfight with this slapped-together team. The only comfort he had was the knowledge that this crew had drilled over a hundred hours together during the last two weeks.

"Okay," he said, and pulled out a second burner phone. He dialed the preset number and listened while it rang.

"Hey, baby. How are you doing? You must be tired," said his make-believe wife.

Is the team ready?

"Actually, I feel great for some damn reason," he laughed. "I should be tired, but I'm not. Wanted to see how you're doing before it got too late."

We're on station, ready to prep. Do we have a green light?

"Well, I'm great, but the kids are still awake for some reason. I'm waiting for them to fall asleep, and then maybe I could call you back? It should only be a few more minutes. Maybe you should get ready for bed, and then I'll call before you fall asleep."

Not yet. The team is still analyzing data. Move into position, and we'll call you back with the go.

"No problem," he said. "I'll get ready for bed, watch the news, and wait for your call."

I'll move the team into position and stand by for instructions.

Dempsey hung up. "Position and hold," he said to the group. "But it looks like we should be a go."

He climbed out of the driver's seat, and Wang immediately jumped in to take his place. Wang's grin and nervous gusto confirmed his inexperience with field ops, though for an IT nerd, the kid had done well on the tactical driving module last week. Dempsey wondered how Wang would do when terrorists started shooting real bullets at him. He slapped Wang on the shoulder. "Don't leave without us."

"And miss the after-party? Never," Wang said, but his voice cracked.

At the rear of the SUV, Smith had already pulled out the large duffel packed with all their gear. He stood waiting with it slung across his back, like a seasoned gladiator primed for battle in the Coliseum. "You're lead," he said to Dempsey. "On your order."

Dempsey nodded, gave the hand signal to move out, and led his team into the woods to go rescue Sarah Reed.

CHAPTER 24

Sneaking through the shadows, an old familiar rush washed over Dempsey. His senses felt keener, his heartbeat stronger. The air tasted sweet, rejuvenating him with every breath. He smirked at the irony of it all. He'd endured weeks of browbeating from Jarvis and Smith on the fact that *Ember was not the teams*, and how being a clandestine operator was not just about *kicking in doors, clearing rooms, and evacuating survivors off the X . . .* What a bunch of bullshit. Tonight's mission was textbook Tier One operations, and they knew it. Which is exactly why they needed him. At the end of the day, all the psychological, secret-agent mumbo jumbo was nothing more than foreplay before the romp in the sack. He'd seen it time and time again on the teams—in the end, guts, muscle, and superior firepower rule the day.

Dempsey stopped at the tree line behind the warehouse and took a knee just inside the boundary of moon shadow. The others pulled up beside him and did the same. Smith slid the bag off his shoulders, unzipped the main compartment, and divvied out the gear. The soft, black tactical vests had no SAPI plates tonight, but the blended Kevlar-Dyneema weave would stop up to a .44 Magnum hollow point.

Dempsey slid the vest over his head and then clicked on the MBITR encrypted radio. He set the radio to channel three, slipped the small earpiece into his left ear canal, and lowered the thin boom mike into position by the corner of his mouth. Next, he slipped three thirty-round rifle magazines and three fifteen-round pistol magazines into the pouches on his vest. He grabbed two flash-bang grenades, handed one to Mendez, and then dropped the other into the pouch on the left side of his vest. Last, he snapped a drop holster onto his belt and adjusted the Velcro straps around his right thigh to hold one of the Sig Sauer P229 pistols Smith was handing out.

Once everyone had handguns, Smith moved onto the heavy stuff. By request, the Sig516 assault rifles went to Dempsey and Mendez. Dempsey had come to like the rifle over the last couple of weeks. It was similar to his SOPMOD M4, but it felt lighter and somehow more solid. With its 7.5-inch barrel and 5.56 x 45 mm NATO ammunition, it was perfect for heavy, close-quarters action. He clicked on the red-dot holographic sight and checked that the magazine was securely engaged in the weapon. He pulled the slide back far enough to confirm a round was chambered, checked that the safety was off, and then slung the rifle across his chest in a combat carry. Satisfied with his weapon, he watched Grimes and Smith ready their smaller H&K MP7A1 submachine guns. The H&Ks were more pistol than a combat rifle in Dempsey's mind, less accurate and less lethal with their 4.60 mm rounds. However, click the mode selector to Auto Fire, and suddenly those problems went away—probably a good thing for the redhead, Dempsey figured.

Quickly and quietly they buddy-checked one another's gear and then performed sequential "double-click" radio checks to ensure they were all on the same frequency. Dempsey tapped his mike with a finger, and they all twisted the knob on their radios to go to "hot mikes," meaning the radios were now voice activated. Last but not least, Smith nudged Dempsey and passed him a small black case with the compact C4 charge he would need to breach the warehouse door. Dempsey slipped the case into the left thigh pocket of his cargo pants and closed the Velcro flap.

He looked at Smith. "I say no to NVGs tonight. Plenty of moonlight and we're going in with lights on. You agree?"

Smith flashed Dempsey his trademark lopsided grin. "This is your rodeo, John. I'm just a cowboy waiting for his eight-second ride."

"All right, then, whenever you're ready," Dempsey said, gesturing toward the house.

Smith gave him the thumbs-up and signaled to Grimes it was time to go. Dempsey watched them disappear into the trees as they began their short trek through the woods around to the front of the property. He checked his watch. Kitting up had taken under a minute.

Excellent.

"Five—Lead—you up?" he said softly into his mike.

"I'm almost to the corner," came Wang's voice over the radio. "I'll be in position in just a sec." Wang sounded tactically nervous, but not "lose your shit" nervous, which Dempsey could live with.

He watched the clock for two minutes, enough time for Smith and Grimes to circle around to the front of the house. When time was up, he signaled to Mendez to make for the building. Moving in a tactical crouch, Mendez ran from the safety of the tree line to the side of the warehouse, while Dempsey covered him. Dempsey followed a split second later, angling to stay clear of the oversize window in the back of the warehouse. As he closed on the building, he noticed that the window was blacked out by a heavy blanket, a low-tech but effective countermeasure against snooping eyes. Dempsey signaled Mendez to reposition to the east entry point around the corner. Keeping low, they moved quickly, rounded the corner, and both took a knee on either side of the weathered metal door. A seam of light glowed through a warped gap in the upper corner, confirming for Dempsey he'd made the right call about the night vision.

While Mendez scanned the yard for threats, Dempsey retrieved the C4 kit from his pant-leg pocket. With practiced efficiency, he pressed the hunk of C4 into the crevice between the lockset and the door frame, and then inserted the red-and-black leads into the gray Play-Doh. He motioned for Mendez to clear the blast zone, and they both backpedaled, Dempsey unspooling the detonator wire as he moved. Dempsey gave himself five feet of lateral separation from the door and pressed his back against the wall. He turned his head to look at Mendez. Mendez, mirroring his position on the opposite side of the door, gave Dempsey a thumbs-up.

"Lead—set," Dempsey whispered into his mike.

"Two—set," Smith replied in his headset.

Dempsey waited and listened. Although muffled by the structure of the building, he definitely heard two men arguing inside. A moment later, over the top of the shouting, he heard the shrill timbre of a woman's voice. He couldn't make out what anyone was saying, but words or no words, Dempsey knew what fear sounded like.

"Mom—Lead. We're set at the target. Disturbance inside. Are we green?"

"One moment, Lead," came the woman's voice, now all business where love had been before.

Dempsey anxiously tapped the side of the plastic trigger box wired to his breacher charge. Inside the warehouse, the argument was turning hot and angry. All three occupants were screaming on top of one another. The woman's voice was being drowned out by the male voices now—voices so filled with rage that he knew what was coming next.

Fuck this.

"Mom, we need a go. The package is in immediate danger." He moved his finger to the trigger. "We need a green now."

"Negative, Lead," came Jarvis's voice, deep and collected. "Pull back and hold. Mission abort. I say again, abort."

A scream of pain from inside the warehouse sent a surge of anger through Dempsey's body.

Maybe Jarvis was willing to let the girl die, but he wasn't.

"Two—Lead, we're going on my mark. Three—two—one—*go, go.*" On the second go, Dempsey pressed the trigger. The breacher charge went off with a resounding thump, blowing a ten-inch hole in the door where the latch and lock had once been. A half second later, he heard the thud from Smith's charge at the front of the house. Thank God, Smith had followed his lead. Mendez slid to the edge of the doorway on a knee, banged the door open with his elbow, and then rolled a flash-bang into the room.

Dempsey reflexively shielded his eyes from the blinding flash as the bang went off, rattling the corrugated metal wall he was leaning against. He dropped into a crouch and burst through the door, moving left and clearing left, door to corner. After confirming he couldn't be flanked, he charged forward, scanning and sweeping over his rifle barrel sights. In peripheral vision, he saw Mendez finish clearing right and fall into step two meters away. At his ten o'clock, Dempsey sensed movement in the white smoke. Muzzle flashes lit up the haze, followed a split second later by the "tap, tap, tap" of a semiautomatic pistol. He brought the human silhouette in line with his holographic sight and squeezed the trigger twice—the figure lurched backward and collapsed to the ground. A woman shrieked, and he had to stop himself from calling out Sarah Reed's name. Clenching his teeth, Dempsey crept forward in the haze, scanning.

Scanning.

Scanning.

The sound of gunfire in the distance registered in his consciousness, and he knew it was coming from the house out front.

Suddenly, the smoke recoiled, as if the warehouse itself had just inhaled, and two new silhouettes materialized in front of him. He saw the girl, cowering behind a male who was crouched low to the floor.

"We're American military," Dempsey shouted. "The house is surrounded. Throw down your weapons."

The crouching male stood, one hand in the air, the other at his side, clutching a rifle. Dempsey put his red targeting dot in the center of the man's face. "I'm not fucking around here," he growled.

The man hesitated, contemplating surrender or certain death. He chose life. The rifle clattered to the ground as he raised his hands into the air.

"On the ground," Dempsey shouted.

The man complied, sprawling himself on the concrete floor facedown. Mendez moved in swiftly and put a knee on the back of the kidnapper's neck. The Marine kicked the rifle out of reach with his other foot and turned to Sarah Reed, who was still crouching beside her fallen captor. "It's okay," Mendez said. "We're the good guys. We're here to rescue you."

"Lead—clear—package secure," Dempsey said into his mike after sweeping the room one last time for additional threats. Satisfied the warehouse was secure, he straightened up and moved toward Mendez and Senator Reed's trembling daughter.

What happened next caught him off guard. The young woman whirled and surged toward Mendez, screaming with incoherent terror. This was either a panic attack or a complete psychological meltdown. She stayed low, but moved with enough speed that Dempsey realized she would likely topple Mendez over, freeing the terrorist pinned under his knee. He surged forward to grab her, but she veered, rolled, and scooped up the rifle that Mendez had kicked aside.

"Allahu Akbar!" she screamed and trained the rifle on Mendez. She fired twice. Mendez grunted and sat back onto his haunches, not falling over, but releasing the terrorist who had been under his control.

Dempsey raised his rifle to shoot the girl, but before he could fire, two loud bursts of automatic gunfire echoed throughout the cavernous warehouse. Sarah Reed arched her back, screamed, and pitched face forward onto the ground. He looked down at the girl, writhing and whimpering on the concrete floor. Blood poured from her left side, making a purple lake beneath her. A moment later, she stopped moving.

Smith and Grimes charged to his side, the barrel of Grimes's H&K submachine gun still smoldering. Dempsey looked at the terrorist's rifle on the floor next to Sarah Reed. With a bellowing roar, he kicked the damn thing across the room so hard he worried he'd broken his toe. Then he went to Mendez. He grabbed the Marine by the shoulders and turned him to inspect the damage. Mendez pressed his palms into his chest and pulled them back dripping with bright-red blood. He looked up at Dempsey, eyes wide with confusion.

"What the fuck?" the Marine croaked.

Dempsey's throat tightened. *Oh God, not again . . .*

"What the fuck indeed," echoed a baritone voice, loud and angry.

A standby electrical generator roared to life somewhere outside. Half a dozen halogen lights turned on, and ventilation fans began to whir overhead, clearing the lingering smoke from the room in seconds. Dempsey ignored all this and stood dumbfounded as a square-shouldered figure strode into the light. He pointed his rifle at the new arrival, just as the familiar voice spoke again.

"At ease, Dempsey."

Jarvis?

"Everyone stand down," Jarvis ordered as he stepped into the middle of the room. "This exercise is finished."

"Exercise?" Dempsey said, lowering his weapon. "What the hell are you talking about?"

He looked at the dead woman on the floor, and watched with disbelief as she opened her eyes, got to her feet, and walked to stand beside Jarvis. Jarvis handed her a brown towel, which she used to mop the "blood" from her chest and arms.

"I'm not shot?" Mendez asked, still staring at his blood-soaked hands.

"Not this time," Jarvis said, tossing another towel to Mendez. "No thanks to your team leader. The low-velocity training rounds broke simulation blood packets inside your vest."

"Shit," the Marine hissed as he wiped at the fake blood with trembling hands.

Dempsey felt his face flush with anger. "You mean this whole thing was some bullshit training exercise?"

"And thank God it was, since you fucked it up royally," Jarvis barked. "In this simulation we briefed ambiguity about the relationship between the package and her abductors, but you ignored that and latched onto Sarah Reed's sorrow-filled backstory. You pitied her and dubbed yourself her protector and rescuer—like a knight in shining armor from some fucking fairy tale."

Dempsey stared at the girl next to Jarvis. The resemblance to Sarah Reed was uncanny, but now he could see that this woman was not the senator's daughter. The shape of her eyes, the size of her nose, the line of her jaw—all slightly different from the photographs he'd spent hours staring at. She blew him a kiss, then reached up with her right hand and pulled off a blonde wig. Fuming, he watched as she ran her fingers through her real, mousy-brown locks.

"But your biggest failing as team leader, John, was not trusting your team," Jarvis continued.

"What are you talking about? Every one of these guys had my back. Hell, Grimes even took out the package before she could turn her gun on me."

"I'm not just talking about the assault team. Baldwin and his guys back at the TOC are among your most valuable weapons. Sometimes the remote analysis team uncovers information they can't communicate to you in the field. If you're ordered to abort, you need to trust your teammates and respect that decision."

"But she was screaming," Dempsey muttered, looking at the actress beside Jarvis.

"Yes, she was screaming. And you acted on that single data point and got a teammate killed," Jarvis shot back. "You made a unilateral decision that sunk an operation where we had the option to leave the principals in play. If you had not intervened, the simulation would have resulted in you working your way up the food chain, locating the terror-cell leadership, and stopping them before they detonated a dirty bomb in Norfolk. The real-time mission is only one piece of the larger mission. Today you failed, and by the simulation playbook, tens of thousands of people will pay the price."

Dempsey clenched his jaw and said nothing. He caught Smith's eyes and the former Delta man winked. Dempsey shook his head.

"The cleanup team will be here in five mikes," Jarvis said. "Pack up your gear and we'll meet at the airfield. Wang could use the practice, so let him drive you out as part of the exercise until you get to the highway. We'll debrief on the plane." He paused for a moment, holding Dempsey's eyes. "Remember this disaster, because training is *now* officially over. We're not going back to Newport News. Wheels up in forty-five minutes for Frankfurt. There've been some recent developments that require our attention. Effective immediately, we're on mission . . . our real mission."

And with that, Jarvis spun on a heel and disappeared into the night, leaving Dempsey alone with his team and his shame.

PART III

"The problem in defense is how far you can go
without destroying from within
what you are trying to defend from without."
—*Dwight D. Eisenhower*

CHAPTER 25

"You gonna ring the bell?"

Dempsey looked up to find Smith staring down at him. "Excuse me?"

"I said, 'You look like hell,'" Smith said, popping a handful of roasted almonds into his mouth. "What did you think I said?"

Dempsey shook his head. "Something else . . . it doesn't matter."

"You know, John, this bird has a full-size shower. You could use one." Glancing at his watch, Smith added, "You still have fifteen minutes until we start the brief."

"Good idea," Dempsey said, extending his right hand. "This chair swallowed me. Help me up."

Smith gripped his right wrist and pulled him out of the butter-soft leather lounger he'd been dozing in for the past hour.

"I'll send Grimes back to join you," Smith said as Dempsey shuffled past. "Maybe she can help you work the kinks out."

Dempsey flipped Smith the bird over his shoulder.

Two minutes later, he was standing inside a marble-tiled shower with steaming hot water pulsing onto his aching back. The airplane was ridiculous. *Ridiculous.* For the tenth time, he had to remind himself he was flying forty thousand feet over the Atlantic Ocean and not in a luxury condominium in San Diego. Where Jarvis got these toys was beyond him. The stateroom suite—which occupied the rear third of the fuselage—was palatial, with a king-size bed, dressing room, and a bathroom worthy of the Ritz-Carlton. In addition to the stateroom, the plane housed a bunkroom designed to sleep eight, with desks and chairs for four. The midsection of the jet was outfitted with a conference room that rivaled what they had at the Ember hangar, including flat-screens, secure computers, oversize leather chairs, and a wet bar. Next was the richly appointed "common room," where Smith had found him. The common room housed a sixty-inch LED television, a sofa, four leather lounge chairs, and a library wall. Attached to the common room was a private office, where Jarvis had been holed up since takeoff. Finally, just behind the cockpit were the aircraft's galley and two additional bathrooms. All told, he guessed this 787 VIP luxury jet had close to three thousand square feet of living space. Talk about waste, fraud, and abuse. What the hell was Jarvis doing with a plane like this? There are perks and then there are "perks." This fell into the latter category, which made Dempsey uncomfortable. Not that he wanted to spend the rest of his life as a back-of-the-bus guy, but seriously, this was absurd.

He closed his eyes and told himself he should be grateful. He could be in the back of a C130 camped out on a square of metal floor, freezing his ass off, and wearing sound-canceling headphones. No leather lounge chairs or hot showers on those sons-of-bitches, either. As the water drummed against his skin, he cleared his head and willed the muscles in his back and shoulders to slowly unclench. He let his mind drift, and it took him to a place he did not expect.

Coronado . . .

"You gonna ring the bell? You gonna quit, fish? Go on, ring the bell. You know you want to. You know you're never going to make it through this program. You're not one of us; you'll never be a SEAL. Ring it, fish. Ring that bell!"

His memory of Hell Week during Basic Underwater Demolition/ SEAL training was a blur. Four hours of sleep in a week does that to a mind. There was one moment, however, that he remembered with perfect clarity. They were on the beach, dressed in fatigues—wet, teeth chattering, and chafed raw everywhere a man can chafe. His fingers were split and bleeding, and the inside of his mouth was pocked with canker sores. The instructors had them in the sand, doing push-ups after thirty minutes of carrying the boats. Everywhere they went during Hell Week, if they were on their feet, there was a boat on their heads—crushing them, literally and figuratively. He'd fallen asleep in the middle of a push-up. Maybe two seconds of blissful unconsciousness was all he got before the Master Chief was in his face. The man's mouth was two inches from his cheek—showering him with spittle on every syllable. He looked up and saw the bell. During Hell Week, the instructors brought that shiny brass bell everywhere. They made it easy to quit. BUD/S was voluntary training, after all. Just three rings brought unlimited access to sleep, food, and warmth. Just three rings to end the pain and misery. So simple. So shiny. With his body at its weakest and his mind delirious, he had wanted to do it. He almost did.

Almost . . . but Jack Kemper wasn't a quitter.

Would John Dempsey have rung that bell?

He tried to remember the Master Chief's face, but the only face he could conjure was that of Kelso Jarvis. His mind teleported him from Coronado to Roanoke—to the warehouse where he'd botched the simulated hostage-rescue operation. He replayed the ass-ripping Jarvis had given him. One sentence stuck with him. One sentence burned, even worse than the charred flesh on his neck and shoulders:

"Your biggest failing as team leader, John, was not trusting your team."

Ironic, because he was a team guy. Trust and brotherhood was what had gotten him through BUD/S. No man can carry those damn boats alone. It took the team. That was the point of Hell Week. You succeed as a team; you fail as team. You live as a team; you die as a team. After hundreds of ops as a Tier One SEAL, why had he forgotten this now? Why had he made the one mistake he never made as a SEAL?

Because *this* world, this new fucked-up world Kelso Jarvis had dragged him into, was not BUD/S. It was not SEALs. It was a world incompatible with his personality, his training, and his skill set.

Maybe it was time to ring the bell now.

He spun the temperature-regulating handle in the shower all the way to cold and then braced himself. He leaned forward and pressed the crown of his head against the wall—he could almost feel the RIB boat pressing down on him. Almost hear the shouting of his dead SEAL brothers: *Don't quit on us. Don't ring the bell. Avenge our deaths. Don't let it all be for nothing.* He was shivering, but the cold made him feel alive. He felt the energy course back into his shoulders and arms.

He was a SEAL, goddamn it.

And SEALs don't quit.

Dempsey looked at his Suunto watch—seven minutes until he was due in the conference room. He turned the water off and stepped out of the shower onto the heated marble floor. He wrapped himself in a towel and hustled out of the bathroom to get dressed.

In the stateroom, he stopped midstride. Elizabeth Grimes stood there in her bra and underwear, changing clothes. He surveyed her lean, muscular legs, washboard stomach, and breasts before meeting her eyes. "Sorry, didn't realize you were in here."

"It's fine," she said, stepping into a pair of black 5.11 cargo pants. When the waistband met her hips, she did a little shuffle to work them up over the hump. Then she looked him up and down, the same as he had done to her.

"You're carved up pretty good, Dempsey," she said, noting his battle damage.

"Yeah," he said, tossing her the folded black T-shirt laid out next to her go bag. "But everything still works. I've been lucky. A helluva lot luckier than . . ." He didn't finish the thought.

She caught her T-shirt in midair and pulled it on.

"So how's that feel?"

"How's what feel?"

"How does it feel to be lucky? How does it feel to be the one guy who lived, when everyone else got incinerated?"

Dempsey tensed, his temper sparking. "What the hell is your problem, Grimes?"

"What's my problem?" she echoed with a condescending smirk. "I'll tell you my problem, Dempsey. My problem is you."

"Me?"

"Yes, you," she said stepping toward him. "Don't you think that you—as the sole survivor of your unit—have a responsibility to identify all the men responsible for your brothers' murder?"

"How can you ask me that question? That's all I care about. It's why I joined Ember, and it's what I'm doing right now!"

"No, it's not," she said, wiping his spittle from her cheek. "You're still wearing your Tier One blinders—the same blinders Smith, Mendez, Wang, and Baldwin are wearing."

Dempsey snorted. "Okay, thanks for clearing that up. For a second I was worried you just had a problem with me, but now my earlier suspicion is confirmed. You hate fucking everyone."

"No, that's where you're wrong. I don't hate you, Dempsey—just your blind, unquestioning devotion to Kelso Jarvis."

He had no rebuttal. This girl was nuts. What the hell was she talking about?

"See, case in point," she said. "You're so naive, you can't even comprehend what I'm talking about."

"I've known Kelso Jarvis for fifteen years. The man is the finest warrior I've ever met. He's a patriot and a hero, and if you know what's best for you, you'd do well to keep your mouth shut."

Grimes shook her head. "Wake up, Dempsey. He's playing you. He's been playing you for fifteen years."

"What the hell are you talking about?"

"Kelso Jarvis is a chameleon. He has every one of you completely duped. For you, he's the consummate Navy SEAL commander. For Smith, he's a covert-operations tactician of paragon proportions. For Baldwin, he's a closet cryptologist and statistician who broke the mold and earned a command. For Wang, he's the first agency boss who not only appreciates his IT prowess but also understands that victory is impossible without cyber . . . Don't you get it? Ember is nothing more than a fraternity of highly decorated yes-men toting big guns. I feel like I walked into a cult, and the longer I stay, the more I'm in danger of losing my head."

Grimes was shaking—literally shaking—with emotion.

Dempsey unclenched his jaw. "What is he to you?"

She crossed her arms across her chest. "Niccolò Machiavelli with a license to kill."

"And that frightens you?"

"What frightens me is that you haven't even considered the possibility that Kelso Jarvis is the man responsible for your friends' murder. It was the JIRG that aggregated the intelligence on Yemen. It was the JIRG that spearheaded the Tier One tasking for JSOC. And it was the JIRG that got it all wrong. I simply don't understand how you can be a member of this task force and not question the motives and faculties of the man in charge."

Her words were a slap to the face. She was trying to take a sledgehammer to the cornerstone of his ivory tower—something he simply could not tolerate. In his universe, SEALs made mistakes, but their integrity was immutable. Could Jarvis have been duped by faulty intelligence? Yes. Was Jarvis capable of gross negligence? No. Was Jarvis a candidate for treason?

Never.

She hasn't served with him.

She hasn't bled with him.

A powerful calm enveloped Dempsey, and for the first time he caught a disconcerting glimpse of himself through her eyes. Grimes saw him as an operator with blind allegiance, but a SEAL's allegiance is never blind. It's earned through blood, sweat, and brotherhood. With time, she would come to understand this.

"Why are you here, Grimes?" he asked, his anger tempered. "Everyone knows why I'm here, but what's your story? Why did you join Ember?"

"I'm here because . . ." Her watch alarm went off. She glanced at it, then looked up at him with a sadness in her eyes that seemed incongruous with the fiery assault he had been fending off over the last few minutes. "You'd better get dressed, Dempsey. The brief starts in one minute."

He glanced down at his Suunto, confirming the obvious, and then reached for his clothes.

Instead of leaving, she watched him. And when she spoke again, the judgment was gone from her voice. "Jarvis set you up on the training op. You know that, right?"

"It's obvious now, in retrospect."

"It always is, after the fact," she said. "When I was waiting with Smith at the front of the house, I told him that if you didn't blow your door and go in, by God I would. There was no way I was going to let those bastards have their way with that poor girl. Anyway, for what it's worth, I was with you one hundred percent."

"For what it's worth, thanks."

She gave him a nod, turned, and left him alone.

He finished dressing and made his way to the conference room. Stepping into the space, he surveyed the faces of those gathered—leadership, ops, security, IT, data analytics, and Special Activities. The full complement of Ember principals sat waiting.

"Nothing like a shower to wash away a mission, eh, Dempsey?" Jarvis said, glancing at Dempsey while ignoring Grimes altogether. His voice and demeanor were calm and subdued—even bordering on warm—a marked change from the impatient teacher in Roanoke.

"Yes, sir," he said as he collapsed into the vacant chair next to Smith.

A pop-up workstation was open at his position. Yes, it was the twenty-first century, but damn it, he was a paper guy. He shut it immediately, folding the screen and keyboard seamlessly back into the polished mahogany table. He estimated the table cost more than he had paid for his last truck.

"Jarvis told me you're a pen-and-paper guy," Smith whispered, and slid him a leather binder. "Happy birthday."

He nodded his thanks to Smith and flipped open the binder. Inside, he found a memo pad, ballpoint pen, and the edge of a grainy picture tucked into an inside pocket. As he slipped the photograph out of the pocket for a look, the same picture, de-pixelated and enhanced, appeared on the flat-screen monitor mounted on the cabin wall behind Jarvis.

"Meet Behrouz Rostami—our target in Germany. There, he is known as Reinhold Ahmadi—a naturalized German citizen and venture capitalist who specializes in real estate and energy investments throughout the Middle East. His employer, Erde Energie out of Frankfurt, has extensive holdings in Dubai, Saudi Arabia, and the UAE, and is heavily invested in promoting both energy and desalination technology throughout the region. The company is real, though we doubt anyone in management knows Rostami's true identity or suspects his connection to VEVAK."

"Are you sure Erde Energie is not a VEVAK front company?" Grimes asked, tapping her heavy pen on the side of the table.

Jarvis gave her a tight, condescending smile. "In the interest of saving everyone's valuable time, let's try to keep the second-guessing and interruptions to a minimum during the brief. If I had information indicating Erde Energie was a VEVAK-sponsored front company, I would have said so. Everyone will have an opportunity to ask questions in a moment—if that works for you, Elizabeth."

With flushed cheeks, the redhead looked down at her hands. From what he'd gleaned of her personality so far, Dempsey knew this was her being angry, not abashed. He looked over at Smith, who was looking at his own hands, but grinning. Dempsey wanted to revel in her admonishment, too, but suddenly laughing at her felt wrong. Something had changed. The argument in the stateroom had altered his view of her. She was tough and perceptive, much tougher and more perceptive than he had given her credit for. In Roanoke, *she* had been the one with the smarts and the balls to shoot Sarah Reed when everyone else balked. Her comment about mission solidarity there at the end was her attempt at an olive branch. Her explosive little diatribe about Jarvis had clearly been percolating for weeks, and she'd taken it out on him. He realized now that Grimes probably felt more alone and isolated in Ember than he did.

Maybe it was time to cut the girl some slack, he decided. He refocused his attention on the brief.

"Herr Ahmadi, or Mr. Rostami, is a middle-level operative for VEVAK," Jarvis continued. "He is implicated in several bombings that VEVAK helped finance and support via Al Qaeda surrogates in Europe. He has also been active in the UK, where we have evidence that he was involved in the failed suicide-bomber plot known as Operation Pitsford. He was also involved in the more successful 2005 London bombings and the 2007 letter bombs."

Why the hell is this guy still walking around? Dempsey wondered.

"The JIRG was looking at him last year, but we were encouraged to leave him in play to support an operation being spearheaded by our allies in the region."

While Jarvis talked, Dempsey looked at Shane and raised an eyebrow. *You left him in play.*

Smith nodded. *Not my call.*

"I can see from the body language in the room that not all of you agree with that call, but I stand by the decision. Rostami is a midlevel operative now, but the consensus is that he is a hot-runner. We see him advancing in the ranks quickly, someone who can be exploited to gain access to higher levels of operational intelligence from within VEVAK."

To Dempsey that sounded like a risky move. He understood the head-of-the-snake philosophy, but vipers like Rostami were too damn dangerous to leave slithering around. Then, the inevitable question exploded in his brain: *Was this asshole tied to the Tier One massacre?* Would Rostami's elimination last year have saved the lives of his brother SEALs?

He felt Smith's eyes on him and willed himself not to look.

My mission is in the future, not the past, Dempsey told himself, and shook the thought from his head.

"Our friends in Tel Aviv have an asset in Frankfurt who is actively engaged in HUMINT collection on Mr. Rostami. After what happened in Yemen and Djibouti, I reached out to a trusted contact in the Mossad to see if the Israelis perceived a connection between Rostami and the Tier One massacre. The short answer is no. However, that doesn't mean he can't be valuable to us. In fact, as a key player in VEVAK's European operations, we believe Rostami is our best lead to others in VEVAK who may have actionable intelligence."

Jarvis clicked a button on a remote control. The picture of the terrorist disappeared and was replaced by a split screen displaying two pictures of a woman about twenty-five years old. In the headshot on the right, she was smiling, her pretty face and blue eyes framed by a short blonde bob and wire-frame glasses. The left picture was a candid shot, taken of her working behind a bar, pouring a shaker into a cocktail glass. In this picture, her hair was cropped short and shaved on the sides. A single, long, tightly braided strand—dyed purple with a feather tied to the end—hung next to her left ear. Her conservative prep-school top and sweater in the right picture were replaced with a skintight tank top. A tattoo of a kraken climbed up her shoulder, the tentacles reaching up and onto her neck. She had a nose ring and at least half a dozen other piercings along the pinna of her left ear.

"This is Effi Vogel," Jarvis said. "Sixteen months ago she was a full-time student at Fachhochschule—aka the University of Applied Sciences—at Frankfurt am Main. She was studying biochemistry but had submitted a transfer application to the Sankt Georgen Graduate School because of a budding interest in religion and philosophy. About that time, she also started working at Luna Bar on Stiftstrasse, bartending part-time. That was when she met Rostami. His influence over her was swift and absolute. Within three months, she had dropped out of school and started working full-time at Luna Bar. Within six months, she had cut off all communication with her family and friends and began studying Islam."

"Wait," Grimes interrupted. "Did this transformation occur before or after she became a managed asset for the Mossad?"

"Before," Jarvis replied.

"So something happened?" Grimes said, more of a statement than a question. "He wounded her."

"Your intuition is spot-on, Elizabeth," Jarvis acknowledged. "The Mossad has been trying to lure Rostami into a relationship with multiple female assets for over two years, but Rostami has consistently rebuffed all female suitors. So, they decided to change tactics. Instead of trying to lure Rostami, they decided to go after Vogel. After Vogel nearly overdosed on heroin, the Mossad approached her about working for them. Vogel accepted within twenty-four hours. Our friends in

Tel Aviv tell me that all Rostami's documented relationships follow the same pattern—physical subjugation, moral corruption, and emotional ruination of beautiful, young, Christian Westerners."

"He's a sadist," Grimes said. "Someone needs to end this sonuvabitch."

Dempsey felt his throat tighten. He failed to see how the behavior of the Mossad—or Ember, for that matter—was any better than that of the enemy. The idea of capitalizing on the continued ruination of this girl at the hands of a known terrorist was repugnant. Their moral obligation was to rescue Effi Vogel, not exploit her weakness.

"I agree with Grimes," Dempsey heard himself say. "Rostami is a monster; the dude needs to die."

Jarvis exhaled with exasperation. "Look, I appreciate where you're coming from. Really, I do. The story of Effi Vogel is wretched, but I need you to keep several things in mind. First: Vogel is not our asset. The longitudinal surveillance of Rostami in Frankfurt is not our operation. How the Mossad chooses to manage their assets and their operations is not our business. Second: Vogel volunteered for the job, and in doing so she's taken control of her destiny. She is no longer alone. She is no longer powerless. She has the full backing and support of one of the world's most elite counterintelligence agencies behind her. And third: It is because of the courage and sacrifice of Effi Vogel that we have access to Behrouz Rostami. Make no mistake, Rostami will have his day of judgment, but until you hear otherwise from me, you will leave Vogel, and the Israeli operation, intact."

Jarvis flicked his gaze back and forth between Dempsey and Grimes, making sure he had their complete submission. The situation took Dempsey back to another life, when SEAL commander Captain Jarvis had used a similar speech to put Dempsey in his place. He held Jarvis's gaze only long enough so as not to challenge the man, then dropped his eyes to his fingers on the desk.

Jarvis tapped his pen on the desk. "That being said, our friends from Tel Aviv are giving us full access to this target. By that I mean they understand the importance of our mission and are willing to sacrifice Mr. Rostami if doing so is vital to our success."

"Are you saying we can snatch him?" Smith asked. "Time is our enemy on this one, boss. We don't have weeks to sit back and hope Rostami says something interesting."

"Indeed," Jarvis said with a nod at his Operations Director. "If we decide to take him, it must be in a way that can't be traced back to us or Israel. How are you and the Dream Makers coming along on your story lines?"

"They put together something that I think you'll like," Smith said.

"Good, because our advance SIGINT team has turned over data indicating Rostami may be planning a trip, possibly leaving Frankfurt for a significant amount of time. Once he's in the wind, he takes everything he knows with him. I do not intend to let that happen. Be ready. This mission could transition to a snatch-and-grab on a moment's notice."

Jarvis paused and scanned the faces around the table—for more than just dramatic effect. He was reading the expressions, assessing confidence levels, and hunting for indecision.

Grimes raised her hand. "Are you taking questions now?"

An odd grin spread across Jarvis's face, and Dempsey realized that Jarvis enjoyed these little games with Grimes. "Yes."

"Let's say we take Rostami, and we successfully move him to a black site for questioning. Then what? Do you think he'll simply rat out VEVAK?"

"We'll be persuasive," he said flatly.

"Translation—you plan to torture him." It was a statement. Based on her expression, Dempsey couldn't tell if she found the idea objectionable or preferable.

"There are many forms of enhanced interrogation, Ms. Grimes, including techniques that don't appear in the classified briefings on the Hill or in the OSTP. Some of these techniques were invented by, and known only to, members of this team who served in the JIRG. Do you have a moral issue with enhanced interrogation techniques? If so, I need to know your objections now."

"No," Grimes said. "I just want to make sure that the risk matches the reward. No point in risking lives and an international incident to grab Rostami if our leadership doesn't have the stones to harvest information from an uncooperative target." The ice in her voice sent a shiver along Dempsey's spine.

The corners of Jarvis's lips curled into an almost imperceptible smile. "It appears we're on the same page on this matter," he said, tabling the discussion. He turned to Smith. "Shane, why don't you tell the team what to expect when we arrive in Germany?"

Smith nodded and turned to the group. "The Signals and Surveillance team, who've been deployed in Frankfurt the last two weeks, is waiting for us at the airport. As soon as we land, they'll brief us on their findings and Rostami's current status. Based on that briefing, we'll develop our mission plan for the next thirty-six hours. My preliminary thinking is that we'll deploy Dempsey's tactical team immediately for additional surveillance and to vet the extraction scenarios. By the end of day two, we should be in hot standby waiting for a green light on the grab."

"And the girl?" Dempsey blurted out, unable to help himself. He needed to know they weren't so fucking cold that this girl was disposable, or whatever term spooks used for innocent collaterals.

"Is to be protected at all costs," Jarvis said firmly. "Not only as a courtesy to the Israelis, but also because it is the right thing to do. Okay?"

Dempsey nodded. "Yes, sir."

Jarvis looked at his watch. "That's enough for now. Those of you in the Special Activities Unit have been in the field for nearly twenty-four hours. I want you in your racks, lights out in ten minutes. Six hours of sleep, and then we eat and reconvene here when the wheels are on the ground."

"Yes, Dad," Smith said with a good-natured chuckle. Turning to the group, he said, "Rest is a weapon, people. If your mind is racing, grab me for some Ambien now. No point wasting the few precious hours we have tossing and turning."

Everyone stood.

Jarvis disappeared through a door into the executive office. Dempsey watched the door swing shut, then he shifted his gaze to the picture of Effi Vogel—the "before" picture on the right, the one of the young, pretty girl with blue eyes and an infectious smile.

He felt a hand on his shoulder—a light touch.

A woman's touch.

"I know what you're thinking," Grimes said.

"How's that?" Dempsey said, keeping his gaze on the screen.

"Because I'm thinking it, too."

He looked down at her. "Ambien?"

She nodded. "Ambien."

CHAPTER 26

Frankfurt, Germany
May 21, 1510 Local Time

"Hold on," said Dempsey, certain he must have misheard. "Did I just hear you say that the plan is to run over Rostami with an automobile?"

"Yes," Jarvis replied, his expression deadpan.

"Seriously? Hitting the target with a car is the best plan your Dream Makers could come up with?" Dempsey shook his head. "Who are these Dream Makers anyway?"

Of all the principals packed into the tiny flat serving as their temporary TOC in Frankfurt, only Smith raised his hand.

"You're a Dream Maker?"

"I'm the head Dream Maker for Ember."

Dempsey screwed up his face. "Then who are the others?"

"The original Dream Makers are a TS think tank funded by the CIA. We used them regularly when we were the JIRG. When we disbanded the JIRG and stood up Ember, I had to sever ties. Jarvis wants to replicate their methodology in-house. So, I put together a little group," Smith said. "Quinton Thomas is a Dream Maker."

"QT?" Dempsey laughed. "The guy with a neck as big as my thigh?"

"That's right," said Smith. "Don't let his looks and demeanor fool you. Quinton is intellectually gifted."

"He's a grunt."

"A grunt with a one hundred and thirty-seven point IQ."

"Aw, shit," Dempsey said with an incredulous huff. "Don't tell me *I'm* the dumbest guy on the team?"

Smith looked at Jarvis, who cracked a smile so wide that everyone else in the room started to chuckle.

"So it's true," Dempsey muttered. "I'm the dumbest guy on the team."

"Not every day," Smith said. "For example, on Tuesdays when the cleaning crew shows up . . ."

"Oh, screw you, Smith," Dempsey said, trying to sound angry, even though he, too, was now laughing.

"Sounds like fun," Grimes said. "Brainstorming crazy scenarios and then trying them out in the field."

"Fun? Really? Have any of you ever actually been hit by a car?" Dempsey scanned their faces. "No, of course not. Members of MENSA are too smart to be hit by cars. Well, I've seen plenty of unlucky bastards get hit by all kinds of motor vehicles, and guess what—it doesn't end well. The vehicle always wins."

"Relax, Dempsey," Jarvis said. "This is a controlled scenario, and Shane will be driving. We're going to hit Rostami with just enough force to require his evacuation by ambulance—*our* ambulance. Besides, I don't see what the big concern is. By the time we're done with that sonuvabitch, he'll be in the hurt locker anyway. What's a few more cuts and bruises?"

"Fine," Dempsey said. Turning to Smith, he added, "Just make sure you don't kill the dude."

"I'll limit my speed of impact. Any other concerns, John?"

"Actually, yes. Why are we waiting until after Rostami meets with Vogel? It puts the girl at unnecessary risk. We should nail him while he's en route to meet her."

"Too many variables," Jarvis said. "Rostami could be early; he could be late. He could approach from the north; he could approach from the south. The BMW and the ambulance have to be perfectly positioned and waiting. Our ambulance has to be the first responder on the scene. Effi will signal her Mossad handler the moment Rostami leaves the hotel room. Then we'll have three minutes to get into position."

Dempsey nodded. He knew Jarvis was right. It was the best way to make sure they controlled the scenario. But it still felt wrong to put the girl at risk. And it bothered him that Jarvis seemed unperturbed by this.

"You on board?" Jarvis asked.

"Of course I'm on board. It's not the worst plan I've ever been tasked to execute. Just the most absurd."

"Any other comments or objections?" Jarvis said.

No one spoke.

"All right, moving on. The ambulance will stop here, en route to the hospital." Jarvis pointed to a waypoint on the map displayed on the computer monitor. "We swap out Rostami for our dead John Doe— provided compliments of our friends in the Mossad—and we egress directly to the airport. Wheels up upon arrival. By the time anybody figures out Rostami is missing, we'll be back in Virginia."

Smith checked his watch. "Field team, you have ten minutes to gear up and check comms, then it's showtime."

Twenty minutes later, Dempsey was sitting on a bench in one of Frankfurt's hipster districts, sipping a steaming cup of Starbucks coffee. Like McDonald's, Starbucks had become ubiquitous. Tampa, Dubai, Newport News, Frankfurt—it didn't matter. The little green mermaid was always beckoning him. Drinking Starbucks abroad was very American, but that was okay. As Smith had aptly pointed out this morning, trying to pretend he was anything but an American was a fool's endeavor. Better to embrace the idea and make it part of his cover. For the next hour, he would walk, talk, and behave *very* American. He shook the page of the *Financial Times* he was reading—loudly vocalizing his displeasure with an article criticizing US foreign policy. With a huff, he folded the paper, tucked it under his arm, and pretended to be irritated while simultaneously surveying his surroundings.

The bench where he sat was located next to a fountain in a square lined with shops, cafes, and bars. The fountain was only a short walk from Luna Bar, where he and the team had watched Effi Vogel sling fancy drinks to German yuppies for the past two nights. Luna Bar's signature pounding techno music was not to his liking, but the German *doppelbock* on draft certainly was. John Dempsey, like Jack Kemper before him, was a beer man. To drink the fufu martinis favored by the club's hipster patrons would be a violation of Man Code.

The first night of surveillance had been a bust—no Rostami—but last night the dirtbag had finally made an appearance. With great difficulty, Dempsey had resisted the urge to drag Rostami into the men's room and choke the life out of him. *Patience,* he'd silently reminded himself. *Complete the mission, and the time for choking will come soon enough.* Besides, the men's room at Luna Bar was completely unsuitable for choking someone to death. It was more like a woman's day spa, replete with burning candles, soft music, and a woman—yes, a woman—handing out hand towels and splashes of cologne from small glass bottles. The night had passed predictably, with Rostami lingering in the bar until the end of Vogel's shift, then the two of them departing together.

Dempsey adjusted his suit coat, propped an ankle across his knee, and took a sip of coffee. He checked his watch twice in the span of three minutes—sighing audibly to complete the portrait of the impatient American businessman waiting for a colleague. The time was twelve past three. Vogel should be on the move and headed toward the Hotel InterContinental, where she would meet Rostami for their biweekly tryst. According to the Mossad report, Rostami would reserve a room the day before, always in her name. She would arrive first, pick up the key, and order coffee service to the room. While Rostami rambled about his made-up business, he required her to give him an hour-long massage followed by fellatio and then sex. Afterward, Vogel would feign sleep until Rostami slipped out of the room, always without a good-bye. Once her Mossad watcher confirmed Rostami had left the hotel, Vogel would furiously thumb-type every detail she could remember from the conversation on a note-taking app on a burner phone. Upon departing the hotel, she would proceed to one of seven rotating locations—a local café, bar, or bookstore—and drop the burner in a restroom trash can for retrieval by a female Mossad asset. Then Vogel would go to her apartment, scrub herself clean of the animal she'd shared her bed with, and cry herself to sleep before heading to work at Luna Bar for the night shift.

Dempsey would take great pleasure in excising Rostami from Vogel's life.

He glanced again at his watch. He should have heard from Grimes by now, which meant Vogel was running a few minutes late. If Vogel followed her usual pattern, she would cross this square before walking east toward the Hotel InterContinental, which sat a block off the river. Grimes was in trail now, and she would follow Vogel until the handoff to him in this square. He unfurled his newspaper, resumed reading, and waited.

Grimes's voice sounded in his earpiece less than a minute later. "Echo Victor moving south," she said, all business. "Approaching Victor-two."

Echo Victor was Effi Vogel. Victor-one was Vogel's shitty little apartment three blocks north. Victor-two was Luna Bar. Victor-three was the Hotel InterContinental, and so on for the six marker positions for the op.

The earpiece transceiver buried in Dempsey's left ear was the latest technology. According to Wang, the device utilized both sound waves and bone-conduction vibration for transmission and reception functions, generating crystal clear sound quality. Even more remarkable, the transceiver's minute size and clear plastic construction made it nearly invisible. It was so small Dempsey wondered how he was going to fish the damn thing out of his ear. Every time he moved his jaw, it seemed to migrate deeper and deeper into his ear canal, like a squirmy little bug burrowing toward his brain. Resisting the urge to probe for it with his fingertip was torture, but he knew sticking his finger in his ear repeatedly would defeat the purpose of the stealth technology, reminiscent of spies talking into their sleeves in the old spy films he secretly loved.

Dempsey stood and stretched. He slung his leather bag over his shoulder by the strap and shoved the folded copy of the *Financial Times* into the outside pocket. He looked again at his watch, sighed impatiently, and dialed a number on his mobile phone.

"Hallo? *Guten Morgen. Wie geht es Ihnen?*" said the voice on the line.

"It's Jim Purcell," Dempsey replied with great annoyance. It was distracting to hear Smith speaking German in his earpiece and in the phone speaker with a half-second delay. "I've been waiting twenty minutes for you. Did I have the time for our meeting wrong?"

"*Nein*—No, Herr Purcell. My apologies, I am running a little late. I should be there in fifteen minutes or so. Do you wish to reschedule?"

"No, no," he said with mock irritation. "I'm only in town for another day. Let's make it thirty minutes. That will give me time to grab another coffee. I'm still on East Coast time and feeling pretty tired."

"Of course," Smith said with a thick German accent. "May I suggest you try World Coffee by Gross Rossmarkt? It is very good and quite close to the property I wish to show you on Kleiner Hirschgraben."

"That's quite a walk," he said, and looked again at his watch. As he did, he saw Effi Vogel heading toward him, walking south on Stiftstrasse, her small leather backpack pulling her tank top tight across her braless chest while her unbuttoned denim shirt flapped open immodestly in the breeze. If not for the piercings, tattoos, and partially shaved head, the girl would be smoking hot. "Don't you Germans drive anywhere?"

Smith laughed. "The traffic is terrible in Frankfurt; it is much quicker to walk. But if you prefer, I can pick you up?"

"No," Dempsey said, and began to walk toward the intersection at Stiftstrasse and Zeil. "Perhaps we can chat about the property while I walk?" A man talking on a cell phone about a possible real estate deal seemed far less suspicious than one trolling along behind a young girl. As Vogel turned right on Zeil, he fell in among the thin crowd of pedestrians a few yards behind her. Grimes was still in trail somewhere behind him, and he resisted the urge to look back. In a half block, she would peel off into Pohland Exklusiv—a very upscale clothing store— her part of the tail and handoff complete. They had practiced the exact technique over and over in Williamsburg during their Farm training, but Dempsey still had to concentrate. It would take months in the field before it became second nature. He could breach and clear a room while picking out guitar chords in his head for a new country song, but this simple technique required all his attention.

In his peripheral vision, he noted he was passing Pohland Exklusiv on his right. Once Grimes dropped off, Vogel was his sole responsibility. He kept the conversation going with Smith, asking questions about the office building on Kleiner Hirshgraben, where his company wished to purchase two floors of space. Smith read him information about the building. He asked a question about renting out half of the property to help offset the cost. All the while, he maintained his distance and kept Effi Vogel in sight.

At the corner just beyond the Zeilgalerie indoor mall, Vogel made an anticipated left turn onto An der Hauptwache.

Dempsey paused at the corner, glancing both ways as if lost. He glanced at the German street sign. "Do I turn left on Ender-Hopped-Wacky?" he asked, mispronouncing the street name badly.

"Ja," Smith said, his tone suggesting that Americans were a pain in the ass. "Left on An der Hauptwache. Do you see a big brown cathedral?"

"Yes."

"Good, walk toward that. The street will become Rossmarkt and then change names to Kaiserstrasse several hundred meters farther."

The pause allowed Dempsey to let out some line on the girl before turning left on An der Hauptwache. "Why do you guys change the name of your streets every damn block?"

"Germans are proud, and so we have many families who wish to be honored," answered Smith, a patient German businessman dealing with another ugly American.

A few minutes later, Dempsey arrived at World Coffee on Kaiserstrasse, thanked his German business partner for the navigation help, and stuffed his mobile back in his pocket. He stood for a moment in front of World Coffee as if trying to decide which one of the available café tables he should occupy under the maroon-colored umbrellas. He watched Vogel continue southeast to an intersection, where Mendez was waiting by yet another fountain in yet another square. The Germans loved their fountains. Mendez would follow Vogel through the intersection at Friedenstrasse and Willy-Brandt-Platz, where Smith would pick her up just before Gutleutstrasse and follow her the rest of the way to the Hotel InterContinental. Wang would be in the lobby and would confirm her check-in and then commence the SIGINT on the executive suite on the twenty-first floor that Rostami perpetually reserved. Wang would be using listening devices already put in place by Mossad, which apparently he was unhappy about for some reason.

At least that was how it was supposed to happen.

Dempsey was in the middle of dialing a number in Texas to check in with his "wife" when things went wrong.

Effi Vogel unexpectedly crossed to the other side of the street and turned left on Bethmannstrasse, before passing the square where the handoff would happen with Mendez.

Shit! She was supposed to stay straight onto Friedenstrasse. What the hell is she doing?

Dempsey took a step, then forced himself to pull back, silently cursing himself for the mistake. That step alone could alert a watcher conducting surveillance detection.

"Crazy fucking city," he mumbled. The words would be picked up by the microphone in his ear, and now everyone on the team knew something had gone wrong. He watched Vogel disappear around the corner and dialed a new number. Smith answered immediately.

"Guten Morgen," he said.

"Hey, it's Purcell again. Is that *other* property we talked about on Bethmannstrasse? Every street in this damn city looks the same. I was thinking about walking down there to check it out?"

"Nein, Herr Purcell. I am nearly to the coffee shop. Let me meet you there, and we can look at both properties together. I don't wish for you to get lost. I have another colleague who is researching that property for your needs, and he will let me know if it is worthy of a visit."

Dempsey looked toward the square and the fountain where he saw a young man with a backpack start toward the corner—Mendez. The Marine was dressed like some metrosexual college student on holiday.

Hurry the hell up, dude. You're gonna lose her.

If they lost the girl, they would lose the opportunity to grab Rostami. Sweat trickled from his armpits down his sides, and Dempsey felt his nerves getting the better of him. He paced, looking at his phone, debating whether to place the call to his "wife" and alert Jarvis directly about the situation. He knew Jarvis was monitoring all the comms from their makeshift TOC—a black-site apartment on loan from the Mossad—but the SEAL in him felt compelled to interface up the chain of command. Phone in hand, he spun on his heel and collided with a uniformed policeman walking up the street behind him.

"Eh, eh, *achten Sie darauf, wohin Sie fahren*?" the officer said, scowling and gripping the sleeve of his jacket. *"Was machen Sie denn hier?"*

"I'm sorry," he said, and unconsciously pulled his leather satchel in tight against his side.

This made the officer shift his gaze from Dempsey's face to the bag—a bag with a Sig Sauer pistol in the bottom easily visible under his "business papers."

"Ich spreche kein Deutsch," Dempsey said, butchering the words. *"Sprechen Sie English?"*

"*Ja*, I speak good English," the young man said, still eyeing the bag. "What is in *Ihrer Tasche?*" The officer paused and looked up, as if looking for the proper English words floating in the air. He raised a finger, proud of himself, but he still hadn't let go of Dempsey's sleeve with the other hand. "What you having in you case—in you bag with you?"

Dempsey looked at his bag. "A real estate contract waiting for signature. If I lose these papers, my boss will kill me." He smiled. In his peripheral vision, he saw Mendez disappear around the corner onto Bethmannstrasse.

"I have her." Mendez's voice was low and quiet in his left ear. "Hold on . . . she's going into a building."

What building? Dempsey thought, distracted.

"May I see into your papers, please?" the policeman said, snapping Dempsey back to the moment.

Dempsey played out scenarios in his mind for incapacitating the police officer and the "run like hell" escape that would follow. Assaulting a German police officer would transform him from an asset to a liability for the rest of the mission in Frankfurt. He needed to buy more time.

"My what?" he asked, stalling.

"*Guten Morgen*, Officer," Smith's voice said from behind him. Dempsey turned to see his partner dressed in a tight-fitting suit, tailored in the European fashion. A BMW sedan was parked along the curb. *"Ist Alles in Ordnung mit mein Freund?"*

"You are to know this man?" the officer said, wanting to show off a bit more of his English.

"Ja," Smith said. *"Ich spreche Deutsch."*

Smith and the policeman spoke for a moment in quick, clipped German, and Dempsey understood nothing. Unable to help himself, he looked toward the corner where he'd last seen Mendez.

"Echo Victor went inside an apartment building over a women's boutique and a little café," Mendez said in his ear. "The address is 50 Bethmannstrasse. She had to code herself into the building. The building has an underground parking garage. From my current position, I have no way of knowing if she ducks out another exit. She could also exit using a vehicle from the garage. Do you want me to breach?"

"Negative, three," said Jarvis over the open channel, his voice cool and collected.

Dempsey smiled awkwardly as Smith and the policeman started laughing, no doubt at his expense. The officer released his hold on Dempsey's sleeve. Dempsey took the cue to join them in the revelry— let's all laugh at the good-natured American buffoon.

"Five is heading your way with ears. You're college buddies meeting after a prolonged absence. Be excited to see him. One and Two should be back in play momentarily," said Jarvis, indicating that Wang was en route to Mendez with SIGINT.

Jarvis sounded more optimistic than Dempsey felt. He wondered how this would impact their grab plan. Perhaps Rostami had changed the rendezvous location with Vogel. If so, would the Israelis be able to reposition the ambulance in time? The plan was already a lot of moving parts, and it seemed difficult to move to a new location.

He returned his attention to his immediate situation. Smith and the German police officer had moved a step away and were laughing at something Smith was pointing at down the street. With all drama and suspicion thoroughly defused by humor, the policeman turned to Dempsey and said, "Hope you are to having a good day, sir." With a tip of his cap, and a wink at Smith, the young officer headed off.

Smith smiled at Dempsey and gestured to the BMW. "I was worried I would not be able to find you, Herr Purcell. You sounded quite lost on the mobile phone."

"The streets keep changing names," he grumbled, walking to the car.

"Well, you have a guide now, *mein Freund*," Smith said, and held the passenger door open for him. "Let me drive you on a tour of this area, then we will head over to the property on Moselstrasse. I think you may like that location better, but let us have a look here first."

Once in the car, Smith pulled them away from the curb, and because of the one-way streets, they were forced to backtrack the long way. They wasted five precious minutes circling back to Bethmannstrasse. When they rolled past the coffee shop, Dempsey spotted Mendez and Wang sitting together by the window. Wang was tapping away on a laptop, while Mendez was thumb-typing on his smartphone. Two young technophiles having coffee and paying more attention to their devices than to each other. *Sadly realistic,* Dempsey thought.

Smith pulled into a taxi queue on the right side of the street and put the transmission in neutral. Dempsey looked up through the BMW's glass moonroof at the austere-looking apartment building across the street. His gut told him Vogel was now inside one of those apartments, alone and waiting, without Mossad's ears to safeguard her.

"Thanks for the save back there," Dempsey said, dropping his gaze back to street level. "It was about to get ugly."

"Yeah, it was. In hindsight, a concealed waist holster would have been prudent," Smith said. "But together, we defused the situation. Adapt and overcome, right?"

Dempsey pursed his lips and nodded. Easy access to the weapon in the bag had been Jarvis's mandate, but he kept the comment to himself.

"Rostami changed the meet location," Dempsey said, craning his neck to scan the windows and balconies of the apartment building for some signal from Vogel. A piece of laundry hung on a railing, a quick appearance on the balcony, a window opening and closing twice . . . anything.

Nothing.

"So it seems," Smith eventually said.

"I don't like it."

"Neither do I."

"Maybe we spooked him. Do you think he knows we're here?"

"Unlikely. If he did, he would have canceled the rendezvous."

"Then why change locations?" asked Dempsey, scratching his neck. "The motherfucker did it for a reason, Shane. That much I'm sure of."

Smith was silent for a several long seconds before answering. "We'll just have to wait and see."

CHAPTER 27

Ember Local TOC
Apartment at Mosselstrasse and Taunusstrasse
Frankfurt, Germany
May 21, 1650 Local Time

Jarvis had an overpowering urge to pace, but he refused himself the luxury.

Instead, he forced himself to stand at parade rest—feet apart, hands clasped behind his back—a position of disciplined military waiting.

Directly in front of him sat the TOC mission controller—Rachel Loren, a young Israeli woman on loan from the Mossad. Loren was the person most familiar with the equipment in this particular apartment, as she was already Levi Harel's mission controller in Frankfurt. She sat on a roller stool at a rectangular desk, working three computer monitors with two keyboards while simultaneously fielding all telephone traffic. The headset she wore made her look more like a telemarketer than a member of the most elite covert operation in the world. Loren's presence in the TOC during the mission was the only concession Jarvis had been forced to make for the Mossad's unrestricted cooperation in Frankfurt. Jarvis couldn't help but smile at the irony. His two most generous benefactors, Robert Kittinger and Levi Harel, had employed identical strategies—pick the most beautiful, competent, loyal young woman on the payroll, stick her inside Ember, and order her to report the unit's every move. The brilliance of the strategy was that it worked perfectly. The request was not one he could refuse, and both Grimes and Loren had entwined themselves like English ivy into the trellis of his operation in no time. Thankfully, he didn't have anything to hide. He was doing exactly what he said he would do—hunting down the bastards responsible for annihilating the Tier One SEALs. The only secret he cared about protecting was the secret existence of Ember itself, and neither Grimes nor Loren had the power or incentive to jeopardize that.

"Five is bringing the camera feeds online now," the Israeli girl said in her soft and accented English. "Patching external vid to monitor number one."

Jarvis looked at the leftmost video monitor. The screen flickered, then switched from a traffic camera outside the Hotel InterContinental to the feed of a store security camera on Bethmannstrasse that Wang has just tapped. The glare was terrible because of the angle of the sun, but both the image clarity and camera position were exceptional. He saw Mendez and Wang sitting at a bistro table, ideally located for surveillance of the apartment and parking-garage entrances.

"Apartment feeds coming up on monitors two and three," she said.

The middle and right flat-screens switched to eight window splits with feeds from various hallway security cameras inside the apartment building. Jarvis glanced at the digital mission clock; it had taken Wang less than two minutes to tap into all the feeds. God, he loved the new generation of networked surveillance cameras; it made life so much easier.

"There she is," Loren said, her voice smooth and without emotion. "Victor Echo stepping out of the stairwell onto the fifth floor."

"Find me all apartment owners and leases for fifth-floor units," Jarvis said to Loren.

"Yes, sir."

"One and Two, report?" Jarvis said into his mike.

"One and Two are covering the back of the building from our vehicle," Smith's voice said. "Any word on our Romeo?"

"Negative," Jarvis said. "But we have Victor Echo on a fifth-floor hallway security vid."

"Roger that. One out."

"Which apartment did Vogel go into?" Jarvis asked the Israeli controller.

"Sixth door down on the right, but we don't have a camera that can read the number."

"Which number can you read?"

"Only the closest one to the camera. Apartment 502."

"Then enlarge the window with that feed, and count the damn doorknobs," Jarvis said, gesturing to the image of consecutively smaller doors in one of eight windows on the middle monitor.

Loren did as instructed. "It should be apartment 508," she said.

"Find out who owns apartment 508."

"Yes, sir. I have an asset in a Frankfurt real estate firm who I hope can help us."

"Good, make the call." Jarvis shifted his gaze from Loren to the left video monitor, where Wang was plugging a piece of hardware into a USB port on his computer. He instantly recognized this device. He waited for Loren to finish her call with her Mossad real estate contact, and then he touched her shoulder. "Give Five the phone number for the burner phone Vogel is carrying."

"Yes, sir," she said, and sent a text message with the number to Wang's phone.

Jarvis saw Wang glance at the mobile phone resting on the table screen-up beside his computer and then continue typing.

"What is Five doing?" Loren asked.

"Improvising. Right now he's tapping into Vogel's burner phone using T-Mobile's GSM network. He'll activate the phone's microphone for continuous data transmission and configure it to leak the data over a secure Wi-Fi hotspot he just set up outside the building. Vogel's phone will stay logged in to Wang's Wi-Fi network, but there will be no indication of this on the phone's display. Also, this technique leaves the phone free to make and receive calls normally."

"Zero, Five. We've got ears," came Wang's voice over the radio a minute later.

"Excellent."

"Sir, I have an Ian Baldwin holding on the secure line for you," Loren said.

"Tell him I'll call him back in a few minutes."

"Yes, sir."

In the left monitor, Wang's fingers were flying across the keyboard of his laptop, but he seemed to have no trouble multitasking—smiling and laughing in conversation with Mendez about some girls they had met at Luna Bar. The IT whiz had proven to be even better in the field than Jarvis had suspected. As long as his hands were on a computer, he didn't appear nervous. Rookie field operatives typically find a security blanket; for Wang it was his computer.

"We've got Romeo One on monitor one," said Loren, her voice brimming with excitement.

Jarvis looked at the left screen, too late to be sure that the man exiting the frame was indeed Rostami.

"Confirm, Romeo One," Mendez whispered over the radio.

The upper-left square on monitor two showed a man stepping into the apartment lobby. He was clean shaven and wore an expensive suit. Jarvis smiled as the man removed his dark sunglasses, revealing himself to the camera for a split second before stepping out of the frame.

Behrouz Rostami.

"Gotcha, asshole," Jarvis said. He tapped Loren on the shoulder. "Anything on apartment 508 yet?"

"Not yet."

He gave in and began to pace. Nervous energy coursed through his body like electricity. His mind was amped up, and his synesthesia was going crazy. Decision trees with probability-based determinants were whirling in his head. Numbers had flavors, and words were changing colors. Bethmannstrasse was a one-way street, limiting ambulance arrival and departure routes and jeopardizing the precision timetable necessary for success. How long would Rostami stay in the apartment? What if he decided to spend the night? What exit would he use? Would he hire a car? Or worse, what if he kept a vehicle in the parking garage? So many new variables to contend with. The probability of success for the op was falling precipitously.

He watched Rostami pass the camera at the top of the stairs on the fifth floor, just as Vogel had done five minutes ago. There was something about the man's smile that pissed Jarvis off. Interrogating this sonuvabitch in an "enhanced" fashion would be very enjoyable.

Rostami retrieved a key from his right front pants pocket and used it to unlock and open the door to apartment 508. He stepped inside. The door shut.

"He has a key," Jarvis said to Loren. "Has he used this apartment as a residence before?"

"Not during my tenure," she said. "His primary residence is a flat in Westend-Süd and a small safe house in Walldorf, near the airport."

"Then whose apartment is this?"

"I don't know, sir. I'm still waiting to hear back from my contact."

"We've got ears in the apartment," came Wang's voice on the open channel. "Here comes the stream."

"Put it on speaker," Jarvis said to Loren.

She did as instructed, and a man's voice speaking flawless, assertive German sounded from the desktop speakers. A woman answered in

German, her voice cowed and tremulous. Then the man's voice again. Rustling. A click and then silence.

"What the fuck just happened?" Jarvis barked. "Five, Zero, we lost audio."

"I know," said Wang. "I lost the link to Victor Echo's burner . . . trying to reestablish the connection now."

"It's no use," the Israeli controller said, shaking her head. "Rostami is meticulous and paranoid. He makes her take the battery out of her phone whenever they meet at the InterContinental."

"Damn it," Jarvis shouted. "Give me options, Five."

"Working on it," said Wang.

"My real estate contact is calling in," Loren announced. She fielded the call: *"Ja . . . Ja . . . danke."* She spun on her stool to face Jarvis. "Apartment 508 is registered as a rental property owned by Grunde AM. Grunde has leased the property to a single tenant for the past two years—Zephyr Power Limited, a wind energy development company in Berlin."

"Okay, how is Zephyr Power connected to Rostami?"

"Zephyr Power was purchased eight months ago by Rostami's employer, Erde Energie," explained Loren. "And one more thing. The lease expires on Monday."

Dempsey's voice rang over the comms circuit: "The bastard is skipping town. That's why he didn't renew the lease."

"Copy," said Jarvis.

"Copy, my ass," Dempsey came back. "If Romeo is leaving town, that means he's tying up loose ends. Zero, we've gotta get the girl outta there."

Jarvis rubbed his temples, but he did not answer.

"Zero, Two, did you copy my last?"

"Sir," said Loren, swiveling on her stool and looking up at him, worry lines furrowing her brow. "Ian Baldwin is on the secure line again."

"Tell Baldwin not now. I'll call him back when I'm goddamn ready."

"I tried, sir, but he insists it's urgent."

Jarvis blew air through his teeth. Baldwin was not the type to pester; for a statistician to say something was urgent meant either someone had just solved the Riemann hypothesis, or the end of the world was imminent. "Put him through," Jarvis said, and yanked off his headset.

The Israeli handed him a modified iPhone from a docking station on the desk. The phone's native processor had been replaced with an aftermarket chip that made the phone's outgoing transmissions impossible to decrypt. The phone generated an annoying, high-pitched squeal that the tech division had assured him was well outside the range of human hearing. That was bullshit, of course, because every time he used the phone he ended up with an excruciating headache.

"Talk to me, Ian," he said, holding the phone a few centimeters from his ear.

As his chief analyst began to talk, Jarvis pressed the phone against his ear and stepped several paces away from Loren.

"Do you know the target?" he asked. "Did you verify the source? Thank you, Ian. Tell Chip and Dale dinner is on me tonight."

Jarvis ended the call and slipped the iPhone into his pocket. He let out a long, heavy sigh and put his wireless headset back on. "All stations, this is Zero," he said. "Stand down. I repeat, stand down. I'm scrubbing the mission."

"You're canceling the grab?" Loren asked, clearly perplexed.

"Yes," Jarvis said. "Romeo is to remain in play."

Dempsey's angry voice rang in his ear. "Zero, Two, you can't do this. He's gonna kill her."

"We don't know that."

"We damn well do."

"Two, Zero, your objection is noted. The mission is secure. Stand down," Jarvis said. "That's an order." He looked down at Loren and met her big brown eyes. "Pull everyone back and get my people to the airport. Wheels up in five hours."

"Yes, sir," she said, and began the process of sending encrypted text messages with instructions to all the operatives in the field.

Jarvis left Loren to finish the administrative cleanup while he stepped into another room. He fumed a moment over losing the opportunity to interrogate Rostami, but the priorities had changed. Something big was going to happen in Geneva, and leaving Rostami in play was their best chance to figure what it was and when it would happen. Moreover, grabbing Rostami now would not go unnoticed by VEVAK. Finding out what had happened to his asset in Tehran would have to wait.

As far as Effi Vogel was concerned, he hoped that Dempsey was wrong. He hoped that Rostami would not kill the girl, but the probability function in his head said otherwise. Vogel's fate was in her own hands now. She knew the risks when she signed on with Mossad. Her safety was neither his responsibility nor his obligation. Collateral damage was regrettable, but in counterterrorism it was a mathematical eventuality. His moral imperative was to serve the greater good. He would deal with the inevitable fallout with his new head of Special Activities later, try to help Dempsey understand the grand chess game Ember was playing. If he couldn't, then maybe he'd misjudged his old LCPO. Disobedience and moral divisiveness among the ranks was something he simply could not tolerate.

Using the special iPhone, he dialed the number for Levi Harel's secure mobile phone. He had an obligation to share this latest intelligence with his old friend. He owed Harel that.

How much he shared was another matter.

CHAPTER 28

Apartment 508
Bethmannstrasse 50,
Frankfurt, Germany
May 21, 1745 Local Time

Rostami popped the battery out of Effi's mobile phone and set it on a console table by the front door of the apartment. He turned to catch her staring at him with an expression he did not like.

"You don't look happy today, Effi," he said. "Is something wrong?"

"Why did you insist on meeting here instead of our usual suite?" she asked in German, folding her arms across her chest.

"This will be our last time together for a very long time. I wanted it to be special," he replied in German, shrugging off his suit coat. Effi had been studying Arabic, but her vocabulary was limited and her accent abysmal, making the conversation so painful he refused to practice with her anymore.

"But the InterContinental is nicer, and they have room service."

"Yes, my love, but here we need not restrain our passion. You can be as loud as you want."

"I don't like it here," she said, pouting. "Can we please go to the hotel?"

"No," he snapped. Then, in a softer tone he said, "I have a present for you."

The right corner of her mouth curled into a half smile. "What kind of present?"

"The kind that sparkles." From his left pants pocket he retrieved a small black jewelry box. He opened the clamshell-style lid to reveal a gold necklace with a diamond pendant.

"It's beautiful," she said, staring at it.

He had paid €5,000 for the necklace, which was more than Effi would make in three months tending bar. "I would like to see you wear it," he said.

"Okay," she said, turning her back to him. "Will you put it on me?"

"First, take off your clothes."

"What? Why?" she said, blushing.

"I want to dress you in gold and diamonds and nothing else."

She gave a nervous laugh, and after a hesitant pause, she undressed in front of him. "Happy now?" she said, putting her hands on her bare hips.

He devoured her supple, young body with his eyes. Even though she was an infidel, he was going to miss fucking this girl. "Very happy," he said. "Now, turn around."

She did as instructed, and he carefully clasped the delicate gold chain around her neck.

"Thank you, Behrouz," she said, holding the diamond pendant up between her thumb and index finger for a closer look. "It's beautiful."

"A beautiful gift for a beautiful woman," he said, and walked into the bedroom with Effi in trail like the trained puppy that she was. He sat down at the foot of the queen-size bed and kicked off his $2,000 handmade Italian loafers. Then he began to unbutton his dress shirt. She straddled his left leg and caught his fingers with hers.

"Let me do that," she said.

He let her undress him. When they were both naked, she said. "Would you like a massage?"

He glanced over at the black leather case he had staged in advance on the nightstand. Inside, the kit contained a rubber tourniquet, two syringes, and enough heroin for a soccer team.

"Don't you want to get high first?" he asked, flashing her the devil's grin.

She looked at the hit-kit. Something—revulsion?—washed over her face, but she tried to hide it with a smile. "Not today, lover."

"I thought you preferred to fuck when you're high."

"I want to remember our last day," she said, and pushed him backward onto the mattress.

Her refusal irritated him. It had been weeks since she'd shot up, and he did not like her newly discovered willpower. Intelligent women were so much easier to control and corrupt when they were addicts. Addiction was a critical element of his breakdown process. All of Effi's piercings and tattoos he had forced upon her when she was so high she could barely walk. The black-and-red kraken tattoo accosting her neck had been his masterstroke. The morning after that wild night, she had been horrified when she saw herself in the bathroom mirror; she'd cried for hours. There was no hiding the monstrous, gnarled tentacles that stretched up just below her right ear—not even with a turtleneck. Even the heavily tattooed punk crowd stared at Effi's neck. He'd corrupted her so completely that her father had disowned her.

What did her defiance matter now?

Rostami rolled onto his stomach, readying himself for her touch. He still hadn't decided how the night would end, and to mull over her fate now would ruin the sex. When the time came, he would know what to do. He closed his eyes and let himself relax as she applied massage oil to his skin. With her soft, small hands, she worked the knots from the muscles in his back. Against his will, his mind drifted to the apprehensions he harbored about his trip to Geneva. His task was to provide last-minute training to the Iranian ambassador on the tradecraft of terrorism—deception and misdirection, how to handle a firearm, and the concealment and deployment of explosives. Skills that had taken him a decade to learn and master, he was supposed to teach to a spineless bureaucrat in twelve hours. How a man as incompetent and weak as Masoud Modiri could be the brother of a man as brilliant and powerful as Amir Modiri boggled Rostami's mind.

Amir Modiri's plan was brilliant, but it would fail. Masoud Modiri was a paper link being slipped into an iron chain.

Still, the decision had been made, and there was nothing he could do about it but adapt and overcome.

"Is this good?" asked Effi.

"Yes, love," he replied. "Perhaps a bit lower."

He grunted as she slid over his warm, oil-coated buttocks before settling into a position straddling his thighs. As she kneaded his buttocks, she rubbed her cleanly shaven crotch rhythmically up and down his legs. He felt himself harden. When she tried to slip one oily hand between his legs to cup his manhood, he squeezed his legs together. Lately, it seemed, she was in such a hurry. Her hands returned to his lower back, but she ground herself more vigorously against him. He felt her lean forward, her breasts brushing his buttocks, and she began to kiss him along his spine. She slipped her hand between his legs again.

This time he let her.

He rolled over, and she squirmed her way to his hips, straddling him and using a hand to guide him into her.

Always in such a hurry.

Always like a man, trying to control our sex.

He let her gyrate on top of him until he became so disgusted by the masculine way this small woman dominated their sex that something snapped inside him. He reached up, grabbed her by the hair, and flung her off him. He was on his knees in a flash, forcefully flipping her onto her hands and knees. Then he took control.

Clutching her with both hands about her waist, he thrust madly into her. She yelped louder and louder with pleasure, and he felt himself nearing climax.

"Tell me you love me, Effi," he huffed, the words more command than request. There was a pause—longer than it should have been—and he reached up with his right hand and pulled her head back by her hair.

"I love you," she choked—in the throes of orgasm, he told himself, certainly not in pain and disgust.

No matter. He came anyway.

He let go of her hair and saw that she was shaking. Sobbing, actually. He pretended it was because he was leaving. Her crying both excited and angered him. In this moment, he possessed her, no matter what her true feelings. He arched his back and cried out like a beast. As he did, he collapsed onto her back, using his bulk to force her facedown onto the mattress. She complied, a limp rag doll lying on her stomach, her chest heaving with each sob. Lying on top of her, he decided her fate.

She should not have cried.

He reached with his right hand off the side of the bed for the blade hidden in the gap between the mattress and box spring.

As his fingertips found the hilt, Rostami kissed her neck.

"There, there, don't cry," he whispered softly in her ear, before sitting up—his muscular thighs straddling her petite, narrow waist. "True love never dies, no matter how far apart we may be."

In a flash, he plunged the blade into the space between the top of her neck and the base of her skull. Her body shuddered, and hot blood spurted onto the back of his right hand as he twisted the knife. With the signals from her brain to her body now severed, her spastic shuddering stopped, and she went limp.

Rostami rolled the girl over and looked into her eyes, where he saw life. And terror. A bloody bubble expanded from her dark-red lips—perfect lips that had pleased him so many times. The bubble popped, and he kissed her forehead. He closed her eyelids with his thumbs.

Death should come in the dark.

Suddenly feeling anxious, he scrambled from the bed. After wiping the blade on a pillowcase, he tossed the knife into his briefcase and washed the blood from his hands. He dressed quickly and found a mirror in which to fix his necktie and smooth his hair. After casting one last glance at the girl's body, he pulled his mobile phone from his pocket. He dialed a number from memory.

"*Ja,*" said the voice.

"I have an apartment that needs cleaning," said Rostami.

"When?"

"Now."

"Where?"

"Apartment 508, Bethmannstrasse 50, Frankfurt."

"The price is double because I'm in Hamburg."

"Fine. I don't care."

"Wire the money and it will be done."

Rostami ended the call and strode toward the front door. Suddenly remembering the diamond necklace, he paused at the threshold. For an instant, he almost went back for it.

The girl's body and the murder weapon would never be found, but even if the German police investigated him for the crime, it wouldn't matter. He would never set foot in Germany again. After completing Amir Modiri's next grand operation, he would return to Persia with the honor and accolades deserved of a hero. For all the sacrifices he had made for Allah and his nation over the past decade, his reward would be an assistant director–level position in VEVAK.

As he took the stairway down to the parking garage, where a driver was waiting in a BMW to take him to the airport, he said a prayer to Allah. He prayed not for forgiveness, nor for Effi Vogel's soul, nor even for success on his next mission. He prayed for a wife—an obedient Persian woman with black hair, copper skin, and a fertile womb. A young woman from a respected family who would cater to his whims, give him pleasure in bed, and bear him many, many sons.

CHAPTER 29

Boeing 787
May 21, 1910 Local Time

Jarvis wanted to change the subject. He wanted to change the subject so badly that he had to clench his teeth together to keep from interrupting his Operations Director, who was debriefing him from the other side of the polished rosewood desk.

". . . And you're lucky he was in the car with me, or he would have done it again," Smith said, his bloodshot eyes and unwashed hair completing the raving-madman metaphor as he stalked about the VIP 787's executive office. "I had to lock the doors and drive away to keep him from charging into the apartment with guns blazing. It felt like Roanoke all over again."

"What are you saying?" Jarvis asked when Smith paused for a breath. "That he's a liability to the team? Do you think we made a mistake bringing him on board?"

"No, no, that's not what I'm saying," said Smith, running all ten fingers through his sandy-blond hair. "Just that he's still so raw. He's driven by emotion and his sense of duty. He still views himself as a protector. An avenging angel. As long as he's part of Ember, we can never lose sight of that, and we must deploy him accordingly."

Jarvis clasped his hands together, propped his elbows on the table, and stared at his prodigy.

"What?" Smith said

"Sit down."

"I can't. I'm too wound up."

"Sit," Jarvis said. *"Please."*

Smith collapsed into one of the two leather chairs facing the desk.

"Now take a deep breath."

Smith scowled but did as instructed.

"Better," Jarvis said, without condescension. He had put his team through the wringer the last three weeks, and even Smith's nerves of steel were starting to get frayed. "I know it seemed that way, but the truth is that Dempsey did show restraint. For all his blustering and threats, he followed orders this time. That *was* him standing down."

Smith cocked an eyebrow at him.

"Don't give me that look. If Dempsey had wanted out of the car, do you think a door lock could have stopped him? Hell no. What you witnessed was Dempsey battling himself. That was Dempsey falling in line, contemplating the bigger picture. Your presence helped him find the self-control to walk away from a young woman in mortal danger."

Smith nodded his head slowly.

"I view it as a positive," Jarvis said decisively. "Dempsey made progress today."

"Yeah, I suppose I hadn't thought of it that way," Smith said. He exhaled long and slow, then asked, "Do we know what happened? Did Vogel check in with her handler?"

Grim-faced, Jarvis shook his head. "Rostami killed her. Mossad went in after he left. They found her body in the bedroom. Stab wound between C1 and the base of the skull."

"Jesus." Smith ran his fingers through his hair again. "Dempsey was fucking right."

"Yeah, he was."

"Are you going to tell him?"

"Yes, but not today. I need him focused. And I need you focused, too. You gotta put it out of your head, Shane. Can you do that?"

Smith nodded, worry lines streaking his forehead. "Yeah, I can do that."

"Good. Now go gather the troops. I need to bring everyone up to speed on why I scrubbed the op and what I want out of Geneva."

Three minutes later, the team was assembled in the conference room. Instead of standing at the bank of flat-screens at the head of the table and lecturing, Jarvis took a more relaxed tack and sat himself in a plush chair next to Mendez. Grimes, who was seated between Dempsey and Smith, whispered something under her breath that made Dempsey roll his eyes, but at least he smiled. He whispered something back, and she shook her head and flipped him the bird, but this time without the fury he was accustomed to seeing in her eyes. Did he just witness the beginning of budding respect between Dempsey and Lady Grimes? It was too early to call today a turning point for the team, but he was encouraged by the subtle shifts he'd witnessed in Ember's two most volatile members.

"I know you're all curious about the short fuse change in tasking," Jarvis began, "so let me fill you in. But first, let me say thank you for trusting the judgment of those of us in the TOC." He looked specifically at Dempsey and nodded.

His Special Activities Director nodded back and forced a tight smile.

Jarvis gave pause—just enough to give Dempsey an opening to ask about Vogel—but Dempsey let the opportunity pass.

"As you all know, our analyst team back home has been working 24-7 processing SIGINT collected on Rostami. This morning Baldwin had a breakthrough, which he reported to me during our op. When I combine Baldwin's findings with the break in routine we observed today, it all points to something big." He leaned forward, propping his elbows on the conference table, his hand folded under his chin. "As Dempsey adamantly and correctly deduced, Rostami is leaving Frankfurt, permanently. We are ninety-five percent confident he has new tasking in Geneva, and I intend to find out what it is. That is why I made the call to leave Rostami in play. Period."

Jarvis saw Dempsey fidget, but the SEAL did not interrupt. "You have a question, John?"

Dempsey looked at Smith and then Grimes. They both gave him encouraging nods.

"Yes, sir," Dempsey said. "The three of us were wondering if we aren't wandering off task here. How is what Rostami does in Geneva related to our mission? In fact, what does a midlevel VEVAK operative in Frankfurt have to do with the massacres in Yemen and Djibouti at all? We know those hits were orchestrated by Al Qaeda and their affiliates, right? Shouldn't we be passing all of this Rostami intel on to other fine agencies with three-letter names so we can stay focused on our mission?"

"All fair questions," Jarvis said, and took a deep breath. "Sometimes I forget that half of the people seated at this table were not with us in the JIRG. To understand my thought processes, the first thing you have to do is ditch the paradigm that Al Qaeda is the terrorist equivalent of CIA or FSB. Al Qaeda is not an umbrella organization with hierarchical staff marching in sync under a Westernized command-and-control architecture. Al Qaeda is a tangled affiliation of sects, with power struggles, ideological differences, and local political agendas. Al Qaeda has money problems. Al Qaeda has leadership problems. These problems have always been present, but with the rise of ISIS and its ability to conduct acts of terror on a global stage, these problems have multiplied for Al Qaeda. Subsequently, they are an organization ripe for exploitation.

So I ask you, what if state-sponsored terrorism is being planned and exe-cuted using regional Al Qaeda affiliates as puppets? What if Al Qaeda is being supported by someone with money, weapons, and counterintel-ligence that Al Qaeda would not otherwise have access to?"

"What do you mean by state-sponsored terrorism?" Mendez asked.

"Hypothetically speaking, let's suppose Iran wants to wipe out the Tier One SEALs because the SEALs are a royal pain in their ass. They plan the mission at VEVAK. Then, they use Al Qaeda to do their dirty work. It's the terrorist equivalent of a false-flag operation."

"Wait. Are you saying Iran, and not Al Qaeda, was responsible for what happened in Yemen and Djibouti?" Dempsey said, leaning forward.

Jarvis could see the rage growing in the SEAL's eyes. He chose his next words carefully. "I'm saying it has become my leading theory, which is why I care very much about where Mr. Behrouz Rostami goes and who he talks to next."

"Jesus," Dempsey growled. "If what you're saying is true, we're talk-ing about an act of fucking war by Iran."

Jarvis nodded.

Dempsey was on the edge of his seat now, his hands balled into fists. "We need to sort this out now, right now, because I'm ready to take the fight to the Iranian bastards responsible."

"That's what we're trying to do, John," Jarvis said, watching his former Lead Chief Petty Officer closely. He thought briefly about the concerns Shane had voiced earlier. He reminded himself that Dempsey was at the very ragged edge here. "But we have to keep our heads. Methodical intelligence collection is our first priority. Before we can act, we need proof."

Dempsey looked at Grimes, as if to say, *Did you know about all this?* She shook her head.

Jarvis dimmed the lights using a remote control on the table. He pressed a button, and a picture appeared on the middle screen. The dark-skinned, bearded man in the picture looked familiar to Dempsey, but he couldn't place him. The official-looking headshot was anything but candid. "Does anyone recognize this man?" Jarvis asked.

"Masoud Modiri," Grimes said softly.

Dempsey glanced at her and raised an eyebrow, impressed.

"He's the Iranian ambassador to the UN," she said.

"He's more than that," Smith interjected. "Masoud Modiri is the brother of Amir Modiri, who we believe is the Director of the Foreign Operations Directorate for VEVAK."

Jarvis waited to see if anyone else would chime in, but when they all turned to him for an answer, he said, "The JIRG had a source inside VEVAK providing solid actionable intelligence prior to Yemen. That source provided confirming evidence that Al Qaeda was gathering in Yemen. That source went dark after the Yemen massacre. So if nothing else, we know at a minimum that VEVAK was tied into the Al Qaeda chatter. We also know Rostami is VEVAK. Rostami gets unexpectedly pulled from Frankfurt and ordered to Geneva. At the same time, Baldwin starts scouring the intelligence data streams for other high-level Iranian operatives and diplomats also traveling to central Europe. That pooled data indicates Masoud Modiri is already in Geneva, and Amir Modiri may have left Tehran for Geneva today."

"Pooled data?" Grimes asked.

Jarvis smiled. "You don't want to know."

"Data I *borrowed* from the NSA," Wang chimed in, garnering chuckles around the table.

"So Rostami and both Modiri brothers are going to be in Geneva at the same time?" Dempsey said.

Jarvis nodded. "And if these guys are meeting, then I want to know everything they have to say."

"There is one additional development to mention," Smith added. "Chip and Dale have been picking up increased chatter throughout the

Al Qaeda networks from SIGINT. Could be coincidence, or it could mean that VEVAK is sponsoring another operation."

"Shit, that's not good," Mendez said.

Jarvis had a flash of déjà vu. He was back with the JIRG briefing the JSOC Commander on events that would ultimately set in motion the massacre of the Tier One SEALs. "Following Rostami to Geneva may be our best shot at determining whether VEVAK is conducting state-sponsored terrorism against the US and our allies. If Iran is using Al Qaeda to do its dirty work, and if VEVAK is planning another attack, we are the only US intelligence asset in a position to ascertain what the target is and when the attack is going to happen. We cannot screw this up, people. Understood?"

"Do you think the target could be the UN itself?" Smith asked. "Helluva coincidence that they're meeting in Geneva."

"Impossible to say," Jarvis said. "Which is why no matter what happens, we can't lose Rostami. If and when Rostami meets with Amir Modiri, we're going to be there—listening to their every word."

Dempsey slapped his palm down on the table. "Then what the hell are we waiting for? You heard the boss—we have an op to plan."

Jarvis stood, and then so did the others. "This is a short hop, people. We'll be on the ground in less than twenty minutes. As soon as we land, the number one priority is to locate and track Rostami. We adjust our game plan from there."

Nods all around.

"All right, then, let's get to work."

He watched them file out. Smith lingered for a second, but Jarvis waved him off, and he hustled to catch up to Mendez, Grimes, and Dempsey. Jarvis returned to his private office, locking the door behind him. He flipped open his laptop screen and logged on to the high-side server. He had three status-update requests from Kittinger in his inbox. He glanced at the draft message he had been working on before the brief.

"Ahhhh, hell," he muttered to himself. He enlarged the window and started rereading what he'd drafted so far.

A moment later the screen flickered and Ian Baldwin's face appeared in a pop-up window. Baldwin's face was so huge in the window that Jarvis could have counted nose hairs, but then his chief analyst settled back in his chair.

"Hey, boss," Baldwin said, looking more like an MIT professor than the spook analyst that he had become.

"Ian, you look surprisingly chipper," Jarvis said. "How are things coming on our special project?"

"Big news," Baldwin said, grinning like a kindergartner with a secret. "The program works—I mean the software. It's a much more powerful tool than I originally anticipated."

"Wait—are you saying you found my missing asset in Tehran?"

"I think so."

"How? He was very careful never to call from the same location twice. You spent days trying to reconstruct this after he went dark. What changed?"

"Remember the variables I told you about—the pings on the burner phones, the episodic activation of local Wi-Fi by the smartphones themselves, the triangulation of the tower signals?"

"Yes, of course."

"Well, that was all data based on calls made from his burner phone to your burner. That wasn't enough to give me anything concrete. But, when I reran the program with the new list of burner phone numbers that Mossad turned over to us—Rostami's phone and seventeen other possibles—then things got busy. It was just as you suspected: your contact used that same burner to make other calls before he started interfacing with you. The thing is, we didn't have that data before, so thank you, Levi Harel. Anyway, the point is that even smart, careful people develop certain habits, and they are constrained by the clock, geography, traffic, personality preferences, et cetera, et cetera."

"Yeah, yeah. I'm with you, Ian. Just give me the punch line."

Ian smiled broadly. "It was a blind—a fiction from the start. Your asset never existed, boss."

Jarvis screwed up his face. "What do you mean?"

"The communications from that burner phone form three clouds when you plot them on a map of Tehran. Think Venn diagram. The biggest cloud is floating around VEVAK, no surprise. A second cloud is floating around influential residential areas of the city where government employees live—again, no surprise. We assumed your guy worked for VEVAK. But the last cloud floats around an address I would never have thought to plot if you hadn't mentioned the name Masoud Modiri as part of the Iranian traffic in Geneva. Lo and behold—in the middle of that third cloud is the ambassador's residence. Once I realized that, I had my boys start digging and, bam, *Amir* Modiri's address is located smack-dab in the middle of the second cloud. With eighty percent confidence, I predict your asset was Amir Modiri, Director of Clandestine Operations for VEVAK."

Jarvis leaned back in his chair and looked up at the ceiling. He did not want Ian to see the anger burning inside him—anger at Amir Modiri, of course, but mostly at himself. He couldn't believe it. Not only had he been played, but he had been played by VEVAK. It made so much sense now. Amir Modiri had been fishing for years and finally caught a whale. "It was my fault," he muttered.

"What's that, boss?"

"Nothing," Jarvis said, and refocused his gaze on the monitor. "Great work, Ian. Excellent, excellent job."

"Wait, there's more," Ian said. "For fun I ran the program again on the other end of the comms. Just trying to be complete."

"And you found me?" Jarvis said, unable to keep the condescension from his voice.

"Yes. Yes, of course," Ian said, and his hand got huge on the screen as he flapped it around as if shooing away an annoying insect. "Only, not *just* you."

It took a moment for what Ian had said to sink in. Jarvis raised an eyebrow.

"There were two of you," Baldwin said, dragging him along.

"Modiri was sending information to someone else in the States?"

"Not sending," Ian said. "Receiving. Eleven encounters with another burner phone stateside."

"Voice or data?"

"Both. Someone else was communicating with Modiri during the mission-planning phase for the Yemen operation. The last communication was after you and Smith had left for Djibouti."

"Who?" Jarvis asked, anger now rising to displace the shock and disbelief.

Ian pursed his lips. "Don't know yet," he said. "I'm really damn close, though. The calls were made from the DC metro and Virginia area. If you could give me a list that's shorter than the federal employee directory to feed into my program, it would help a ton. If the list is less than fifty names, I can play some *What-if* games. I'm certain the second phone is a burner, but if you give me authorization, I can call the phone, see if the bastard answers, and get a voice ID."

Jarvis leaned forward and tapped the keyboard, Ian now shrinking into a small box in the upper-right corner. He opened the high-side e-mail and began typing.

"I'm sending you a list of ten numbers. Start with the first one," Jarvis said, and clicked "Send." It was almost impossible to believe, but what if it was true?

Ian looked away, reading the e-mail he had just received, and his eyebrows arched. "Can I try to get a voice ID?"

Jarvis was about to say yes, but he stopped himself. He needed to be smart. He needed to tread lightly; he couldn't afford to spook any of the players just yet. "I'll get back to you on that."

"Understood," Baldwin said. "Anything else?"

"No," said Jarvis, his mind already onto the problem. "Just keep up the good work, and keep me informed."

"Roger that," said Baldwin, and the chat window disappeared.

Jarvis stared at his distorted reflection in the glossy computer screen.

You got played, he said to himself, *this time.*

But never again . . .

CHAPTER 30

Céligny, Switzerland, North of Geneva
May 22, 0701 Local Time

Dempsey rolled out of the Mercedes GL 350 SUV like he was rolling off the side of a RIB during a water INFIL with the SEALs. He moved quickly, leading Grimes, Wang, Smith, and Mendez from the Route de Suisse highway into the tree line. Once they were deep enough to be invisible from the road, he dropped to one knee. Smith tossed their gear bag onto the pine-needle-carpeted ground in front of Dempsey, and they all fell into a tight circle around it. Dempsey took out a handheld GPS and located their position. Smith handed out pistols, leaving the assault rifles, NVGs, and grenades in the duffel. It was daylight. The woods were much thinner than Dempsey had hoped, and they were patrolling along the residential shoreline of Lake Geneva. The risk of counterdetection was off the charts, which meant kitting up now was out of the question.

"The lake house is just over half a kilometer in that direction," he said, chopping a hand to his right. "There is one estate between us and the target, so we'll drift a little west and give ourselves a wide berth before we close."

Everyone nodded.

A bird shrieked and took off from a low branch nearby, causing Wang to jump and spin around, scanning the woods behind them.

"It's all right, dude," Dempsey said with a smirk. "It's just a bird."

He slipped a Sig pistol into the holster at the small of his back, stood, and set off deeper into the woods. Wang hung annoyingly close to his left side, Smith fell in behind him, hauling the duffel backpack-style, and Grimes brought up the rear. Dempsey scanned the woods in sixty-degree sectors as they walked. They moved swiftly and quietly, except for Wang's unbelievably loud breathing.

"Wang, bro," Dempsey whispered, "quit breathing like a horse. Use your nose."

"Sorry," Wang whispered back.

As they closed on the rented lake house, Dempsey marveled at how quickly Ember had pinpointed Rostami's whereabouts. With DHS co-managing the INTERPOL Washington bureau, getting expedient access to the INTERPOL facial-recognition database had been a cinch. Video streams at Geneva customs had picked up Rostami, and the Swiss customs records showed that Rostami had used his German NOC for the trip. This was useful information for two reasons: First, it meant the Iranian was not running scared, and Ember had retained the tactical advantage; second, it made it easy to track his rental-car transaction. Wang had hacked the Eurocar database in less than fifteen minutes; a minute later he had the VIN number, plate number, and LoJack codes for Rostami's rental car, which he fed to Baldwin stateside. Baldwin "borrowed" some satellite time and picked up the vehicle from the LoJack GPS signal just as it arrived at an estate property on Lac Leman, presumably rented. None of Jarvis's "friends" had ears inside the property, which meant they needed to get Wang as close to the house as possible. There was no telling how long the meeting would last, and Ember's next move would rely heavily on whatever dialogue Wang could snoop.

A rustle at his ten o'clock pricked Dempsey's ears. He held a fist over his head, took a knee, and was pleasantly surprised when Wang did not bump into him. He listened, waited, and watched for movement. After a few seconds, a red deer crept cautiously into view and then froze. The doe's right ear turned toward them. They made eye contact. She gave a snort and dashed away into the woods.

Dempsey gave the signal, and his four-person team was on the move again. After another fifty meters, he noticed the woods were thinning, so he drifted farther east, trying to keep to the denser cover as long as possible. God, how he wished he had an overflight drone to mark security along the perimeter of the lake house. Ideally, he wanted to position Wang at the southern corner of the estate so if they got ambushed, they had two egress options: back into the woods or a sprint to the lake. Dempsey had insisted that Mendez rent a motorboat to give his team a water EXFIL option in case of emergency. The Malibu Wakesetter 23 LSV Mendez had found wasn't a RIB, but the 555-horsepower engine would definitely get the job done. At this time of year, the famous lake in the Alps would be frigid, but that was the least of his worries.

They closed another fifty meters, and the dark-blue water of Lake Geneva came into view through the gaps in the trees. The forest extended all the way to the shore, but the trees had been cleared on the estate property to make an immense, manicured lawn. This was as close as he dared go. Dempsey knelt again and leaned back toward Wang.

"Is this close enough?"

Wang nodded, slipped his backpack off his shoulders, and squatted. He opened his laptop, plugged one of his magic boxes into a USB port, and then donned a pair of noise-canceling headphones. In moments Wang was lost in another world, his fingers dancing on the keyboard and touchpad. Twisting, multicolored lines marched across his laptop, and Dempsey noticed that Wang was manipulating and adjusting them with his keystrokes. Like a cowboy corralling a herd of rowdy steers,

Wang coaxed and nudged the unruly colored strands into an organized, cooperative pattern.

Wang turned to Dempsey, grinned, and gave him a thumbs-up.

"Zero," Dempsey whispered, his left hand subconsciously feeling for that old familiar boom mike on his cheek, but finding none. "Data coming in a moment."

"Copy," Jarvis's voice answered in his wireless earbud. "We'll try and clean it up and stream it back to you with minimal delay so you can listen in if you like."

"Copy."

"Keep sending until we pull you out."

"Roger."

Dempsey felt a tap on his shoulder and turned his head.

"Rifles?" whispered Smith.

Dempsey weighed the pros and cons and decided to err on the side of firepower. As long as they were stationary, the team was vulnerable. He nodded, and Smith pulled three Sig516 rifles from the duffel—one for each of the operators. Dempsey surveyed the woods, the lake, and what he could see of the lake-house property through his binoculars. He was no stranger to the waiting game. As a SEAL, his team would often stake out a target for hours—sometimes days—at a time.

"Triangle perimeter around Wang," he said, and motioned Grimes to reposition left and Smith right. He took point.

Now, all they had to do was wait, listen, and not get caught.

CHAPTER 31

Amir Modiri put his hand on Rostami's shoulder. "Don't worry, my brother can do it."

Rostami glanced at the bathroom door, still closed with the light streaming out beneath the gap at the floor. "He's been in there a long time," he said, his expression doubtful.

"Have faith."

"I have faith in Allah, I have faith in Iran, and I have faith in you," said Rostami. "But I do not have faith in *him*."

"My brother is strong, but not in the same ways that you and I are strong. Words are his weapon, not guns and explosives. He has no training or experience in the ways of war. I'm counting on you, Behrouz, to guide and protect him."

Rostami grunted disapprovingly.

Amir grabbed Rostami by the arm with such speed and force that it surprised his lieutenant. "You are trying my patience. I will not tolerate your insolence a moment longer. Maybe you've been in the West too long? Maybe I should take you off this operation and send Turan Al-Abid in your place? You can go to Pakistan—or maybe Iraq—for a two-year tour to recalibrate your faith and commitment."

"I apologize, sir. I was disrespectful and have forgotten my place," Rostami said through gritted teeth.

Amir released him with a shove. "I kept you in Europe too long. You've become infected with the same presumptive arrogance as the Germans."

Rostami bowed his head. "Forgive me. I swear to do all that you ask of me and more."

Amir stared at Rostami.

The truth was that he dare not substitute Turan Al-Abid for Rostami on this mission. Rostami was a sadist and a sociopath, but he was unflappable under pressure. Without question, Rostami was his best field operative, and the plan would likely fail without him. This dressing-down was a much-needed recalibration, but both men knew it was nothing more than posturing. "Very well," said Amir, his voice low and hard.

Rostami looked up and met his eyes. "Once your brother sets off the charges, I can handle the rest, but Masoud is the trigger for the entire operation. He cannot fail on this task."

"I understand. He won't fail," Amir said with conviction.

"How many Al Qaeda men will I have under my command?"

"Assuming everything goes according to plan, which never happens, but assuming it does, you'll have six men inside the UN—two suicide bombers and three snipers in buildings across the street. The ranking AQ operative for the mission is Mohamed Assaf. He was just informed that you'd be running the operation. He was not happy with this development. By the way, how is your Arabic these days? Your accent needs to sound Saudi, not German."

"Maybe I should be asking you, where is your faith?" Rostami said, and then rattled off the same sentence with perfect Saudi Arabian MSA.

"Good," said Amir. "When is the last time you saw Assaf?"

"Three years ago in Dubai. To be honest, I'm surprised he volunteered for this mission. He has risen high in the ranks since then."

Amir smiled. "An unexpected development from the victory in Yemen. Most of the men in the compound were respected veterans in their sects. Their martyrdom has shamed their peers who abstained. Now, Assaf feels compelled to make his mark, as much for Allah's will as his own pride."

Rostami nodded. "In a sense, I can relate."

"Let us review the plan together: After the first detonation, there will be much death and confusion, but do not lose sight of the fact that *our* mission is not the same as Al Qaeda's. Iran must be perceived as much a victim of this tragedy as the other nations. Your only priority is to separate my brother and the American and British ambassadors from the rest of the group in the Assembly Hall. Move them at gunpoint to the emergency-egress tunnel system. All the ambassadors have received terrorism-event and emergency-evacuation training; Masoud knows the way. Once you are in the tunnels, Masoud will resist and make an attempt to fight back. Have you instructed him how and when he is to disarm our Al Qaeda brother?"

"Yes," Rostami said. "I will scout ahead, leaving him alone with the brother who is prepared to martyr himself. I thought it was best to lie, otherwise he might hesitate in the moment."

"That was a wise decision," said Amir.

Amir met Rostami's eyes. "It is imperative this part of the plan is carried out. Masoud's heroism must be noted by the American and British ambassadors. For the plan to succeed, Persia must be perceived as a victim of terror, and also as a hero in the fight against it."

"I understand. It will be done."

"Most of the infidels will be executed in the main chamber, but we have a safe house on Long Island where you will hold the British and American ambassadors for the hostage negotiation."

"You realize that the NYPD will close down all roads around the UN Complex. It will be impossible to get off the grounds, let alone Manhattan Island."

"No, not impossible," Amir said with a wry grin. "During the renovations, the UN built secret evacuation tunnels. One of these tunnels leads to a maintenance and ventilation access door inside the Queens Midtown Tunnel. When the NYPD shuts down the entrance, we will already have a car waiting inside that encounters 'mechanical problems' at the access point."

Rostami eyed him suspiciously but said, "I understand."

"Once you reach the safe house, you will hold the ambassadors for the duration of the 'hostage negotiation.' Ultimately, Tehran will negotiate their release, and Masoud will be praised by his Western colleagues as a hero. The US president will be pressured by the international community and the media to lift all remaining sanctions on Iran as a gesture of goodwill, and the UN Security Council will follow suit. Iran will gain new standing in the international community while simultaneously gaining more freedom to continue our work paving the way for the caliphate."

Rostami nodded.

"You look skeptical," said Amir.

"If you had asked me four months ago, I would have said it cannot be done," Rostami replied, rubbing his clean-shaven chin. "But after what you pulled off in Yemen and Djibouti, it is clear that you are Allah's chosen general."

Amir nodded. It was time to give his soldier his pride back. "There is no one I trust more with this task than you, Behrouz. Your service will be greatly rewarded."

Rostami bowed his head deferentially.

The bathroom door latch clicked. Both men turned and looked as Masoud pushed open the door and stepped out in the hallway. His brow was dappled with sweat, and his hands were trembling. "I can't do it," he said, looking down at his shoes.

Amir smiled and walked to his brother. "Of course you can."

"No, I can't," said Masoud, shaking his head. "What you ask of me is wrong. It is unclean. As a man . . . as a Muslim . . . I cannot."

Amir laid his right hand on Masoud's shoulder. "It is the only way."

Masoud looked up, his eyes pleading. "Why can't I just swallow it? Put the explosive in capsules, and I can vomit into the toilet when it's time."

"No, Masoud," said Amir, shaking his head. "The stomach empties into the small intestine within hours. Once the material moves into your small intestine, it cannot be regurgitated. Then, we are stuck waiting for an indeterminate amount of time until it reaches your colon—anywhere from twelve to twenty-four hours. This is not acceptable. You need to be able to access the material at will. Also, the explosive material is highly toxic. Our scientists have worked very hard to find methods to concentrate the compound and enhance yields. If the latex were to leak or rupture inside your intestine, it would poison you. I'm sorry, Masoud, but it must be the other way."

Masoud took a deep, defeated breath. "I can't."

Amir sighed. He had anticipated this. A demonstration would be necessary to convince his brother, so he had taken laxatives the night before in preparation. No matter the challenge, if he crossed the bridge first, Masoud would eventually follow. It had always been that way. He was the leader, his big brother a reluctant disciple.

Amir walked into the bathroom, turned to face Masoud and Rostami, and then unbuckled his trousers. He let them fall to the floor and then dropped his underwear. Standing naked from the waist down, he picked up the tied-off latex condom packed with eight one-inch balls of concentrated plastic explosive. Grabbing the tube of lubricant from where it sat untouched next to the sink basin, he liberally applied the clear, viscous gel to the upper half of the condom. Gripping the base of the condom with his right hand, he bent at the waist and reached around behind his buttocks. Without a grunt or a grimace, he pushed the fully packed condom inside himself. After an inch, the sensation was so repugnant he wanted to gag, but he kept going with stoic determination. When the deed was done, he took a deep breath, dressed himself, and walked out of the bathroom. Amir could feel that his face was flushed, but he was proud that he had not even broken a sweat. Standing face-to-face with his brother, he said, "You see, Masoud, it can be done."

Masoud nodded penitently.

"Now, we change the condom and you try."

Masoud returned to the bathroom, and this time was gone but a few minutes. When he returned, his face was pale and his shirt collar soaked with sweat, but it was clear from the look in his eyes that he had succeeded—yet again—in matching his younger brother. It was like playing soccer in their youth, or the climb over the nine-foot wall into the neighbor's courtyard, only this time Masoud had not broken a bone, just his pride.

They sat together in the sunroom, and he allowed Masoud to collect himself. Amir crossed his legs at the knees and sipped his tea, feeling sympathy for his older brother.

"Do you wish to review the plan and your mission again?" he asked.

His brother nodded softly and smiled tightly. His color was returning.

"He is ready," Rostami replied for him. "He is truly a warrior in the service of Allah. He brings much credit to your family and Persia. You should be proud of his role in fighting the Great Satan."

Amir tried not to be annoyed with his lieutenant, who no doubt wished to bolster his image after their earlier misunderstanding. He set his tea aside and looked at his brother. "I have faith in you, Masoud. You alone can provide the access we need to the UN. You will use your gift—the gift of discourse that Allah has blessed you with—to engage the American and British ambassadors in conversation in the far corner of the room. This is crucial." He leaned forward to be sure that Masoud was paying attention.

"I understand," his brother said. "I must direct the ambassadors to the corner so that our brothers in jihad will be able to isolate us quickly."

"Correct," Amir said, satisfied. "This will allow us to gain control of the General Assembly Hall quickly. From there, you will be marched at gunpoint to the tunnels. Rostami does not know the way, so you must lead him while making it appear that he is leading you. At the same time, you must resist him. You will be defiant, condemning his actions. You must put your gifts as an orator to work and convince the world that Persia is a victim, too."

Masoud nodded.

"Do you remember your lesson from last night—how to disarm a man and how to fire a weapon?"

Again the nod, but this time his brother looked up with uncertain eyes. "There is no way around shooting this man—my fellow Muslim?"

"No," Amir said. "This will make you the hero. There will be heroes and there will be martyrs. It is an honor to be martyred for Allah, and the brother's reward in Paradise will be great."

A final nod.

"You are ready, Masoud," Amir pronounced rather than asked. "Do not fear. It is a blessing to have been chosen to serve Persia and Allah on this mission. You will not fail."

"Will I be in the tunnels with Rostami before . . . before the executions of the other diplomats begin?"

"You will," Amir promised, feeling annoyed that his brother did not have the stomach to witness the judgment of infidels. "The world must see that those who serve as the pawns of America and the Zionists will be judged and punished in the name of Allah."

"After it is done, how long will I be held hostage?" Masoud asked.

Amir tried not to sigh. He had explained this several times already. "It will not be long, I promise. I will look after your wife and your affairs while you are away. You are ready," he proclaimed, and kissed his brother on the cheek. "It's time to go. The schedule is tight."

"For Allah," Masoud said.

"For Persia," chanted Rostami.

Then Amir led his brother and Rostami to the driveway where the cars were waiting.

CHAPTER 32

Lake Home Estate
Céligny, Switzerland
May 22, 0952 Local Time

Tap, tap, tap.

Tap, tap, tap went his index finger against the trigger guard.

A rustle behind Dempsey made him turn. Wang had pulled his headphones off and was packing up his computer. Feeling Dempsey's eyes on him, he looked up and dragged a hand across his throat. "Leaving," he whispered.

"Did we get what we needed?"

Wang shrugged. "Don't know. It was really dirty. Zero never streamed anything back. The geek squad must still be cleaning it up."

"EXFIL," came Jarvis's voice in his ear, sounding calm and confident. "We got everything we're gonna get. Satellite has Rostami's rental car on the move. Confirm?"

Dempsey lifted his compact binoculars to his eyes and scanned the lake-house driveway. He glimpsed the rear quarter of Rostami's rental sedan turning out of the drive onto Route de Suisse highway. A moment later, he saw a second sedan following the rental car up the drive.

"Two vehicles leaving the house," Dempsey whispered. "No ID on the passengers."

"John!"

He looked at Wang. From the pallor of the kid's skin, he knew they had a problem. Keeping as still as possible, he followed the vector of Wang's terrified gaze.

Standing at the edge of the estate property and peering into the woods was an Iranian security guard. He wore dark jeans, a turtleneck sweater, and sunglasses. He held a submachine gun tight to his chest, with his index finger poised and ready on the trigger guard. Even at twenty meters away, Dempsey could make out the compact radio on his belt and a microphone cord clipped to the epaulets of his sweater. The sunglasses made it impossible to tell exactly where the man was looking, but obviously the guard had not seen them yet. Judging from the Iranian's posture, this was a "Shoot first, ask questions later" kind of guy.

In slow motion, Dempsey dropped to the ground, disappearing into a patch of brush. Wang crawled in beside him. Dempsey put a finger to his lips and gestured for Wang to stay put. The tech's eyes widened with uncertainty, and for one awful moment Dempsey thought Wang might bolt. With the calm assurance of a lifelong operator, Dempsey looked him in the eyes and mouthed, "It's okay." Some of his confidence must have rubbed off, because the kid nodded and settled down.

Dempsey looked back at the Iranian sentry. The man was on the move, drifting closer to their position but still hugging the tree line. He paused to listen. Then he took a tentative step into the woods.

Cursing under his breath, Dempsey slithered backward silently, moving deeper into the woods. He crept to the west, wondering if Smith or Grimes had seen the sentry yet. It could be a problem if two of them made a move against the Iranian at the same time. Since the patrolling guard was now in Dempsey's area, he prayed that his teammates had the good sense to leave the unpleasant task ahead in his capable hands.

Dempsey paused in the middle of his flanking maneuver, sighting through the forked trunk of a tree. The sentry took two more steps into the woods, closing on Wang's hiding place. Dempsey watched and waited, both hunter and prey, given his position. The SEAL in him wanted to drop the asshole with a headshot, but the clandestine operative knew better. Sniping this sentry solved the immediate problem, but gunfire would bring more security guards on top of them, compromising the op and their escape. Radio calls would be made. Rostami and Modiri would know that *someone* had been watching them, unraveling everything. He couldn't let that happen.

Easy was not an option.

The sentry paused. Clutching his weapon, he scanned the woods in a broad, sweeping arc. Seemingly satisfied, the man turned around. He'd only taken a single step back toward the lake house when a rustle from Wang's position stopped him cold.

Dempsey's heart sank.

The sentry whirled, training the barrel of his submachine gun on the clump of brush where Dempsey had left Wang. Then the Iranian stepped cautiously forward, moving deeper into the woods.

Dempsey scowled and silently unsheathed the knife strapped to his left thigh. He moved like a ghost, circling behind the Iranian. Each footstep was a tactical operation in and of itself. The mat of pine needles that blanketed the forest floor was a blessing and a curse—muffling his footfalls, while concealing dry, brittle kindling. A single twig, in snap or silence, would decide the fate of three men.

As the sentry closed in on Wang's position, Dempsey's heart began to race. The geometry wasn't right yet. The Iranian would be on top of Wang before he got close enough to make the kill. He ducked his torso, pinned his rifle to his chest with his right hand to preserve his stealth, and changed his vector, from flanking to closing.

The sentry stopped five meters from the clump of brush. He made a move for his radio, but then suddenly changed his mind. He took a half step forward into a firing stance, brought his submachine gun up to his shoulder . . .

Dempsey closed the gap in a flash.

The sentry tried to spin left, but it was too late. Dempsey clamped his right hand over the sentry's mouth and jerked the man's head back. The sentry reached up with his left hand to key his mike, but Dempsey's knife was already on a collision course with the man's neck. The blade threaded the gap between the third and fourth metacarpal bones in the sentry's hand, exited through the palm, and continued on into the side of the man's neck. Dempsey yanked the blade free, and hot blood spurted in a high arc, spattering the trunk of a nearby pine. The sentry shuddered and kicked, but Dempsey held firm. He brought the knife down again, this time cutting across the sentry's throat from right to left, severing both carotid arteries and splitting the trachea in half with a hiss of air. Neck muscles and ligaments splayed as the sentry's knees buckled. Still gripping the man's jaw, Dempsey whipped the man's head back to an impossible angle, ending with a crunch. He squatted and gently laid the dead man on the pine-needle floor, blood still spurting in all directions.

Dropping to a knee beside the dead man, he scanned the forest for the next threat, lifting his Sig516 into a firing position. Grimes closed from the east, and Smith from the west, but no other threats appeared. After finishing his scan, he spotted Wang lying prone, half-buried in pine needles behind a bush three meters away.

Wang scrambled to his knees and put a hand over his mouth as if to stifle a sob. He approached Dempsey and the dead sentry hesitantly, eyes wide, tears streaming down his cheeks.

"I thought I told you not to move," Dempsey growled.

"I know," Wang whispered. "I'm not sure what happened. I was scared."

"Are you okay?"

Wang stared at the Iranian's butchered neck but said nothing.

"First time?" Dempsey asked, wiping the blood off his knife.

Wang nodded.

"The first time is the hardest. You'll be fine."

Smith and Grimes huddled in beside Wang.

"Did he get a transmission off?" Smith asked.

Dempsey shook his head.

"SITREP," a voice demanded in his earpiece. It was Jarvis.

"Zero, this is Two. We have one Tango down," Smith said softly. "No compromise."

"Are you positive?"

"Yes. One made sure of that."

Dempsey heard Jarvis sigh heavily on the line. "He'll miss check-in, but that's all they'll know. Sterilize protocol. No evidence, no clues left behind. Then, egress to the pickup coordinates," said Jarvis, his voice hard and tense. "You have ten minutes."

"What's going on?" Smith pushed.

"We cleaned up the audio. This is a short fuse. They're going big."

Dempsey and Smith exchanged glances.

"How big?" Dempsey asked.

"Big. Now move. Zero, out."

Dempsey knelt next to the dead man. "You got duct tape in that duffel, Smith?"

Smith shrugged the bag off his shoulders, fished inside, and tossed him a roll of EB green.

"Lift his leg while I tape." Dempsey turned to Grimes and Wang. "You two, go find as many rocks as you can. Hurry."

Smith lifted the dead man's left leg off the ground by the boot, and Dempsey looped the roll around the bottom, taping the dead man's pants legs closed at the ankle. Satisfied, they moved on to the right leg and repeated the process. In the meantime, a pile of rocks had materialized beside the dead man's right shoulder, Grimes and Wang bringing back every-size stone they could find. Without needing to be told, Smith started stuffing rocks down the dead Iranian's pants.

"Four, One. Copy?" Dempsey said.

"One, Four. Go ahead," Mendez came back, his voice barely audible over the sound of the wind howling and the boat engine roaring in the background.

"In five mikes, be at the shore, a half-click north of the surveillance point. Have a towline ready."

"Roger that."

"Is that enough rocks?" Grimes asked, scanning the forest for threats over her gun sight while Dempsey and Smith packed rocks.

"Should be," Dempsey huffed, taping a seal around the dead man's waistband.

"You gonna sink him?" Wang asked.

"Yep. I'll have Mendez tow me out, and I'll take the body down deep. You guys EXFIL to the road, and I'll ride with Mendez to the marina. We'll meet you at the rendezvous."

"Someone could spot you dragging him out of the woods," Grimes said.

"If you have a better idea how to make this body disappear in the next five minutes, I'm all ears, otherwise it's Davy Jones's Locker for this SOB."

Grimes chewed her lip.

"All right, we do it my way," Dempsey said, taping the dead man's rock-laden legs together at the ankles. "Smith, help me. Shoulder carry, like he's a fucking training log."

Together, Dempsey and Smith ran the body through the woods to a spot a half-click north of the lake house where the tree line pressed to the water's edge. Mendez was waiting with the idling Malibu Wakesetter, ideally positioned on the blind side of a small peninsular outcropping, bow out with a towline flung onto the rocky shore. Dempsey moved swiftly, dragging the dead man across the rocky shore into the glacier-fed waters of Lake Geneva. He wasted no time, forcing the dead man below the surface in three feet of water. Holding the body down with his boot, Dempsey looped the towline around the dead man's torso three times and then knotted the loose end to the line. Bubbles streamed upward from the dead man's open mouth and air pockets in his clothing.

Dempsey looked back at Smith, Grimes, and Wang, who were watching from the cover inside the tree line. With a chattering jaw, he said, "You guys owe me one for this."

After settling down to his neck in the frigid water, he gripped the towline with both hands.

"Ready?" Mendez called, looking back over his shoulder.

Dempsey gave a nod. "Take us out. Nice and easy."

CHAPTER 33

Route de Lausanne, Southbound Toward Geneva
May 22, 1019 Local Time

Dempsey cranked the thermostat control in the Mercedes SUV to max heat. He was still in his wet 5.11 Tactical clothes and shivering like mad, but he had nothing to change into, and they didn't have the time to stop.

"Your lips are blue, dude," Mendez said, glancing over at him from the driver's seat. "You look like a corpse. You sure you're okay?"

"I'm fine," Dempsey said nonchalantly. "Hey, do you think if I turn on the seat heater, it will electrocute my ass?"

"Go for it, bro," Mendez said. "I know CPR."

Dempsey pressed the button for the seat heater and then pretended to convulse in his seat.

Mendez slammed on the brakes before he realized that Dempsey was kidding.

"You asshole," Mendez growled.

Dempsey opened the dry bag at his feet and retrieved his wireless earbud and mobile phone. "I'm gonna check in. We don't even know where we're going."

"They sent me coordinates, bro."

"Okay, then where are we going?"

"To the coordinates," Mendez said emphatically.

"Like I said," Dempsey quipped, inserting his earbud. "We don't know shit."

He dialed Smith, who answered on the first ring. "Smith."

"Now that my brain has thawed, bring us up to speed," Dempsey said.

"How'd it go?" Smith asked, sounding more concerned about the dead guy than whatever "big" event was about to go down.

"I took him down deep, and he's not coming back up. It will be a long time before anybody finds him."

"How deep?"

"As deep as this old, fucking Navy SEAL can free-dive, okay. He's deep," Dempsey said, irritated. "Now tell me what the hell is going on?"

"We're still waiting on the call from Jarvis; he wants to brief everyone at the same time."

Dempsey ripped the portable GPS off the windshield mount and zoomed to the coordinates Mendez had entered. "We're headed to the Palais des Nations?" he said. "What's that?"

"The United Nations of Geneva," Grimes said, her voice more distant. "They're targeting the UN, Dempsey."

"Like the UN itself? The building?" Dempsey couldn't believe it. Ambassadors or staff in Geneva was one thing, but the UN building itself?

"Holy shit," Mendez said. Dempsey saw the Marine's knuckles go white as he clenched the steering wheel tighter.

"That's Jarvis calling," Smith said. "Hold on, I'm gonna patch him in."

After a short, silent pause, all their phones were in conference.

"The intercept data was shitty," Jarvis began. "Baldwin is struggling to clean it up, but we have enough snippets to make an educated guess about their plan. We have a positive voice ID on Rostami, and there were two others."

"Both Modiri brothers?" Dempsey interrupted. Then he squeezed his eyes shut. "Sorry, Skipper. Go ahead."

"Yes, we think so. We have a positive ID on Masoud Modiri, and we're nearly certain that the other vehicle leaving the estate in Céligny had Amir Modiri inside. We're hoping to confirm Amir's attendance with a second run at voice recognition. The first set of data is pretty filthy, but even so we got a seventy-eight-point match.

"I'm sending you a transcript. You'll see lots of breaks. It's not redacted, just dirty. You'll have it in a second. Everyone look at it; find anything we're missing."

Dempsey reached back to the second-row seat and grabbed the strap of Mendez's backpack. He pulled the pack up and onto his lap, opened the main compartment, and retrieved Mendez's 4G-enabled tablet computer—the same one he and every other Ember operative had been given. The tablet showed a push notification from the secure high-side server. Dempsey clicked the notification, downloaded the file, and opened the document. To his mind, it was unintelligible. Strings of random words, seemingly unrelated most of the time. He did see the words *UN*, *infidels*, *United Sta*tes, *brothers*, and *Allah* rather frequently, but that could mean anything.

"Looks like nothing but random words."

"Hang on," Jarvis said. "Keep looking and try to imagine filler for the long gaps—common words and phrases, as if you were talking on mobile with a bad connection. This is the raw file. I'll send you the enhanced version with computer-generated fillers using Ian's statistical algorithm, but I want you to look through the raw transcript first."

Dempsey had no idea what that meant but continued to scan the widely spaced words.

Jarvis continued. "I believe that there is an attack imminent on the UN. It appears to be an Al Qaeda operation, but sponsored and planned by VEVAK. The attack will involve executions as well as hostage taking. This jells with some recent traffic we're getting from various affiliates we're monitoring."

"Keep in mind that Ambassador Modiri works at the UN," Grimes said in his earpiece, playing devil's advocate. "There could be any number of things the UN references could pertain to. Without more data, it's a stretch."

"I'm sending the enhanced file now," Jarvis said. "Look this over and I will be back online in a moment. I have calls in to Levi Harel, the local CIA station chief, and the Swiss FIS to look for confirming data."

"Shouldn't we alert UN security?" Smith asked. "And perhaps our own State folks in Geneva?"

"Not yet," Jarvis said. "Keep looking this over. If we're wrong and we lock down the UN, we alert Modiri that we're tracking him. Then both he and the whole op will be in the wind. I'll be back in a moment, and we'll talk tactical response."

A second push notification chimed, and Dempsey opened the new file. Where the enormous gaps in the text had once been, there was now purple-colored text. Words became phrases. Snippets were now sentences. As he read through the new, more robust transcript, he got a chill up his spine—not the kind related to his hypothermia-inducing swim in Lake Geneva. There were now phrases such as: *"Masoud is the trigger for the entire operation,"* and *"Six inside the UN, two suicide bombers, and three snipers in buildings across the street."*

As he scanned the remaining five pages, he found more bits of disturbing conversation: *"An unexpected development from the victory in Yemen . . . there will be heroes and there will be martyrs . . . fighting the Great Satan . . . those who serve as the pawns of America and the Zionists will be judged and punished in the name of Allah."*

The evidence was damning, except for one problem: 75 percent of the text was generated by a computer. He didn't care how good Baldwin's statistical algorithm was. Before he went charging into the

UN with guns blazing, he needed something concrete. Something solid. Something intrinsically irrefutable.

He waited for Jarvis to return. He waited to ask the question that had been bothering him for the past twelve hours, but he had been too afraid to ask.

Jarvis chimed back into the call. "I'm back up," he said. "We're the only ones with intel on this, but I have the CIA station chief coordinating—"

"Sir, I have a question," Dempsey interrupted. "What is the status of Effi Vogel?"

"I don't see what Effi Vogel has to do with the situation at hand, John," said Jarvis. "Let's not lose focus here."

"Well, that's where you and I differ, I guess. Because in my mind, Effi Vogel has everything to do with the situation at hand. You're about to launch a full tactical intervention based on a *computer's* interpretation of a conversation between the Iranian UN ambassador, the VEVAK's Ops O, and Behrouz Rostami. Call me old-fashioned, but I'd rather make my decision based on empirical evidence of character."

An uncomfortable silence hung on the line for several seconds. "He killed her. I'm sorry, John."

Mendez glanced at Dempsey.

Dempsey asked the question with his eyes: *Did you know?*

Mendez shook his head and whispered, "I swear, I didn't know."

Dempsey looked down at his lap and noticed that both his fists were clenched. "All right," he said. "I'm convinced."

"Hey, guys," Grimes interjected. "On page five, there's a line where Modiri is talking about gaining *'the access we need to the UN and the US and British ambassadors,'* and then there is something about isolating them in a room."

"There is also reference to a hostage negotiation on page three," Dempsey added, scrolling back to a reference he'd remembered seeing.

"What do you think Masoud Modiri means when he asks, '*How long will I be held hostage?*' That doesn't make any sense," Grimes said.

"Then after that, someone, presumably Amir, says, '*I promise. I will look after your wife and your affairs while you are away,*'" Smith added.

"Does anyone else feel like the US and British ambassadors are to be targeted for kidnapping by Masoud Modiri?" Grimes asked, her voice hesitant with conjecture. "I know it sounds crazy, but . . . hold on, I want to check something."

"What's your theory, Elizabeth?" Jarvis asked.

"Call it off," she said, her voice now strong and confident. "They're not targeting the Palais de Nations! Call off the response teams or we'll spook them."

"If they're not targeting the UN, then what is the target?" Smith asked.

"They're targeting the UN, just not the UN in Geneva," she said. "Are we still tracking the LoJack on Rostami's rental?"

"Yes," Jarvis answered. "They're well ahead of you on Route de Lausanne."

"Are they past Route des Romelles?" Grimes asked.

"Still a couple of kilometers north. Coming up on it in a minute. Why?"

"Give me a minute," Grimes said. "I'm looking something up." Dempsey could hear the tapping of her fingers on a keyboard in the background.

"You think they're going to the airport?" Jarvis asked.

"Just a second."

There was an agonizing pause, during which Dempsey looked furiously at the broken transcript, trying to see just what the hell Grimes saw that he didn't. When she came back, she sounded excited but still a little unsure.

"Why do we think the attack is today?" Grimes asked, leading them.

Smith chimed in. "Because the transcript shows Amir saying, '*You are ready. It's time to go. The schedule is tight . . . for Allah . . . for Persia.*' That's it, then they leave."

"Yes, but according to the UNOG online calendar, the only noteworthy meeting today in Geneva is the Committee on Economic, Social, and Cultural Rights in Sub-Saharan Africa," Grimes said. "The US and British ambassadors are not going to be at that committee meeting. Because . . ." Dempsey heard more tapping on her laptop. "The Nuclear Nonproliferation Conference is scheduled for tomorrow at the UN Headquarters in New York."

"The attack is in New York City," Dempsey said.

"Rostami just took the exit to the airport," Jarvis said. "Good work, Elizabeth."

"Thank you, sir."

"All right, everybody, you heard the lady. Change of plans. Wheels up as soon as we get runway clearance. We're heading home."

CHAPTER 34

United Nations Headquarters
New York City
May 22, 1250 EDT

Masoud Modiri wiped the sweat from his brow and tried to pay attention to the conversation he was having with the Jordanian ambassador. While this sounded simple in theory, the fear and the discomfort he was suffering made the task nearly impossible. He had been carrying a condom filled with plastic explosives inside his rectum for hours, and he was terrified that at any moment he might lose control. As they approached the security checkpoint inside the new South Screening Building, it was all he could do to smile, squeeze, and walk with a normal gait.

While he waited in the short security queue, Modiri noticed a bronze bust of Wallace K. Harrison prominently displayed on a nearby marble pillar. The irony of locating the bust in this South Screening Building was not lost on Modiri. Harrison had served as the lead architect of a multinational coalition of architects responsible for the design of the United Nations Complex in Midtown Manhattan. The coalition's design had represented the hope and idealism of a world freed from the terror of Nazism and war. Openness and transparency had served as guiding design principles, resulting in a facility that—by modern standards—was easily accessible and vulnerable to attack. In light of the events on 9/11, the safety shortcomings and strategic vulnerabilities of the aged complex were an impetus for a massive internal renovation. The renovation team had the dubious task of trying to preserve the spirit of the coalition's design while implementing modern, antiterrorism defenses. As one of the renovation architects had explained to Modiri during the "reopening" cocktail party: "Our job was to create the illusion of transparency and accessibility while simultaneously turning the UN headquarters into a citadel." When Modiri had recounted this to his brother, Amir had laughed and said, "The two visions are mutually exclusive. Remember this man's name, so later you can tell him that his glass citadel cost the lives of many."

After seven years, and hundreds of millions of dollars in budget overruns, the internal renovation was now complete. In the weeks preceding the grand reopening event, all the ambassadors and their staffers had been forced to sit through an hour of training summarizing the improvements to the complex. The renovation had included systematic upgrades to the safety and security of the UN headquarters, including the installation of biochemical airborne samplers in the ventilation system, upgrades to the video-surveillance systems, and the replacement of all exterior and observation windows with explosion-resistant ceramic glass. It also introduced the new South Screening Building—reminiscent of TSA security checkpoints in airports—as well as a major upgrade to the underground tunnel complex linking the Secretariat, the General Assembly, the Conference & Visitor's Center, and the Dag Hammarskjöld Library buildings. In addition to the training, all representatives had been asked to participate in a series of emergency-evacuation drills, utilizing the upgraded tunnel system. Modiri had taken detailed notes during these sessions and turned the information over to his brother for the planning of the attack.

Modiri had suggested the grand reopening ceremony itself as the focus of the attack, but Amir had deemed the risk too great. With an unprecedented number of Secret Service, FBI, NYPD, and UN security personnel swarming the complex, VEVAK had calculated the odds of success in the single digits. Now, one month later, it was a perfect time to strike. With the euphoria and the paranoia of the reopening all but forgotten, the UN was back to business as usual.

"Mr. Ambassador, sir," a young security officer said, interrupting his thoughts. "Can you please swipe your badge, empty your pockets, and place your personal belongings on the X-ray conveyer? You do not need to remove your shoes or your belt."

"Why is the Delegates' Entrance closed today?"

"I don't know, sir. I only do what they tell me," the guard said without humor. "They also closed the Visitors' Entrance at Forty-Sixth Street. All traffic in and out of the complex must come through this gate today."

Modiri could feel his heart pounding in his chest. Something was wrong. They knew something, or why else would they close the Delegates' Entrance?

"Sir, if you could please swipe your badge and place your belongings on the belt," the guard prompted again.

Modiri did as instructed, emptying his pockets and placing his mobile phone and briefcase in a plastic bin on the conveyor. Next, he swiped his security badge through the card reader. The card reader beeped, and an LED flashed green.

"Do you have any medical implants—such as a pacemaker or insulin pump—on or inside your person?" the guard asked.

"No," Modiri said.

"Do you have a prosthesis—such as an artificial leg or hip-replacement joint—that might preclude you from passing through the scanner?" the guard asked, reciting the words with the practiced efficiency and boredom of a veteran.

"No."

"Very well," said the guard. "Please walk normally through the tunnel. Do not stop. You may pick up your belongings on the other side."

"Is this really necessary?" Modiri said, gesturing at the latest and greatest whole-body-scanning monstrosity the Americans had dreamed up. "I am an ambassador. Don't you see the badge clipped to my jacket?"

"Yes, sir, Mr. Ambassador," the guard said without a trace of humor or intimidation, "but these procedures are in place for your protection."

Modiri sighed and walked into the tube. This new scanner was supposed to be less intimidating and intrusive by allowing you to keep your belt and shoes on during the walk-through. He said a silent prayer to Allah and clenched his sphincter muscle with all his might as the machine bombarded him with backscatter X-rays, giving the guard the ability to peer beneath his clothes like Superman. Amir had assured him that the waves bounced off his skin, and the device could not see anything inside his body.

A bead of sweat trickled down his temple.

He hoped his brother was right.

"Clear," said a guard holding a tablet computer at the exit. "Next."

Modiri stepped out of the scanner tunnel, turned left, and walked over to the baggage conveyor to retrieve his briefcase and belongings. The belt was stopped, and the guard sitting at the computer screen had summoned another guard over to his workstation. Modiri could not hear what they were saying but he saw the first guard pointing at the screen. The second guard spoke, and then the first guard turned and pointed at him. Modiri felt his breath catch in this throat. The detonator was disguised as an MP3 player and a pair of earbuds. Amir had assured him the device would be indistinguishable from the real thing. The pressure in his rectum was building in step with his fear.

The second guard said something to the first, and the conveyer started moving. Then, the second guard—apparently a supervisor—approached Modiri. "Sir, is this your briefcase?"

"Yes," said Modiri.

"Can you open it please, sir?"

Modiri pressed the right and left latch-release mechanisms with his thumbs, and the lid to the briefcase popped open. Inside were a stack of folders, several ink pens, a notebook computer, and the MP3 player with headphones.

"Sir, I need to run your computer through the scanner separately."

"Very well," Modiri said, trying to sound astonished at the request.

"Thank you," said the guard, taking the computer.

Modiri's heart skipped a beat when he saw the guard swiping the computer with a round, white paper disc. He had been careful to handle the explosives only wearing nitrile gloves, but if a trace chemical signature had somehow . . .

"Sorry to trouble you," said the guard, returning with his computer. "You're free to go, Mr. Ambassador."

Modiri nodded, repacked the laptop, and closed his briefcase.

In the time it had taken to screen the case, Modiri's three staffers had cleared security and were hovering around him in a semicircle. He ignored them, gathered his things, and headed as quickly as he could toward the General Assembly building. The day's conference on nuclear nonproliferation included forty of the delegates and their staffers, which made the General Assembly Hall the only space large enough to accommodate the session.

The plan was for the first suicide bomber to lay waste to the South Screening Building entrance, giving access for the attack team to enter the facility while AQ snipers outside provided cover fire. In the ensuing calamity, he would detonate his explosive in the bathroom located on the perimeter wall of the General Assembly building, blowing a gaping hole in the side of the building. This would give a second assault squad access to the north side of the building, even with the building on lockdown. For that to happen, however, he had to pull off the most dangerous task of his entire life, and do so without detection.

By the time Modiri reached the lobby of the General Assembly building, he felt like he was going to burst. He walked to the men's restroom at the north end of the building. "Wait outside," he barked to the three young men accompanying him—none of whom were read into his brother's plans for this day. In fact, one or more of them would likely die today, a thought he pushed from his mind as an irrelevant distraction. They nodded and waited obediently.

Inside the bathroom, Modiri selected the end stall and latched the door shut. Extracting the packet of explosives was not a problem; his body *wanted* it out. Retrieving the thin yellow bag coated with his own excrement from the toilet, however, proved far more difficult for him. An angry self-reminder of the price his dead son, Kamal, had paid gave him the willpower to accomplish the disgusting task. Three minutes later he was cleaned up, with the empty condom flushed down the toilet.

Modiri retrieved a pair of nitrile gloves from a hidden pocket in his jacket and proceeded to knead the plastic explosive into a flat, rectangular lump. With great care, he pressed the explosive clay against the concrete wall behind the base of the toilet, obscuring it from view. Next, he retrieved the MP3 player and headphones. Each earbud unscrewed at the base to reveal a bare copper lead. He plugged the auxiliary jack into the MP3 player, then pressed the MP3 player's power button, and the LCD screen came to life with a menu screen. Buried seven menu levels deep, he found the setting to activate the player's embedded cellular chip and antennae, turning the device into a fully functional 4G-enabled detonator. On his mobile phone he pressed the preprogramed phone number for the detonator listed under a false name in his contact list. The detonator received the call and activated without complication. Using the menu function, he reset the device. Modiri dropped to his knees, and with shaking fingers he pressed the copper leads from the MP3 detonator deep into the clay.

The world did *not* explode.

Modiri exhaled, wiped the sweat from his forehead, and took a seat on the toilet. He took several deep breaths to center himself. His mind went to young Reza Pashaei—the boy who had called himself "June" in Djibouti. A wave of nausea washed over him as he imagined the awful courage and abject terror required to detonate explosives inside one's own body. During every second of every minute of every hour he carried the bomb inside him, all he could think about was getting it out. Now that it was out, the sense of relief was unlike anything he'd ever known. Poor Reza had been given no such luxury—the explosive had been surgically implanted in his abdomen. The only solace to temper Modiri's guilt and pity over what Reza had been forced to experience was knowing that the Mahdi had gotten Reza's final request at the well of the Jamkaran Mosque.

Reza, like all the martyred brothers before him, was basking in Paradise now.

Before leaving the stall, Modiri repacked his briefcase and said a prayer to the Mahdi. He asked the Twelfth Imam to bless Reza, to bless Persia, and to bless the act of jihad he was about to commit. In prayer, he found both the affirmation and courage he needed. He stripped off his gloves, unlatched the stall door, and stepped out. To his surprise, he was alone in the bathroom. He buried the nitrile gloves at the bottom of a wastebasket under layers of refuse. Then he walked over to the sink, and after washing his hands, splashed cold water on his face. He patted his cheeks and forehead dry with paper towels and checked his suit in the mirror.

He could not look himself in the eye.

Gripping his briefcase in his right hand, he marched out of the restroom and toward the General Assembly Hall, his staffers in tow. Now, all he had to do was figure out what to tell the American and British ambassadors so they would talk exclusively and privately with him for the next twenty minutes.

CHAPTER 35

Newark Airport, Corporate Terminal, FBI Hangar
May 22, 1315 EDT

Dempsey fell in behind Jarvis as the Ember Director took the lead.

Smith and Mendez followed on Jarvis's left, while he and Grimes stayed right. The Ember Special Activities Unit ran five abreast from their "borrowed" VIP 787 to the figure waiting across the tarmac for them. A refueling problem at the Geneva airport had delayed their departure by seventy minutes. Even pushing the speedy Boeing Dreamliner to the limits, they couldn't catch the Iranians in their Gulfstream 650, which held the title of the world's fastest corporate jet. Now, every second wasted mattered.

"Are you Captain Jarvis?" asked the man behind the Ray-Ban shades.

"Call me Kelso," Jarvis said. "You must be Special Agent Hansen."

"Get in," Hansen said, nodding at the GMC Yukon Denali XL parked behind him. "We'll do introductions en route."

Dempsey surveyed the SUV; it looked eerily similar to his own—black paint, tinted windows, and a strained suspension thanks to the bulletproof glass, armored doors, and undercarriage shielding. Three identical GMCs were lined up behind it, idling and ready to go. Dempsey studied the lone operator standing by the front bumper of the lead vehicle. With his green flight suit, body armor, and SOPMOD M4s slung combat-style across his chest, this guy had to belong to the FBI Hostage Rescue Team. Besides Ember, HRT was the only nonmilitary unit he could imagine being a part of. HRT recruited heavily from the pool of military operators; Dempsey knew several Tier One SEALs who'd joined HRT after retiring from the teams.

Hansen made a circle in the air with his index finger and yelled, "Let's roll."

Thirty seconds later, they were packed into the seven-passenger beast, with Hansen behind the wheel, screaming toward Manhattan at eighty-five miles an hour.

"Thanks for meeting us at the plane," Jarvis said from the second-row, right bucket seat. Dempsey had the left bucket seat, while Smith, Grimes, and Mendez were crammed in the third-row bench seat. A stoic HRT operator occupied the front passenger seat.

"I go where I'm told—especially when the call is from the DNI," Hansen said, making no effort to conceal his irritation.

Dempsey eyed Jarvis, but the seasoned Skipper shrugged off Hansen's undertone. They were all big boys here, and Jarvis was the type of leader who found pissing contests utterly unproductive.

"This is John, Shane, Sal, and Beth," Jarvis said, motioning to Dempsey and the team. If Hansen found it strange to be introduced to the team using only first names, he showed no sign of it.

"You're the ones I'm supposed to embed on the HRT?" Hansen asked, eyeing them skeptically from the rearview mirror. Dempsey noticed the Special Agent's gaze settle on Grimes, who was wedged between Smith and Mendez. She responded by resurrecting her trademark glower, a look Dempsey realized he hadn't seen once in at least twenty-four hours.

"Thanks for having us, sir," Dempsey said diplomatically. "In my former life, I sometimes had strangers forced on my team—so I know how much this situation chafes. But we've got one hell of a clusterfuck brewing at the UN, and we appreciate your help more than you know. We won't be a drag on your tactical operation."

"It's not me you need to worry about," Hansen said, and tilted his head toward the front-seat passenger. "That's my tactical squadron leader riding shotgun. He's a former SEAL, and someone you do not want to fuck with."

Dempsey contained his grin.

Hansen glanced at Jarvis in the rearview mirror. "Captain Jarvis, will you be going in?"

"No," Jarvis said. "I assume you have a mobile TOC of some sort?"

"I deployed it an hour ago. It's parked at the end of East Forty-Third Street, overlooking United Nations Plaza."

"Then that's where I'll be," said Jarvis.

"Very well," Hansen said. With a jerk of his thumb toward the caravan of SUVs trailing behind them, he said, "The rest of you will be teamed with two of my guys, making a six-man team. You're Team One, and there will be three others. We're gonna stage at Ralph Bunche Park, which is directly across the street from the Secretariat building. You guys look like you kitted up on the plane, but I'll ask the question anyway—do you need any gear?"

"Just encrypted radios set to your preferred freqs," Smith said from the back.

Hansen nodded. "No problem."

"Has Ambassador Modiri passed security at the UN yet?" Grimes asked, but made a point of looking at Jarvis instead of Hansen.

Dempsey saw Hansen's mouth twist with annoyance in the mirror, but the lead agent called in the question over his radio.

The call came back loud enough for all to hear. "Yes, sir. Five minutes ago. Processed Modiri through the South Screening Building with all the other ambassadors and staff. He was clean. But whoa, mama, you should see the SSB—talk about a bunch of pissed-off diplomats."

"What was your screening protocol for Modiri?" Hansen asked, all business.

"Walked him through the whole-body scanner, ran residue swipes, and x-rayed his gear. Why?"

"Just making sure he got the full treatment."

"Sure did. Everything but a body-cavity search," the voice on the other end said with a laugh.

"Thanks," said Hansen. "Keep me posted if you pop any red flags."

"Roger that, sir."

Hansen turned and looked at Grimes. "There's your answer. That *is* what you were hoping to hear—right?"

"Yes," she answered while inserting her wireless earbud in her right ear canal. "But unfortunately, I don't think you fully appreciate what these assholes are capable of."

CHAPTER 36

General Assembly Hall
UN Headquarters Complex
May 22, 1330 EDT

The best lie is one so exquisite and so tempting that both the deceiver and the listener yearn for it to be true. The lie that Masoud Modiri told US Ambassador Felicity Long and British Ambassador David Cochran was such a lie.

As he spoke, Modiri felt the spirit of the Mahdi flowing within—energizing his body, enlightening his mind, and guiding his tongue. Every word, every beat, every inflection, was perfectly timed and executed, erasing any hint of pretense, insincerity, or deception from his message. His offer to share military intelligence and begin a new era of cooperation with the West to combat terrorism enraptured his enemies so completely that fifteen minutes passed in the blink of an eye. When the South Screening Building exploded—obliterated by the first Al Qaeda suicide bomber—Modiri was so deeply engaged in the discourse that the detonation actually took him by surprise.

His immediate reaction matched that of his contemporaries—shock and wide-eyed disorientation.

A hush fell over the General Assembly Hall.

Someone's mobile phone rang, piercing the silence.

Then another.

Then many mobile phones began to ring, and the grand hall erupted like a symphony of nightmares.

That his own mobile phone was *not* ringing was the trigger that reminded Modiri he had forgotten to detonate his charge. He retrieved his mobile phone from his pocket and pressed the "Redial" button. The call rang once, twice, and then connected. He immediately began rambling in Farsi, pretending to be talking to his security detail.

The next blast was loud—much louder than he expected. The percussive wave rattled the hall, momentarily silencing the frenzy, before it erupted again with twice the cacophonic intensity.

Everyone began screaming.

Running and shoving.

Alarms blared.

Pandemonium.

Modiri felt someone grab his upper arm. He whirled, hot with anger, and locked eyes with his senior staffer.

"Sir, we have to get you out of here," said the young man.

"Where am I supposed to go?" he yelled. "Where is the next bomb going to explode? Which exit is safe?"

This comment seemed to grab the attention of everyone in a ten-foot radius, including Ambassadors Long and Cochran.

"He's right," said Ambassador Long. "We need to follow the emergency-evacuation protocol. UN security personnel will escort us to the basement, and from there we'll take the tunnels to safety."

Everyone nodded.

Automatic weapon fire cracked in the hall, reverberating in triplicate in the great dome over the rostrum.

Modiri ducked, squatting in the aisle between two rows of delegate desks. He grabbed Felicity Long by the wrist and pulled. "Get down," he barked.

She hesitated a half second before cowering next to him. Modiri looked up at the wide-eyed British ambassador and tugged on his pant leg. The man looked down and then dropped to his knees beside them as well.

He was amazed at how quickly the Al Qaeda assault team reached the hall after his breacher charge blew.

More gunfire and screaming echoed in the hall.

"Where is US Ambassador Long?" a stern male voice shouted in heavily accented English. Modiri recognized the voice—Rostami.

The American ambassador gripped Modiri's hand. He met her gaze and saw that she was paralyzed with fear.

"Get ready," he said.

"For what?" she choked.

"To have courage," he said. "He's going to threaten to kill hostages until you identify yourself. If you don't, he will kill many of us. If you do, lives may be spared."

"Where is US Ambassador Felicity Long?" the terrorist yelled again; this time his voice was closer.

"He's going to kill me . . . isn't he?" she said, her voice wavering.

"Perhaps. Perhaps not." He squeezed her hand. "I will stand with you. We do it together."

"No," said Ambassador Cochran, grabbing his arm. "Stay down. We must be quiet."

Modiri shook off the man's hand in disgust. He was weeping like a woman.

A burst of automatic weapon fire made them both flinch.

There was a scream again and the sound of a body crumpling to the floor. Through the legs of the chairs, Modiri saw a woman facedown and motionless, several rows up from where they crouched. A pool of dark blood spread out from her head.

"Oh my God," Ambassador Long sobbed beside him. He looked over and saw her eyes riveted to the corpse. Modiri squeezed her hand tightly.

"We will be strong together," he promised. "I will stand with you and protect you."

"If the US ambassador does not show herself in five seconds," Rostami bellowed, "I will continue executing delegates. Five . . . four . . ."

Modiri stood up and pulled Ambassador Long to her feet beside him. "I'm here," she said, her voice no louder than a squeak.

"Three . . . two . . ."

"Here," Modiri called loud enough to be heard over the commotion. As he spoke, he stepped in front of Long, shielding her with his body. "Ambassador Long is here, with me."

The terrorist, Rostami, whirled 180 degrees and leveled the barrel of his submachine gun at them. Then, he tilted his head and squinted, as if to get a better view. "There you are, Ambassador Long. I almost didn't see you," he said mockingly. "Tell me, who is your brave and foolish friend?"

"I am Ambassador Masoud Modiri of the Islamic Republic of Iran," said Modiri, puffing out his chest. He reached down and pulled the British ambassador by the arm. The older and considerably frailer man rose beside him, shaking with fear. "This is Ambassador Cochran from the United Kingdom, and we stand with Ambassador Long."

The arrogant, amused look on the terrorist's face morphed into a ghastly scowl. "Why would you—a Muslim of Persia—protect this daughter of the Great Satan? There is only one reason I can think of. You are a traitor and an infidel, Masoud Modiri. Which means that your fate is now tied to hers."

Modiri swallowed the urge to cringe at the words. This was acting, nothing more. He looked beyond Rostami at the massive, golden UN emblem set above the grand marble rostrum. The globe, as seen from the North Pole, cradled by two olive branches. It was an atypical cartographic perspective of the earth; it was the Creator's perspective. "You bring shame to Islam with your bombs and your guns," he said. "Islam is a religion of enlightenment and peace."

Rostami laughed. "You're a fool, old man." He gestured with the barrel of his automatic weapon for them to clear the aisle. A second terrorist, younger than Rostami, stepped into the aisle behind them, using a flanking position to herd them toward Rostami.

"Move," the boy said, jabbing the British ambassador in the back with the muzzle of his machine gun.

The ambassador sandwich—Modiri in front, Long in the middle, and Cochran at the rear—shuffled reluctantly toward Rostami. When they reached the aisle, Rostami glared at them. "You will follow me to the tunnels. If any of you try to escape, Modiri, the traitor of his faith, dies first."

The look in Rostami's eyes was so convincing, Modiri began to question whether the man was acting anymore. Perhaps it was his role that was the ruse. Perhaps they meant to martyr him for Iran. Would that not achieve the same political result? As Rostami led them toward the stairwell to the basement, he called to Mohamed Assaf, the ranking AQ operative for the mission. "Give us three minutes to get to the tunnels, then you can send them all to Hell."

CHAPTER 37

Lead GMC Yukon
First Avenue, Manhattan

Dempsey wondered if they'd gotten it wrong.

Was their perception of the threat skewed by Baldwin's augmented lake-house transcript? The original transcript—the raw translated dialogue—had contained only isolated words and short fragments of the Iranians' conversation. The persuasive parts had come from the chief analyst's statistical algorithm, which in Dempsey's mind was just a fancy term for computer guesswork.

Dempsey had defaulted to trusting his gut, but was his method any more scientific?

No, probably not.

The tactical lead of the FBI's elite Hostage Rescue Team updated everyone *again* that absolutely nothing suspicious was happening at the UN.

Although it was tempting, Dempsey didn't take the bait.

After ten seconds of silence, the now chatty HRT man said, "Are you guys OGA or what?"

"Or what," Dempsey said reflexively. Then, he remembered how much it had pissed him off when some civilian asshole showed up at the X barking orders and tossing around useless bits of cryptic intel like they were golden nuggets. Dempsey cleared his throat, and with as much sincerity as he could muster, said, "Sorry, sir, but I'm sure you get it."

The former SEAL in the front passenger seat grunted and then mumbled, "Fucking spooks. You guys better not fuck up my TAC team, is all."

"I'm a former team guy," Dempsey said. "Don't worry, sir. I know how to keep a team in line."

Dempsey knew he'd revealed too much, but he felt like the guy deserved to know he was a real shooter. If they found themselves in the suck, it was important for the head of the HRT unit to know the quality of his embedded assets. Fair was fair.

The HRT operator swiveled in his seat and stared at him—undoubtedly trying to place Dempsey's face.

Dempsey smirked.

Good luck, buddy. Only Kate would know me with this face . . .

"We should probably—" Smith began, but stopped midsentence when Hansen held up a hand to silence him.

"Say again?" Hansen said, his usual gruff intonation suddenly going strange. "Roger, execute protocol Echo Orange. HRT time to target, three mikes." Hansen turned on the Yukon's lights and sirens and punched the accelerator. The Yukon's V-8 engine roared, and the chassis lurched as he piloted the oversize SUV like a Formula One race car toward the UN.

"Everyone come up on TAC Two on your radios," the HRT team leader barked.

"What happened?" Jarvis yelled over the sirens.

"A suicide bomber just blew up the SSB," Hansen said. "The UN is under attack."

CHAPTER 38

Nothing sobers like a bomb.

Every petty thought, every carnal want, every physical distraction—these all vanish when something goes boom.

Dempsey ceded control of his heart, his mind, and his body to the single-minded warfighter who, for the next hour, would simply be known by the radio call sign *One*. "How long until we're on target?" he asked.

"Less than a minute," Hansen answered from the driver's seat.

"We've got sniper fire," the HRT leader said, repeating the comms report on TAC Two for anyone in the SUV who had not tuned in yet. "Three confirmed shooters, firing from buildings on the west side of First Avenue."

Dempsey imagined an aerial view of the United Nations complex and surrounding streets, which occupied a sizable chunk of real estate on the east side of Midtown Manhattan. "From that location, they can hit anyone going in and out of the General Assembly and the Secretariat buildings."

Hansen pressed his hand against his ear. "They just hit the General Assembly building . . . blew a hole clear through the north wall."

"Holy shit," Mendez cried from the backseat. "How many assholes are we dealing with here?"

"My spotters are reporting two separate terrorist assault teams converging on the General Assembly building—one from the south moving toward the lobby, and one from the north moving for the breach. The snipers are providing cover fire—hitting UN security forces inside the fence and an NYPD cruiser on First Avenue."

"We're heading north on First Avenue, right?" Dempsey asked.

"Yeah."

"Isn't there a traffic tunnel that goes under UN Plaza?"

"Yeah. The First Avenue Tunnel. First Avenue goes bi-level at Forty-Second Street. Above ground it becomes United Nations Plaza; below ground it's the First Avenue Tunnel."

"How many blocks long is that tunnel?" Dempsey asked.

"Five, I think. Why?"

"I want you to take it."

"What the hell for? You can't access the UN from down there, if that's what you're thinking," Hansen came back.

"I realize that," Dempsey said. "Let's use the tunnel to duck under those snipers and then INFIL from the north."

"Through the same breach the terrorists used?"

"Exactly."

Just then, Grimes passed him a tablet computer with a SAT image of the UN complex and surrounding streets that she had pulled up.

"You read my mind," Dempsey said, taking the tablet. The imagery matched what he remembered, but now he had all the details. "Hansen, when you come out of the tunnel at Forty-Ninth, make a U-turn to the east. Then come back south. There's a set of gates between Forty-Fifth and Forty-Sixth Streets. You're gonna hit those gates, drive this fucking Yukon up the steps, and drop us off as close as possible to the building."

"You agree with that plan?" Hansen asked his tactical lead.

"Better than getting carved to shit rushing the front door," said the former SEAL, "but I'll reassess at the target before deploying our teams."

As the Yukon angled down into the First Avenue Tunnel, Dempsey caught a glimpse of smoke rising above the UN complex and people running away. With sirens blaring, they flew through the tunnel. To Dempsey's surprise, traffic parted like a zipper in front of them. Even the normally belligerent, unyielding NYC cab drivers moved out of their way. Smith handed out weapons, and by the time Dempsey was holding his Sig516, they were flying out of the tunnel like a shell fired from a cannon.

Dempsey glanced at Jarvis, who had been oddly silent during the drive from Newark.

"Sure you don't want to kit up and come with us?" Dempsey asked.

"I'm saving myself for the next one," Jarvis said with a smirk. "Besides, somebody needs to keep Hansen company when the snipers turn this Yukon into a block of Swiss cheese."

Dempsey nodded.

"Provided we don't get shot to hell, Hansen and I will try to make it back to the mobile TOC," Jarvis said, and put a hand on his shoulder. "Good luck, John. Go take care of business."

Hansen hit the U-turn so hard the SUV rolled up onto two tires for half a second. They rocketed south—driving the wrong way against the northbound traffic on First Avenue. Through the windshield, Dempsey could see the flashing lights of multiple NYPD cruisers setting up a roadblock to the south, presumably at Forty-Second Street. Out the left-side passenger window, the iconic parade of flags—the colors of the world—zipped past in a blur.

"Passing Forty-Sixth," Grimes yelled from the back. "The gates are on your left in a hundred meters."

"I see them," Hansen yelled. "Everybody hang on."

Hansen braked, swerved, and piloted the Yukon onto a collision vector with the ten-foot-tall black iron doors set into the perimeter fence. The big SUV hopped the curb with a double thud and careened onto the sidewalk. The snout of the Yukon smashed into the fence with a sickening crunch, and the gates crashed open, swinging wildly on their hinges. A half second later, they hit the concrete steps. The big SUV bottomed out and shuddered, but the XL wheelbase and twenty-inch wheels devoured the ramping staircase with the ease of driving up a loading dock. The next thing Dempsey knew, they were skidding to a stop five meters from a gaping hole in the side of the General Assembly building.

"Left side exit. Stay low and behind the vehicle," Dempsey yelled, as the first sniper round hit the right-side B-pillar with a resounding thud.

Everyone crawled out the left-rear passenger door, except for Jarvis and Hansen.

Three more sniper rounds smashed into the armored SUV in rapid succession.

The other two black SUVs, loaded with the men of the FBI's elite HRT, arrived a split second later. A swarm of FBI operators—in their green flight suits and matching green kit clad—formed up behind the column of SUVs. The modified Yukons' armored skin and ballistic windows served as their shield.

Dempsey grabbed the closest two HRT operators and pulled them into a huddle with his Ember teammates. "This is Team One. We INFIL through the breach, then work our way to the General Assembly Hall. Radios on TAC One. Expect anything from a hostage standoff to suicide bombers. Drop anyone with a weapon. Ready—on my lead."

"Hey, wait a goddamn minute," the HRT leader hollered.

"Sorry, boss," Dempsey said, without a hint of apology. "We need to move. If you could use the number-three Yukon to distract those snipers for a few seconds, I'd be most grateful."

The scowling HRT leader gave Dempsey a grudging nod.

Dempsey crabbed forward until he was squatting beside the lead Yukon's front left tire. He spied an eight-by-eight-foot smoking hole fifteen feet away, with a geyser of water spraying upward that suggested the breach was through a wet wall—most likely a restroom. The two HRT organic team members hesitated at first, but fell in next to Grimes, Smith, and Mendez.

Thirty seconds later, he heard tires squealing behind him.

"Now," Dempsey yelled, and ran in a tactical crouch toward the jagged void. A bullet whizzed over his head just as he slipped through the breach into the building. He cleared the opening and took a knee inside what remained of a men's bathroom. Grimes arrived next, followed by an HRT operator, and then Mendez. Dempsey heard a dull shout outside. He peered through the breach and saw one of the HRT operators fall. Smith, who was bringing up the rear, slowed. Another burst of fire spit up turf harmlessly only two feet in front of him. A still target would be dead in seconds—long before the HRT shooters outside could ID the point of fire.

"Move it, Smith. Into the breach," Dempsey yelled.

In midstride, Smith grabbed the fallen FBI agent by the vest straps and jerked him to his feet. The man grunted and hobbled with Smith toward the breach. They arrived at the wall, and Dempsey yanked Smith into the hole so hard that both Smith and the FBI operator fell down. Dempsey helped the injured man into a seated position, his back against the concrete wall.

"One is clear," Dempsey said into his mike.

Smith: "Two."

Grimes: "Three."

Mendez: "Four."

There was a long pause, and then, "Guess I'm Five," said the uninjured FBI agent, but he did not sound happy about it. "It's so awesome to be on Team One with whoever the hell you crazy fuckers are."

"I'm Six," came another strained voice. "And Six got fucking shot."

Mendez moved toward the downed agent, pulling a medical blowout kit from his left cargo-pants pocket. Dempsey had no idea what Mendez's real combat time was, but as a MARSOC Marine with ten years' tenure during the war on terror, he figured Mendez had done this more than once. Within seconds, Mendez had combat gauze pressed against the agent's left thigh and groin.

"Rear upper-thigh entry and exit just below the groin. Missed the femoral artery," Mendez reported. "Move your foot," he said to the man, and then, "No nerve injury, it appears."

Dempsey looked at the downed HRT man. "Keep pressure on that wound and you won't bleed out. Help is coming."

Dempsey led the team across the remains of what was a restroom—the marble floor now cracked, the mirrors in pieces, and the toilet stalls a jumble of tile and steel. They waded through several inches of water to the door. Dempsey cracked the door open and peered. The hallway outside was deserted.

He heard a burst of gunfire and screaming coming from the General Assembly Hall.

Time to move.

Dempsey led his team of five out of the bathroom. In the hallway outside, he spied a fire-escape placard on the wall. He ripped it off and studied the building diagram. They had entered on the ground level, but the building actually had four levels. Due to the stadium seating of the General Assembly Hall, the main entrance was located on Level Two. What appeared to be a ground-floor entrance to the General Assembly Hall meant that with any luck, they would surprise the terrorists inside.

"Team Two is coming through the breach in the wall," a voice said in his headset.

Perfect, I'll send them to the fourth-floor balcony press boxes. We'll have these assholes high and low from multiple angles.

"Team One standing by to storm GAH from west ground-level entrance," he said into his boom mike. "Team Two proceed to Level Four and provide cover fire support from the balconies. Radio when you're in position."

He looked back over his shoulder at his teammates. "We go on my mark. Shoot to kill."

CHAPTER 39

Modiri ducked his head and hunched down as he stepped through the four-foot-tall entrance to the newest and most unpublicized modification to the UN complex—the series of emergency-evacuation tunnels. The Dag Hammarskjöld Library, the Secretariat, and Conference buildings were already connected via underground tunnels, but none of these tunnels facilitated escape from the complex itself. This new tunnel connected the General Assembly building to the existing tunnels and included two new secret spurs—one giving access to the FDR Drive, which passed directly under the UN complex itself, and the other bisecting the Queens Midtown Tunnel south of Forty-Second Street. The tunnel entrance point for the General Assembly building was located in the basement and was camouflaged to look like a maintenance access panel rather than a doorway. Of course, the designers probably had not envisioned a scenario in which one of the terrorists was a permanent delegate to the UN—the very body of people the new tunnel system was meant to protect.

Rostami's Al Qaeda companion poked Modiri in the back with the muzzle of his automatic weapon. "Move," the young jihadist barked.

Modiri turned and eyed the Al Qaeda fighter. Minutes ago, inside the General Assembly Hall, the young jihadist's eyes had been full of murder, and for a moment, Modiri had actually feared for his life. Now, the young man scowled convincingly enough, but Modiri saw a complicity in his eyes. Perhaps the plan would unfold exactly as Amir had envisioned. So far, everything had progressed without complication. He focused his mind on the task at hand: *Stay calm, appear strong in front of the other ambassadors, and time my rebellion according to the plan.* When Rostami scouted ahead—that would be the signal. He prayed silently for the strength and courage to carry out his orders. He thought of his wife, Fatemeh, and his only living son, Cyrus.

What I do, I do for them. After all I have done already, this last mountain I can climb. But if I do fail, it will be my honor to die for my family, for Persia, and for Allah.

He reached back, took Felicity Long's hand, and helped her through the low entryway. Her delicate fingers trembled in his grip, and her cheeks were streaked with tears. Modiri steeled himself and showed her a brave and chivalrous face. He hoped that in the decadent West, women could still recognize such things. This thought made him wonder how Felicity Long felt about trying to live the life of a man now.

Behind her, the elderly British ambassador, David Cochran, followed. Gripping the metal frame of the entryway, he tried to step over the four-inch-tall lip at the bottom, but the toe of his wingtips caught the edge, and he stumbled through the hole. His knee struck the ground on the other side, and he cried out in pain.

"Silence," Rostami hissed, and struck the man in the back of the neck with the butt of his AK-47. The British ambassador bit his lip, holding in another cry, as tears streamed down his cheeks. Normally, Modiri would have found the Brit's display of weakness both feminine and disgusting, but given his own fear, a wave of empathy for his ambassador colleagues washed over him. Instead of rejecting the feeling, Modiri decided to harness it and use it to legitimize his performance.

Rostami shoved Cochran forward.

Modiri caught him by the shoulders, steadying the man and keeping him from another painful fall. "It will be all right," Modiri whispered in the man's ear.

Cochran met Modiri's gaze with grateful eyes.

Rostami herded them deeper into the tunnel, which was tall enough for them to stand upright. Sterile, blue-light emergency beacons glowed at regularly spaced intervals, giving the corridor an unnerving alien atmosphere. The tunnel curved to the right. After thirty meters or so, they came to a junction—one corridor continuing straight, the other angling off to the right. The left tunnel was labeled **FDR DRIVE/ EAST RIVER ACCESS**. The right tunnel was labeled **UN CONSOLIDATION TOWER/MIDTOWN TUNNEL**.

"Go right," Rostami said, shoving Modiri in the back.

They walked for at least five minutes. When Modiri glanced over his shoulder, he could no longer see the entrance to the fork behind him.

Suddenly, Rostami grabbed him roughly by the collar of his dress shirt and jerked him back. "Stop," he commanded.

Modiri stopped.

Rostami walked around the group from the back to the front. "Against the wall, all of you," he commanded.

The three ambassadors complied. Modiri was delighted when Ambassador Long reached out and desperately gripped his arm. He patted her hand, but then softly released her grip. He would need to be unencumbered to accomplish his next task. Thirty seconds of violence and then it would be over. After that, he could again go back to using his intellect and gift of oral persuasion to serve Allah. During the ensuing period of captivity and hostage negotiation, he would be the strength for the group and become instrumental in convincing his captors to accept Tehran's terms of release.

"Watch them," Rostami commanded his young accomplice. "I'm going to scout ahead."

That was the signal. As soon as Rostami disappeared from view, he would rush the young jihadist. He would wrestle away the AK-47 and shoot the martyr. It was an honor to die in the service of Allah. On hearing the gunshot, Rostami would return and disarm him. Modiri hoped the "disarming" would not be too painful. Amir had made Rostami promise to show restraint when inflicting violence on Modiri, but Modiri had never trusted the man.

He would count to ten and then launch his assault.

"Stay behind me," he whispered to the US ambassador, and began his countdown.

CHAPTER 40

Dempsey clutched the door handle in his left hand and his Sig516 in his right.

His radio crackled, and a voice in his ear said, "Team One, this is Team Two. In position and waiting for your signal."

"Copy. In three, two, one, go."

Dempsey pushed the door open to the General Assembly Hall. The first thing he noticed was the tripod set up in the center aisle of the hall, pointed at the rostrum, with its black-marble podium and towering, gilded rear wall. Twenty-five hundred square feet of hand-laid gold leaf was about to be ruined by automatic weapon fire. He didn't care. Standing on the rostrum, front and center, were four terrorists—two on each side—flanking a dozen delegates kneeling beneath the Al Qaeda flag. The flag of murder and terror covered the iconic United Nations emblem symbolizing peace and unity. Behind the delegates, a man clad in a black robe and mask stood with his arms folded across his chest. A long, curved knife dangled from the black sash tied about his waist. Dempsey's worst nightmare had come home to roost. Al Qaeda was about to broadcast the ritualized beheading of the world's ambassadors of peace for the entire planet to see.

Dempsey took all this and more in during the fraction of a second before he cleared his corners. As his teammates fanned out to his left and right, gunshots rang out in the massive eighteen-hundred-seat auditorium. Team Two's HRT sharpshooters in the press balcony were going to work.

Straight ahead, a jihadist brought his rifle up to his shoulder. Dempsey squeezed off two rounds, finding the terrorist's neck and forehead. Blood, bone, and brains painted gruesome modern art on the wooden wall panel behind the man. He dropped to a combat crouch and scanned over his Sig516, one eye focusing through the EOTech Holosite. A man in a bulky vest screamed and ran toward a large cluster of delegates huddled together to Dempsey's left. With a three-round burst, he removed the suicide bomber's head from his body. The terrorist manning the video camera in the center aisle fumbled for his rifle, but there was a loud *pop pop* from Dempsey's right, and the man's head disappeared in a pink puff of bloody smoke. From the corner of his eye, he saw the jihadist in the black robe swinging his knife at the neck of a panicked delegate, but Grimes dropped him with a double tap to the chest.

His team of five—four from Ember and the one HRT operator—moved forward, each engaging and firing at targets in their fields of fire. At the same time, the FBI Team Two shooters in the balcony provided cover fire and hit targets of their own. In less than ten seconds, it was over. The jihadists lay in crumpled heaps, while kneeling hostages and other delegates were frozen with shock.

There was a moment of eerie silence as the five operators scanned the room thoroughly for other targets. Then a woman began to scream. Several of the people kneeling at the front of the hall collapsed forward, fainting.

"Team One in the main hall," Dempsey announced into the radio. He swept a full arc, sighting through his Holosite, while the rest of the team did the same. "Main hall secure."

As they advanced toward the rostrum, Smith hollered, "We're the FBI hostage rescue team. We're here to help you. Please stay calm. Everything is going to be okay."

Several of the hostages looked up now for the first time, and from the front rows, dozens of people got up from their seats and began moving toward the center aisle. Dempsey knew that in a moment the room would be chaos.

"Team Two entering the main hall," called a voice from the main entrance. Dempsey looked over his shoulder and saw his new buddy, the HRT unit lead, walking down the steps. Someone nudged his left arm, and Dempsey turned around and found Smith standing shoulder-to-shoulder beside him.

"I don't see Felicity Long," Smith said, holding a laminated photograph of the US ambassador in his hand.

"Ambassador Masoud Modiri—Ambassador Felicity Long— Ambassador David Cochran—this is the FBI," Dempsey shouted. "We are here to rescue you. Show yourselves." He scanned the room but saw nothing except the panicked mob of people now moving up the center aisle toward them.

"We're about to get mobbed," Smith said.

"They took them," said a tiny voice to Dempsey's right. Standing in the row of seats next to him was a middle-aged woman of Asian descent—a tiny voice for a tiny woman. "The terrorists took Ms. Long and the others to the tunnels."

"Show me," Dempsey said. She pointed at a blue light flashing over a set of double doors in the corner of the hall. "Thank you," Dempsey said, moving into the row in front of her, sidestepping his way toward the far wall. "Team One on me," he hollered over his shoulder.

His team followed him into the delegate seating area, just as the surging crowd of hostages made it to where they had been. He looked back and saw Team Two's green-suited FBI agents trying to pacify the swarming crowd.

At the end of the row, Dempsey sprinted toward the blue flashing light. He skidded to a halt at the exit and cautiously opened the left side door. After a quick scan, he entered the hallway with his team in tow. At the end of the hallway, he saw a staircase leading down to the basement.

"They have the US and UK ambassadors, so fire with discipline," he said. "I have the lead."

He charged down the concrete steps into the basement. After a quick scan, he spied the entrance to the tunnels—a hatch-style door swung ajar on its hinges. He sidled up next to the edge of the frame and glanced inside.

"Clear."

He stepped through the hatch and into the tunnel. Scanning over his rifle, he cleared both directions then advanced five paces in a low crouch. He drifted left until he hugged the wall and paused for his team to join him. He chopped a hand forward, and they moved in unison—he and Mendez on the left wall, and Smith, Grimes, and the HRT operator on the right. They moved swiftly and silently for fifteen meters, then the tunnel began to curve to the right. Pools of shadow between the emergency blue lighting seemed to be getting bigger as they went. As he approached the end of the bend, Dempsey raised a closed hand over his head and took a knee.

Fifteen meters ahead, the tunnel split—one corridor continuing straight, and the other diverging to the right. This deep underground, their radios and mobile phones would be of little use. That meant no guidance from Jarvis and Hansen in the mobile TOC. He looked at Smith and shook his head.

Through clenched teeth, Dempsey said the four words every team leader dreads most. "Time to split up."

As he read the paint-stenciled letters for the left tunnel, he mumbled the words, "FDR Drive, East River access." He glanced right. "UN Consolidation Tower, Midtown Tunnel."

"Whatcha think, John?" Smith said.

Dempsey closed his eyes and listened, hoping to hear footsteps or voices echoing in one of the tunnels, but all he could hear was the whir of the ventilation fans and the buzz of the emergency lighting fixtures.

When in doubt, go right, Kate always used to joke.

He opened his eyes.

"Smith and Mendez, take the left tunnel," Dempsey said. Turning to the HRT operator and Grimes, he said, "You two come with me."

"Rendezvous back here?" Smith asked.

Dempsey shook his head. "If you hear gunfire but you ain't in the fight, then you're in the wrong tunnel."

"Roger that," Mendez said with a smirk.

"Move out," Dempsey said, and advanced into the right tunnel. He hugged the left wall, Grimes took the right wall, and the HRT operator walked the middle, lagging a few paces to form a *V*.

Ten meters in.

Twenty.

At twenty-five meters, the tunnel doglegged, obscuring his line of sight. He paused at the corner and looked at Grimes. *Ready?*

She nodded.

They crept around the bend and spied the three missing ambassadors with their backs pressed against the wall. A single terrorist holding an AK-47 paced in front of them. The jihadist was looking off to his right, down the tunnel. Suddenly, the Iranian ambassador sprang forward and grabbed the stock and barrel of the terrorist's rifle.

What the fuck is he doing?

The two men wrestled over the weapon, but then the terrorist seemed to give up and practically handed the weapon to Masoud Modiri.

Dempsey advanced in a tactical crouch, keeping a red dot on the Iranian ambassador's forehead as he closed the gap. "FBI—drop the weapon!" he hollered.

Both the terrorist and Modiri whirled toward him, shock on their faces. Modiri looked confused and looked back at the terrorist, then

back at the team as they surged down the corridor. Through his holographic sight, Dempsey watched Modiri point the machine gun at the
terrorist and squeeze the trigger.

The roar of the AK-47 discharging in the tunnel was deafening. The
left side of the young jihadist's face evaporated in a cloud of blood and
bone. The terrorist bellowed a dissonant, gurgling scream as he pitched
backward against the wall. With a violent spasm, he slid to the ground,
leaving a wide trail of blood and something else on the wall behind him,
and ending in a lifeless pile at Modiri's feet.

The team moved in on the three ambassadors.

"Drop the weapon, Modiri," Dempsey called out, his voice cool
and collected. Grimes continued down the right wall, closing off the
tunnel to encircle the group.

Modiri looked at him, his face a twisted mask of confusion and fear.

"What are you doing?" Ambassador Long shouted, moving between
Dempsey and Modiri. "He's with us. He just saved us."

Dempsey pushed the woman aside with his left forearm and stepped
in front of her, placing himself between her and Modiri. Ambassador
Cochran stayed pressed against the wall, his head jerking back and
forth between Modiri and Dempsey, his mouth open and his hands
over his head.

"Drop the weapon," Dempsey ordered again. He held the targeting
dot in the middle of Modiri's face—the red light from the laser designator blinding the Iranian. Grimes had shifted farther on her arc to the
left, clear from his field of fire. He saw her red dot on the side of the
Iranian's head. Modiri raised his arms in the air, but the AK-47 was still
clutched in his right hand by the grip, index finger still on the trigger.

"I am the Iranian ambassador to the United Nations," Modiri said,
raising his chin in defiance and puffing out his chest. "Lower your
weapons."

"I know exactly who you are," Dempsey said.

"What the hell are you guys doing?" the HRT operator said.

Dempsey ignored the FBI man. Modiri was stalling, and it set his nerves on fire. He tensed his right index finger, putting pressure on his trigger.

"If you don't put the weapon—"

A muzzle flash behind Grimes and the deafening thunder of another AK-47 discharging in the tunnel drowned out his voice and sent the standoff straight to hell. To his horror, Grimes screamed and pitched forward. She hit the ground facedown. The US ambassador screamed and started running in the wrong direction. The British ambassador fainted and slid to the floor.

Events shifted into slow motion.

The HRT operator ducked and scrambled toward where Grimes lay on the ground.

Dempsey locked eyes with Modiri, who was still clutching the AK-47.

In that moment, time froze. Like a slide show in his mind, the smiling faces of his Tier One SEAL brothers flashed through his mind. Thiel manning the BBQ grill; Spaz and Pablo arguing about which superhero made the best operator; Gabe, Rousch, and Gator doing the chair dance at Zach's bar mitzvah, Helo sucking on a beer . . . all gone. All gone, thanks to this man and his brother.

Modiri's eyes went wide, and his lips curled with rage. "Alluhu Akbar!" he screamed, his face twisting in a homicidal fury. The Iranian brought the rifle to his shoulder but aimed at the US ambassador instead of Dempsey.

The round from Dempsey's Sig516 hit Modiri just above the bridge of his nose, silencing the homicidal scream and splitting the top of the man's head apart. Modiri stumbled backward, looking like someone who had just been hit in the forehead with an ax. Dempsey fired again as the body fell, the second bullet hitting the Iranian in the middle of the chest.

He was aware of a series of pops to his left as the HRT guy, crouching over Grimes, engaged the target retreating down the tunnel. He was aware of the whispered cries from Felicity Long: "He was going to shoot me. Why was he going to shoot me?" He was aware of these things, but his only concern now was Elizabeth Grimes. He flew to her side. He wouldn't lose another teammate. Not today.

The tunnel was silent now.

"Clear," the HRT guy said. "The shooter is down."

Dempsey quickly scanned Grimes's body and the ground around her for blood. No blood, but he did find a jagged hole in the back of her vest, just below her left shoulder blade. He hunched over to see her face. Her eyes were open, and her mouth was pulled back in a grimace.

"I'm gonna roll you onto your back," he told her. As he did, she winced—a good sign.

"Wow, that fucking hurts," she hissed. Dempsey stroked the hair out of her face, and she looked up at him and tried to smile. "Thanks for the tip about wearing my SAPI plate," she said, and then coughed. "Still hurts like a bitch, though."

Dempsey flashed her smile. "Yeah, trust me, I know."

Footsteps echoed in the tunnel behind him. Dempsey spun around, his Sig516 trained down the tunnel. In his ear he heard Smith's voice. "One, this is Two. Coming to you."

At the same time, Mendez hollered, "FBI. Don't shoot!"

Dempsey lowered his weapon and looked over at the HRT guy, who was now standing and staring down at him.

"You shot the fucking Iranian ambassador," the agent said, pale-faced with disbelief.

Smith fell in beside Dempsey, surveyed the scene and said, "No, *you* just shot the mastermind of the biggest terror plot since 9/11. HRT uncovered the plot, and you shot the leader and rescued the US and British ambassadors. You're a hero, my friend."

The HRT operative stared at him, completely perplexed.

"And we were never here," Dempsey added.

Smith slipped a USB memory stick into the agent's right chest pocket. "Turn this over to Agent Hansen. Tell him that everything he needs to know about the plot is on here," Smith said in a hushed voice.

"Who the hell are you guys?"

"No one," Mendez said, and slapped the man on the back. The agent looked at him, realization spreading slowly across his face.

Dempsey looked up at Smith, grateful for his friend's perfect timing.

"Rostami?" Smith asked.

Dempsey nodded down the tunnel. "Our HRT friend here said he bagged him, but we should probably confirm."

"Agreed," Smith said. He looked at Grimes. "You all right?"

"Yeah," she said with a grimace. "You boys go. Mendez can keep me company till you get back."

Dempsey stood. "You heard the lady."

"Age before beauty," Smith said, gesturing down the tunnel.

Together, Dempsey and Smith advanced down the tunnel, weapons at the ready. After a few meters, when he didn't see a crumpled body sprawled on the ground, Dempsey's heart rate picked up. He glanced at Smith.

"I don't see a body," Smith whispered.

Dempsey nodded.

They pushed on, and Dempsey felt like he had that night on the deck of the *Darya-ye Noor*. Same stillness. Same eerie "This was too easy" feeling.

He felt an ambush coming.

Five meters . . . seven meters . . . ten . . .

On the ground, two feet in front of him, he spied what looked like a small puddle of oil. He stopped next to it, knelt, and dipped his left index finger in the liquid. He held his finger up for inspection, and then rolled the liquid between his thumb and fingertip to check the viscosity.

Not oil.

In the dim blue aura of the tunnel's emergency lighting system, blood looked black.

"Blood?" Smith asked.

Dempsey nodded and got back to his feet. Two feet away, he saw another drop, and then another. They followed the trail of blood until it suddenly stopped. Dempsey surveyed the tunnel walls for possible exits or alcoves, but found nothing.

"He must have stopped the bleeding," Smith whispered.

"Too bad. I was hoping to find the bastard bled out."

They pushed on until they reached another fork in the tunnel. This time the right fork was labeled **UN CONSOLIDATION TOWER**, and the left fork was labeled **MIDTOWN TUNNEL**.

"Split up?" Smith asked.

"No way. Not this time," Dempsey said.

"Agreed."

"When in doubt, go right?"

Smith rubbed his chin. "Construction on the Consolidation Tower isn't even close to finished. My money says that tunnel dead-ends at a construction wall."

Dempsey nodded. "Left it is."

They took the left tunnel, and after a few meters the background noise began to increase in volume. As they advanced, the whir of ventilation fans became so loud that Dempsey lost the sound of his footsteps and breathing. Ahead, the passage ended at a steel door. He tightened his grip on his rifle and dropped into a tactical crouch for the approach.

At the door, Dempsey studied the doorjamb and the handle. The door opened "in." He gestured for Smith to open and he would clear.

Smith nodded and mouthed a silent count—*One, two, three*—and pulled the handle.

Dempsey glided through the opening—clearing while sighting over with the barrel of his Sig. The next room was tiny—a closet, really, no bigger than six feet by six feet—and smelled of enamel paint and engine exhaust. Directly facing him was another door, the same configuration as the last, but this one was labeled DANGER—TUNNEL ACCESS.

Smith stepped up beside him. "Let's do it again."

Dempsey nodded and readied his weapon.

One, two, three . . .

Smith pulled the handle.

Dempsey took a step but immediately caught himself, nearly tumbling headfirst into the Midtown Tunnel. "Jesus Christ," he bellowed.

Smith jerked him backward by the straps on his vest.

"Thanks, dude," Dempsey said, gawking at the two-lane underground highway in front of them.

"Don't mention it."

The tunnel was empty, not a single vehicle in sight.

"What the fuck?" Dempsey said.

"This is the eastbound spur," Smith said. "The NYPD must have shut down the entrance. Emergency protocol for any terrorist attack. Any cars already down here would have been oblivious to the closure and exited into Queens."

"Shit," Dempsey said. "The motherfucker got away."

Smith nodded. "Yeah. This was their end game. This was how Rostami was going to get the ambassadors out."

A knot formed in Dempsey's stomach. "I really wanted to put a bullet in that psychopath's head," he said. "For what he did to that poor girl in Frankfurt."

Smith put a hand on Dempsey's shoulder. "I know, bro. Me, too."

"I'm gonna find that sonuvabitch," Dempsey said.

"And I'm gonna help you," said Smith, and let the door slam shut behind them.

CHAPTER 41

607 Horseshoe Drive
Williamsburg, Virginia
May 26, 2100 EDT

The buzz of his mobile phone vibrating on the table interrupted dinner.

Jarvis was dining alone, as usual, which meant there was no one to offend by checking it. The text message was from Ian Baldwin:

```
Urgent. Sent u e-mail on the high side.
Call after you read—Ian
```

He stood, left his half-eaten plate of grilled salmon and vegetables on the table, and walked to his personal TOC in the basement. After satisfying the biometric security sensor, he pushed open the hidden panel door, stepped inside, and inhaled the cold, odorless air. The computer monitor on his desk showed a push notification of the waiting e-mail. He logged in to his secure high-side server and then minimized all the OPSEC briefs and security updates he had yet to read. He clicked on his e-mail login and tapped in his username and password.

At the top of his inbox, with a red exclamation point marking the message as time sensitive, was the e-mail from Ian. He scanned the text in three seconds.

He had expected this.

In the partitioned corner of his mind, his own cerebral, intracranial TOC, Jarvis had already made plans for this scenario. He felt nothing—not surprise, not anger, not rage, not even hatred. He had already battled these emotions when Ian first briefed him on the second burner phone during the flight from Frankfurt to Geneva. All he felt now was the compulsion to act.

Baldwin had dutifully copied Dempsey, Smith, and Quinton Thomas on the e-mail string. That was standard procedure for a message such as this—one containing sensitive information with safety and security implications for the team. Still, Baldwin's rigorous adherence to protocol was incredibly inconvenient. Jarvis checked his watch and quickly calculated his head start:

Geographical proximity to the target: + twelve minutes

Preparation: + seven minutes

Tactical planning: + thirty minutes

Group consensus and debate handicap: + eleven minutes

Inebriation handicap: +/– ten minutes

The "Dempsey Factor" offset: – ten minutes

TOTAL ESTIMATED HEAD START: forty to sixty minutes

Jarvis closed the e-mail without responding. For urgent messages, the system would generate a time stamp and an automated reply to the sender with notification that the message had been read.

He expected calls from both Smith and Baldwin any minute, but he would let them go straight to voice mail. He tapped a code in a small dialog box in the upper-left corner of his center computer screen, and a flat, black glass biometric reader hissed open beside his keyboard. He scanned his thumbprint. A pop-up window opened on his screen.

ARE YOU SURE YOU WANT TO ENABLE SYSTEM
LOCKDOWN?

He clicked "Yes."

Every monitor in his TOC went dark.

From his pocket, he retrieved a stainless-steel Kershaw tactical knife. A flick of his thumb and the talonlike blade arced open. With his right index finger, he probed the skin along his left side above his hip. Finding the lump he was looking for, he plunged the point of the blade into his flesh and gave the knife a twist. He withdrew the blade, and blood immediately mushroomed from the hole. Using his right thumb and forefinger, he milked the tissue until a bloody lump the size of a camera battery popped to the surface. He used the knife to cut it free from a scar-tissue tether and held it up for inspection in the light. Satisfied he'd gotten the right implant, he dropped the micro GPS tracker next to his tactical phone on the desk, where both items would remain for the next several hours—perhaps longer—until he returned. If he returned. He pressed a sterile dressing against the hole in his side and walked out of his personal TOC. He had chitosan-based wound dressing in the med-kit in his car. The stuff burned like hell, but it worked, and the chitosan polymer would stop the bleeding almost immediately for such a small wound. This was something he could take care of on the way.

He walked past his Ember-modified GMC Yukon to his personal vehicle. His work truck needed to stay in the garage tonight; it would take a helluva lot more than a knife to remove the Yukon's tracker.

He climbed into the driver's seat of his silver BMW X5, pressed the ignition start button, and shifted the automatic transmission into drive.

Time to go have a conversation with his boss.

CHAPTER 42

Dempsey leaned back on a deck chaise and told himself he didn't feel his age.

He took a long pull from his beer and smiled.

All was not right in the world tonight, but given the constraints of his new life, this was probably as good as it would get.

The air smelled of honeysuckle and fresh-cut grass, and occasionally he'd catch a waft of smoky BBQ as the breeze blew past the Weber cooling in the corner of his deck. It was the perfect night for a cookout, and he'd called the gang over to his place at the last minute. Jarvis had declined, Wang never responded, and Mendez said he had a hot date. So it wound up being just the three of them. Smith leaned against the railing, staring at Grimes's ass as she bent over the Igloo to fish three more longnecks from the icy slush. He decided he liked his new team, especially these two. They had grit and attitude. And they were both damn good operators. Originally, he figured that after he got his vengeance, he would drift off into the sunset—on a sailboat, or a fishing boat, or some damn thing. Now, he realized he was home.

"Here," Grimes said, handing him another beer. She sat down on the twin chaise beside him, set her beer down on the deck, and tossed the remaining beer to Smith. "Yaoow," she said, wincing and clutching the left side of her chest.

"How are the ribs?" Dempsey asked as he watched her hiss a short breath out of clenched teeth.

"Hurts like hell," she said, taking a long swig.

"Mendez and Wang should be here," Smith said.

"Yeah, if they're too cool to hang with us," Grimes said with a laugh, "then fuck 'em. Just means more beer for us." She extended her arm to clink bottles with Dempsey and winced again.

"Mendez claims to have a hot date," Dempsey said. "And Wang is probably off playing Dungeons and Dragons somewhere."

Grimes gave him a funny look. "Dungeons and Dragons? Jesus, how old *are* you, Dempsey?"

He laughed. "Okay, fine, maybe Wang is off playing Assassin's Creed on his Xbox—is that better?" This time he clinked her bottle with his.

"What do you think will happen to Ember?" she asked, her tone turning serious.

"Don't look at me," Dempsey said. He nodded toward Smith. "There's the man you need to ask."

Smith shrugged. "This last mission was our charter, but that doesn't mean we're done. We uncovered the UN plot and stopped Masoud Modiri, but Amir Modiri and Behrouz Rostami are still out there. Hell, there's plenty of other counterterror work that needs to be done. I think, with Dempsey on board and the Special Activities Unit concept, Ember could be the next evolution of Tier One operations." Smith took a long pull from his beer. "But, that being said, we all need to prepare ourselves for the most likely scenario—that Ember will be shut down."

Dempsey felt a surge of frustration. Like so many times in the past, he just wasn't ready to ring the bell. Not in BUD/S, not on the white-side SEAL teams, and not during his tenure in Navy Tier One. He realized now that he couldn't ring the bell on Ember, either. "Did Jarvis say anything specific to you after New York? Anything about going after Amir Modiri and his VEVAK minions?"

"Nope," Smith said. "He has a meeting in DC tomorrow with our sponsor, but until then, even he doesn't know our fate."

"Wait, you're telling me the all-knowing, all-powerful Kelso Jarvis is actually in the dark about something?" Grimes said, trying to lighten the mood. "I call bullshit."

This time they all laughed and clinked their three beer bottles together.

Dempsey watched Grimes smile and pull her legs up beneath her in the chair. Tonight he was getting a glimpse of the girl beneath the armor—feminine, playful, and young. When they first met, he'd con-sidered her a nuisance. Over the past month, his opinion had morphed three times: from nuisance to adversary, from adversary to liability, and finally from liability to asset. During that time, he hadn't devoted any time to ruminating about what was beneath the surface—what filled her with such motivation and anger. He'd been so focused on his own rage that he didn't give a shit about the reason for hers. Everything they'd been through had changed that.

"Mind if I ask you a personal question?" Dempsey said.

Grimes hesitated a beat before answering. "You can ask. Doesn't mean I'll answer it."

"What's your story? Why did you join Ember?"

She shook her head. "Sorry, off-limits."

"All right," he said. "Then your NOC, Elizabeth Grimes, did you pick that?"

"Yep."

"Any significance?"

Her lips curled into a wry grin. "Of course."

Dempsey took a pull from his beer. "Care to share?"

"Only if you promise not to laugh."

He drew an *X* across his chest with a fingertip. "Cross my heart."

She shifted her gaze to somewhere in the night sky. "Elizabeth was my mother's name. She wasn't in the military, but she was the strongest woman I've ever known—mentally, emotionally . . . spiritually. She was diagnosed with breast cancer when I was sixteen. I was so scared, but she fought it and beat it. We became best friends after that. But four years later, the cancer came back, and this time they found it in her liver, too. They said she would last three months, but she made it thirteen. I . . . uh . . . I pray every night that I can live with half the courage she did."

She took a sip of her beer.

"I think you do," Dempsey said. "What you did at the UN is proof of that."

She shrugged. Her eyes were wet now.

"And Grimes? Where'd that come from?"

She laughed, while wiping her eyes with the back of her wrist. "Grimes I borrowed from *The Walking Dead*."

"The zombie show?" Smith asked. "Are you serious?"

"Yeah, the lead character, Rick Grimes, is a total badass. He never quits. No matter the odds, no matter how miserable and terrible and hopeless it gets, he just kills every fucking zombie who tries to hurt his family . . . That's what happens when someone goes after *my* family."

After a long pause, Dempsey said, "Sounds like Rick and I would get along."

"Most definitely," she said, then got up and walked over to the deck railing, putting her back to both of them.

Dempsey glanced at Smith.

Smith nodded. "Mind if I check my high side?" he asked, but he was already heading toward the sliding glass doors.

"My house is your house—I mean, like, literally, they're exactly the same," Dempsey said. "Sure, knock yourself out."

After Smith disappeared inside, Dempsey asked, "What will you do if they shut us down?"

"It's hard to think past tomorrow," Grimes said, not turning around. "I burned a lot of bridges to get here. I don't know if going back to my old job is an option. Even if I could go back, I don't know if I want to . . . What about you? Will you go back to the teams?"

Dempsey shook his head. "Can't," he said simply.

She turned around.

They locked eyes, and he felt a twinge in his chest.

"John?" came Smith's voice from the house, interrupting the moment. From the somber intensity of his voice, Dempsey knew something was wrong.

They followed him to the TOC in Dempsey's basement, where Smith pointed to the middle of three computer screens.

"What's wrong?" Dempsey asked.

"Read this," Smith said, and slid out of the way. Grimes crowded in beside them. "Just Dempsey," Smith said, putting a hand on her shoulder.

"Fuck that," Dempsey said, pulling Grimes in closer by a belt loop on her low-riding jeans.

He began to read, unsure at first what he was seeing.

"Ian sent it to Jarvis, but he copied the department directors."

"What the hell is he talking about?" Dempsey asked. The message rambled on and on about intersecting lines among satellites and cell towers, and graphing them against the movement of subjects from some list Jarvis had given him. Then, there was a math equation in the middle of the text that made Dempsey's head hurt. "Shane, what are you showing me?" he finally said with irritation.

"It's an algorithm to figure out who was messaging and sending data from a series of burner phones," Grimes said.

"To who?" Dempsey asked.

"Amir Modiri," Smith said.

"So what?" Dempsey asked, standing up. "Do we go to the hangar and see if they match the burners we recovered off the Al Qaeda shit-heads in New York?"

"These calls are all dated much earlier," Smith said.

"Before the massacres in Yemen and Djibouti," Grimes added, her voice now a whisper.

Smith leaned in and scrolled down in the message.

They read the last paragraph together. The evidence was damning. The White House chief of staff, Robert Kittinger, had communicated with Amir Modiri on eleven different occasions, the last call placed ninety minutes before launching the raid in Yemen. This was more than just an OPSEC violation; Kittinger had compromised the entire mission by providing time-sensitive information, communication frequencies, and status reports to the enemy.

"We need to call the boss," Smith said, and reached for the secure phone on the desk. As he reached for it, his secure cell phone rang. "Smith," he said. He listened for a moment. "We just saw it. Did you talk with the boss?" Another pause. "Understood. We'll head in . . . Okay, I'll keep trying, too. What happened to the detail?" He chuckled. "Well, that's Jarvis, right?"

Smith shoved his phone back in his pocket and turned to Dempsey. "That was Quinton Thomas. We're on full recall. He wants everyone at the hangar until this is sorted out." He fished out his phone again and started to dial. "I'm gonna call Ian and see if he knows where the boss is. The stamp on the e-mail shows Jarvis has read it, so he already knows what's going on."

Dempsey felt an eerie calm envelop him, followed by a vision of perfect clarity. He knew now the answer to Grimes's question. He knew what he needed to do next, and when he was done, there would be no *after*.

He shoved past Smith and opened the heavy glass door to his weapons room. He selected a form-fitting backpack—one he had worn on countless operations with the teams—and opened it on the countertop. He pulled two handguns from the shelf—the Sig Sauer 229 and the more compact 239. He thought of these two weapons as an extension of himself. He had carried them in Iraq, Afghanistan, Yemen, Egypt, Somalia, and at least half a dozen other shithole countries—countries where he had fought and bled and cried for his nation while that fucker Kittinger ate steak at the Old Ebbitt Grill in Washington. He took the short-barrel Sig516 and grabbed a PEQ-4 IR target designator and snapped it onto the rail.

"What are you doing, John?" Smith called to him.

Dempsey didn't turn around. "Ending this," he said, and slipped the bag with his night vision gear into the backpack. "Completing the goddamn mission and fulfilling our charter."

"Slow down. We need to think this through," Smith said. "We're talking about the chief of staff to the president of the United States, for Christ's sake."

"He's just a man."

"What you're talking about is treason, John."

"Yes, exactly. Kittinger is a traitor—a crime punishable by death."

Smith ran his fingers through his hair. "We need to talk to Jarvis."

"Fine, call Jarvis," Dempsey said. He stripped off his black T-shirt and then slipped on his low-profile body armor, dragging the rough Velcro straps over his bare skin. "You guys can talk about this all night long, but I'm going to take care of fucking business."

"I'm going, too," Grimes said, and reached for a pistol from Dempsey's top shelf.

"Like hell, you are," Dempsey said, grabbing her by the wrist.

Grimes shook off his hand and shoved him backward.

He recoiled and took an uncertain step toward her.

"Fuck you, John," she said, pushing him again. "This is my mission, too. I deserve to be here—just as much as you do!"

Dempsey felt his body surge with anger. "This has nothing to do with you wanting to play dress-up and pretend you're an operator. I don't give a shit about your pedigree or whoever the hell you're trying to impress. They were my brothers, Grimes. This is my justice to serve."

"He was my brother, too, goddamn it!" she screamed, her spittle splattering his face.

She tore her wrists free with a Krav Maga move he should have seen coming and pounded her fists against his chest.

Instead of stopping her, he let her pound on him. A silent voice whispered epiphany in his mind. He grabbed her in a bear hug and pulled her close.

"Who are you?" he whispered, his lips by her ear.

"I'm Kelsey Clarke," she sobbed. "I'm Jonathan Clarke's sister."

SO1 Jonathan Clarke, USN. Tier One SEAL. Spaz, to his teammates. Fuck.

"I didn't know," he whispered. "I didn't know . . ."

At that, she stopped squirming and let him hug her.

Dempsey looked at Smith over a tousled mess of auburn hair. "She's coming with me," he said.

Smith threw his hands up in exasperation. "What the hell is wrong with you guys?"

"Jonathan Clarke was one of mine," Dempsey said, releasing Elizabeth from his grip. "He was in the TOC in Djibouti when it blew." He turned his back on Smith and resumed packing his bag. Grimes moved next to him and went to work, snapping an EOTech Holosite onto the top rail of a SOPOD M4. Dempsey handed her a night vision kit, and she slipped it into the bag. "I'll get you body armor," he said. He returned a moment later, adjusting the Velcro on one of his spare vests so it would fit her better. Grimes pulled her T-shirt over her head with no shame, and then pulled the body armor on over her head, her face tight with pain from her two fractured ribs beneath the black bruise on her otherwise perfect skin. She pulled her black T-shirt back on and selected a tactical knife with a long, folding blade for her pocket. Dempsey put a hand on her shoulder and then looked over at Smith, who was back on the computer. "What did Jarvis say?"

"I still can't reach him," Smith said. "Which is weird. I've tried his high-side and low-side phones, I've texted him, and sent an urgent e-mail—nothing."

"What did you tell him?" Dempsey asked. He selected his own tactical knife and then zipped the backpack and slung it over both shoulders. He checked the right panel for the two medical blowout kits he always kept packed. Hopefully he wouldn't need those tonight.

"That I urgently needed to speak with him," Smith said, snapping the lid of the laptop closed. He stood up. "But I have a feeling that doesn't matter now."

"Where are you going?" Dempsey asked.

"With you," Smith said. "You'll need eyes and ears. I downloaded what I could find on the house. I also pulled the details I need to hack the security system and tie into the cameras."

Dempsey placed a hand on Smith's shoulder and looked his *new* brother in the eyes.

Smith met his gaze. "We're a team. If we do this, we do it together."

Dempsey nodded and turned to leave, but Smith caught him by the shoulder. "Hold up," he said, jogging back to the weapons room. He returned a minute later with two tiny pistols that Dempsey wouldn't even consider for paperweights. "For this mission, you might want to reconsider your hardware selection." He handed one baby Sig to Dempsey and the other to Grimes, along with a threaded suppressor for each.

"What the hell is this?" Dempsey asked, looking disdainfully at the cap gun in his palm.

"That is a Sig P232 22LR, my friend," Smith said. "And that is what you're going to use to shoot Kittinger."

CHAPTER 43

John Dempsey ran his fingertip along the place where the jihadist's dagger had cut him. The scar wrapped his forearm like a serpent. It was an old wound, pearly white and smooth, all the pink and tenderness bleached away by sea, sun, and time. But now, in the dark of night, it burned. Burned with pride and prejudice. Burned with retribution.

Even in the dark, a man cannot forget his scars.

Dempsey waited, his NVGs tilted up and off his eyes. Grimes waited with him. He looked over at his battle buddy, his gaze drawn to her taut, muscular arms—pale and defined in the moon's shadow. They were hiding in the bushes that surrounded the bureaucrat's manicured lawn. She didn't notice his gaze because she was scanning the residential street with her NVGs.

They had conducted surveillance for over an hour, from these bushes and other equally scratchy and annoying shrubbery locations. Through the windows they had watched Kittinger drink scotch in his office, and they had watched the bureaucrat's two-man personal-security team depart around eleven thirty, a half hour after Mrs. Kittinger had retired upstairs for the evening. That left a roving patrol, which they would have to rely a bit on luck to avoid. They had all agreed they would take their own casualties rather than permit collateral damage. The chief of staff was a traitor, but the security guys were just doing their jobs.

While they waited, Smith acted as OTC in his SUV, giving them reports over their encrypted comms circuits about everything he saw inside the house. To Dempsey's surprise, Smith had managed to hack into the home security system and was streaming the video feeds on his laptop. Dempsey made a mental note to rib him about spending too much time with Wang.

"Just a few more minutes," Smith said in his earpiece. "I expect his security detail to do a drive-by."

"They already left," Dempsey whispered in his mike.

"I know, but typical protocol is to circle back after a little delay."

Dempsey clicked twice.

"I'm searching inside the house," Smith came back.

Smith is annoyingly chatty tonight, Dempsey thought.

"There's no camera in the bedroom, and I can't get a signal from the one in the library. I had it earlier . . . not sure what happened."

Dempsey clicked twice, hoping Smith would just shut up until it was time to go.

"Weird. I can't tell you where the target is . . . No motion in the house. Nothing on the parabolic . . . Lights are all out since the wife went upstairs. He's either in the library or the bedroom, because I sure as hell don't see him anywhere else."

Dempsey's mind flashed back to something Jarvis had said during their training: "*This is an entirely new world for you, John. This is making someone disappear from bed while his wife is sleeping beside him.*" Tonight it might come to that, but one way or another he was sending Kittinger straight to hell. They would clear the library first and hope the fucker was there, sleeping on the oversize leather couch they had seen before the library camera went dark.

In his peripheral vision, Dempsey saw a car drive down Kittinger's street. Grimes tracked it until it disappeared into the night. She turned to look at him, tilted her NVGs off her face, and gave him a thumbs-up.

"Zero, Two," she said. "Confirm security detail second pass."

"Roger," Smith said. "Sweeping the yard and the street now. Go on my count."

Dempsey adjusted his posture to a knee-down crouch, and Grimes did the same beside him. He snapped down his NVGs, and she did the same. To Dempsey's present regret, Smith had somehow convinced them to leave their SOPMOD M4s in the trunk, and so they were carrying the ridiculous .22-caliber, silenced peashooters. When Smith advised that he leave his P229 behind as well, Dempsey had refused. No way in hell was he going on a mission without a real pistol.

"Go," Smith said.

Stooped in a combat crouch, Dempsey led Grimes across the side yard, around to the back of the house. He hoped that Smith had interrupted the camera or inserted a loop or whatever he intended to do for any exterior cameras. He stopped at the backdoor access to the garage.

"We're at the door," he whispered.

"No cameras in the garage, but try and be quiet," Smith said.

Dempsey pulled a pry bar from his pack and wedged the angled tip into the gap between the lockset's faceplate and strike plate.

"You should try to pick it first," Grimes whispered.

He popped the pry bar. The old wooden door frame yielded with a satisfying crunch. "Consider it picked," he whispered, and followed her inside the two-car garage.

"Okay, we're in the garage," Dempsey said into his mike.

They made their way past a Lexus RX and a Cadillac CTS to the house door. He stopped by the door, slipped the pry bar back into his pack, and retrieved a MIC kit.

"Whatcha doing now?" Grimes whispered.

"Can't pop this one," Dempsey said. "Reinforced striker plate with a deadbolt."

"Are you crazy?" she said, looking at his hands as he prepped the material. "A breacher charge will wake the entire neighborhood."

"It's a MIC, not a breacher."

"What's a MIC?"

"An intermolecular composite—aka super thermite," Smith said over the channel. "It uses nanoparticle chemistry to create a high-energy, oxidizing, exothermic reaction."

"In other words," Dempsey whispered, inserting two wires into the yellow lump of polymer, "I'm going to burn the shit out of this lock."

Grimes grinned at him in the dark.

"Zero, One. I'll burn on your mark," Dempsey said.

"Security is interrupted for the next twelve seconds," Smith said. That was the maximum power surge tolerated by the system without tipping the alarm. "Burn it."

Dempsey started to press the MIC polymer into the lockset, but when he did, the door moved, swinging slowly open. He looked at Grimes, who stared back at him through her NVGs, mouth agape.

Dempsey pulled his Sig229 from his thigh holster, grabbed Grimes, and pulled her through the open door into a mudroom. He eased the door shut behind him, while Grimes drew her P232 with suppressor. She gave him a *"You're using the wrong gun"* look, but he ignored her. The mudroom was connected to a butler's pantry, which he presumed led to the kitchen. He scanned ahead, but he could only see part of the room. He crept forward, crouched low, and peeked into the kitchen.

Nothing.

Behind him, Grimes slid a wedge into the bottom of the garage entry door to keep it in place.

"Everything okay?" Smith asked.

Dempsey didn't answer. Something was terribly wrong, and they needed to be completely quiet. He raised a hand, and they moved silently into the kitchen, leading with their pistols.

"I see you in the kitchen," Smith said. "Tell me what you're doing."

Again, Dempsey stayed silent. He and Grimes cleared their corners—his to the left and hers to the right. He felt terribly uneasy without his rifle and PEQ-4 infrared designator. There simply was no substitute for a proper weapon with a holographic sight and a clip holding lots of bullets.

"Okay, fine, be that way," Smith said in his ear as they moved into what Dempsey guessed was the dining room.

"Kitchen camera is off. I'll kill the dining-room feed and bring the kitchen back online after the count," Smith said. "I'll call the play-by-play and try to stay ahead of you. After the dining room, clear the living room. Then, into the library. If he's not there, we'll head upstairs. Five seconds . . . four . . . three . . . two . . . one."

Dempsey kept them ahead of Smith's count, and they entered the dining room. He moved to the left to lead them away from the French doors, to prevent anyone who might be watching outside from seeing their shadows move across the thinly curtained glass.

"Ten seconds to cross the room. Next is the living room, and you'll move to the right. You'll see a set of wood-panel double doors on the far wall that leads to the library. The main staircase leading upstairs is across the foyer. Six seconds . . . five . . . four . . ."

Dempsey moved across the living room toward the double doors leading to the library. When he saw that the right-hand door was cracked open almost six inches, he slid left and pressed his back against the wall. Grimes did the same in mirror image on the opposite side. She looked at him for instruction. Dempsey pointed to his ear.

"Three . . ."

Dempsey thought he heard something—like the soft rustle of clothing.

"Two seconds, guys."

He thought of his dead brothers, and hot rage surged through every fiber of his body. On the other side of those doors, justice would finally be served.

"Go," Smith said.

Dempsey pushed the door open with his foot and cleared left, while Grimes followed and cleared right. After clearing his corner, Dempsey angled toward the desk. In the center of the room, behind a colonial period wooden desk, sat the president's chief of staff, Robert Kittinger. Dempsey stared at the man's chubby face, which was lit up from below by the light of the notebook computer monitor open in front of him. His head was tilted back against the backrest of his chair; the man's piggish nose and heavy jowls made him look like a contemplative bulldog dressed in a bathrobe. Dempsey put his pistol's night sights in the center of the man's chest.

He hesitated, waiting for Kittinger to startle or speak or snore, but the chief of staff stayed perfectly still.

Dempsey took a cautious step forward, his weapon a steady, unwavering platform in midair. He advanced to the edge of the desk. The man's eyes were open and staring at a spot somewhere over Dempsey's head. Then he noticed it—a thin tendril of black dribbling down Kittinger's right cheek from a black hole at the edge of his temple.

Black in the world of night vision.

Red in the light of day.

"Hello, John," a voice whispered to his right, freezing Dempsey in place. "I thought you might come—both of you."

He spun to his right, while Grimes backpedaled. In the corner of the room, steeped in shadow, a figure sat cross-legged and motionless on the floor, his back resting against a file cabinet. It took a moment for Dempsey's brain to register that the gray-green face he saw through his monocular night vision belonged to Kelso Jarvis.

"Skipper?"

With gloved hands, Jarvis collected the mess of folders spread out on the floor around him into a tidy stack. He shoved all but one of them into a bag propped against his leg. Then he stood.

"We should go," Jarvis said. "I'm sure you were in like the night, but time's up. I interrupted the surveillance feeds and auto-alarm features, but the alarm company *will* notice eventually."

Jarvis opened a file folder in front of the corpse at the desk and spread the pages out. Then he pulled a pistol from his belt, squeezed it into Kittinger's lifeless right hand, and raised the muzzle until it lined up with the hole in the man's right temple. He let go. The dead man's arm dropped to his side, and the pistol clattered to the floor.

"Time to go," Jarvis said, heading for the double doors.

Dempsey, finally recovering use of his faculties and his voice, said, "Hold on, Smith will lead us out."

Jarvis smiled. "Of course, Shane is here," he said, with what almost sounded to Dempsey like fatherly pride.

"We're a team, what did you expect?" Dempsey whispered back. "Zero, One. Ready for EXFIL. Library to rear entry. Give us the count and lead us out."

CHAPTER 44

International House of Pancakes
Manassas, Virginia
May 27, 0410 EDT

He should be happy, Dempsey told himself. He should feel a sense of satisfaction and vindication, but these were not the emotions he felt. Jarvis had taken the kill away from him, and he was struggling to accept it.

Was that selfish?

Yes.

Was he pissed about it anyway?

Absolutely.

He had deserved this one. He and Elizabeth . . .

"You haven't touched your food, John," Grimes said. "Are you okay?"

"Oh, he's just pissed that Jarvis took his kill," Smith said, shoveling a forkful of pancakes into his mouth.

Grimes looked from Smith to Dempsey. "Seriously?"

"Hell yes," Dempsey growled, breaking his fifteen minutes of silence. "Kittinger should have been mine."

Grimes shook her head. She took a sip of orange juice and said, "There are some things I will never understand about men, and that's one of them. The asshole is dead. Justice is served. End of story."

Dempsey turned to look at her. He had intended to glare at her like the big, grumpy brute that he was, but when he looked at her—attacking a piece of bacon like it was the last morsel of meat on planet Earth—all he could do was smile. Elizabeth Grimes, aka Kelsey Clarke, aka Spaz's kid sister, was finally at peace.

"You're right," he mumbled.

She looked up at him and made an exaggerated gesture of cupping her right ear with her hand. "Excuse me, I couldn't hear you. Could you please say that again?"

"I said you're right," he repeated, this time in a normal voice.

Smith joined in, cupping his hand over his ear. "But I couldn't hear you—say again?"

Dempsey laughed and yelled, "I said you're right."

The waitress at the counter looked up and shot him the stink-eye, which sent Grimes and Smith into an adolescent laughing fit.

Collecting herself, Grimes reached out and patted Dempsey's hand. "He didn't do it to steal your thunder," she said. "He didn't do it for any of the reasons your testosterone-charged, Navy SEAL brain would ever think of."

"Oh really," he said, taking his first bite of food. "Then, please, Your Highness, enlighten me with your royal wisdom."

This made her smile. "Jarvis was trying to protect you," she said, and then shifted her gaze to Smith. "And you . . . and me. All of us. He knew we'd go after Kittinger. So he acted first. That way if things went wrong, he'd take the fall. Him and him alone."

Dempsey looked at Smith. "You've known Jarvis a long time. What do you think?"

"I haven't known him as long as you, but that sounds like the Jarvis I know."

Dempsey raised his coffee cup. "To our fearless leader, Kelso Jarvis, who tried to take one for the team tonight."

"To Kelso Jarvis," Grimes and Smith said in unison, clicking mugs.

A comfortable silence fell over the group and lingered while they ate. *Comfortable* silence between teammates was a good thing, Dempsey had come to realize over the years.

When the sole waitress stepped outside the otherwise deserted pancake house to have a smoke, Dempsey spoke up. "There is one thing that still bothers me," he said in a hushed tone. "VEVAK must have had something on Kittinger . . . unless they bought him. Why else would he do it? It must have been blackmail, right?"

Smith shook his head. "I don't think so. I think Kittinger was a patriot. I think he truly believed he was securing our nation. I think the president wasn't listening to his advice on Iran, and he wanted to force Warner and the United Nations to see what we all know to be true—that no matter what President Esfahani says, or what agreements have been signed, Iran hasn't changed. The country is controlled by the Supreme Leader, and his followers believe that Iran is destined to rule the world at the head of a great Islamic caliphate. Maybe Kittinger understood this and feared a strengthened, emboldened Iran. Maybe he understood VEVAK's success manipulating and organizing the activities of Al Qaeda factions to serve Iran's hidden agenda, and wanted to expose VEVAK with a story the media couldn't possibly ignore. And maybe he saw the United States being lured into complacent appeasement of the Esfahani regime. I think Kittinger hoped to use the massacre of the Tier One SEALs to rally the president, Congress, and the Pentagon to take military action against Iran."

"If you truly believe that Kittinger was a patriot," Grimes whispered, "why did you help Dempsey and me go after him? If you thought the man's heart was in the right place, why take him out? Motive matters, right?"

Smith took a deep breath. "I don't know. I guess I got wrapped up in the moment."

"That's bullshit, Smith, and you know it," Dempsey said. "There are rules and there are lines. Kittinger crossed the line and made unwitting, nonconsenting martyrs of our brothers. That's the difference between a jihadist and a warrior. Kittinger *thought* he was an American patriot, but in reality he was an American jihadist. For that, he needed to be held accountable. You came with us tonight because in your heart, you felt the same."

He noticed Grimes was staring at him. "What?"

"Nice speech. Maybe you're not as big a meathead as I thought you were," she said with a sly grin.

"I have my moments."

"And Ember?" Grimes asked, looking back at Smith. "Why would Kittinger task us like he did?"

Smith ran his fingers through his hair. "That's a forty-million-dollar question."

"What's the forty-million-dollar answer?"

"This is me talking now, not Jarvis," Smith said, eyeing them both.

"Understood," Dempsey and Grimes replied in uncanny unison.

"He needed an experienced task force to collect enough evidence to prove VEVAK was the puppet master behind Yemen and Djibouti. Without evidence, he couldn't pin unequivocal blame on Tehran and make Iran enemy number one in the eyes of the world. But he also needed complete control and leverage, which is why he dissolved the JIRG and offered Jarvis a deal he couldn't refuse."

"But he had to know there was a chance we'd find out about his communication with Amir Modiri."

Smith shook his head. "Kittinger was an arrogant bastard and probably thought we wouldn't start digging in our own backyard. But he was no fool. You don't become chief of staff without knowing how to make deals and cover your ass. Ember was born in the black and outside the

DNI's purview, giving Kittinger complete autonomy and control. If something went wrong, all he had to do was pull the plug, deny Ember's existence, and mop up the mess. And don't forget about the ace in his back pocket."

"What ace?" Dempsey asked.

"Leverage," Smith said.

"On us?" Dempsey asked, confused.

"On some more than others." Smith reached into the messenger bag on the seat beside him, retrieved a folder, and slid it across the table to Grimes.

"What's this?" she asked, looking the folder.

"Leverage," he whispered, eyeing the waitress, who had just stepped back inside. "Jarvis asked me to give this to you. He told me to tell you, quote, 'This should take care of what the bastard had on you,' and that you would know what he was talking about."

Dempsey shook his head. That wasn't the only folder he remembered seeing Jarvis take from Kittinger's study.

Grimes snatched the folder off the table and clutched it defensively to her chest. "Thanks," she said, not meeting Smith's eyes.

"Don't worry, Elizabeth," Smith said. "I didn't look at it."

She looked up at him and then at Dempsey.

"Of course if you want to tell us . . . ," Dempsey said, grinning at her and crossing his heart with his fingertip.

"Maybe someday," she said, flashing him a tentative smile. "If you're lucky."

CHAPTER 45

Tehran, Iran
May 28, 1040 Local Time

Amir Modiri gently stroked Fatemeh's hair as she wept. He'd expected this visit to be difficult, but he had not imagined it would be *this* difficult.

For both of them.

He had known his brother's wife for as long as he could remember. They had played together as children—he, Masoud, Fatemeh, and her younger brother in the streets of their neighborhood in Mashhad. In adolescence, Masoud had claimed Fatemeh as the object of his affection, and Amir had respected that claim. In the forty years since, he had loved her as a brother loves a sister. Now, in the same kitchen where they had shared tea and laughed about trivial things just weeks ago, he broke the news of Masoud's valiant death during the terrorist attack at the UN in New York City. The tale he told her was the same one being broadcast on the government-controlled Iranian news programs:

Ambassador Masoud Modiri, of the Islamic Republic of Iran, died a hero, defending the lives of his brave Muslim staffers and fellow ambassadors during an unsanctioned attack on the United Nations by a radical splinter cell of Al Qaeda.

Flowers lined the sidewalk along the perimeter fence of the ambassador's official residence—a residence from which Fatemeh would soon be evicted to make room for her husband's replacement. Amir had selected the choicest bouquets and brought them inside with him, but she would not look at them. For ten minutes, her face had been pressed into his chest, and he wondered if he would ever be able to let her go. After Kamal's death, she had unloaded all her anger and grief onto Masoud. His brother had taken her burden and added it to his own. That was the type of man he was. With Masoud gone now, Fatemeh had only her youngest son, Cyrus, to lean on. But Cyrus was eighteen, enrolled in university, and living away from home. Thankfully, Cyrus had come to the ambassador's residence this evening at Amir's request. He had decided it would be best if both mother and son heard the story directly from him. Also, he felt better knowing his nephew would spend the night in the same house with his grieving mother.

Just in case she . . .

Amir looked over at the boy, who was sitting on the opposite side of the table, looking lost. He had always liked Cyrus, and Cyrus had worshiped him as the uncle who brought tales of adventure and comedy into the reserved Masoud Modiri home at holiday gatherings. Unlike Kamal, Cyrus showed great intellectual promise. Where Kamal had been the hot-tempered warrior, Cyrus showed the cool acumen of a tactician. The boy's handsome face, affable nature, and mind for mischief had always reminded Amir of himself. The youngest Modiri male would make a perfect candidate—when the time was right.

Amir gently disengaged from Fatemeh, scooting his chair back so that she could not lean against him without falling out of her chair. She sensed this and pulled away, hugging herself while she tried to control her sobs. In this state, she looked so very childlike, not the proud matriarch he had become accustomed to in recent years.

"I don't understand," she murmured. "I don't understand people whose only mission in life is to spread death and fear around the world. These jihadists claim to be loyal servants of Allah, but Allah is the God of Peace. The murder of innocents is not the way of Islam, but that is what Al Qaeda signals to the world. No wonder the Christian West fears Islam."

"The jihadists are misguided—"

She talked over his comment, lost deep in her own thoughts. "That is why Masoud dreamed of being ambassador. He wanted to be the voice of a rational, peaceful Islam. He wanted to represent the real Iran—a learned country with noble people and a noble past. We are not a people of hate and aggression, as portrayed in the Western media. He wanted to spread that message to all the nations of the world." She paused and looked down while wringing her hands. "I cannot tell you, Amir, how many nights Masoud and I lay awake in bed, talking about the UN and the path to global peace. My husband was a dreamer. Did you know that about him? He was a pious man, a brilliant philosopher, and a rare candle of hope in a world so bent on snuffing all candles out."

Amir reached out and squeezed her hand. "Masoud was the wisest man I've ever known. I am proud to have called him my brother," he said, his voice cracking at the end.

She gave the back of his hand a pat. "Thank you, Amir. I know Masoud is watching us from Paradise, and he is grateful to you for coming to comfort me. The road of sorrow ahead is long, but knowing that you and Maheen will walk beside me gives me the strength and courage to make the journey."

He hugged her one last time, and she began to weep once more. He stood, and looked at Cyrus. The boy looked up at him with wet, angry eyes.

"Before I go, Cyrus, I would like to talk with you as men," Amir said.

Cyrus nodded and followed him to the stone courtyard. Amir gestured to one of the two aluminum benches and took a seat on the other, while experiencing a terrible sense of déjà vu.

"I expect you to watch after your mother," he said, his tone compassionate but firm. "The coming weeks will be difficult for her, and you are the man of the household now. Do you understand what that means?"

"Yes, Uncle," said Cyrus.

"I also expect you to honor your father. Do you know what that means?"

Cyrus crossed his arms across his chest. "You want me to speak at his funeral?"

"No, that honor falls to me," said Amir. "I'm talking about what you must do after the funeral."

Cyrus's mouth twitched at the corner. "In that case, I'm not sure what you're talking about."

"That's all right," said Amir, nodding his head slowly. "I will teach you."

EPILOGUE

J&G Steakhouse
515 15th Street NW, Washington, DC
May 28, 2115 EDT

Jarvis swirled the full-bodied red wine around in his glass—a 2011 Justin Isosceles, a wine he loved for the name as much as for its long finish. The triangle and the wine were congruent—both all about symmetry. He took a long, slow swallow and pretended not to feel the other man's eyes on him. The Director of National Intelligence was waiting patiently for him to answer, and the DNI was not the type of man who was accustomed to waiting.

"I appreciate the compliment, Director Philips," he said at last, meeting the other man's eyes. "There was, as is so often the case, a lot of luck involved."

"Call me Ed," the DNI said. "And luck had nothing to do with it, Kelso. We're both Annapolis grads; you don't have to kowtow for me."

"Okay, Ed, but I'm guessing you didn't ask me to this dinner meeting to reminisce about the good ol' days on the yard," Jarvis said. He set down his wineglass and leaned back in his chair.

"Quite right," Philips agreed. He held Jarvis's eyes with a hard stare, looking very much the ex-fighter jock Naval aviator that he was.

Jarvis had read once that Philips had earned a Distinguished Flying Cross for action at the tail end of Vietnam, and another for a mission twenty years later in Gulf War I. He was a true warrior and a kindred spirit . . . so Jarvis hoped.

"Too bad about Kittinger," Philips said, casually taking a sip of wine.

"Tragic," Jarvis agreed, without blinking. "So senseless," he added. "Does metro PD or the Secret Service have any leads? Bob didn't seem the suicidal type."

"No leads," Philips said, setting down his glass but watching Jarvis closely. "I don't believe he even left a note."

"That's what I heard. His sudden death must be quite a loss to your office, I'm sure."

At that, Philips chuckled and shook his head. "No," he said, leaning in as if to confide a secret. "Bob's heart may have been in the right place, but clearly he harbored some misguided ideas about how to safeguard our great nation. The president will be well served to replace him with someone who will provide more sound advice to the administration."

"Clearly," Jarvis agreed.

"It was time for him to go, I'm sure we agree."

"We do," Jarvis said, unable to resist this arrogant last step in the waltz of words they were dancing. He carved off a hunk of his Wagyu strip steak with the razor-sharp serrated knife.

The moment gone, Philips now cut into his own enormous, twenty-ounce bone-in ribeye. "So, Kelso, where would you like to go from here?" the DNI asked.

"After the failure of the JIRG and my resignation, there aren't a lot of places left for me to go," Jarvis said, engaged but cautious. "And without a sponsor, I suppose it's probably time to shut down Ember."

Something flashed across the DNI's face and then disappeared. "Have you fulfilled your charter?"

"Technically, we're mission complete," Jarvis said, watching for another hint in the DNI's expression. He got none.

The DNI took another generous bite of steak and made Jarvis wait an excruciatingly long two minutes while he chewed before finally speaking. "There will be no more inappropriate short chains within the White House, I assure you. The obvious illegality of it aside, it is an unsound way to get things done."

Jarvis nodded and said nothing.

"In your report, you wrote that Behrouz Rostami avoided capture and is still at large."

"Correct, sir," he said.

"And that the mastermind of these latest offensives, Amir Modiri, is still serving as the Director of the Foreign Operations Directorate at the Ministry of Intelligence and Security."

"Yes, sir, he is."

The DNI wiped his mouth with his napkin. "In that case, I don't see how you're mission complete on your charter. It seems to me that you still have work to do, Director."

"Yes, sir. I suppose I do," Jarvis said, forcing himself not to smile.

"You work for me now, but Ember will continue to have the autonomy you earned when you ran the JIRG. I've spoken with the president and made him aware of what your people did at the UN. I have his full support for this arrangement." Philips took a sip of wine. "How do you like your team?"

"They're the best I've ever had," Jarvis said.

"Good," the DNI said. He reached down into the briefcase on the floor beside him and retrieved a sealed yellow envelope. He set the envelope on the table but rested his hand on top of it. "While Ember focuses on satisfying its long-term charter, there is something else pressing that I could use your assistance with."

"We would be happy to help, sir."

Philips smiled and slid the envelope over to him. "You will report only to me, understood?"

"Understood."

"In that case, please get to work." Philips stood up from the table. He extended his hand to Jarvis.

The dinner was apparently over, at least for him. Jarvis gave one last glance at the balance of his fifty-eight-dollar steak, stood, and shook his new boss's hand. "Thank you, sir. I'll get the team right on this."

"See that you do," Philips said, returning to his dinner. "There's a car waiting for you outside."

Envelope in hand, Kelso Jarvis, former Navy SEAL Commander, now Director of the nation's best-kept Tier One secret, headed out into the early summer rain.

GLOSSARY

- AQ—Al Qaeda
- BDU—Battle Dress Uniform
- BUD/S—Basic Underwater Demolition School
- BZ—Bravo Zulu (military accolade)
- CASEVAC—Casualty Evacuation
- CENTCOM—Central Command
- CIA—Central Intelligence Agency
- CO—Commanding Officer
- CONUS—Continental United States
- CSO—Chief Staff Officer
- DNI—Director of National Intelligence
- Ember—American black-ops OGA unit led by Kelso Jarvis
- EXFIL—Exfiltrate
- FARP—Forward Area Refueling/Rearming Point
- FOB—Forward Operating Base
- HALO—High Altitude Low Opening (parachute jump)
- HRT—Hostage Rescue Team (FBI)
- HUMINT—Human Intelligence
- IAEA—International Atomic Energy Agency
- IC—Intelligence Community
- INFIL—Infiltrate
- IRISL—Islamic Republic of Iran Shipping Lines

- IS—Islamic State
- ISIL—Islamic State of Iraq and the Levant
- ISIS—Islamic State of Iraq and al-Sham
- JCPOA—Joint Comprehensive Plan of Action (Iran treaty)
- JCS—Joint Chiefs of Staff
- JIRG—Joint Intelligence Research Group
- JMAU—Joint Medical Augmentation Unit
- JO—Junior Officer
- JSOC—Joint Special Operations Command
- JSOTF—Joint Special Operations Task Force
- JTF—Joint Task Force
- LCPO—Lead Chief Petty Officer
- MARSOC—Marine Corps Special Operations Command
- MBITR—Multiband Inter/Intra Team Radio
- MEDEVAC—Medical Evacuation
- MIC—Military Incendiary Compound
- MOIS—Iranian Ministry of Intelligence, aka VAJA / VEVAK
- MOSSAD—Israeli Institute for Intelligence and Special Operations
- NAVSPECWAR—Naval Special Warfare Command
- NCDU—Naval Combat Demolition Unit
- NCO—Noncommissioned Officer
- NOC—Nonofficial Cover
- NSA—National Security Administration
- NSA—National Security Advisor
- NVGs—Night Vision Goggles
- OGA—Other Government Agency
- OPSEC—Operational Security
- OSTP—Office of Science and Technology Policy
- OTC—Officer in Tactical Command
- PD—Police Department
- PJ—Parajumper/Air Force Rescue

- QRF—Quick Reaction Force
- RIB—Rigid Inflatable Boat
- SAPI—Small Arms Protective Insert
- SCIF—Sensitive Compartmented Information Facility
- SEAL—Sea, Air and Land Teams, Naval Special Warfare
- SECDEF—Secretary of Defense
- SIGINT—Signals Intelligence
- SITREP—Situation Report
- SOAR—Special Operations Aviation Regiment
- SOCOM—Special Operations Command
- SOG—Special Operations Group
- SOPMOD—Special Operations Modification
- SQT—Seal Qualification Training
- TOC—Tactical Operations Center
- UNOG—United Nations Geneva
- USN—US Navy
- VEVAK—Iranian Ministry of Intelligence, analog of the CIA

ABOUT THE AUTHORS

Brian Andrews is a US Navy veteran who served as an officer on a 688-class fast attack submarine in the Pacific. He is a Park Leadership Fellow and holds a master's degree from Cornell University. He is the author of *The Calypso Directive*, the first book in the Think Tank series of thrillers. Born and raised in the Midwest, Andrews lives in Tornado Alley with his wife and three daughters.

Jeffrey Wilson has worked as an actor, firefighter, paramedic, jet pilot, and diving instructor, as well as a vascular and trauma surgeon. He served in the US Navy for fourteen years and made multiple deployments as a combat surgeon. He is the author of three award-winning supernatural thrillers: *The Traiteur's Ring*, *The Donors*, and *Fade to Black*. He and his wife, Wendy, live in Southwest Florida with their four children.

Andrews and Wilson are also the coauthors of the Nick Foley Thriller series.